Date: 11/4/21

LP FIC KANTRA
Kantra, Virginia,
Beth & Amy

BETH & AMY

BETH & AMY

VIRGINIA KANTRA

WHEELER PUBLISHING
A part of Gale, a Cengage Company

GALE
A Cengage Company

LIBRARY OF CONGRESS CIP DATA ON FILE.
CATALOGUING IN PUBLICATION FOR THIS BOOK
IS AVAILABLE FROM THE LIBRARY OF CONGRESS.

ISBN-13: 978-1-4328-8298-3 (hardcover alk. paper)

Published in 2021 by arrangement with Berkley, an imprint of Penguin
Publishing Group, a division of Penguin Random House, LLC

Printed in Mexico
Print Number: 01   Print Year: 2022

For the daughters, especially
Jean Elizabeth.

And to Michael.
Most of what I know about love
I learned from you.

Bunyan, North Carolina, Then
The screen door slammed.

Amy ran down the back porch steps clutching her sketchbook. "Wait for me!"

Her sisters were already loading the car. Meg carried a beach mat. Jo lugged the cooler. Beth toted an old plastic pail and shovel — as if they all weren't too old for sand castles now.

"What took you so long?" Jo asked.

"I had to wash my hair."

"Why? We're going to the beach," Jo said. "You'll just get it wet again."

Jo never cared how she looked. Or what other people thought of her. Amy stuck her nose in the air. "Aunt Phee says appearances are important."

Jo grinned. "Too bad about your face, then."

"Jo, don't be mean," Meg said.

Their mother emerged from the barn, two

7

of the baby goats — Hector and Hermione — trotting at her heels like puppies. "All set?"

Meg nodded.

"Good. Drive safely," Momma said.

Not, *I love you.* Not, *I'll miss you.* Not, *Have a good time.* But there was a note in her voice — wistfulness? — that caught at Amy's heart.

Come with us, she almost said.

But she didn't. Momma wouldn't. Their mother never took a day off. Not since the girls were small. Besides, the trip wouldn't be the same if their mother came along. Amy was practically a teenager and she was tired of being treated like the baby. She couldn't go to the beach with her friends like Meg did. But going *with* Meg felt special. Grown-up.

"Don't worry, Mom," Meg said. Responsible, as always. "I'll be careful."

She was driving the old Ford Taurus that belonged to their father. Daddy was away serving in Iraq, on his second tour as an army chaplain.

"I'm your mother. It's my job to worry." Momma's smile flitted across her face. "I expect you all home for supper. Don't be late."

"Yes, ma'am. No, ma'am," they all said,

8

and Bethie kissed her.

"Right," Jo said when their mother went back to her goats and her chores. "Let's go!"

Giddy with freedom, they loaded the car.

"Hey, March girls."

Amy turned, clasping her sketchpad to her chest. It was Trey — Theodore James Laurence III, who lived in the big house a mile down the road from their farm. He sauntered up their drive, his dark, curly hair matted with sweat, his lean chest bare and faintly golden. His running shorts drooped from his hips, exposing his striped boxers.

"Hey, Laurence boy," Jo said. "What are you doing here?"

"Thought I'd get my run in early." He and Jo were on the cross-country team together. "Want to come?"

"Sorry. Can't," Jo said with brief regret.

"We're packing," Beth said.

"So I see. Got your sketchbook," Trey said to Amy.

She glowed at his attention. "Mrs. Wilson said I should work on my portfolio this summer."

Jo snorted. "Who wants to draw at the beach?"

"You're going to the beach?" Trey asked.

"We're on our vacation," Beth explained.

Not a real vacation. Not like other families

who went to Disney World. "Just for the day," Amy said.

"Momma said we all deserved a day off," Beth said.

"She wanted us out of the house," said Meg.

"Out of her hair," Jo said.

Amy didn't say anything. She heard Meg and Jo talking to each other in low tones late at night, when they thought she was sleeping. Since Daddy's deployment, Bethie's stomachaches were back. Momma thought this trip to the beach would make her feel better.

Trey leaned against the side of the car. "Sounds like fun. Maybe I could come, too."

Totally casual. Cool. That was Trey. But something in his eyes reminded Amy of their mother. Like he was on the outside, looking in.

She glanced at her sisters. It sucked that their father was away again. And Momma, since moving them all out to the farm, seemed to be busy all the time. But at least both their parents were still alive. It couldn't be easy for Trey, living alone with his grandfather.

"Of course you can come!" Jo said. Meg raised her eyebrows. "What? We packed enough food."

"He doesn't have a swimsuit," Amy said.

Trey grinned. "We can go skinny-dipping."

Jo socked him in the arm.

He held up his hands in an I-come-in-peace gesture. "Kidding. I'll swim in my shorts."

"You can share my towel," Beth said.

"Don't you have to tell your grandfather where you're going?" Meg asked.

"He won't care."

Meg, looking remarkably like Momma, leveled a look at him.

"Fine." Amy watched as Trey fished his phone — the new flip kind — from his pocket. Even Meg wasn't getting her own phone yet. Not until she went away to college next month. *Why should I pay for another line when we live under the same roof?* their mother said.

Trey left a message for his grandfather and tucked the phone away. "All set." He reached for the front door on the passenger side.

"Shotgun," Jo called.

"You can sit in back with us," Beth said to Trey. "I'll take the middle."

"I'll sit in the middle," Amy said. "You get carsick." Besides, that way she could sit next to Trey.

In the car, their legs almost touched.

11

Trey's knees were big and knobby, his thighs dusted with dark hair. He smelled different from her sisters. Good different. On the hour-long drive, she let herself imagine what it would be like if it were just the two of them going to the beach together; if she were older, sixteen or seventeen, and he was her boyfriend.

"Your face is red," Meg said to Amy as they unloaded the car. "Do you feel all right?"

Amy nodded. The sun beat down on the parking lot, baking the asphalt and the top of her head. Cars shimmered in the heat. But beyond the short line of beachgoers at the public restroom, past the puddles on the concrete by the outdoor showers, a splintery walkway cut over the dunes. Sea oats bowed and waved their plumes in the breeze from the water. The wind lifted Amy's hair, cooling her hot cheeks.

Beth sighed. "Smell the ocean!"

"Don't forget your things," Meg said.

"Oh, hurry!" said Jo.

They bumped and shuffled along the weathered walkway, Meg with her mat, Trey and Jo carrying the cooler between them. And then the dunes crested and fell away. The sand tumbled to the shining sea, stretching to the curving horizon. White foam curled and sparkled on the waves. Happy little clouds floated across the sky. Amy caught her breath, wishing she had the talent to paint it all.

"Come on!" Jo said.

They trudged over the hot sand past the lifeguard station, setting up camp on a broad, nearly empty stretch of sand near the water's edge.

Meg promptly oiled herself and spread out on her bamboo mat to get the full effect of the sun. Beth tucked the corners of the big beach blanket in the sand to secure them against the wind. Jo and Trey ran, whooping, to the water, plunging through the surf into the waves. Amy followed them. But the water was cold. The tide was too rough. She was not that strong a swimmer.

After being pummeled, dragged, and dunked by the waves, she retreated to the blanket and her sketchbook, her hair a salty wet tangle. Beth wandered the shoreline, collecting shells as Jo and Trey played in the water, sleek as otters. Amy pushed her hair from her eyes, determined to capture the scene in front of her, everything alive with color, light, and movement.

But it was no good. She was no good. After a few attempts, she stopped, frustrated by her failure to draw what she saw. What she felt. Maybe if she'd brought watercolors with her, or chalk . . . She was sure she could do better. If only she were old enough for oil paints!

She doodled in the margins — a silly crab with elongated eyestalks, a cartoon gull in a sunbonnet. But Mrs. Wilson said she would never be a real artist if she didn't take her art seriously. Mrs. Wilson said that the study of the human form was the best way to learn how to draw.

Amy flipped a page and started to sketch Meg, motionless on her mat. Meg had curves. Real breasts, instead of mosquito bumps. Amy stuck her tongue between her teeth, dividing her sister into lines and shapes as if she were assembling a quilt.

Jo staggered from the surf and collapsed, dripping, on the blanket, reaching with one arm for the cooler.

Amy shrieked, covering her sketchbook. "You're getting my paper wet!"

"Relax. I just want food. I'm starving."

"Why don't we all eat lunch?" Meg suggested. She stood and called down the beach. "Beth! Bethie! Lunchtime!"

"Whatcha drawing?" Trey asked, leaning close to see. A single drop of water slid from his nose and plopped onto the page. "Is that Meg? Nice."

Amy brushed the drop away, angling her paper so he could see. "Do you really think so?" she asked breathlessly.

"Yeah. Looks just like her." He smiled, and her heart melted like chocolate in the sun.

Beth returned with her treasures. The four sisters and Trey sat around the cooler, eating gritty peanut butter and jelly sandwiches, balancing their drinks in the sand.

"Everything tastes better at the beach," Beth said with a contented sigh.

Jo stuffed a cookie into her mouth. "Because we worked up an appetite."

Amy licked Cheetos crumbs from her fingertips, hoping she wouldn't leave orange smudges on her paper.

Trey tossed a chip to a hovering gull.

"Don't feed it," Meg warned. "You'll only attract more."

"Too late," Jo said as four more gulls swooped on the scene. She stood, scattering birds and sand. "Who wants to go swimming?"

"You should wait an hour before you go into the water," Meg said.

"Fine." She flopped back down on her stomach, rummaging in the beach bag for her book.

Trey angled his head to peer at the cover.

"*Frankenstein,*" he read aloud.

"It's on our summer reading list," Jo said. She and Trey were in AP English together. "Haven't you started it yet?"

"I watched the movie."

Jo snorted. Trey rolled to his back, linking his hands beneath his head. "Man, this is the life," he said contentedly, gazing up at the sky. "We should do this every day."

"We can't. Summer's almost over," Beth said sadly.

"And some of us have to work," Meg said.

Poor Meg. She was babysitting the horrible King children this summer to earn money for college in the fall.

"You're not working today," Beth said.

"Yes, I am," Meg said in a virtuous tone.

"On what?" Amy asked.

Meg smiled. "My tan." Trey laughed. "How are your applications coming?" Meg asked him.

He shrugged.

"I've already started my essays," Jo said. "College deadlines will be here before you know it."

"I don't want to go to college," Trey said. "Not right away. I want to take a gap year — maybe a couple of years — and travel, the way my father did. Go to Europe."

"That sounds wonderful," Amy said. "I

16

would love to go places. Paris. Rome."

"We would miss you," Beth said shyly.

Trey smiled at her. "I'm not saying I'd stay away forever. I just want a chance to live first. All Granddad cares about is me going to school and making money."

"There's nothing wrong with making money," Meg said. Meg was going to be an accountant. "At least you don't have to worry about finding a job after you graduate."

"Or student loans," Jo said. "You're lucky. You can apply to any school you want."

"You sound like my grandfather. Like I should be happy being a landlord or selling cars for the rest of my life."

Old Mr. Laurence owned most of the commercial real estate in town, including the big car dealership along the highway.

"Well, what do you want to do?" Meg asked practically. Meg was always practical.

He grinned. Shrugged. "Maybe I'll become a famous music executive and discover the next Maroon 5 and never worry about money or business again."

Jo touched his arm. "You're smart enough to do anything. Momma says you just need the right motivation."

He gave her a sideways look. "You could be my motivation."

Jo scowled and dropped her hand. "Don't be stupid. The minute I graduate, I'm moving to New York to be a writer."

Something flickered in Trey's eyes when he looked at Jo. Amy squirmed. Like she shouldn't have seen . . . whatever it was. Or maybe she didn't want to see.

Beth had wandered away from the discussion and was quietly digging where the waves came in. They were too old to play in the sand. But suddenly anything was better than sitting on that blanket. Amy got up and plopped herself by Beth. Seizing a handful of wet sand, she let the silt dribble through her fingers, building a spire drop by drop, a fantastic gloppy tower at the water's edge.

"You need to work on the foundation first," Meg said. "You can't live in your castle if it collapses."

Amy ignored her.

"Here." Meg stood. "I'll show you."

Jo jumped up. "Give me the shovel."

Meg smiled. "Nope."

Jo grabbed the pail instead. The four sisters worked together, digging and directing, laughing and bickering. Jo shored up the walls as Meg packed sand into towers. A bridge or a rampart? A pyramid or stairs? Trey was everywhere, helping everybody.

Or in the way. It wasn't the grown-up day at the beach Amy had dreamed of. It was better, like a scene from their childhood, the last week of summer, their last shared adventure before Meg went away to college and forever.

"Watch where you step!"

"I need the bucket."

Shadows lengthened as the tide crept closer. Finally, sandy, sweaty, and sunburnt, they stood back to admire their creation.

Meg tilted her head to one side, considering. "It needs something."

"A feather?" Beth suggested.

"A shell," Amy said. She ran to Beth's pile of treasures and chose the prettiest, curliest shell she could find.

"I'll do it." Jo took the shell, leaning over to stick it in the window of the tallest tower.

Amy sighed. "I wish we lived in a castle."

Meg smiled. "It would be awfully sandy."

They watched a curl of water lap at their castle's foundation. A bit of the wall crumbled away.

"And dangerous," Beth said. "When the tide comes in."

Jo put her arm around Beth. "It's still good to dream. 'Build your castles in the air. That is where they should be,' " she declaimed.

That was probably a poem or something, Amy thought. Jo had read more than anybody else, and wanted you to know it.

"I don't need a castle," Meg said. "Although I would like a big house on the river like the Gardiners'. And somebody to clean it."

"So . . . a castle with servants," Jo said.

"What's wrong with that?"

"Going to college to find your prince?" Trey asked slyly. Jo punched him in the arm. "Ow."

Meg turned pink. Or maybe that was sunburn. "I'm going to get an education," she said with dignity. "But if I meet someone, that's great. I want a family, one day. Like Momma and Daddy. I want to get married."

"Not me. I want to be in control of my own life. I want to have *purpose*," Jo said.

"I thought you wanted to be a writer," Amy said.

"Daddy says writers can change the world," Jo declared. "I'm going to write a *New York Times* bestselling novel. And then, when I'm a rich and famous author, I'll come home and buy you all presents."

"I don't care about presents," Beth said. "As long as you come home."

"What's your dream?" Trey asked.

Beth ducked her head. "I don't really have one. I just want us all to be together."

"Bethie's going to be a famous musician," Jo said. "You can discover her."

"I would like to learn to play guitar better," Beth said.

"I have lots of dreams," Amy said. "Like, I want to be the best artist in the whole world. Or win *Project Runway* and have my own fashion line and see all my dresses on the red carpet."

Jo rolled her eyes.

"What?" Amy demanded.

Trey grinned. "Jo wants to change the world, and you want to make it pretty."

Amy's heart burned. Everybody always thought Jo was so awesome, interesting, and important, and Amy was just a kid. Shallow. Spoiled. But she had dreams, too. One day she would show them.

"It's a nice dream," Meg said kindly.

The surf rippled in, foam fanning over the hard-packed sand. Water breached the wall, filled the moat, and drained away.

"I wonder if any of our dreams will come true," Jo said.

Beth sighed, resting her head on her sister's shoulder. "I guess we'll have to wait to find out."

21

Amy scratched at a bug bite. "I hate waiting."

A guard tower slumped as another chunk of the facade slid into the water. The sisters watched as the tide rolled in, wave by wave, and washed their castle away.

"Time to pack up," Meg said at last, and so they did, arriving home in time for supper.

But the memories lingered.

And the dreams never went away.

CHAPTER 1
AMY

It's always a mistake to sleep with a man who's in love with your sister. Even in Paris. Even if they'd broken up again — for good this time, he said. Even though I'd been in love with him since I was eleven years old.

But I was young and dumb and homesick. So. Whatever. I had a one-night hookup in a foreign city with Trey Laurence, the rich boy next door, after my sister broke his heart.

Three years later (*Thirty-three months, if I were counting. I was totally counting*), I was older and a whole lot wiser. But returning home for my sister's wedding was still going to be all kinds of awkward.

Oh, I'd been back to North Carolina before. For holidays, and that awful time when Momma got sick, and when my nephew Robbie was born. I still saw my sister occasionally when she came to New York to visit her publisher or the restaurant where she'd once worked. But even though Jo was about to be married to another man, I still couldn't face her without a squirm of guilt. I'd had *sex* with her *ex* — a clear violation of the Sisters' Code. As for the other guilty party, Trey . . . Well. Just because he'd found a way to forgive himself didn't mean I had to forgive him. Or myself. Mostly I avoided him.

Which was going to be a lot harder to do now that we were members of the same wedding party. (And no, my heart wasn't holding on to some pathetic hope that since Jo was finally marrying somebody else, Trey would pull his head out of his ass and realize it was me he loved after all.)

But maybe being a bridesmaid in Jo's wedding would bring me and my sister closer. Maybe this was my chance to prove to Trey — or at least to myself — that I was over him. I had better things to do with my life than obsess over a stupid childhood crush. My handbag business, Baggage, had taken off. Meghan Markle herself had recently been photographed carrying one of my totes, and demands for the rechristened "Duchess" bag were pouring in, threatening to flood my Bedford Park apartment in the Bronx.

"It's like a goddamn rainbow puked in

here," my assistant, Flo, had said before I left New York. She zipped tape across the top of a carton, adding to the boxes of custom orders packed and stacked for pickup by the door.

I glanced from her Frida Kahlo T-shirt to her natural hair, tipped this month in fiery red. "Yeah, I know how much you hate color," I said, making her laugh.

I skirted a rack of bins to get to my worktable, piled high with wallets waiting for snaps and trim. Purses, totes, and cross-body bags in bright colors and various stages of assembly overflowed every surface. I was already renting storage from the dry cleaner's downstairs. My bedroom was so filled with bolts of vinyl and leather, I couldn't find my mattress. Not that I had much time to sleep anyway.

The truth was, we needed a bigger workroom. A second sewing machine. More shelving. More light. Maybe even a little retail space, although a storefront in Manhattan was totally out of my price range, at least for now.

I reached for a punch tool. "You sure you're all right filling these orders while I'm gone?"

"Mamey." *Easy.* Flo Callazzo was a real New Yorker, a proud Afro-Dominican-

Puerto-Rican daughter of the Bronx.

Me? Not so much. In Paris, my schoolgirl French had marked me as irredeemably "other." I'd thought being back on American soil would feel like home. But my first week in the city, I'd realized my down-home accent made me stick out among the fast-talking Yankees all around me. Waitresses asked me to repeat myself. Buyers assumed I was uneducated. Guys figured I was easy. Or naive. A dumb hick blonde.

Which worked to my advantage, sometimes.

"You're not getting out of your sister's wedding on account of me," Flo said.

"I'm not trying to get out of anything." I busied myself inserting a snap. "I already rented a car and everything. I drive down Wednesday."

"Faster to fly."

"I thought I'd stop along the way. Take a day to do some store checks."

I didn't actually need to visit clients on my way to my sister's wedding. But I needed the car to transport her wedding present, draped across the backseat.

Anyway, I loved walking into a store and seeing my bags, my brand, displayed on the gleaming shelves. #bagsinthewild #ownit I loved the expensive smell of the boutiques,

26

citrus, sandalwood, jasmine, the fragrant scent of bergamot oil. The accounts were always happy to see me, flattered I'd gone out of my way to visit.

Not like going home at all.

Not that my family didn't love me, I told myself as I left the last client store in Raleigh and hit the highway for my mother's farm. They did. All of them, even Jo. But my sisters were too busy with their own lives to care much about mine.

Our mother, who never took a day's vacation in her life, had encouraged all of us girls to work hard and follow our dreams. Meg was the perfect mother to two perfect children. Jo was a bestselling author. Beth was a budding country star. And I . . . I made accessories. It didn't matter how many Instagram followers or employees I had. In my family's eyes, I was still little Amy, playing with scraps from Miss Hannah's quilting bag.

And yet . . . There was comfort in the familiar landscape rushing by, the tall pines stretching to the wide blue sky, the sunlit ditches full of cattails and turtles, the poppies blooming by the side of the road. I turned up the gravel drive marked SISTERS' FARM, the stones spitting beneath my tires. The square frame house, the old mule barn

27

turned creamery, the child's playset in the baby goats' paddock.

Home.

Too bad nobody was there. No car. No truck. Nobody.

I got out of the car and took a deep breath of country air scented with hay and the river. Also . . . goats. Brown goats, black goats, striped and spotted goats, all sizes, smelling like cheese left out on the counter too long. They crowded to the fence, bleating and bumping for attention, the babies skipping around the paddock like they were auditioning for YouTube. Cute, if you liked that sort of thing.

Our mother loved them. Not more than she loved us girls, of course.

Our mother, Abigail March, could do anything — drive a tractor, make a pie crust, refinish a table. Find anything — toys, shoes, missing homework. Fix anything, except a broken heart. She made sure we got our shots and permission slips on time, taught Meg to cook and me to sew, and came to all our school performances. But her time and attention were always rationed between us and the farm.

Meg said things were different before Daddy quit his job as a minister and went to Iraq as an army chaplain. I remember I cried when we left the parsonage and all my friends in town. But I was only ten when our mother moved us girls out to the farm. Most of my memories were of her working.

It wasn't like her to be gone in the middle of the day.

I didn't expect to see our dad. Mom had asked him to move out almost three years ago. But I felt his absence like poking at a missing tooth with your tongue.

Stupid. Meg and Jo were grown and gone when I was still in high school. I should be used to coming home to an almost empty house by now.

I leaned against the front fender as I called Momma's cell. She didn't pick up. Typical. *"Why would I ignore somebody standing right in front of me to answer the phone?"* she liked to say. But I could call Meg, my oldest sister. Meg was busy, too — her twins were about to turn five, and she kept the books for several farms and businesses in town. But she always found time for me.

A guy walked around the corner of the barn. Tall and rough-looking, his face seamed with sun and hard living behind a don't-mess-with-me beard.

I kept a hand on my phone just in case he turned out to be, oh, a serial killer or something. Living in New York had taught me caution. And out here in the country, nobody was around to hear me scream. "Hi."

He nodded in greeting. The strong, silent type, obviously. Beneath the beard, he looked vaguely familiar. Which . . . Yeah. Everybody looked familiar in Bunyan. Because of inbreeding, Jo said. But it was more that everybody had a cousin who used to go to your daddy's church or went to school with your sister, strands of connection twined and knotted like macramé.

I tried again. "Do I know you?"

He looked at me, no expression at all, like a New Yorker. Or a Frenchman. "Dan Harkins."

I smiled encouragingly, waiting.

"I work for your ma."

So he knew who I was. Or at least that Momma was expecting me. I relaxed my grip on the phone.

Our mother came from tough Scottish stock, too proud — or too cheap — to pay somebody else to do her work. But after she was hospitalized a couple years ago, she'd hired some of Dad's vets to do the heavy lifting. Mom was better now, but as her herd and business grew, she'd kept on some of the new hires.

"Where is my mother?" I asked.

"Over at Oak Hill." A pause. "Helping your sister."

Jo, being Jo, had taken a casual approach to her wedding. She and her love, Eric Bhaer, were already living together, dividing their time between New York and North Carolina. They had three kids — baby Rob and two teenage sons from Eric's previous marriage. It was only now that Eric's ex-wife was deployed and his younger son Alec was coming to live with them that Jo decided it was finally time to get married. "I don't need a poofy dress and a big, fancy wedding," Jo said when she called me. "I just want to marry him."

So. No poof. No bachelorette parties, no bridal showers, no save-the-date cards or hair and makeup trials. It wasn't quite an elopement — our great-aunt Josephine had offered her big old house at Oak Hill for the wedding, and all the family would be there — but it was pretty close.

I thought of the garment bag in the backseat, hung from the hook on the passenger side. I had to give it to Jo sometime. And there must be a million things to do before the ceremony on Sunday. Food. Eric was a chef. Maybe I could help with the flowers or something.

"I guess I'll go give them a hand," I said.

Because nothing says *I'm so sorry I slept with your old boyfriend* like a flower arrangement. Anyway, spending time with my sister couldn't be more awkward than hanging out here with Silent Sam.

With a little wave, I got back in the car, flipping down the visor to check my Parisian Red lipstick. The little flick of eyeliner I'd applied so carefully this morning was only slightly smudged. Good enough, I decided. It wasn't like I was going to see Trey. And Jo didn't care.

But Aunt Phee would, I thought as I turned down the long sandy lane toward Oak Hill. Nothing mattered more to our great-aunt than appearances.

Our father grew up in the big white house on the hill. When Daddy deployed to Iraq, Momma refused to move in with our father's aunt Phee, moving us instead to her parents' small farm. Over the years, Oak Hill's land had been sold off to developers and the Coastal Land Trust, but the manor and some of the original outbuildings remained. Too much space, Aunt Phee said, for one old lady. Our father had moved into the carriage house after Momma kicked him out.

I could see signs of recent activity as I approached. The dark magnolias had been

32

trimmed back from the house, the columned porch freshly painted, and the grass mowed all the way down the long slope to the duck pond. Azaleas and early roses bloomed everywhere, clouds of pink, red, and white transforming the scrubby gardens into the perfect wedding venue.

I pulled into the long, circular drive and parked behind our mother's battered blue pickup under a mature live oak draped in Spanish moss. A white van with The Taproom logo — Eric's new restaurant in town — was parked by the side of the house.

And there was my sister Jo, laughing and chasing Robbie on the grass. He was grinning at her over his shoulder as he pushed a toy lawn mower, his fat little legs moving as fast as they could go.

Gladness and guilt surged inside me. And maybe . . . a pang of envy? She looked so *happy.*

"Jokies!" I cried, getting out of the car.

Which is what I called her. We had always been rivals, for Dad's attention and, later, for Trey's. She didn't confide in me the way she did in Meg. She didn't baby me the way she did Beth. But we were sisters. The funny pet name was my way of establishing a special bond between us.

Robbie looked in the direction of my

voice, stumbled over the mower, and fell.

"Oh shit. I'm sorry."

"It's okay. You're okay," Jo said. *To which one of us?* She scooped up her baby, smooching his cheeks and propping him on her hip. She smiled at me over his head. "Hey, Ames."

I hugged her awkwardly, the baby between us. He peeped at me from her neck, his shy smile revealing a string of little pearl teeth. He had his daddy's dark skin and curly hair. Eyelashes to die for. "Hello, handsome." I kissed his forehead gently. "You're getting so big," I marveled.

"Nineteen months." Jo shifted his weight. "Good to see you. Mom wasn't sure when you were getting in."

"I wanted to come early to help. Not that you need it," I added. "Everything looks wonderful."

"Thanks. Wait till you see the inside," Jo said.

I thought of fetching her wedding present from the car. But her arms were full with Rob, and anyway, it was her turn to show off. I trailed her up the wide, shallow steps to the high, shaded porch. Planters of ferns flanked the leaded glass door.

Oak Hill manor was built in 1852 in the Greek Revival style. Aunt Phee's taste in furnishings was almost as old. But the faded velvet drapes and most of the oriental carpets were gone, the pine floors refinished, the walls painted a creamy neutral. The whole effect was light, bright, and inviting.

"Wow." I surveyed the changes. Tables had been set up in the living and dining rooms. Dining chairs were stacked in the hall. "I thought you wanted a simple wedding."

"Oh, it's not for the wedding." Jo's face lit with excitement. "Tell her."

Only one man brought that light to my sister's face. I turned to see her honey, Chef Eric Bhaer, striding from the direction of the kitchen. Arm Porn Guy, I'd dubbed him when they first got together. He kissed Jo and hefted their baby in the air, making him squeal with delight, before wrapping me in a big bear hug.

"Amy! *Spatz*!" *Sparrow*, in German. I felt a little glow at the special pet name. "It's so good to have you here."

Here was the welcome I'd hoped for. Eric was such a great guy. There was a time I couldn't imagine how Jo could possibly reject Theodore James Laurence III in favor of, well, any other man. But obviously my sister had made the right choice. Which only proved — didn't it? — that I was over Trey. "Tell me what?" I asked.

35

"Eric's opening a restaurant," Jo said.

"Another one?" I asked.

Jo nodded, beaming. "Here at Oak Hill."

"But you just opened The Taproom."

"A year ago," Jo said.

"I wanted someplace for everyone to go year-round," Eric said. "Casual dining, but good food."

"And ever since The Taproom opened, we've been mobbed," Jo said. "Especially on weekends during the tourist season. So Eric got the idea for Oak Hill. Fine dining, in season, weekends only."

"What about Gusto?" His restaurant in New York. The one that launched his best-selling cookbook.

"I will still consult, yeah? But I have been in New York for ten years. When I started, my restaurant is something different. Now there are restaurants like Gusto on every corner. Here in Bunyan, I am making a difference again."

"Eric started hiring teens at The Taproom. Training them," Jo said. "But now he has the chance to do more. He's hired a whole new staff. Local kids who can't afford culinary school. Working at Oak Hill will give them a chance to learn the high-end food business — everything from busing and dishwashing to cooking and hosting —

36

without going into a bunch of debt."

"I do not do it alone. Your sister is teaching them life skills, how to budget, how to write a résumé."

"Jo wants to change the world," Trey had said one summer long ago. *"And you want to make it pretty."*

"It's a great idea. But how on earth did you get Aunt Phee to go along?"

"It was her idea," Jo said. "She wants Oak Hill to stay in the family, and she wants us to spend more time in North Carolina. So she offered us Oak Hill."

"But where will she live?" I asked.

"She's moving into the carriage house. At least for now."

"Aunt Phee is going to live with *Dad*?"

Jo hesitated. "I think they're still working that part out."

"She is in the library with your mother now," Eric said. "They will be glad to see you."

"They were arguing about a seating chart for the reception when I left," Jo said.

"Oh." Well. Definitely not the time to spring my surprise on Jo. "I'll go . . . referee."

Jo grinned. "Better you than me."

My sandals tapped and echoed on the polished pine floor. ". . . have a responsibility," Phee was insisting as I came down the hall.

"Not anymore." My mother's voice was flat.

I blinked. Abby March was all about taking responsibility.

"He's still your husband," Phee said, and my stomach sank.

They weren't talking about the wedding. They were arguing about Dad. I pasted a smile on my face and pushed open the door. "Hey, Momma," I said brightly. "Hi, Aunt Phee. Am I interrupting?"

Phee glowered. She and my mother faced off across the library desk. My mother's hands and lips were pressed together, a sure sign she was angry. But she smiled when she saw me.

"Hey, sweetie. What are you doing here?"

Like I needed another reason to feel de trop. I felt my smile slipping and dragged it back. "I thought I'd come in early. To help." I gave Momma a quick hug before going around the desk to kiss Phee's cheek. The little dog in her lap growled.

"What about your work?" my mother asked.

"Flo's handling orders while I'm gone. That's the advantage of owning your own business," I said. "I can take time off." As long as I paid for the extra help and checked in three or four times a day.

If my mother was impressed by my entrepreneurship, she didn't show it. "Jo doesn't want a lot of fuss."

Don't fuss was our mother's motto. I pictured it embroidered under an imaginary coat of arms: two goats on a green field with a pricker bush.

"I thought I could help with the flowers," I said.

"Meg ordered the bouquets already. She's coming over later."

"What about table arrangements?"

"I'm picking up flowers when I go to the farmers' market on Saturday." Something must have shown in my face, because our mother added, "You could arrange those. You did such a nice job for Meg's wedding."

Phee sniffed. "You want to make yourself useful, you can take Polly for a walk."

"Nice to see you, too, Aunt Phee."

I eyed the bad-tempered Yorkie on her lap. The dog didn't seem any more excited at the prospect of a walk than I was. But I was obviously in the way here. Besides, our family owed Aunt Phee. She had paid for my postgraduation trip to Europe. She had opened her home to Dad. And she was doing such a generous thing for Jo and Eric, letting them have the wedding here. Letting them have Oak Hill.

Hm, I thought as I clipped the lead to Polly's collar. I wasn't jealous. Exactly. But if Phee was going to invest in her great nieces, why not me?

Polly and I meandered toward the duck pond, the little dog stopping frequently to sniff. The sun sparkled on the flat water. A faint breeze rippled the surface, stirring the reeds at the water's edge, loosening a shower of petals from the nearby apple trees. All the scene needed to be perfect was Colin Firth in a wet white shirt. In spite of the smell of pond decay.

Polly growled and quivered. A family of Canada geese was browsing on the bank, the adults standing at attention over five little goslings.

"Don't even think about it," I told her sternly. "They'll eat you for lunch."

Polly snorted and busied herself with a stick. Let her. I didn't care if she made herself sick.

While Polly rootled at the ground, I contemplated the azaleas, wondering how long the blooms would last if I cut some branches to use in the wedding arrangements. A burst of yapping grabbed my attention. Polly tugged against my hold on her leash. There was a squawk. A honk. A splash.

I looked. Polly had seized one of the goslings by the neck and stood with her struggling prize on the bank, triumphant and seeming slightly bewildered by her success.

Shit. I started forward. But not before Momma and Poppa Goose lunged, necks outstretched, black beaks open and hissing.

"No!" I shouted. "Polly, stop! Drop it!"

Wild-eyed, the dog obeyed. Or maybe the gosling freed itself. Peeping in distress, the bird ran for its mother. But it was too late. As Momma Goose shepherded her baby to safety, Poppa attacked.

Polly yelped and stumbled under the rush of the bird's wings, tumbling into the water.

"No!" I yelled again. "Shoo!"

The goose paid no attention, fixing its beady eyes menacingly on the dog.

Crap, crap, crap. I ran into the pond, my sandals sinking in the muck, and scooped up Polly. The Yorkie bit me, drawing blood. The indignity of it — after I'd rescued her, the little monster! — slapped my senses. The goose advanced on us, hissing, head moving side to side like a snake's. I clutched Polly to my chest.

And then, apparently deciding I wasn't

worth it, the big bird folded its wings and launched past me, rejoining its family in the center of the pond.

The ripples faded in its wake. I stood there, dripping and shaking with shock. In my arms, Polly shook, too.

"I thought I heard a commotion," said Trey's voice.

I swayed. I was hallucinating. Unless . . . I turned. Nope. There he was, in the flesh, on the bank, golden-skinned and lean and perfect, the only boy I'd ever loved.

Of course he would show up *now*, I thought. When I was wet, muddy, and bloody. At a total disadvantage. History repeating itself.

Our gazes locked. "Little Amy." He smiled crookedly. "I should have known it would be you."

My vision grayed. And I realized two things.

One, I was quite possibly going to faint.

And two, I wasn't over him after all.

CHAPTER 2
BETH

Life was not, after all, like a country song.

"Three chords and the truth," songwriter Harlan Howard famously said about country music. But I was mostly living a lie these days.

I swished and spat from the bottle of mouthwash the makeup artist carried ready in her kit. There was always a bucket positioned in the wings in case I threw up again. Three weeks into the tour, the stage crew wasn't taking any chances. One of the guys — Jason — whisked it away. The rest went on with their jobs, big men in black shirts moving purposefully in the shadows.

Sharla, the makeup artist, took the wet washcloth she had pressed to the back of my neck and handed it to an assistant. "Better?"

I nodded, feeling lighter. Relieved.

"Good. Eyes up."

I swallowed, trying to focus on the lights

overhead and not the crowd milling in the pit, bellowing along to "County Road." From the corner of my eye, I could see the blue-and-gold glow of the big stadium screen — Colt, looming above the audience, larger than life. In his element.

Only four more shows, I told myself. Only three more days before we went home for my sister Jo's wedding.

Not that I grudged Colt one moment in the spotlight. He was so talented. I still couldn't believe he had plucked me from the chorus of a Christmas show to be his. Every singer-songwriter's dream, right? Every country music fan's fantasy.

The assistant fussed with my hair as Sharla repaired my makeup. We had a routine down now.

"Don't say anything to Colt," I said.

Without comment Sharla ran concealer stick under my eyes.

"I don't want him to worry about me," I added.

She met my gaze. "Honey, Colt worries about Colt. You should take care of yourself."

My mouth jarred open. The assistant adjusted my headset over my hair.

"Lips," Sharla said.

I pursed obediently. The band launched

into the final rollicking verse of the song, accompanied by stomps and screams from the crowd. Rodney, the stage manager, tapped his headset and held up one finger. I swallowed. It was time.

"All set." Sharla tucked the gloss into the black apron at her waist. Somebody on the sound crew repositioned the boom at the corner of my mouth. "Go get 'em."

I ran the gauntlet in the semidarkness — sound crew, lighting crew, backline crew. I could barely hear Colt's voice in my earpiece through the roar of the audience, the buzz in my head. I paused, blinking, blinded by the stage lights.

Rod nudged me forward. I stumbled past the backup singers, earning a resentful look from Mercedes.

Someone grabbed my elbow. Isaiah, at the mic. "Steady, girl."

I squeezed his hand, grateful for his support. Glanced anxiously at Colt, in the spotlight. He smiled with warm encouragement, only the faintest twitch betraying his annoyance at my clumsy entrance.

"Audiences love you 'cause you're real," he liked to say. Well. He used to say it.

"Hello . . ." My voice trailed off. *New York? No, that was last week. Saratoga Springs to Wantagh to . . . Were we in Virginia now?* I swallowed. Waved weakly at the blur beyond the lights, feeling like a fraud. "Hello, everybody."

Hollers, punctuated by whoops and whistles. Andy, the roadie, handed me my Gibson Hummingbird. I clutched the guitar gratefully, immediately feeling less naked.

"Let's give them what they came for, angel," Colt said, taking control, the way he always did. He winked — for my benefit? for his fans? — and launched into the opening chords of the next song, a song I wrote for him, our second Grammy-nominated hit, "Smooth as You."

The audience responded with an animal roar. I flinched, leaning into the Gibson to check the tuning. Nodded to Andy, who plugged me in. I swallowed, fixing on Colt's face with painful intensity, struggling to hold on to his voice in my ear. Trying to find the harmonies through the noise of the crowd and the insect whine in my brain.

"The way you go down easy . . ."

The crowd fell away as I found myself in the music. Singing always steadied me. Grounded me. With every note, every breath, my voice and my nerves grew stronger.

"All the things you do . . . Hit me like eighty proof . . ."

Our voices rose and blended, rough and smooth, strands of melody wrapping us in a magic cocoon. My hands stopped shaking on the strings. My confidence swelled as the Hummingbird sang in my arms. *"One taste and I'm addicted . . . never be whiskey quite as smooth as you."*

Our eyes held. The last note lingered. The light from a thousand cell phones danced like fireflies in the dark. As the audience erupted, Colt gave me a little nod and a smile. I smiled back, relieved. Forgiven. No matter how bad things got, the music brought us together.

And then I turned and puked all over Mercedes's shoes.

The first time I got sick at school, Momma picked me up from the nurse's office. A stomach bug, the nurse said when she called home. My mother tucked me into bed in the room I shared with Amy, and I watched TV all afternoon, cuddling with the kittens, feeling safe and cherished while she brought me saltines and Coke on a special tray and Jell-O and pretzels for dinner.

Then when Daddy left for Iraq, I was so sad my stomach hurt all the time. Everybody at school kept asking, *"Are you all right?"* and I had to say *"Fine,"* because soldiers' daughters are brave and a minister's daughter could not lie. But if I were sick, I thought, I could go home.

So one day after lunch in the school cafeteria, I went into the girls' bathroom and locked myself in a stall. I gagged and gagged until my face was hot and my eyes ran. It was really hard, then. But finally I stuck my finger down my throat and made myself throw up in the toilet.

And Momma left the farm and came to get me. Riding beside her in the truck, I felt ashamed and comforted and oddly powerful. She babied me for the rest of the afternoon, until Amy came home.

I didn't throw up again for a long time after that.

But the hollow in my stomach didn't go away, and the possibility was always there, a constant companion, a shadow awareness. Whispering. Tempting. Like a friend who tries to talk you into playing hooky.

Not a friend Momma would approve of.

A secret friend. Mine.

Even then, I knew I shouldn't listen to temptation. But it felt so good to have something to cling to. Something all my own. This one thing I didn't share, even with my sisters.

Colt was late coming back to the tour bus. After a show, he needed a drink and a shower. He usually hung out with the band in the stadium locker room, grabbing a couple of beers with Zeke, the road manager, and chatting with the production crew. He'd sign autographs for a few lucky fans, meet with the VIPs and promoters, the local DJs, and the press.

I stayed away, avoiding the lines of people and tables of catered food. After Colt had seen all the people he needed to see, there was time for us.

"Everybody else wants a piece of me," he told me once. "You're different."

He stood in the doorway of our private bedroom, watching as I did crunches at the foot of our king-size bed.

"You must be feeling better."

"I'm fine." I got self-consciously to my feet, aware of my sweat-dampened hair, the shirt clinging to my ribs. "You were wonderful tonight," I told him.

"You put on quite a show yourself."

I flushed, reaching for a towel to blot my face. "Sorry."

"The guys were all talking. Some reporter

dude asked if that tabloid story was true. If you were using. Or pregnant."

"I can't be." I'd taken a pregnancy test a few months ago, when my period stopped, locking myself in the bathroom, shoving the wrappers down in the trash. Three tests. One line. *Not pregnant.*

"It does happen," Colt said.

"I know. My nephew Robbie is a surprise baby."

"So we're going to a shotgun wedding?"

"Oh no. Robbie's a year and a half old already. I just meant . . . Something I ate must have upset my stomach."

It slipped out so easily, a lie worn smooth by repetition.

"That's what I told them." Colt gave me a brooding look. "At least if you were expecting a baby, it would be over in nine months."

Not the way I hoped the man I loved would talk about our future family. But Colt's big plans for our life together didn't include having kids. At least, not yet.

I understood.

My childhood wasn't perfect. I only remembered it that way. Colt didn't even have memories to sustain him. The first time he took me to dinner, to a quiet little restaurant where everyone pretended not to recognize him, he'd told me with tears in his eyes about his hardscrabble childhood, his uncaring mother, his absent father.

It would take time for him to open up to the idea of family. To convince him that my dream — the front porch swing, the home overflowing with kittens and music and curly-haired toddlers and love — could come true for both of us.

"I'm sorry," I said.

"Don't apologize. Not for that, anyway." He moved restlessly away from the door, but there was no room to pace in the back of the tour bus. Nowhere to go. "The insurance company wants you to get drug tested."

"What? No."

"It's a liability thing." He shrugged. "You got a problem with it, talk to Zeke."

"Zeke works for you."

"That's right. I pay him to handle this shit. Anybody else, he'd take care of it. But I told him I wanted to tell you personally."

I was not going to argue. Arguing made everything worse. "I'll do whatever you want."

He shot me an exasperated look. "I *want* you to be with me. But, angel, you've got to be *with* me. One hundred percent. Not puking onstage. Not hiding on the bus."

"I'm . . . ." *Sorry.* Don't say *sorry.* "Not

51

like you," I said. "I don't like everybody staring at me."

"But you're beautiful," Colt said.

He said that all the time. *You're so beautiful. You're so talented.* I loved his belief in me. But I had trouble believing him. It was getting harder and harder to perform, to pretend, to be perfect. To look perfect for his fans and the selfie line. I'd stopped going with him to promo events. Stopped singing an opening set. And with each failure, each withdrawal, he got a little more impatient, a little less understanding.

"I'm uncomfortable," I said.

"You need to get over it," he said. "You could be a star. Hell, you are a star. You got two Grammy nominations and a CMA award."

"That was you," I said, giving him the praise he craved. "Best Male Vocalist. *And* Album of the Year."

"You wrote the songs, angel."

I felt like an impostor. "That's different. I'm no good at this, Colt. Being onstage all the time."

"Not if you're going to throw up." Colt ran a hand through his sun-streaked hair. "Look, babe, this sucks. But Zeke and I were talking. Maybe you should go home."

Home. The word wrapped around my

heart and squeezed.

"We are going home." I smiled at him, but my face felt wrong. "On Sunday."

"Not me. You." His eyes met mine. "We're three, maybe four, hours away. Jimmy can drive you there tomorrow."

"But . . ." I sank down on the bed. I couldn't have heard him correctly. "You're coming with me."

"I have back-to-back shows. Charlotte. Raleigh. I can't take off because you want somebody to hold your hand."

"But the wedding . . . Colt, my sister is getting married on Sunday."

Everyone was expecting to meet him. He was the first man I'd ever loved. The only one I'd had sex with. He *had* to come with me.

"Which is why this is such good timing," he said. "I can tell everybody you're going home for your sister's wedding. That should shut up the rehab rumors, at least."

Controlling the story. I understood that, too.

"Do you want me to go?" I whispered.

He sat beside me, his weight sinking the mattress. I could smell the beer and pizza on his breath. "This isn't about what I want. I'll miss you, you know that. Nobody can sing your songs like you do. We got chemistry, babe. Magic. But there are fifty people on this tour. I can't let them down."

What about letting me *down?* a selfish voice protested.

I shushed it. I loved that Colt cared about his crew. "I could stay on the bus," I offered. "We could tell everybody I'm sick."

"Again?" Colt shook his head. "Face it, angel, even without all the shit in the tabloids, you're a distraction. It'll be good for you to get away. Rest up. Take a little break." He played with the ends of my hair.

Colt liked to make love when he was coming down from the adrenaline high of performing. There was never any shortage of girls around the band, begging him to sign their concert shirts, their arms, their chests, throwing their hearts and panties onstage. But he loved me. He had chosen me.

"Because you're the only person who doesn't give a shit who I am," he said when I asked him why.

My lips felt stiff. "What about us?"

"Don't worry about us. Nothing's going to change."

But something already had. I felt it in his occasional flashes of frustration, the way his gaze dropped to his phone or searched the room behind me when we were together.

My fault. If only I were prettier, skinnier, braver, he wouldn't send me away.

"I wanted you to meet my family," I said.

"And I will," he promised. "As soon as things get better."

Things. Me.

I felt the beginnings of panic, like a shadow plucking at my sleeve. "I don't like leaving you."

"You're still with me. Hey, all your songs are still in the show."

His music before me was the life he knew, or celebrated, all mud tires and tailgates, booze and boots and good times. My ballads were a chance to draw breath, for him and for his audience.

"Maybe . . . Maybe while I'm gone Mercedes could sing my part," I suggested. I needed to do something for her, to make amends for ruining her shoes.

His touch paused. "Sure. Whatever you want." He resumed stroking my hair.

But that tiny, betraying hesitation told me everything. Of course Mercedes would take over my songs. Colt had made that decision before he even got on the bus.

I hugged my knees, afraid to leave him. Terrified of losing him by insisting I stay.

"It's only temporary," Colt was saying. "I need you, angel."

55

For how long? I wondered. But I didn't ask. I didn't want to risk pushing him further away.

"We cut the new album in September," he said as if he could read my thoughts. He glanced at the notebook on my side of the bed. "You can work on your songs."

"September?"

"Could be sooner."

The panic spread. "I can't write under pressure."

"The Suit says you can have two tracks. More if you want." The Suit was Dewey Stratton, who oversaw artist development for the record label. "It's for your own good."

"For *my* good."

"Yeah." He grinned, quick and charming. "And mine. We're a team. The bad boy of country rock and the girl who's gonna win him another Grammy."

My gut twisted. "Colt . . . That's not really me."

"Sure, it is." He pressed a kiss to my shoulder. "Just give me some of that sweet thing you're so good at."

He eased me down onto the mattress. I shrank inside my skin, needing a shower, wanting . . . His hands slid under my shirt, distracting me. I twined my arms around

56

his neck as he pulled on my zipper, as he lowered himself over me.

At least in this way, we could be together. I could be who he wanted.

CHAPTER 3
AMY

The first time Trey rescued me, I was twelve. He and Jo had taken the boat out on the river, and I had tried to follow, tipping our father's canoe and almost drowning. Jo said it was her fault because she wouldn't turn back for me. But I knew better. Besides, she'd tried to save me after I fell in.

The second time, when I was fourteen? Also my fault.

We had a good childhood, my sisters and me. We weren't rich like the Gardiners or the Moffats, the families who lived in gated communities along the river with boat slips and hired help to look after their yards and their children. But we had a place and a position in town — we were the Reverend March's girls, from the parsonage by the white-spired Methodist church.

All that changed when we moved to the farm.

My mother's people were Curtises, small-time farmers and homesteaders. After Daddy deployed and Momma took over running the farm, it was like we became Curtises, too.

Meg could at least drive. She had all her friends from when we lived in town and was leaving soon for college. And Jo didn't care. She was still the smart one who ran cross-country, wrote the school play and for the school paper, and was obviously going places. Beth . . . Well. Beth never wanted to go anywhere. She actually liked living on the farm.

But I hated it.

It wasn't so bad while Meg and Jo were still at home. They'd take me into town sometimes, if I asked nicely or Mom insisted. And sometimes Miss Hannah's kids, James and Daphne, crossed the fields with their mother to help in the cheese room or play in the barn.

But high school pretty much sucked. I hated getting on the bus with the farm kids and the others, the ones from the trailers with dirty screens and sagging porches, moldering away between the tobacco barns on the outskirts of town.

My friends all lived in solid homes with sidewalks, flags, and flower beds or in neat subdivisions with pools and two-car garages.

So when Jenny Snow invited me to a sleepover at her house the Friday before homecoming, of course I said yes. We did manicures and face masks, swapped lip gloss and eye shadow, ate pizza and waited for Mr. and Mrs. Snow to go upstairs.

"Let's play a game," Kitty Bryant said after they had gone to bed.

Mary Kingsley smiled cruelly. "Chubby Bunny?"

Kitty flushed. She wasn't fat. But there was a softness to her face, a tiny roll at her waist when she bent over, that was different from the other girls'.

"We could dress up," I suggested.

Mary rolled her eyes. "Oh, please."

"Like *America's Next Top Model*," I said. "We could do a photo shoot."

"A lingerie shoot!" Jenny said.

We posed in pajamas and underwear like we were competing for *America's Next Top Model. Head back, tits out, booty tooch.* Mary snapped pictures on her new iPhone.

Jenny took off her bra. "Porn shot!" We all shrieked with laughter. "You next," she commanded Kitty, who reluctantly complied. One by one, the girls all flashed for the camera.

Jenny turned her smile on me. "Your turn."

"Oh, I don't . . ." My mother would kill me. My father was an army chaplain serving in Iraq. I glanced at the bedroom door. Closed, thank God. "What about your brother?"

"Don't worry. He's out with his stupid friends."

"You have such a cute figure," Kitty said.

"It's not like you have that much to show anyway," Mary pointed out.

"Everybody else is doing it," Jenny said. "Don't be such a baby."

So I posed, too.

But the following Monday, my picture was the only one circulating at school. Faceless breasts with the caption: *Whose boobs are these?*

For a while it was a game, played phone to phone. Every time I passed a knot of boys hunched over a screen, I cringed inside. At least nobody knew that headless torso was me.

And then the whispers started.

"Little titties."

"Dude. You think it's a dude?"

"I heard . . ."

"Easy A." Snickers.

A is for Amy.

Boys — who had mostly ignored me — now made comments in the hall. They blocked my locker. Bumped into me in the classroom. Jenny Snow wouldn't speak to me at lunch. Kitty Bryant couldn't meet my eyes.

I burned with shame and betrayal. It was Jenny's idea. Mary's phone. Kitty was my *friend,* my best friend since second grade. Why would they do this to me?

The next Friday was homecoming. The plan had been for me to attend the game with Jenny, after which we were going to her house to change before the dance.

Mom dropped me off at school in the battered pickup she used to haul goats and feed. "You all right?" she asked with a searching look.

I nodded, a lump in my throat. I didn't know how to tell my mother that the plan had changed. Or why. That because of one stupid picture, I didn't have any friends anymore.

After the game, Jenny and Mary bundled into Mrs. Snow's car without a glance in my direction. Kitty Bryant blushed guiltily as she let herself be pulled away.

I stood alone in the shadow of the bleachers, trying to ignore Jenny's brother Davis and his friends nudging one another in the stands.

"Hey, Little Bits. Nice tits."

I flinched, and the boys all laughed.

I missed my sisters. Especially Meg. Nobody made fun of me when Meg was around. Beth had chosen to stay home that night. Which made her either an even bigger loser or smarter than me.

Half the town had turned out for homecoming, parents stopping to chat on the track, their arms full of discarded coats and water bottles, former students here to see the game or catch up with friends. A group of older boys — college boys — sauntered by, heading for the parking lot. I shrank against the wall. What if they pointed me out? What if they laughed at me? Amy March, the stupid freshman with the tiny tits.

"Hi, kid."

"Trey!" I almost fell into his arms. "What are you doing here?"

Trey and Jo were sophomores at the University of North Carolina at Chapel Hill. Jo had a scholarship. Trey had a car.

"Drove down for homecoming," he said.

I scanned the crowd behind him. "Is Jo with you?"

Even Jo would be a comfort. Nobody

dared mess with Jo.

Trey's face shadowed. "She had to study."

I nodded. Jo was always studying.

He smiled, shaking off whatever mood had temporarily seized him. "What about you? Going to the big dance?"

I shook my head, swallowing the lump in my throat. "I'm not dressed."

"Right." He eyed the bag I was holding with my dress inside.

I raised my chin. "Besides, nobody wants to go with me."

"Trey! You coming?" Ned Moffat called.

"In a minute." Trey regarded me a moment. "Get changed. I'll walk you inside."

"I . . . I couldn't," I stammered. "You can't."

He grinned. "Mrs. Ferguson's chaperoning, right?" The AP English teacher. "She'll let me in."

"But your friends . . ."

He glanced over his shoulder. "You guys go on. I'll meet you at Sallie's."

There was some good-natured grumbling and then they left.

"Off you go," he said to me. "I'll wait."

In a daze, I went to the girls' locker room, empty except for some girls from the marching band changing out of their sweaty uniforms. Outcasts, like me. At least they had one another.

I listened enviously as they chattered and laughed, fixed their hair and their faces, borrowed lip balm and gum.

". . . in the wrong place," the short girl complained. "Every time."

"At least he's consistent," her friend said, and they all laughed.

I edged around them to get to the mirror. "Excuse me."

"No problem."

"Is that . . . ?" A whisper.

"Amy March."

"Oh. *Oh.*"

"Didn't she . . . ?"

"Ssh."

"I like your dress," one of them said kindly. Her face was vaguely familiar. A friend of Beth's?

"Thanks," I said with dignity.

Momma said we couldn't afford a fancy new dress I would wear only once. So I'd altered Meg's dress from five years ago, when she was on homecoming court. I'd taken in the bodice (a lot), shortened the skirt, and hand-stitched a ribbon of bling at the waist.

"Little Amy," Trey said when he saw me. "You clean up good."

I glowed at the compliment.

Beauty is as beauty does, our mother liked to say. Which wasn't much comfort if you were fourteen years old and worried that your nose was too big and your chest was too flat and you were never going to catch up with your sisters. Our father called me "Princess," but he was always quicker to teach or preach than hug or approve. *" 'Charm is deceitful, and beauty is vain, but a woman who fears the Lord is to be praised.' "* Anyway, Jo was his favorite.

But floating into the gym on Trey's arm, wearing Meg's old dress, I felt for a moment like Cinderella going to the ball.

Or like Carrie before she got hit with a bucket of pig's blood.

The gym was decorated with the balloon arch from the football field and crepe paper streamers in the school colors, blue and gold. Lights swirled over the ceiling. Dancers milled on the floor. Music pulsed and bounced as we wended our way through the press of bodies around the door, under the noses of Jenny and her court, past Davis and his horrible friends.

"Pss pss pss."

"Hey, hey, it's Easy A."

"Show us your tits."

Followed by snickers.

Trey stopped.

66

I put a hand on his arm, embarrassed. "It's okay."

"It's not." His black gaze scanned the boys by the door. "You guys always this stupid or is today a special occasion?"

Stephen Campbell smiled weakly. "Hey, Trey."

"We didn't mean anything."

"Then shut the fuck up," Trey said.

"What's your problem?" Davis said, aggrieved. "It's not like she's got anything to see there anyway."

Trey's arm turned to iron under my hand. He was only two years older than the seniors, almost thirty pounds lighter than Davis. But their faces were softer, their features unformed. Trey looked harder. More finished. Almost . . . dangerous. My avenging knight. I felt a little flutter of fear or attraction.

He took a step forward, into Davis's space. "Davis, right?"

"Yeah. So?"

"I know your dad. He works at the dealership. Good guy," Trey continued almost conversationally. "What happened to you?"

Davis went white.

Trey smiled. Not a nice smile. "Family's really important. It's all who you know, right? And this girl, Amy, she's like family

67

to me. Like a sister. How would you like somebody to talk like that about your sister?"

Davis's gaze darted around. "I guess . . . I wouldn't."

"Right." Trey grabbed a fistful of Davis's shirt and pulled him close, his voice low and intense. "Like a sister, asshole. I'm looking out for her. If I hear you've done anything — if you've said anything — to upset Amy March, or any of the March girls, I will find you and hurt you. Got it?"

I was *not* Trey's sister. But still, it was oddly thrilling to have him come to my defense.

I'd never forgotten.

Trey's concerned face pulled me back to myself.

I clutched my aunt's beastly little dog to my chest. Briefly, I calculated the advantages of sinking into a graceful swoon. I was pretty sure Trey would catch me. He had played the knight for most of my childhood. But we weren't kids anymore.

Anyway, the women in our family did not faint. Granny Curtis — the one I was named after, the one who didn't have any money — used to wring a chicken's neck for Sunday dinner and butcher hogs in the fall. Mom could birth a goat and kill a copperhead. I couldn't do those things. I didn't *want* to do those things. But I had enough of their toughness in me not to lose consciousness over a stupid dog bite.

Or over the shock of seeing Trey again. Bad enough to realize I still . . . Well. Had feelings for him. Much, much worse if he knew.

I sloshed forward. He pulled a handkerchief from his pocket — a crisp, white square, as perfectly ironed as his shirt — and held it out.

I raised an eyebrow. "Who does your laundry?"

A flush climbed his cheekbones. "Give me the dog."

I surrendered Polly and took the handkerchief. I really needed something more substantial to clean up with. Like a towel. Where to start?

"Let me." Trey wrapped his handkerchief around the fleshy part of my thumb. *Ouch.* The pressure hurt. Red seeped through the clean white cotton.

Thank God I wasn't in my workroom today. Bloodstains were a bitch to get out of leather.

I looked away, woozy again at the sight of blood or maybe his hand, cradling mine.

He had beautiful hands, as finely drawn as Adam's in Michelangelo's *Creation,* marred only by a jagged white spot at the base of his thumb from baiting my fish hook when I was twelve.

I swallowed and pulled my hand away. "I'm fine. It's nothing."

"It's a dog bite. You should have somebody look at it." He guided me up the grassy slope with a touch on my elbow, Polly in his other arm. The Yorkie nestled into his hold, pink tongue lolling.

I concentrated on my footing, trying not to be jealous of the dog. "What do you care?"

Trey stopped, fixing me with those dark, almost black eyes. "I've always cared about your family, Amy."

The look, the words, snagged in my heart like another fish hook. Because . . . Yes. Our family *was* his family, his adopted family. I was in fifth grade when Trey had moved in with his grandfather, a mile down the road from Momma's farm. She took him under her competent wing, providing the kind of meals and mothering he didn't get at home. Trey's own parents were dead, killed in a boating accident. At ten, I thought his parents' fate was wildly romantic. Way more interesting than my friends' parents, who were all boringly married or merely divorced.

My family drove me crazy sometimes. Especially Jo, who never cleaned her hair out of the tub and thought she was smarter than anybody else. But I couldn't imagine my life without them.

I'd asked Trey once how it felt, losing both his parents like that.

"Shut up about it," Jo had said, and I'd subsided, sulking. It was only later that I realized Jo was worried about our own father in Iraq.

"They care about you, too," I said now. *I care.* The words stuck in my throat.

If Trey noticed anything missing from my statement, he didn't let on. "Meg's up at the house," he said in an apparent change of subject. "She was asking about you."

"Oh, that's great." The knot in my throat eased. Pretty, kind, sensible Meg could always make me feel better. "I can't wait to see her."

"I figured." A slanting smile. "Jo told me you were down here."

So he'd come to fetch me. Of course. He was the little brother Meg never had, Jo's best friend and coconspirator, Beth's champion. My first crush. He cared about all of us.

71

But it was Jo that he loved.

Nothing I'd ever said or done had changed that.

I started back up the slope. Trey fell into step beside me, still carrying the dog. This time, I noticed, he did not touch me.

Eric pulled a chair from the stack in the hall while Jo fetched the first aid box from the kitchen. I washed my hands under our mother's supervision and then sat under the nineteenth-century crystal-and-bronze chandelier as she applied antibiotic cream.

"You don't need stitches," she said, briskly sympathetic.

"I have stitches. See, Auntie?" Daisy stuck out her chin, revealing a small, silvery scar under her jaw.

I winced as Momma pressed sterile gauze to my hand. "I see. How did that happen?"

She and her twin exchanged glances.

"I signed them up for gymnastics. They were using the chairs in the living room as parallel bars," Meg explained.

"It bleeded and bleeded," DJ informed me.

"That sounds . . ." *Gruesome? Great?* What did you say to an almost-five-year-old? "Scary," I said.

"I wasn't scared," Daisy asserted. "I was

very brave."

"I'm sure you were."

Daisy patted my knee. "You brave, too, Auntie."

Trey grinned. "So brave."

I shot him a death glare.

Aunt Phee sniffed and stroked her dog. "Such a fuss over a little bite. You must have frightened her."

"I rescued her," I protested.

Our mother's mouth was compressed, a sure sign of annoyance. But her hands were gentle as she wrapped my thumb. "Bites get infected. You need to keep it clean. Change the dressing every day."

I regarded the bandage ruefully. "At least it's blue."

Meg smiled encouragingly. "It matches your bridesmaid dress."

"What bridesmaid dress?" Jo asked.

Oops. I looked at Meg.

Jo crossed her arms. "You guys. We agreed. No frills."

"Please," I said. "I don't do frilly."

"They're not exactly bridesmaid dresses," Meg said. "They're totally different styles. We just thought it would be nice to co-ordinate our colors."

"Blue," Jo said, like she was tasting it in her mouth.

73

"Tarheel blue or Blue Devil blue?" Trey asked, naming the colors of the big rival Carolina schools.

"Different shades," I said. I'd pored over my swatch cards, choosing and comparing, texting photos back and forth with Meg and Beth. But now was not the time to get into an explanation of the Pantone palette system.

"We were going to tell you," Meg said.

"It's okay," Jo said. Being a good sport. "I told you all you could wear whatever. I want everybody to be comfortable."

"It's a wedding," Aunt Phee said. "You're not meant to be comfortable. That's why God invented Spanx."

"I'm pretty sure that was Satan," Jo said.

I cleared my throat. "Actually, I wanted to talk to you about your dress."

"If you can call it a dress. Looks like a beach cover-up to me. She found it at the thrift shop," Phee added in deep, disapproving tones.

"She looks fine," our mother said.

"Beautiful," said Eric.

I took a deep breath. "So, the thing is . . . I brought something for you. A dress. It'll have to be fitted, of course, but —"

"Wait. You bought me a wedding dress?"

I had a degree in fashion design from NC

State. "I made you a dress. Sort of a wedding present." Or a guilt offering. Whatever.

"Seriously? Wow. That's . . ." Jo hesitated, at an apparent loss for words.

"Very thoughtful," our mother said firmly. Jo nodded.

"I'm sure it's beautiful," Meg said.

My stomach sank. Twenty-five years old and still seeking my family's approval. Pathetic. "If you don't like it, it's no big deal. I can take it back." Almost six yards of silk crepe de chine at twenty-six dollars a yard. No exchanges, no returns.

"Well? Let's see it," Phee said.

"It's in the car," I said.

"I'll give you a hand," Trey offered.

Good old Trey, always ready to lend a hand or a shoulder, an ear or a few extra bucks. All that attention could make a girl feel special. It took me years to figure out he was that kind to everyone.

I shook my head. "I've got it. Be right back," I promised, and escaped.

I ducked into the backseat of the rental car. As I unhooked the garment bag, a limousine glided around the drive and stopped at the bottom of the stairs.

I turned, cradling the dress in my arms.

The limo door opened and the driver got out, broad shoulders flexing against the seams of his dark jacket. Richard Gere arriving in *Pretty Woman*. Big in *Sex and the City*.

Maybe he wasn't the driver. Maybe he was the limo owner, the wealthy son of a friend of Aunt Phee's. A guest at the wedding.

"Nice dress," he'd drawl, and I'd murmur "I made it" as he pulled me close and we danced to Elvis crooning "Can't Help Falling in Love," while Trey looked on, brooding, and later we'd elope to Vegas and have three children, little artists and trust-fund babies.

Or not.

Still, he was very cute.

I smiled. "Well, hello. You're here early."

He gave me a brief perusal, up and down, and a grin. Very American. "Yes, ma'am."

"The wedding's not till Sunday," I said.

"That's what she said," he said, and opened the rear door for his passenger.

Cowboy boots and skinny jeans. A fall of light-brown hair like water. My heart lifted. "Beth!"

She held out her arms. "Amy!"

All our lives, we'd been paired and compared, the angelic middle child and the spoiled baby of the family, never quite living up to the expectations of our parents or the example of our older siblings.

I did not drop the dress — I'd put at least

twenty hours of work into Jo's gown, cutting the fabric properly on the grain, piecing and pressing and hand sewing — but I did my best to hug around the garment bag. Her shoulders were as sharp and angled as a model's. "I thought you weren't coming until this weekend."

Beth's thin face flushed. "Yes. No. I . . ."

"Bethie?" Jo stood at the top of the stairs, eyes shining. "Oh, Beth! You're here!"

My family swept from the house in a wave, gathered her up, and sucked her in, everybody hugging, laughing, and exclaiming at once, the children running in circles, shrieking, the dog yapping. March Family Madness, Jo called it once. No Dad, but that, too, was typical. Beth was pink cheeked and smiling, the center of attention without even trying.

I had a knack for getting people to notice me. But Beth . . . Everybody loved Beth.

"Look at you," Mom said. "You're skin and bones."

"You can never be too rich or too thin," Phee said.

"Where do you want these?" the driver asked, gesturing with the luggage. Two suitcases and her guitar case, more than enough for a weekend home. She must have packed extra clothes for the wedding.

"This way." I skirted the mob to lead him into the house.

He set the bags at the bottom of the staircase. I draped the garment bag carefully across a couple of chairs, ignoring a pang. It was just a dress. It wasn't like I'd written a Grammy-winning song or spent nine months gestating a book. Or a baby.

We went back out to the noise. Down in the yard, Mom and Aunt Phee were talking to Beth, in the middle of a sister sandwich with Meg and Jo. Eric carried DJ on his brawny shoulders. Baby Rob tagged Daisy across the lawn. Trey was propped against a column of the porch at the top of the stairs, part of and yet apart from the rest of the family. His lord-of-the-manor pose.

"Thanks for bringing Beth," he said to the driver. "What do I owe you?"

"I've got this," I said. He always paid, with the casual generosity of somebody whose family never had to worry about money.

Trey looked surprised. When I'd tagged along with him and Jo to the movies, he used to buy my popcorn. When Mom was facing surgery in the hospital, he'd bumped me up to first class so I could fly home. When I sort of started a fight in a dive bar down by the river, Trey had paid off the bartender.

78

He'd paid when we were in Paris, too. For dinner. For drinks. For a hotel room with a view of the Eiffel Tower . . .

"I don't mind," he said.

"I do. I'm not your surrogate kid sister anymore." Or somebody he had to be nice to because we once had sex.

"Hey, don't worry about it," the driver said. "I'm on the payroll." We both looked at him. "I work for Colt."

"Where is your young man?" Aunt Phee asked Beth.

Jo rolled her eyes.

"He's coming Sunday," Beth said.

Meg said something, lost in the clamor. The driver descended the stairs, leaving me and Trey standing alone on the porch. I was hyperaware of him, the height and heat of his body, the smell of his skin overlaid with clean cotton and citrusy bergamot.

"What about you?" he was asking.

"What about me?"

"I thought you were bringing your pal Vaughn with you." He could have been talking to Beth, his tone light and indulgent.

Fred Vaughn, lead singer of the British boy band Cricket, Instagram influencer, and twelfth Baron Byrne. Because of Vaughn, my Duchess bag was selling out on both sides of the Atlantic. I *owed* Fred. But we didn't have the kind of relationship that would drag him to a family wedding in North Carolina. None of which I felt like explaining to Trey.

"I don't need a date to my own sister's wedding." I slid a look at him. "Where's your plus-one?"

There was always someone — several someones, women — around Trey.

"I don't need a date, either," he said. "Although I could use . . ."

"A wingman?"

Wicked black amusement leaped in his eyes. "A friend." I felt the melting, seductive tug of his laughter. He met my gaze with disarming directness. "Listen, Amy . . . There's no reason this has to be awkward."

The word jabbed my memory. "Because we slept together, you mean?" I asked, keeping my voice low. "Or because you're still in love with my sister?"

He didn't deny it. "Jo is getting married." *To another man.* Another tug, of sympathy this time. He held out his hand. "Friends?"

We couldn't be enemies. He was part of my life, part of my family, my childhood crush, my sister's best friend. "Sure. Whatever." I swallowed and shook. His hand was warm and smooth and firm. I dropped it like I'd been burned. "Excuse me. I've got to hang that dress."

"There's no reason this has to be awkward."

Except for Paris.

CHAPTER 4
AMY

Paris, Then

The light in Paris reflected off the white stone buildings in the most amazing ways, bouncing off the bright awnings, picking out the delicate contrast of graceful iron-work. A young couple — tourists — stopped in the street to take selfies. An older woman leaned on her companion's arm. Sunlight filtered through the trees, painted the scarves and umbrellas, tomatoes and peppers in the street market. I stopped at a produce stall, attracted by the bright piled fruit, and the guy trailing behind me made a suggestion I had just enough French and imagination to translate.

All my life I'd dreamed of Paris. The light, the food, the art, the fashion.

Turned out it was just like high school, a bunch of assholes following me around saying horrible things.

"Les raisins," I said to the stall owner, care-

ful not to smile. Only fools and tourists smiled in Paris. *"C'est combien?"*

Transaction concluded, I fumbled the grapes into my bag, still ignoring the commentary of the guy behind me.

"Amy!"

For a moment, I blocked the sound of my own name. And then the voice registered. And the accent.

I turned, joy bubbling inside me. "Trey!" Tall and lean, dark and bronzed, wearing a pressed white shirt, untucked, and jeans. "When did you get here?"

"Flew in this morning. I went to your apartment. Your roommate — Chloe, is it? — told me you were out shopping."

My potty-mouthed stalker muttered one last observation — something about my breasts and his dick — and blended into the crowd.

Trey scowled over my head. "Who was that?"

"Nobody." I took his arm and squeezed it. "Oh, I'm so glad to see you!"

He looked handsomer than ever, a light scruff on his jaw. "I told you I'd stop on my way to Italy."

"You're so lucky." We walked down the sunlit street, arm in arm. It felt wonderful. Safe. A happy little sigh escaped me. "I've

83

always wanted to see Rome. Milan."

"I'm going to the Ferrari factory in Modena." He took my shopping bag, filled with grapes, *saucisson,* and cheese. "Do the tour, visit the track. We might put together some kind of VIP event."

I raised my eyebrows. "You get a lot of VIP Ferrari customers in Bunyan?"

"You sound like my grandfather."

"Do I?"

"Events like this are an incentive. Not just for the dealership, but on the commercial real estate side."

"Okay."

I didn't know enough to argue with him. I didn't want to argue with him. It couldn't be easy, being old Mr. Laurence's grandson. I had grown up as the Reverend March's daughter, as Meg, Jo, and Beth's little sister. I was so excited to come to Paris, to forge my own identity in a place where nobody knew my family or my high school reputation. *Easy A, the slutty March sister.* I couldn't wait to get away from my mother's advice, from my father's faint, surprised disapproval.

I just hadn't realized how hard it would be to live day after day where nobody recognized me. Or cared.

Raising my phone, I took Trey's picture.

Against the backdrop of plane trees, the light dappling his head, he looked like a print ad for Armani or Tom Ford — lean build, overlong hair, the cheekbones of a model or a poet. But there was a trace of brooding in his eyes, a hint of sulkiness around his mouth.

"There." I flashed the photo. "Something to remember you by."

His expression relaxed as he smiled in the old way. "Nice. Got any more?"

I nodded. "Mostly tourist stuff. Some design ideas."

"Let me see." I handed over the phone, watching as he browsed through shots of storefronts and flowers, stonework and graffiti. Strong lines, bold colors, vibrant bursts of imagination. He looked up, a smile in his eyes. "These are great."

I squirmed with pleasure. "The rest are just family," I said as he continued to scroll.

He paused. I peered over his arm at a photo I'd taken last Christmas, Jo frowning at her laptop in front of the fireplace, hair bundled on top of her head. I'd drawn a lightbulb over her head and captioned it, *Genius burns.*

"That's a good one," he said quietly.

"I'll send it to you," I offered.

"Thanks."

"How was your flight?" I asked as we walked on.

"Okay. We had a delay in New York."

"You were in New York? Did you see Jo?" He nodded. "How is she?"

"The same. Great. Happier than ever." I glanced at him sideways. He looked — not sick, or unhappy, exactly, but oddly serious. He met my gaze, a twist at the corner of his mouth. "We broke up."

I stopped walking. "Oh, Trey. I'm so sorry."

Not sorry. I'd crushed on him for years. He was my Edward Cullen, the sparkly vampire of my teenage fantasies, the one bright spot of my biggest high school humiliation. But Jo was my sister. And Trey . . . He was obviously hurting. So.

I patted his arm in what I hoped was a sisterly fashion. "I'm sure you'll get back together."

That was the pattern, right? For the past ten years. Jo broke up with him, he buzzed around some other girl for a while, and then made a beeline back to her. Sometimes I wanted to smack my sister.

"Not this time," he said. "It's over. I'm done."

I felt a little flutter like hope. Because if they *had* broken up . . . If they *really* were

86

through . . . But I didn't dare complete that thought.

We had reached my apartment. Chloe's apartment. I was paying half her rent for the privilege of sleeping in her tiny outer room on her even tinier couch.

"Do you want to come up?" I asked.

Chloe was in, but maybe she wouldn't mind squeezing an extra guest into a space the size of a bathroom back home. Not if the guest was Trey. She'd probably be thrilled, in a predatory sort of way.

"Let me take you to dinner," Trey suggested instead. "What time should I pick you up?"

I did a quick calculation. "Seven thirty?"

He smiled. "See you then." He bent to kiss me, a brief, brotherly brush of the lips, no more intimate than *la bise,* the standard Parisian double kiss of greeting.

But my heart still pounded.

As soon as I got upstairs, I FaceTimed Meg. There was a six-hour time difference between Paris and North Carolina, which made it late morning back home.

She picked up on the third ring. "Amy! Is everything all right?"

Yes. Maybe. No.

"Can't I just call to say 'hi'?" I asked.

"Not usually," Meg said. The picture

87

wobbled as she wiped her kitchen counter. "What's up?"

"Me, me!" Daisy said, reaching for the phone.

"It's Aunt A-my," Meg said. "Can you say 'A-my'?"

"Mee!" Daisy said, banging her tray table.

"She wants to talk to you," Meg translated.

"Put her on," I said.

Chloe gave me a French eye roll and rather obviously closed the door to her room.

My niece's face, smeared with — Cheerios? — wavered into view. "Hey, Daisy. How are you?"

Silence.

"Daisy and DJ are having a birthday soon," Meg coached in the background.

"I know," I said with more enthusiasm than I felt. "That's so awesome."

Heavy breathing, like the pervert in the market.

"Are you going to be two?" I asked, holding up two fingers.

Daisy dropped the phone.

"Oopsie," Meg said. "Hang on a sec, okay?"

I waited while she washed the twins' faces and hands and released them from their high chairs. "Sorry I won't be home for their party," I said when she got back on the phone.

"That's all right. We're keeping it small. Just family. Bethie's coming."

"What about Jo?" I asked, keeping my voice casual.

"I don't think so. I talked to her this morning." Meg and Jo talked almost every day. "She doesn't want the newspaper to start thinking she's dispensable."

"Did she sound . . . upset?"

"Over missing the toddlers' birthday party?" Meg asked in a dry tone. "Shockingly, no."

"But otherwise? She's okay?"

"She's fine." Meg shot a too-seeing look through the phone. "Why the sudden concern about Jo, anyway? Are you sure you're all right?"

A guilty flush heated my face. "I care, that's all."

"Aren't you sweet." A pause, as if Meg were debating with herself how much to tell me. "She broke up with Trey again."

"Oh no." *Yes.* My heart beat faster. "Do you think they'll get back together?"

"She says not. Well." Meg smiled ruefully. "You know Jo."

I did. Jo had gone to New York for her

MFA and found a job as a features writer. It was hard to imagine her giving up her dream to live in Bunyan.

And hard to imagine Trey anywhere else.

He wasn't born in North Carolina, I reminded myself. He hadn't grown up with the rest of us. But he was part of the fabric of my childhood, woven in with memories of the time before Meg got married and Jo moved away.

"Listen, sweetie, I have to go," Meg said. Changing the subject? "The twins are up to something."

"I don't hear anything."

"Exactly," Meg said darkly, making me laugh before we ended the call.

I took extra care getting dressed for my dinner with Trey. I wanted him to think I looked pretty. That was my value in our family. Meg was responsible, Jo was smart, and Beth was good. I was decorative. So. Yeah. You have to work with what you're given.

Besides, I wanted Trey to see me as something other than a pesky brat following him around, a humiliated fourteen-year-old shamed by her so-called friends.

White lace top. Skinny black skirt. Skinnier belt. I added red lipstick and tied a scarf around the handle of my bag in case it got cooler later. This was Paris, the city of fashion. I might not have money, but I had learned to accessorize.

When the buzzer sounded, I ran down the five flights to the street, breathless even before I saw Trey waiting on the sidewalk.

He smiled when he saw me. "You're ready."

"Don't sound so surprised. I can get ready in under an hour now," I said.

"I see that." The admiration in his eyes warmed me. "I like your top. Is it new?"

Helpless longing for his approval bloomed inside me. I fluffed my hair with my fingers, striking a pose. "This old thing?"

"You look very nice."

"So do you. Very elegant." He wore clean jeans and a navy blazer over another of those perfectly pressed white shirts. "I think I'll call you 'my lord.' "

His grin deepened, which was so . . . Wow.

"Anywhere you want to go?" he asked as we stepped off the sidewalk. Polite as always.

A heady feeling rose in me. "Anywhere?"

"Sky's the limit."

The top of the Eiffel Tower. Epicure. Arpège. All the restaurants I'd longed to go to and couldn't afford. With Trey, there was no danger he expected me to pay for dinner with sex.

"We don't have a reservation," I said.

"I made one at my hotel. In case you didn't want to decide."

According to the online guides, some of the best restaurants in the world were in Paris hotels. But . . . This was our chance to meet as equals, right? I wasn't a kid begging for treats anymore.

"There's a bistro I like. Near the square? We could walk."

He glanced at my black espadrille wedge sandals. "You used to complain about walking everywhere."

After we moved out to the farm, I couldn't run across the street or down the block to play with my friends like I used to. When they told stories about getting together after school or hanging out on weekends, I could only smile and wish I'd been there.

"That was in North Carolina. This is Paris," I said.

We set off. The narrow streets gradually filled with people getting off work or going out for the night, Parisians pursuing their daily lives as if the terrorist attacks of less than a year ago had never happened. Lovers walked arm in arm or hand in hand. Parents pushed strollers. Groups of students, hipsters, and *immigrés* congregated on corners or in doorways. Restaurants were opening for dinner, smells and tables spilling onto the sidewalks.

The bistro was down a battered back street, off from the square, the seating a mix of red vinyl booths and dark metal chairs, the doors flung open to the warm evening. I smiled brightly at the cute maître d', hoping he would remember me and give us a table. I wanted to show off my knowledge of the city and my somewhat improved French to Trey.

And the smile worked, or maybe the man took pity on me, because he nodded and beckoned us forward to a tiny table for two squeezed in by the door.

The bar was full. Trey looked around at the dining room — cozy, crowded, and relaxed — and then at me. "This is great."

I glowed. I suggested favorites from the menu, enjoying playing hostess. But when it came to ordering the wine, I stumbled.

"May I?" Trey conferred with the waiter before settling on a nice bottle of Médoc.

"I didn't know you spoke French," I said after our server departed.

"I don't."

"Your accent is better than mine."

He shrugged. Our table was very small. Our knees rubbed together unless I angled my legs away from his. Which I didn't. I

93

kept stealing glances at him, his lips, his lean, elegant hands. Excitement licked over my skin. Yet at the same time the oddest sense of calm, of comfort, settled in my stomach, a feeling like coming home. Because this was Trey.

"Did you ever speak Spanish at home?" I asked suddenly.

"No. Granddad didn't like it."

"Before, I mean. When you lived in Miami."

He rarely talked about his life with his parents, before they died in a boating accident, before he came to live with his grandfather. But I knew his mother was Cuban.

Trey repositioned his silverware. "Sometimes. With my mother. But my father wasn't fluent, so . . ." He broke off as the server returned with our wine.

"What do you mean, your granddad didn't like it?" I asked when the waiter was gone.

"He didn't like my mother. He was angry at my father for not taking over the business."

Old Mr. Laurence owned the car dealership and half the commercial real estate in town. A pillar of the community, Aunt Phee said. The Laurences had served as soldiers, judges, and state legislators. They'd financed the renovation of the waterfront and the park, donated to the library and the new hospital wing. I could understand old Mr. Laurence being pissed when his son and heir decided not to follow in his family's footsteps.

"But none of that was your fault," I said.

"He didn't approve of the marriage. He basically disowned my dad. Until they died, I'd never spoken to him, except on the phone."

I winced a little in sympathy, trying to imagine being fifteen years old, going to live with some grandfather I'd never met. "What about your mother's family?"

"They didn't approve, either. My grand-mother thought my father was *un vago* — a slacker. So that was the one thing she and Granddad could agree on." He met my gaze, smiling crookedly. "Hey, I'm not blaming the old man. I was the new kid in town. I didn't want to stick out by speaking Spanish."

"That wouldn't matter."

His eyes were black and opaque. "It didn't matter until the first time somebody asked me if my mother was a Mexican."

"That shouldn't make any difference!"

"But it does."

"But . . ." I struggled to reconcile this Trey

with the godlike image I'd carried since middle school. "Everybody liked you."

"Your family liked me," Trey said. "I wouldn't have survived without your sisters. Your mother. Everybody else thought I was some stuck-up rando from Orlando."

I set down my wine. "I thought you were from Miami."

His grin broke, quick and genuine. "Hialeah. We had an apartment four blocks from my grandparents' house."

We. His parents. I wondered if he'd had a chance to grieve their deaths, or if he'd been too busy making himself liked. Making himself fit in. I could relate to that.

"Do you ever think about going back?"

He shook his head. "I haven't been back since I was twelve. Except for holidays."

I frowned, confused. "I thought you were fifteen when you came to live with your grandfather."

"My parents sent me to military boarding school. Outside Philadelphia. Me and the screwups and the drug lords' kids. Granddad paid."

The food arrived then. Chicken with a crispy skin for me, a perfect filet balanced by freshly cut frites and an artfully arranged salad for him.

The noise of the room, the low lights,

wrapped us in a bubble of privacy. Our knees brushed under the table. I had an insane urge to slip off one sandal and curl my bare foot around his ankle. Which . . . No. He was my sister's boyfriend. Ex-boyfriend. Talking was better. Talking was safer.

"That must have been lonely," I said.

He didn't answer.

"Do you ever hear from them?" I asked. "Your mother's family?"

Trey cut his steak. I should let it go, I thought. *Don't spoil the mood.*

"Not really. There's just my grandmother now," he said. "And some cousins."

"She must miss you." *You must miss her.*

Another shrug, to show he didn't care. "She said I was better off living with my grandfather." A quick glance up from his plate. "I remind her of my dad, I think."

Her son-in-law. The slacker.

I could see a resemblance to old Mr. Laurence in Trey's long, straight nose and high forehead. But his golden skin, his wild, dark hair . . . Surely he got those from his mother. I reached across the table and squeezed his hand holding the knife.

Trey switched his grip, giving my fingers a quick press before releasing them. "So, tell me about Paris," he invited, sitting back in his chair. "What have you seen so far?"

I accepted the change of subject, chatting about the museums I had visited, the places I still wanted to go. It was quickly obvious that Trey knew the city better than I did. This was not his first trip through Paris. But he listened as if my adventures, my opinions, mattered, nodding when I talked about the fashion exhibits at the Louvre, smiling at my descriptions of window shopping in Le Marais. We talked about the sculptures in the Tuileries Gardens. I didn't tell him about my attempts to sketch there. I'd quickly learned that sitting alone on the classic park benches was an invitation to be molested by pigeons. Or worse.

Under his attention, I expanded like a flower in a time-lapse photograph. It was so easy to talk to him. No language barriers. No barriers at all. He asked about my plans and listened to the answers like he cared. Nobody in Paris cared.

Extending my postgraduation trip had been more difficult than I'd thought. I had some money saved from working retail in college. But nobody would rent to me without six months' payment in advance, proof of employment, and a guarantee from a French bank.

"I'm hoping for a job in a boutique," I

confessed. "I have experience. And obviously, I speak English."

"I thought you were here to play," Trey said.

"I'm here to learn. I want to be accepted to Louis Vuitton's craftsman training program. But that's not happening, because I'm an American. So . . ." I shrugged. "I'll sell accessories to rich tourists."

"You'll make it work," Trey said. "You're very talented."

"Thanks." I took a breath, returning his smile. "You are, too."

I asked about his trip. Over dessert, he talked about Modena — not about the cars or the track in Maranello, but about the ducal palace and the piazzo in front of the duomo. I watched him greedily, hoarding details for later — the purple-red wine, the bittersweet chocolate, the play of light on his face and hands.

He paid the bill.

Outside, streetlights bloomed against the fading sky. The winding streets were lined with bars and cafés full of people drinking and smoking. "Nice neighborhood," Trey remarked.

"Not much to see," I said. "But lots to do." I didn't tell him I spent most nights alone in the apartment.

99

He smiled, making my heart skip. "Let's do something, then."

I nodded. I didn't want to let the evening go.

We walked through narrow cobblestoned streets toward the Bastille, Trey matching his steps to mine. The first time I had visited the site of the old prison, I'd been disappointed to find a bustling roundabout with cars whizzing by. But at night, the monument in the center of the traffic blazed with light. The golden-winged statue topping the column looked poised to fly. We stopped for a drink on a quiet side street. Strolled along the brown-black canals, enjoying the warm summer evening. Bursts of music, snatches of conversation, drifted from groups of students hanging out on the iron footbridges.

Being with Trey was so fun. So . . . *easy.* No Parisian men calling, *Miss, Miss.* No Parisian women flickering scornful looks at my hair, my clothes, my shoes. Not with Trey beside me.

Like my freshman year of high school. Trey had rescued me then, too, walking me into the high school gym under the noses of Jenny Snow, Queen of the Mean Girls, and her asshole brother and his friends.

By the time we returned to the apartment,

the sky was inky black with an orange haze and my feet throbbed inside my espadrilles.

"Thanks for dinner." I couldn't invite him up. Chloe would be home. And if she weren't there, if we were alone in the apartment . . .

"I had a good time."

"Me, too," I said breathlessly.

He smiled a little. "I'll call you."

He wouldn't. "Sure."

He hugged me, quick and hard, enveloping me in the scent of bergamot, like a cup of Earl Grey tea on a cold day. When he let me go, I shivered, my body protesting the loss of his warmth.

"Tomorrow," he promised, and I ran upstairs, feeling like that statue in the plaza — on tiptoe, my heart poised for flight.

CHAPTER 5
BETH

The sun streamed through the windows of Oak Hill, bathing everything in a warm golden glow. I'd spent the morning outside with my sisters, arranging chairs and flowers on the terrace. Now we crowded into the master bedroom, Momma and Aunt Phee, my sisters and me, to help Jo get ready for her wedding.

She stood in front of the full-length mirror as Amy, on her knees, made a last-minute adjustment to the hem of her wedding gown.

I'd changed my clothes an hour ago, grabbing a moment alone in the bathroom, where no one could see and compare and comment. Without Sharla to supervise, my makeup was simple, mascara and lip gloss.

Every few minutes, I checked my phone for messages from Colt.

"I suppose you're next," Aunt Phee said.

"Next?" I repeated.

"To get married. You and that singer."

"Oh. I . . . No." I blushed furiously, putting my phone away. "He hasn't even . . ." *Asked me.* "Met the family yet."

"Is he here?" Meg asked.

"Not yet."

He had texted late last night, my phone screen lighting up the dark. Great show. Miss you, angel face.

Then . . . Nothing.

He didn't say when he was coming. If he was coming. He'd never actually promised.

"He has a lot of people depending on him," I said.

Our mother shot me a sharp look.

"Stop fidgeting," Phee ordered Jo.

"I feel like I'm getting ready for prom," Jo grumbled. But she stood obediently still as Amy trimmed her thread.

"Think of it like a play," Meg suggested.

When we girls were little, Jo wrote plays for us to perform on the parsonage porch. I remembered changing costumes behind a blanket, and for once, the memory of going onstage didn't make my stomach clench.

I smiled. "Only this time you're the princess."

"Not me. Amy's the princess," Jo said.

Amy narrowed her eyes. "Why am I always the princess?"

Jo grinned. "Because you can't act?"

"Well, today I'm your fairy godmother."

"I'm a fairy, too," Daisy shouted, pirouetting. As she twirled, the blush tulle skirt of her flower girl dress floated around her like a cloud. The photographer Meg had hired snapped a picture. I flinched at the click of the shutter, automatically sucking in my stomach.

But nobody was looking at me. All eyes were on the bride.

Jo turned to study her reflection. "This *is* a great dress."

The heavy cream silk flowed over her curves, softening her angles. Her hair was up — Meg had arranged it in a softer version of her usual messy bun — exposing the jaunty black bow at the back of her neck. The racerback straps emphasized the strong, clean line of her shoulders.

Amy got to her feet. "Thanks."

"It fits," Phee acknowledged.

"It better," Amy said. Her eyes narrowed on me. "We need to take yours in at the waist. Have you lost weight?"

Yes. "No. I like it loose," I protested.

"You look amazing," Meg said. Smoothing things over, the way she always did.

Or proving I'd really needed to lose those extra pounds.

"Beth should be comfortable," Jo said, coming to my defense. "I want everybody to be comfortable."

"You look beautiful," I said. Almost boyish, even though she was a mother now.

"Especially your arms," Meg said. "Have you been working out?"

Jo smiled. "Lifting my little guy."

Amy turned from the bed with a shoe box in her hands. "Speaking of comfortable . . . ."

"I thought I'd wear my old sandals," Jo said.

"Just try them," our mother said.

Jo looked from the shoe box to Amy's hopeful face and sighed. "Sure. Why not?" She tugged off the lid and dug in the tissue paper. "Oh, Ames." Her laugh was choked with emotion. She drew out a pair of white sneakers, adorned with tiny black bows to match her dress. "They're perfect. Everything's perfect."

Whirling, she hugged our sister close. The mirror caught the moment, Jo's dark head by Amy's bright one, the misty smile on Meg's face, the naked love in our mother's eyes. My vision shimmered at the sight of all of us together. Aunt Phee sniffed.

"I never thought I'd say this, but you were right about the dresses," Jo said.

"You all look wonderful," our mother said.

Meg smiled. "We do, kind of."

We looked like sisters, all in blue, the same and not the same. Meg had chosen something off-the-shoulder that hugged her curves. Amy wore a midnight fit-and-flare, the cutouts at the waist and hem filled with dark illusion.

I smoothed the soft blue lace Amy had picked out for me, wishing I had bought a larger size. But Amy had insisted.

Our mother smiled at me reassuringly. "Stop fussing. You look fine."

"You, too, Momma," I said.

Her body, straight and spare as pine, was set off by a sleeveless steel-blue sheath. She looked like Meg would in twenty years, with thick, faded hair and steady eyes, our sister's prettiness stripped down to its essential structure.

"Not bad for an old broad."

"Just wait until Dad sees you," Amy said.

"Ha. Your father hasn't looked at me in years," Abby scoffed. But her cheeks turned pink.

"Hey!" Jo grinned. "My dress has pockets!"

"Don't you dare carry anything but a handkerchief," Meg said. "You'll spoil the line of your skirt."

"Okay." Jo took a deep breath and grabbed

106

the bottle of champagne sitting ready in the bucket Meg had brought up from the kitchen. "A toast!"

The cork popped. The camera clicked and whirred. I didn't even blink.

"Just half a glass for me," our mother said.

"Come on, Mom, live a little. I'm getting married!"

"About time," Phee said.

Momma smiled. "Fine. Fill it up."

"I want to toast," Daisy said.

I passed around glasses. It felt so good to be home, to fade into my familiar supporting role. Not the princess or the fairy or the star. Just . . . me, one of the March girls, the quiet one who brought home strays and sometimes played guitar.

Meg poked a straw into a juice box. "Do not squeeze," she warned Daisy.

"Right." Jo cleared her throat. Raised her glass. "I want to say this now, in case I can't do it properly later. To Aunt Phee, thank you for letting Eric and me have Oak Hill for the wedding, for the restaurant, and to make our home. We'll do our best to make everyone feel always welcome. To you, my darling sisters. Thank you for the flowers and the dress and the cake and, oh, everything. Thank you for making a fuss, even when I said I didn't want one. And

Momma . . ." Her gaze sought our mother's. Her eyes shone with unshed tears. "Thank you most of all. For being there for me. For us. Always."

"To Momma," I echoed softly.

Amy patted her fingertips under her eyes. "No crying," Meg said. "You'll ruin your makeup if you cry."

Our mother passed out tissues while the photographer snapped pictures.

"Time for the flowers!" Amy said.

Meg had ordered seasonal bouquets from the farmers' market, sweet pea and tulips for us girls, gillyflowers and blush roses for Jo.

"One last thing." Our mother turned from the bureau, a box in her hand. Opening it, she lifted a simple pearl brooch from the cotton batting. "It was your grandmother's. Something old to carry on your wedding day." She pinned it to the white ribbon binding Jo's bouquet. "For luck."

"Oh, Momma." Jo threw herself in our mother's arms.

Aunt Phee cleared her throat. "Don't you think you've kept that man waiting long enough?"

Jo grabbed her bouquet. The petals trembled in her grasp.

My heart squeezed in sympathy. "Nervous?"

"Maybe. A little." Jo shook her head, smiling. "Not about getting married. Now that the day is finally here, I can't wait to be Eric's wife. He makes me better. More. More myself, you know?"

I didn't, but I nodded anyway.

Honestly, I never felt I could be entirely myself in Colt's world. There were always too many other people around us, watching. Judging. He was so wonderful. I could never quite measure up in their eyes or my own, never be the equal partner he deserved.

It was different for Jo. She fit into Eric's life. She had worked in his kitchen. They went back to New York all the time, to visit her publisher or his restaurant. But Eric, with his big heart, had chosen to live in her world.

Surreptitiously, I checked my phone again. No word from Colt.

"Because Eric loves you," Meg said.

"He does. And I love him." Jo grinned. "I guess I'm just worried I'll trip. Or forget my lines or something."

"Your father will remind you," our mother said.

"Where is Ashton?" Aunt Phee asked.

"Outside," Meg said. "With Eric. They're all waiting."

"He should be here to give you away."

"That's an antiquated tradition from a time when women were considered property, Aunt Phee," Jo said. "I'm my own person. I don't need my father to give me away."

"Not to mention you and Eric already have a kid together," Amy said.

"Ash is performing the ceremony," our mother said.

"But who will walk her down the aisle?" Phee asked.

"You will. All of you." Jo reached out and took our mother's hand on one side, Meg's on the other. Her smile reached out and embraced us. "All the March women, together."

"Oh, Jo." My voice broke. "That's perfect."

Meg wagged her finger. "Uh-uh. No crying."

"I never heard of such a thing," Phee said. "Tromping down the aisle like a bunch of cows."

Our mother laughed. "Goats, maybe."

"If you can't do it, I'm sure everybody will understand," Amy said to Phee. "I mean, nobody expects you to walk that far at your age."

Phee drew herself up, elegant in lavender silk. "I'm perfectly capable of walking myself down the aisle, thank you, missy."

"So is Jo." Amy smiled sweetly. "But for some reason she wants you."

Phee snorted. "Don't think I don't see what you're doing, young lady. I won't be manipulated."

"But you'll do it anyway." I kissed her cheek. "Because you love us."

"Humph," Phee said. But she looked pleased.

"Right." Jo took a deep breath. "Let's do this thing."

"Daisy, here's your basket," Meg said.

"I'm a fairy. I don't want a basket."

"How about a fairy crown?" Amy suggested.

Daisy nodded.

So Amy bobby-pinned a circlet of flowers to Daisy's head like a crown, and we went out into a garden full of guests and flowers and sunshine. The green lawn rolled away to the water. I hung back behind my sisters, peeking from the shadows of the porch at the rows of white chairs. No Colt. But our friends and family were all there, Eric's parents and his sister from Germany, Miss Hannah wearing her best church hat, old

Mr. Laurence in a yellow bow tie. Eric waited under the wedding arch, Rob clutching his pants leg. His tall sons, Bryan and Alec, stood shoulder to shoulder beside him. Trey and John were next to our father, solemn in his minister's robes.

Trey saw Jo first. His face was white, his eyes very dark. Even though I was so, so happy for my sister, I felt bad for him. Poor Trey. He had loved her for such a long time. But everything happens for a reason, right? I knew Jo was making the right choice.

And I knew Trey. He would never do anything to cast a cloud on Jo's special day.

Eric's eyes were fixed on the porch. His great smile took over his whole face. Jo beamed back at him, starting down the steps, practically floating. Not waiting. Not tripping. The musicians, a flute and guitar hired from church, rushed into the opening notes of "Be Thou My Vision" as the rest of us — my mother and sisters, Aunt Phee and Daisy — scurried after her.

"*Now* she's in a hurry," Aunt Phee remarked to no one in particular, and Jo's wedding to Eric began with laughter and music.

A light breeze sent a scatter of apple blossoms across the yard. The guitar's B string needed tuning, but that slight flaw only made everything more real. More beautiful.

Eric's voice as he spoke his vows was almost too deep and low to be heard, but Jo made her promises in a clear, confident voice, looking him straight in the eye.

Our parents exchanged glances. Meg smiled at John. Aunt Phee dabbed her eyes.

I leaned my head on Amy's shoulder, so happy to be with them, one of them. If only Colt were here, it would be perfect.

"Do you who represent their families rejoice in their union and pray God's blessing upon them?" our father intoned, and we all said, "We do."

"Mama!" Rob said, holding out his arms.

Jo scooped him up to another smattering of laughter.

Eighteen-year-old Bryan dug in his pocket for the ring. And then they were married. Eric kissed the bride. Jo kissed him back enthusiastically, and Trey looked the other way.

I looked away, too, as a long black car slid from beneath the trees and stopped at the curve in the drive.

My heart thumped.

The limo door opened.

Colt. The surge of happiness caught me in the chest. He was here.

Parties had always been agony for me. I was anxious at sleepovers, awkward at school dances, overwhelmed at college parties with their pizza, beer, and random friends-of-friends. After-concert parties were the worst. I never knew what to say or how to penetrate a group. I couldn't eat. I was afraid to drink, because of the rumors. I spent a lot of time in the bathroom.

Eric and Jo's reception was different. At home, no one expected me to make uncomfortable small talk while their eyes scanned over my shoulder for Colt. Guests wandered through the house and garden, filling plates with Eric's upscale barbecue — a whole hog, roasted overnight, with bushels of oysters, potato salad, coleslaw, and corn bread. There was a keg on the terrace, a table of desserts, contributed by the neighbors, in the foyer, and pitchers of sweet tea and lemonade. So much food. So many calories.

A shadow fell over the celebration, rising in my mind: the specter at the feast, hovering around the buffet like an unwelcome wedding guest. I blinked and looked away.

Amy had gone a little crazy with tulle,

twinkling lights, and tin buckets of flowers everywhere. Colt and I sat at a little table, just the two of us. I sipped my water, watching as the photographer moved around the dance floor, taking pictures. Of Jo, bouncing baby Rob. Of sixteen-year-old Alec, rocking out with Amy.

Dad, having done his duty in the father-daughter dance, was listening courteously to Wanda Crocker. Such a saint. Everybody said so. He'd returned from serving as an army chaplain in Iraq to open a storefront ministry for veterans. He was always available to those in need.

That was the problem. His sainthood took him away from us. He was deployed for years. Even after he came home, there were always phone calls and crises and other people requiring his attention at dinnertime or in the middle of the night.

I felt a stab of anger, quickly suppressed. I missed him. I missed our family the way it used to be, the security and support that came with being one of the March girls.

Eventually our mother lost patience with him, I guess. Meg said nobody knew what went on in a marriage except the two people involved.

Trey's grandfather came over to our table. "Beth. It's good to see you, girl."

"Mr. Laurence!" I jumped up, ignoring his outstretched hands to kiss his cheek, breathing in his good grandfather scent of witch hazel and tobacco.

He cleared his throat, patting my back awkwardly. "There's nothing left of you to hug. Don't they feed you in Nashville?"

I forced a smile. "We've been on tour."

"Ah. We've missed you around here." He drew back. "And this must be . . ."

"Colt Henderson." I said.

Why didn't Colt stand? But he shook hands politely enough, used to meeting and greeting fans.

"You should be dancing," Mr. Laurence said. To Colt? To me?

"Oh, I'm fine," I said.

Mr. Laurence shot a look at Colt from under his bushy gray brows. "Of course."

Heat washed my face. Had he been asking *me* to dance? "I'd love to come see you while I'm home," I said.

"I'd like that. Anytime. Bring your . . ." His gaze lingered on Colt. "Guitar."

"I will," I promised.

He nodded shortly at Colt before moving on.

"How do you know Colonel Sanders?" Colt asked.

"Mr. Laurence? He's our . . ." *Neighbor.*

Friend. Grandfather figure. "He gave me my guitar."

"The Hummingbird? Nice." Colt swigged his beer.

I glanced wistfully toward the dance floor. My mother was holding hands with Daisy and DJ, twirling them in circles.

"I wish they'd dance together," I said to Colt.

"Who?"

"My parents."

"I thought they were divorced."

"Separated." My mother had asked Dad to move out three years ago. I wasn't there. *"Nothing to do with you,"* she assured me when she broke the news. But like a little child, I couldn't help wondering if I were somehow to blame. If I hadn't gone to Nashville, if I'd been here when she was sick and needed me, would she have minded so much that our father didn't help around the farm?

"They still love each other," I said.

"Come on, angel. Even you can't believe that."

"Maybe not romantically. But we're still family." That's what our mother said. "Families love each other."

Colt tipped back his beer. "Not all families."

Not *his* family, I thought with a wave of sympathy.

Our tour of his flooded hometown last month had *not* included a visit to his mother. *"She wants to see me, she knows where to find me,"* Colt had said. His father walked out on them when Colt was small. He'd confided once that his dad had called a couple years ago, looking for money. No wonder Colt was sometimes a little cynical.

My family wasn't perfect, but I'd never doubted I was loved. I was happy to be home where I was useful. Where I could hide.

Colt frowned at the photographer, snapping pictures of Eric's parents on the dance floor. "They don't pay any attention to you. It's like you're not even here."

What a nice thought. Like I could simply disappear. "It's my sister's wedding," I explained. "It's not about me."

"Don't these people understand you're a star?"

"You're the star." And then I realized. He was used to being the center of attention. Of course. I reached across the table. "I'm so glad you came."

"Whatever makes you happy."

"Aren't you having fun?"

"Weddings aren't really my thing."

"The ceremony was beautiful," I said.

"It was cute, yeah. I just don't see what difference a bunch of words and a piece of paper makes." He squeezed my fingers and smiled. "The way I see it, if you want to be together, that's what counts."

I held on to his hand and the smile. "A marriage is more than words. It's the commitment. Eric and Jo belong to each other. They're a family now. They have a child together. Children."

"Kids, also not my thing. Not yet." He swiveled his head, surveying the terrace. "Speaking of kids, how old is that DJ? Twelve?"

I glanced toward the DJ's table, willing to be distracted. *Not yet,* he'd said. That meant he was open to children one day, didn't it? All he needed was . . . *A kick in the ass,* said a voice like Amy's.

Time, I told myself. I needed to be patient. I needed to be perfect for him. "A little older than that. He's one of John's students."

Colt looked blank.

"Meg's husband, John?" I'd introduced Colt to my entire family right after the ceremony. I couldn't expect him to remember them all. "He teaches history at the high school."

119

"Yeah, well, somebody should teach that kid how to make a playlist. This isn't exactly a Marvin Gaye crowd."

I looked at Eric's parents, swaying together to "Let's Get It On." So adorable together. Happy. Affectionate. The way I wanted us to be. Jo and Eric were lucky, to have his parents as role models. "Do you want to dance?" I asked Colt.

"We can do better than that." He stood with a jerk of his chin to someone behind me.

I looked at him in confusion.

"Come on, angel." He grinned, making my heart thump. "Let's give your family a show."

My heart started pounding for a completely different reason. "I should see if Meg needs help with . . ." *What?* Daisy and DJ were happily occupied playing hide-and-seek under the tables. For a second, I wished I could join them. "The cake."

It wasn't like I was going to stuff my face with lemon curd and buttercream frosting. But I could help serve.

"Later for that," he said. "Sing with me."

"Colt, I . . . I really don't feel like it."

"So fake it."

Nerves roiled my stomach. "I can't."

Irritation flickered across his face. "Baby,

120

you fake it all the time."

I wanted to die. He *knew*?

He must have seen something in my expression, because he winked. "That's what performing's all about. Fake it till you make it, right?"

On *stage,* he meant. Not in bed. Relief washed over me. I smiled back.

"You'll be fine. You can do this little thing for me." His voice turned coaxing. "Do it for your sister."

A gift for my sister. I could do that.

Jimmy appeared with Colt's guitar, pausing to speak to the photographer. The photographer nodded and raised his camera.

It was all too fast. Too perfect. Too orchestrated to be spontaneous — Jimmy, the guitar, the photographer. Doubt knotted my insides, sharp as a cramp. Had Colt *planned* this? Stepping into the spotlight. Taking control.

His warm blue eyes met mine. "Come on, angel. Let's give them something for You-Tube."

CHAPTER 6
AMY

"Folks, can I have your attention? Attention, please!" the guy with Colt said into the microphone. Jimmy, that was his name. The driver-slash-assistant-slash-bodyguard.

He'd better be making a toast. Because, honestly, drinking was the only way I was going to get through being back in Bunyan, where I had never been voted Most Popular like Meg or Most Likely to Succeed like Jo. Girl Most Likely to Do Something Stupid to Impress Her Supposed Friends, that was me.

At least no one had accused me of being a boyfriend-poaching slut yet.

". . . special surprise for you all," Jimmy finished, handing off the mic to Colt.

Eric looked at Jo, who shrugged. So, a surprise to the bride and groom, too.

John and Trey exchanged glances. No one would ever mistake them for brothers. But something in the way they stood, assessing the newcomer, linked them together and marked them as family. The artist in me admired the picture they made: Eric, big and dark, bearded and tattooed; Trey, lean and golden, elegant in Armani; solid John, with his blond cowlick and appealing dad bod.

Not that I was checking out my sister's honey. Nope. Not ever making that mistake again.

I grabbed my glass to toast the happy couple.

". . . want to thank you all for this wonderful welcome," Colt was saying. "But I wouldn't be here without my angel."

"Laying it on pretty thick," Trey murmured close to my ear.

I managed not to jump. "Maybe he's just trying to give Beth credit. You know, for writing two hit songs?"

Beth had that deer-in-the-headlights look she got before every school concert. Her fingers fidgeted against her side.

"She looks like she's going to throw up," Jo said.

"Stage fright," Meg said.

John draped an arm over his wife's shoulders. "It's been two years. I thought she'd be over that."

"Some things you don't get over," I said

with a glance at Trey.

But he was watching Colt. "What's our Beth doing with a guy like that, anyway?"

His protective older brother routine was pretty funny. And surprisingly sweet.

"She doesn't go into detail," Meg said.

"But they are sharing a tour bus. So . . ." Jo shrugged.

"Did you guys ever consider that maybe Beth got exactly what she wants?" I asked. "She's with a super hot, rich, famous music star who can help her career."

Trey raised his brows. "A regular Fred Vaughn."

"Fred's an influencer. He's been very good to me," I said. "Maybe Colt is good for Beth."

"She's a little young for him," John said.

Eric smiled and said nothing.

"Older than me," I pointed out. Everyone always forgot that.

"Yeah, but you can take care of yourself," Jo said.

Not always. Not when I was a fourteen-year-old high school freshman desperate for acceptance. Trey had rescued me then. But I'd never told him — I'd never told anyone, even Meg — the whole story.

"What is that supposed to mean?"

"She means you are not afraid to go after

what you want." Eric smiled at his wife. "Like Jo."

Trey's brow flexed as he glanced from Jo to me. He smiled. "They *are* sisters."

I tossed my head. "You know what? I'm tired of people always comparing me to my sisters."

Jimmy handed Colt a guitar.

"Ssh," Jo said. "He's going to play something."

Beth's face was flushed, her eyes bright. With nerves? I wondered. Or excitement?

"You don't think he's going to propose, do you?" Meg asked.

John shook his head. "That guy? Not a chance."

"It would be a dick move, anyway," Trey said.

I looked at him in surprise. "Why?"

"It's Jo's day. Jo and Eric's. He should let it be about them."

See, this is why I wasn't over him. Trey was a good man. He always knew the right thing to do.

There was a spatter of applause as Colt began to play. Honestly? I wasn't a huge Colt Henderson fan. He was a little too country for a girl determined to leave Bunyan behind. But he sure knew how to gauge his audience.

125

I recognized the opening of "I Miss You More," the ballad Beth had written, a duet between a deployed soldier and his sweetheart back home. Everyone in these parts knew a father, sister, husband, neighbor who had been deployed. Colt sang it well, in a velvet whiskey voice with plenty of feels. And when Beth joined in, her radiant soprano weaving and throbbing over the melody, the song arrowed straight to my heart.

"In the quiet," she sang.

"When things get rough," Colt answered.

They sang together. *"Your calls and your letters are never enough . . ."*

"That takes me back," Meg said wistfully.

Back to when Daddy went to Iraq, to when Momma first moved us girls out to the farm. Back when we were a family, when I thought they would stay married forever. My eyes stung. Logically, I'd accepted that my parents' relationship wasn't perfect. But the two of them together was all I'd ever known.

"You're not the only one." I nodded toward our parents. In the fading light, I couldn't see their faces. Only the pale flash of our mother's hair and our father's head, lowered over hers.

"They're dancing," Meg said in a troubled

voice. Making herself responsible for everybody's feelings. As usual.

"Honey, it's fine," John said.

"But . . ."

He turned her to face him, resting his
hands on her hips. "It's a wedding. Let them
enjoy themselves for one night."

She sighed and looped her arms around
his neck. Giving in to the moment or the
music or the memories. Eric gathered Jo
close, holding her to his heart. She rubbed
her cheek against his shoulder. All around
me, couples swayed and shuffled. Colt and
Beth sang together, voices twined, gazes
locked.

"If this good-bye is forever . . ."

"I'll still remember."

"And miss you more."

The twinkling lights blurred.

"Want to dance?"

I blinked. Trey's face swam in front of me,
smiling in the old way, easy and affectionate. You would hardly guess his heart was
broken. Of course, he'd had almost three
years to get used to the idea that the love of
his life was marrying another man.

Some things you don't get over, I thought
again.

"Nope. Sorry." *Not sorry.*

Weddings were dangerous. All those feel-

127

ings swirling around in the air. I didn't want my sisters talking about me the way they talked about Mom and Dad. About Beth and Colt. Besides, if I danced with Trey . . . Well. I knew where *that* would lead. Drunken Wedding Sex.

I was not going to be a cliché.

"I have to see Aunt Phee," I said.

Trey lifted his eyebrows. "Now?"

"I may not get another chance. I'm going back to New York tomorrow."

"Fine. I'll come with you."

My mouth dropped open. "You will not."

"To see Phee."

"I . . . Oh." Heat washed my face. "For a minute, I thought you meant you were coming to New York."

His black gaze met mine. "Are you inviting me?"

Longing jabbed me like a needle. I rolled my eyes. "Please. Even you don't have that much time on your hands."

I walked away, leaving him to trail me around the dance floor the way I used to tag after him and Jo.

So much had changed, I thought, with a queer tug of heart.

And so much remained the same.

Some guy loomed in front of me, cutting me off. I got a feeling like a spider crawling on the back of my neck. Davis Snow, older brother of Jenny Snow, meanest of the Mean Girls.

"Amy March. You've changed." Davis looked me up and down, lingering on my now-developed breasts. "I hardly recognized you with your clothes on."

I was aware of Trey behind me, making his way with unhurried ease through the wedding guests. But I didn't need him to rescue me anymore.

"You're right," I said to Davis. "I have changed. Too bad you're still an asshole."

I moved around him to where Phee and her pal Wanda Crocker sat in a pair of straight-backed chairs like two elderly chaperones in a Regency novel.

"Why aren't you dancing?" she demanded as I approached their table.

"I was looking for you." I bent to kiss her Estée Lauder–perfumed cheek, ignoring a yap from Polly in her lap.

"Well, you've found me."

I glanced at Wanda. "I was hoping we could talk."

"Would you like to dance, Miss Wanda?" Trey asked.

Her face lit.

"That was nice of him," I said as he led her off.

129

"He's a good boy," Phee said. "I always thought one of you girls should have married him."

"Excuse me?"

"You should think about it. Now that you're home."

"But I'm not," I said, sinking into Wanda Crocker's abandoned chair. "Home, I mean. I go back to New York tomorrow."

"I suppose it will have to be Beth, then." The old lady met my gaze, a gleam in her eye. "Jo thinks they'd be good together."

Beth? And *Trey*?

For a second, I imagined them as a couple. Trey would make Beth happy. Beth would give Trey the family he'd always wanted. It could work.

Except . . . I hated the idea.

"Beth already has a boyfriend," I said. "And a career."

Phee fed cheese to her dog. "Well, it's too late for Meg to marry the boy. And now Jo's lost her chance, too."

"Aunt Phee! I thought you were happy Jo was with Eric."

"Happiness has nothing to do with it. They have a child together."

"You gave them Oak Hill as a wedding present."

"I'm not giving anybody anything." Her

back was poker straight. "It was a financial decision. An investment in Eric's restaurant. Maybe he can make something of this place. God knows your father never wanted to. Or his father."

I regarded her with affection. "You old softie."

Her lips twitched in what — in another woman — would have been a smile. That was my cue. My chance.

Colt and Beth had ended their duet, shifting on a bridge of bright guitar notes to a rowdy, boot-stomping party song. I didn't have much time before Wanda returned. I scooted my chair closer.

"Speaking of investments . . ." I took a breath. "I was hoping to talk to you about Baggage."

"Your own? Or your company?"

I laughed dutifully. "Ha-ha. The thing is . . . You've always been really generous. Sending me to Paris and everything."

"A graduation present. Your sisters made other choices."

"It was a wonderful opportunity."

"You seem to have made the most of it."

I flushed with stupid pleasure at this rare praise from a family member. "Thanks. The thing is, I have this other opportunity, and I could use your help."

131

"An opportunity for what, exactly?"

"We're doing — Baggage is doing really well. We're in thirteen stores now, and I have more orders than I can handle for the new Duchess tote. It's the perfect time to expand. All I need is a larger workroom." And a few more employees. A second sewing machine. A chance to step back and breathe and actually focus on design, because after the Duchess bag there had to be something else, something new, something fresh. #handbagaddict #ownit

"In New York," Phee said.

"Yes. Ideally. I'd love to get into a little retail space with production in the back." I could picture it, shelves of stock in whimsical designs. Quirky, colorful window displays. A sign over the door in the shape of a handbag, with my logo in jaunty letters. "But that's probably out of my price range. Rents in the city are pretty steep."

"You could relocate."

"I've considered it." Setting up shop in an abandoned warehouse in Newark or some boarded-up storefront in Trenton. Commuting into Manhattan, bundling big boxes of samples on the New Jersey Transit system. I shoved the thought away. "Wherever I go, a move is going to take money."

"Sell more handbags."

132

"That's the plan. But I'm really limited by my space right now." And my cash flow. "Which is why I need a loan. An investment. Like in Jo and Eric's restaurant."

Phee's mouth pulled tight, like the knot on a balloon. "I assume you've been to the bank."

I nodded. "Meg helped me with my application."

"And . . . ?"

"They turned me down." The memory seared my chest. "I don't have enough assets." Just my sewing machine.

"But you have orders, you said."

"Orders, inventory, materials. But none of those are assets. Apparently those things don't have any value unless you're in the business of making and selling handbags. Which the bank isn't."

"Neither am I."

I met the old dragon's gaze, my heart thudding. "But you could be."

"Hmph." She stroked Polly, her wrinkled hands on the dog's silky fur. "An investment," she repeated slowly.

I nodded.

She raised her head, staring across the terrace at Meg and Jo, talking and laughing under the twinkling lights. At our parents, standing very close together in the shadow of a column. (*And what was that about?*) In profile, I could see the aging no amount of moisturizer could smooth away, her drooping neck, her sagging cheeks beneath the mask of carefully applied color. She looked back at me. "There would have to be terms."

I released a breath I hadn't been aware of holding. "Of course. I'd be happy to pay you the same rate of interest as the bank. There are forms online —"

She waved my eager suggestions away. "Perhaps *terms* is the wrong word. I should have said *conditions*."

"What conditions?"

"Come back to Bunyan."

"I'd love to," I lied, guiltily aware I didn't visit as often as I should. "It's just . . . I'm really busy right now. All those orders. Maybe this summer." Everyone left the city in August anyway. Bunyan was hardly the Hamptons, but . . . "I'll come for a whole week," I promised.

It would be worth it, to get a new workroom.

"Not for a visit," Phee said. "For good."

I sat back. "Excuse me?"

"I'll invest in your business if you move it here, to Bunyan. That's my condition."

My mouth dropped open. "You're kidding."

"I never joke about money."

"No way."

"Any amount, at one half point over the rate of inflation," Phee said crisply. "To be repaid over a period of time determined between you and my lawyer."

Shit. She was serious.

"I . . . Thank you, Aunt Phee. But that's impossible."

"On the contrary, I think I'm being very reasonable. Even generous."

"But I'll pay you back!"

"I have no use for your money. It's time you came home."

"But everything I have is in New York!"

"Except your family."

"That's not fair."

"It's extremely fair. It's the same offer I made to your sister and Eric." Phee arched an eyebrow. "*He* didn't argue with me about relocating."

"But . . . *Bunyan.*"

"There's nothing wrong with Bunyan. This town is like me. Our best days may be behind us, but we're not dead yet."

I opened my mouth. Shut it. Our mother always said you could catch more flies with honey than vinegar. I was *not* going to get a loan by arguing with Aunt Phee.

"Hello, March women."

135

Trey was back. Every missed opportunity, every bad decision of my life, standing before me in the flesh.

He smiled, and my poor, stupid heart froze like a squirrel in the path of an oncoming car. "Dance with me?"

My head was spinning. I needed to *think.* "I'm busy. Go ask Jo."

"She turned me down."

Of course. I would never, ever come first with him.

"Go away, Trey. I'm not your consolation prize."

"Never that," he said.

But I had been, once.

Chapter 7
Amy

Paris, Then

"I'll call you," Trey had said when he left me at Chloe's apartment last night. Obligatory guy speak for *good-bye.* He was never going to call, he was taken. Or he wasn't that into me. Besides, he was on his way to Modena.

But all the rationalizations in the world didn't stop me from checking my phone every five minutes like a crazy obsessed teenager. And when his number flashed on the screen, I jumped on it like *Project Runway* was calling.

"Trey! Where are you?"

"I'm at the hotel. I thought we could hang out today."

Yes. Wait. "What about your meeting at the Ferrari factory?"

"I put it off. When you've got money, they'll wait for you."

His cynicism bothered me a little. I wasn't going to criticize him. Not when there was

137

a chance we could spend more time to-gether. But . . . "I don't wait for anybody," I said.

"That's my girl," he said, his voice warm and amused. Or maybe, *Thattagirl*? Over the phone, it was hard to tell. "I can be there in twenty minutes. Let me feed you. Take you shopping."

"The shops are closed. It's Bastille Day."

"So we'll watch the parade. There's got to be a parade somewhere."

"Or a demonstration," I said. This was Paris, after all.

"Whatever you want," he said, still with that smile in his voice. "I'm all yours."

Even though he didn't mean that, not the way I wanted him to, the words were like a dream come true. *Pinch me.*

I clutched the phone, ridiculously happy. "There's a military parade on the Champs-Élysées. And a concert and fireworks tonight at the Eiffel Tower. We could picnic."

There was a moment's silence.

"Unless you'd rather not," I added. *Because of Jo.* The words stuck in my throat.

"Sounds like fun. It's a date."

"Good." My face, my grip, my whole body, relaxed. "Great. That's great. Like homecoming."

"A familiar face," Trey said.

He was that, a reassuring reminder of home. But he was more. "No, I meant high school homecoming." Our first date. "You took me to the dance? I was fourteen."

"Right. I forgot about that."

How could he forget? I remembered everything.

"You saved me," I said honestly. "I survived my freshman year because of you."

He made some sound — acknowledgment? embarrassment? — that tugged at my insides. He was so sweet. "It was a long time ago. Anyway, your family saved me." He cleared his throat. "See you soon."

Of course he was late. The metro stations near the parade route had been closed, and the streets were full of people. We joined the crowd streaming toward the Champs-Élysées.

Trey took my hand. The perfect gentleman, right? Protecting me from the crush.

A strange, sweet pressure filled my chest.

"Wait." I surveyed the densely packed street. We were never going to squeeze our way to the parade route. "Do you really want to see the parade?"

Trey glanced at me, a glint in his eyes. "You got something else in mind?"

My heart beat chaotically. Chloe was out,

139

celebrating with the rest of Paris. *We could go to my place.*

I swallowed the words. "We could go to the Louvre," I suggested. "It won't be that crowded today. Everybody's here."

"Is that what you want?"

I shrugged. "It's free." Because of the holiday.

"I'm not worried about the money."

I narrowed my eyes. "Well, I am. I don't want you to have to pay for me."

His brows rose, just a little. "You March women. So independent."

I flushed. Was he comparing me to *Jo*? "It's just . . . I'm not twelve anymore, Trey. I don't expect you to buy my popcorn."

He smiled crookedly. "Fair enough."

We walked, wandering down side streets to avoid the parade traffic. Trey still held my hand, and it was all sorts of perfect: Paris in summer, layered with color and light like an Impressionist painting. The sun dappled the trees and well-tended grass of the Tuileries Garden with dots of purple and green, speckles of cadmium yellow and titanium white. A formation of military planes roared overhead, streaking the sky blue, white, and red. At the Louvre, sightless kings and courtiers stared down from the palace facade on the great steel-and-glass pyramid that lit the underground galleries below.

"So, are you seeing anybody?" Trey asked.

Like he wanted to know. I resisted the urge to bounce. "Nobody special." *Except for you.* Could I say that? He and Jo had just split up. I didn't want him to think I was hanging around hoping to pick up the pieces of his broken heart. "Anyway, I don't really have time for a relationship right now," I added. "I want to focus on my career."

He smiled a little. "Amy Curtis March, the greatest designer in the world."

A few inline skaters took advantage of the nearly empty courtyard, zipping around tourists with phones and fanny packs.

I wrinkled my nose. "Yeah, that's not happening." *"You'll never be a real artist,"* Mrs. Wilson had said back in seventh grade.

"It could. You're talented. Hardworking."

"Not as talented as Beth. Or as original as Jo. I'm trained in design, and I'm good at marketing. But I'm not a genius. I'll never be great. So." I tossed my head. "I've decided to settle for rich and successful."

He gave a nod — almost a bow, really, an old-fashioned tribute like a character from a novel. "To your success, then." His lovely dark eyes were warm on mine. "And for what it's worth, I think you're pretty great."

I flushed. "Not selfish?"

"No. You're going after what you want."

"Aren't you?" I asked shyly. "Doing what you want?"

He slanted an amused look down at me. "I work for my grandfather. I do what he wants."

I cocked my head. "You know you don't have to work for him, right?"

"What else would I do?"

"I thought you were going to be a hotshot music executive."

"I'm not going to discover the next great rock band at Alleygators." A dive bar down by the river, near the trailer park.

"So go to L.A." *Or New York, where Jo is.* I pushed the thought away.

"I can't leave Granddad."

"Why? Is he threatening to write you out of the will?" I joked.

Trey smiled. "No. But he took me in after my parents died. He could have left me in boarding school. I'm all he has."

And he's all you have, I thought.

"Sorry about your mom and dad," I said.

He shrugged. "Nothing to be sorry for. They died. It sucked. To tell the truth, I was glad when people stopped calling me that 'poor Laurence boy who lost his parents.' "

"I hate that expression," I burst out. "Like you misplaced them somewhere."

He looked at me, arrested. I froze, afraid I had gotten this — gotten him — wrong. "Like car keys," he said.

I relaxed. "Or your phone."

His eyes smiled. "Exactly."

"Trey." I stopped, putting my hand on his arm. "Are you happy in Bunyan?"

"I could have been. With the right person. I thought . . ." He broke off, staring across the sun-washed courtyard.

That Jo would marry him. My heart cracked a little.

"So, what's the plan now?" I asked.

"Jo was the plan. So . . ." He shrugged. "There is no plan. Live. Play. Enjoy myself." He looked back at me, forcing a smile. "What about you, little Amy? Are you happy?"

"I'm happy here." I smiled and took his hand again. "I'm happy now." *With you.*

"Good." His smile was less forced this time. "That's good."

But he didn't say he was happy, too. Maybe coming to the Louvre was a bad idea. This wasn't his first trip to Paris. He didn't need another highlights tour of the museum.

"What do you want to go see?" I asked,

143

my voice too bright.

"What about that exhibit you were talking about last night? The fashion stuff."

The Musée de la Mode et du Textile. "You can't be interested in looking at a bunch of sketches and dresses."

He lifted an eyebrow. "Why not? Isn't that your thing?"

"Actually, I'm more into accessories."

"Jewelry."

"Shoes. Scarves. Handbags." I gave him a straight look. "Beautiful things can be useful, too."

"Okay, Miss Defensive," he teased. "Show me."

We wandered the gallery, looking at leather pouches and silk reticules, at bags made of paper and plastic and linen.

"Men used to carry purses, too," I said. "Before their clothes got pockets in the seventeenth century."

We ambled through displays of sleek bags, shaped bags, bags in every shade and texture. Purses decorated with feathers, beads, and embroidery, or embellished with buckles and chains. Trey was a good listener, leaning forward a little as I chattered about fabrics and designers.

I broke off abruptly. "I must be boring you."

"Nope." He smiled at me with his eyes, with his whole face, and . . . Wow. That was some smile. I flushed like a girl with her first crush. Which, of course, I was.

On our way out, Trey led me through the antiquities exhibit toward the great hall. Under the arched and vaulted ceiling, he stopped. I shivered. Because . . . There she was. Nike, *Winged Victory,* poised halfway up the stairs.

Her impact was irresistible, inescapable — the tits-out headless torso of Samothrace. That stupid boob shot from high school was behind me, but I could hardly bear to look at her. So beautiful, so hopeful, so broken.

"She reminds me of you," Trey said quietly.

My blood ran cold. I was sure — almost sure — he'd never seen me with my boobies out, exposed and inadequate. But everything posted online was public. Permanent. And Bunyan was like the Internet. Your past followed you forever. In Bunyan, I would be Easy A until I died.

"What do you mean?"

"Fearless," he said. "About to take off."

Tears stung my eyes. Was that really how he saw me?

"You okay?" he asked.

145

I smiled at him through my tears. "Never better."

We went out into the gardens. The sun warmed the air, releasing the scent of the grass and the starch in his shirt and his good, male Trey-smell. Puffy white clouds chased each other across the blue sky.

I sighed. "What a perfect day."

"It's been fun."

"We ought to head back. If we want to get a spot for the fireworks."

"Let's eat first."

"I should have packed a picnic."

Trey smiled. "I have a better idea. Let's go to my hotel."

The air thickened. The sun was suddenly hot, spreading warmth from the top of my head to my toes. I could say yes. I'd said yes to other guys, lots of times. But the other guys had never been Trey. The stakes had never been this high before.

"There's a restaurant on the roof that serves dinner," Trey added.

"That sounds . . ." *Dangerous. Tempting.* "Great," I said.

This was Trey, I scolded myself as we walked to his hotel. My sister's boyfriend. Ex-boyfriend. Practically a brother.

But Myself wasn't listening.

The hotel was on a swanky, tree-lined

avenue near the Arc de Triomphe. The foyer looked like something out of a movie with black-and-white marble floors and wood-paneled walls lined with mirrors and oil paintings. We rode the elevator to the terrace.

"Wow. That is some view," I said.

The rooftops of Paris spread out below, wrapped in a golden haze. The Eiffel Tower rose on the horizon, dark against the caramel sky.

"I thought we could watch the show from here," Trey said.

"The fireworks won't start for hours."

He smiled a little. "That's why we're having dinner first."

As we walked through the bar, I saw other women and more than a few men glancing at Trey, at his lean, elegant body and movie star hair. He didn't seem to notice. Like he didn't even realize how gorgeous he was. Or maybe he didn't care.

My toes curled a little in my cheap, flat sandals. At least I was wearing a sundress — inexpensive but appropriate.

We sat in a green alcove, shielded by banks of boxwood and blooming roses. The ground-level stink of Paris, of pee and diesel, wet limestone and the river, seemed very far away. The air smelled expensive, like jas-

147

mine and wine. Our food came, artfully arranged on white plates. I ate chocolate-covered strawberries and drank pink champagne cocktails. Watched as the sun slid down and the lights winked on and the Eiffel Tower lit up, sparkling in the distance. *Magic.*

I let Trey pay for everything. Did Cinderella insist on split checks with Prince Charming?

We talked easily, without the usual awkward getting-to-know-you crap. He had known me since I was ten. I'd loved him nearly that long. But this was almost the first time we were together as adults, out of Bunyan. Out of school. Away from my family.

"So, what's next for you?" he asked as the server cleared our plates away.

"After Paris? I don't know. I don't want to end up another unemployed design student selling dresses at Nordstrom. I'm hoping to establish my own line somewhere. Atlanta, maybe, or Miami."

"Why not New York?"

I shook my head. "New York is Jo's thing." My sister, after a stint in grad school, was working as a features writer for the *Empire City Weekly.* I was tired of following in her footsteps. Of living in her shadow. I met

Trey's eyes. "I am not my sister."

The air charged between us. I felt its static all over my skin.

When the first burst of fireworks lit the sky, Trey took my hand and led me to the stone balustrade. I shivered a little in happiness and excitement. His arms came around me. I leaned back against him, protected and warm, inhaling the citrusy scent of bergamot and starch.

Another bang. Another flare streaked across the velvet dark, red and gold blazing against the invisible stars.

I turned in his arms.

His eyes were dark and serious. "Amy . . ."

I didn't want to hear. I stood on tiptoe to kiss him.

When his lips met mine, showers of sparks rained down behind my closed lids.

I rode the elevator to his room in a glow of fireworks and champagne cocktails.

I wasn't drunk. I knew exactly what I was doing. What we were about to do. And I couldn't wait.

The tiny cage descended, starting and stopping like my heart. *Ping, ping.* The mirror reflected us standing very close together, Trey, dark and intent, and me, pink-faced with sun and anticipation. He stroked the

149

tips of his fingers between my hair and my cheek, his gaze dropping to my mouth. My heart bloomed with happiness.

The elevator jolted to a stop. He pushed open the ironwork gate, and we tumbled into the hall, wrapped in each other, kissing, kissing like we would never stop.

"Prenez une chambre, jeune homme." Get a room, delivered with finely calibrated scorn.

Trey raised his head. A very well-dressed woman stood waiting for the elevator, thin-plucked brows arched high. He grinned. *"Heureusement, j'ai déjà une chambre, madame." Lucky I already have a room.*

Her lips twitched in acknowledgment, scorn dissolving in the face of his charm. I hid my smile against his starched white shirtfront.

He had a room. We were going to his room.

It wasn't like this was my first time. I wasn't as slutty — God, I hated that word! — as my high school reputation made me out to be. *Easy A.* But I'd recognized years ago that the love of my life belonged to my sister. So there had been others. Nice boys, mostly. Just . . . not Trey.

He tugged me down the hall, opened the door in one smooth move, and pulled me into the room. Everything inside me spar-

150

kled like the Eiffel Tower. I turned and wrapped my arms around his neck, ready for him to do me against the wall. On the floor. Anywhere.

He caught my hands, holding them between his own, his gaze dark and seeking. "Is this okay?"

I've loved you my whole life, I thought helplessly. It was more than okay, it was all my fantasies come true.

"It's fine. I'm not a virgin, Trey."

His eyes danced with amusement. "I meant the room."

"Oh." Laughter bubbled inside me. It felt like champagne, or happiness, spilling everywhere. The suite was crimson, rose, and gold with Louis XV furniture and a flat-screen TV. Elaborate sconces cast pools of light on the plasterwork walls. The heavy silk drapes were looped back, framing Paris, lit up like a birthday cake beyond the windows. "It's stunning."

"You're stunning."

I turned. Trey was watching me, arrested laughter in his eyes. My insides turned warm and liquid.

Then — *thank you, yes!* — we were kissing again, his lips smiling against my mouth, and the warmth surged, heavy and golden. His body was hard and lean against mine, all angles and strength. I could feel myself melting, softening to receive him.

We made it to the bed, and it was better than my fantasies. And even then, when our breathing was ragged and our bodies tangled together, he raised his head. His face was flushed, his hair curly with sweat. "You good?" he asked, thoughtful and protective, and if I weren't already in love with him, that question at that moment would have done it.

I kissed his shoulder. "I am excellent."

He smiled into my eyes, creating a sweet ache in my chest. "Yes, you are."

And that was all either of us said for a long time.

Chapter 8
Beth

Backstage, Then

The Branson theater was more like Fellowship Hall back home than the cramped, dark warren of rooms I had imagined. Same white-painted trim and sand-colored walls and carpet. Same granite countertops and oversize coffeemaker in the kitchen. Same double sink next to the stalls in the ladies' room.

I rested my forearm on the porcelain toilet, breathing the mingled scents of pine cleaner and vomit. My gauzy angel costume collapsed around me.

"Beth, honey? You in there?"

It was Mercedes, my roommate. We were both in the chorus, sharing a cheap apartment on the outskirts of town with two other non-Equity performers. "If you're not in the union, the pay sucks," Mercedes said when we moved in together. "But at least you can always find work."

Mercedes was a year younger and a million times more, well, more everything than me. More talented, more experienced, more beautiful, more confident. Her voice was big. Her clavicle flared like wings — the real deal, built in bone, not the limp costume I wore. This was her second season with the Christmas show.

"Be right out," I called through the locked door.

Shakily, I got to my feet. Spit. Wiped. Flushed. When I exited the stall, Mercedes was waiting, leaning against the sink, dressed as a sexy elf in white cowboy boots and spangly red short shorts that showed off her thigh gap.

"Throw up again?" she asked sympathetically.

"It's just nerves." Mostly nerves.

"Gosh, I'd be nervous, too, singing a duet with Colt."

I flushed. I wasn't part of the initial cast. I was an alternate, an also-ran, a *Nice try, sweetheart.* Which was something of a relief, honestly. I'd auditioned for the show only because my voice instructor insisted it would be good practice. But then one of the singers broke an ankle and dropped out of the cast, and Colt heard my song "Leave a Candle in Your Window," and wanted it in

154

the show, and the next thing I knew we were singing onstage together.

I turned to the mirror, blotting my smeared mascara. "I still can't believe he chose me."

"Nobody can." Mercedes grinned to remove the sting from her words. "You sure you're okay now?"

"I'm fine, thanks."

"Because if you need me to go on for you, I can change real fast."

A chill settled in my stomach.

Because there were a hundred, a thousand, girls ready to take my place. Girls who looked the part. Girls who sang at church, who sang at school, who took every opportunity to get onstage and follow their dreams.

"You'd be amazing," I said honestly. "You're so pretty and talented. Sometimes I feel like an impostor."

"Don't be silly. You sound real good." She met my gaze in the mirror, her eyes dark with knowledge. "And at least you'll never be fat."

I was never comfortable eating in public. But I was grateful that on my sister Jo's big day I didn't throw up and ruin my dress. Or anyone's shoes. Or her wedding.

Colt was pleased. "Told you the break would do you good," he said when we got back to the farm. He followed me heavily up the stairs to the little back bedroom I used to share with Amy.

"You can't sleep *here*," I whispered. "My parents' room is right across the hall."

"So?"

"My father is a minister."

"He got a gun?"

"No. Anyway, he's at my aunt's. He and Mom are separated," I reminded him.

"They looked pretty tight to me."

When they were dancing. They'd looked so good together. Like they used to. "Thanks to you."

"You, too." He touched my neck. "You sounded good tonight, angel."

I pressed my cheek into his palm, leaning into his approval. He dropped his hand to my breast.

I jolted. "My mother . . ."

"Can't see us."

"She might hear us."

He grinned, amused. "Didn't you used to sneak boys up to your room when you were a teenager?"

"I was a slow starter."

Now, there was an understatement. Even after I started noticing boys, I liked the ones who looked most like me, thin and smooth. Non-threatening. Sexless.

Colt rubbed my breast lazily through the lace of my dress. "Angel, I didn't leave the tour to sleep alone tonight."

"No, of course not."

"You want me to go?"

Once again, I felt control slipping away. "No."

"So what do you want?"

The pretty blue lace chafed my skin. What did I want?

"Stay," I said.

The gray morning light crept around the edges of the blinds, stealing across the patterned rug and my teddy bear on the floor. I drew a careful breath, raising my head to check on Colt. Asleep. He always slept, after, his body heavy, his face relaxed while I lay still, my mind and heart racing erratically.

Shivering, I eased out of bed, pulling on sweatpants and a sports bra under my sleep shirt before I snuck from the room. I sat on the front porch to tie my running shoes. I ran every morning, even on tour, six or seven miles. Arenas, parking lots . . . The route didn't matter as long as I was burning calories.

157

But it felt good to be home, on familiar roads.

I was in the kitchen when Amy wandered down from Meg's old room, wearing a silky camisole and boxers. "Oh God, are you making coffee? Can I have some?"

"Sure." I spooned more grounds into the filter. "You're up early."

"Couldn't sleep." She sat on the edge of the counter, swinging her feet. Her toenail polish was blue, to match her underwear. Her wrists were so delicate. Her ankle bones stuck out.

I felt a twinge of envy. "Aren't you cold?"

"Nope." She yawned. "I'm surprised you're awake."

I smiled. "Up with the sun, Momma says." Or before the sun, in kidding season. "Do you want me to make you some toast or something?"

"I'm good. But I'll sit down with you if you want breakfast."

"Oh, I already ate."

Amy's eyes narrowed. I tensed. Our youngest sister was more perceptive than most people thought. But then she grinned. "I guess you and Colt worked up an appetite. After all that noise you made last night."

I ignored the tight ball in my stomach. "That wasn't me."

158

She grinned. "Hey, at least you were enjoying yourself."

"But I didn't." Amy's eyebrows shot up. "Make noise," I clarified.

"It's okay. I won't tell Mom."

"Tell me what?" Our mother appeared, wrapped in her bathrobe.

I threw Amy an agonized look.

It's not like we never discussed sex with our mother. After Jo got her period without a word to anyone, Mom sat us down, Amy and me, and told us matter-of-factly what to expect. We could have babies now, she explained briskly, so we needed to be careful. Sex was a gift from God intended to sustain loving relationships between wives and their husbands. Not something casual. Amy had peppered our mother with questions, totally mortifying me. I already disliked my changing, awkward body. I really didn't want to talk about it.

"Tell me what?" Mom repeated.

"I, um . . ."

"Coffee?" Amy asked blandly.

"Thanks, honey." She took down two mugs from the cupboard.

"I've already got mine," Amy said.

Our mother busied herself pouring coffee, not quite meeting our eyes. "It's for your father."

"Daddy?" Amy asked.

"Mom?" Bewilderment thinned my voice. If our father was here . . . Those noises Amy heard . . .

"Oh, for Pete's sake," Amy said. "Am I the only one in this family who didn't have Drunken Wedding Sex last night?"

"Are you . . . Are you and Dad getting back together?" I asked.

Our mother pressed her lips together, stirring her coffee with vigor.

There was a knock on the back door. "I smelled coffee," a man's voice said. Dan Harkins, who helped Momma around the farm.

"You can have mine," I offered.

Our mother belted her robe tighter. "I'll make more. Come in, Dan."

He glanced at Amy, sitting on the counter, idly swinging her long, bare legs. "I don't want to intrude."

She smiled at him like a cat, fluffing her hair with her fingers. "Don't mind us. Everybody's feeling friendly. Very friendly, apparently."

Our mother shot her a sharp look.

He stepped into the kitchen, a tall, rough man in dirty work clothes. "So. How'd things go last night?"

Mom's hand jerked, scattering coffee

grounds across the counter.

"The wedding was lovely," I said.

"I didn't see you there," Amy said.

His gaze rested on her briefly. "Not my kind of party."

"There was lots to eat," Amy said. "And drink."

"I'd rather drink alone," he said straight-faced.

"Ha. Although I . . ." Amy broke off, her eyes narrowing. "Wait. That was you! In Alleygators."

"You were in Alleygators?" I asked. A dive bar. Not at all Amy's kind of place.

Amy nodded. "He hauled my ass out of a bar fight once."

"Three years ago," Dan said.

"Christmas Eve," said Amy.

"When I was in the hospital?" our mother asked.

"I went out for a drink," Amy said. "He rescued me."

Dan shook his head. "I wouldn't say that. Your sister Jo was there. And your boy-friend."

"Amy doesn't have a boyfriend," I said.

"The Laurence guy. The grandson."

"Trey? He's . . ." *Jo's,* I almost said. But of course he wasn't. Not anymore. "He's like our brother."

161

Mom handed him the mug she had poured for Dad. "Was there something else, Dan?"

He regarded her a moment, all expression hidden behind his beard. "Milking's done. I was going to finish the babies and then turn the ladies out."

"I'll be with you in a minute. To help with the bottle-feeding." Was our mother blushing?

He jerked his chin toward the door. "And there's a guy sleeping in a car outside."

Oh no. I glanced outside, where a long black limo was parked next to the barn. "It's Jimmy."

"Friend of yours?" Dan asked.

"He's Colt's driver." Guilt jabbed me. I'd seen the car when I went for my run. I should have realized . . . "I should see if he's all right."

"I'll go with you." Dan looked at our mother. "Appreciate the coffee, Abby."

She gave a short nod, her cheeks faintly pink. I followed Dan outside.

"I'm so sorry," I said to Jimmy. I handed him a cup of coffee through the open car window. "I didn't know you were out here."

"Boss likes me to stick tight. It's fine," he said, catching sight of my expression. "Seat goes back all the way. Not much different from sleeping on the tour bus."

"Trailer's over there," Dan said. "If you want to wash up."

"Thanks, man."

I watched him go, a knot in my stomach. Why didn't I realize Jimmy would end up sleeping in the limo if Colt stayed with me? And why didn't Colt care?

"Everything all right?" Dan asked.

I nodded, still distressed by my thoughtlessness.

He regarded me from behind the beard. "You want to feed some baby goats?"

I did.

Nothing is cuter than a baby goat. Kittens, maybe. Or puppies. But goaties are bouncy and cuddly, with silly ears and adorable little hooves. Our mother left the babies on their mommas during the day, separating them at night and milking the lady goats in the morning. Most of them were good mothers. But a few were new and nervous or neurotic and neglectful, and their babies needed extra care and snuggles.

I curled in the straw with a kid on my lap, feeding it from a bottle. Its solid little body quivered in my arms, furry and alive. The sun warmed my hair, seeping into my bones like happiness.

"I should have known I'd find you here,"

Colt said.

I waited for the baby to suck the bottle dry before scrambling to my feet. "You're up."

"No point in staying in bed alone."

I flushed. "I thought you were sleeping."

"So you snuck out." *Again,* his look said.

"Sorry."

He kissed my cheek. "Hey, you do whatever makes you happy." He could be so sweet. He winked. "As long we get another Grammy."

I tugged on the hem of my sweatshirt.

"You look like the farm girl in a music video. All you need is pigtails and short shorts."

I smiled weakly. "And Sharla to do my makeup."

Jimmy came back from the trailer. "Ready, boss?"

I looked at Colt, noting for the first time the bag in his hand, the wet comb tracks in his hair. "Where are you going?"

"Back to the tour."

A cold fingertip traced my spine. "You don't have another show until Wednesday."

"Angel, I can't spend another night in a twin bed. Anyway, this" — he gestured around at the barn, the fields, the farmhouse — "isn't really my scene."

"I thought you were into country," Dan drawled behind me.

"Colt, this is Dan."

"Nice to meet you. Are you a fan?" Colt asked.

Dan gave him a level look. "Can't say as I am."

Ouch. But Colt was still smiling, secure in his own worth, his attention already moving on.

He'd never intended to stay, I realized dully. "I'll get my guitar. Pack my things."

"No. No, this break is good for you. You sounded great last night. You need to stay until you're a hundred percent."

"What about the tour?"

"Don't you worry about the tour. Mercedes can fill in for you for a while longer. You just concentrate on writing those songs. Dewey's riding my ass for the new tracks. We'll be back in the studio before you know it."

I didn't protest. I was too stunned.

I was off the tour.

He was leaving. Leaving me. I wasn't enough to keep him here. I stood numbly as Jimmy loaded the bag in the trunk, as Colt kissed me and got in the limo and drove away.

"You okay?" Dan's concerned face shimmied in my vision.

I forced myself to smile. "Fine."

Not fine. My head throbbed, little flashes of light at the back of my eyes. My skin was clammy and cold, my palms sweaty. *It's only temporary,* I told myself. *"We'll be back in the studio before you know it."*

Dan was still talking, his voice coming from very far away.

My heart raced. "I . . . What?"

The ground tilted.

"I'm gonna get your ma," Dan said before I fell.

"Honey?" My mother's voice was brisk and warm. Her hand was cool and comforting on my forehead, which was strange, because I seemed to be shivering. "Let's get you up to the house. Amy, you stay here and give Dan a hand with the goats."

Amy widened her eyes. "But I don't know what to do," she said, which was possibly even true. Amy never had liked helping on the farm.

I struggled to sit. "I can help."

"You fainted," Amy said.

"Did you eat breakfast?" Momma asked.

No. "I'm fine."

"The March women's motto," Amy said.

Mom gave her a straight look. "Here's

another one. Take care of your sister."

Amy grinned. "Better Beth than the goats." She put her arm around me. "Come on, Mouse."

I'd always liked my nickname. *Mouse.* It suggested something small, neat, unobtrusive. But now I felt weak and embarrassed. I leaned on Amy as we walked toward the house. "I'm so sorry."

I was the older sister — by fourteen months — but growing up, it never felt that way. Amy always wanted *more,* always rushing ahead while I hung behind, clinging to childhood. I was happy with what we had, still playing with dolls while she paged through teen magazines.

She was surprisingly kind and competent, though, bringing a washcloth for my face as I sat on the edge of the bed. "Can I get you some crackers?"

I shuddered. "I don't need anything."

"How about a drink of water?"

"Yes, please."

I waited until she was gone before I undressed. By the time she returned, I was safely under the covers. "Thanks, Amy."

She adjusted the blinds so the light didn't shine in my eyes. "So, what happened with the boyfriend?"

"He left."

167

"Yeah, I know. I was in the kitchen. Did you guys have a fight or something?"

Amy and I had never confided in each other. Not like Meg and Jo. "He had to get back to the tour."

"Without you?"

My face was hot. "I've been sick."

"You were fine yesterday. And earlier this morning. And you were obviously fine last night." She narrowed her eyes. "You're not pregnant, are you?"

"What? No!"

"You can't blame me for wondering. Not after Jo."

She sounded like Colt.

"Not pregnant." My stomach hurt. I closed my eyes. Turned my head away.

Something soft brushed my arm. My chin.

I opened my eyes in surprise. Amy, tucking my bear under the covers with me.

"Look, I'm not going to judge you. I've done enough stupid shit myself." She sat on the edge of my bed, the mattress depressing under her weight. "But you do look a little run-down. It must be tough, performing every night. Maybe your boyfriend's right. Maybe you do need a break."

"You don't understand."

"So explain it to me."

Funny, how we had shared this room for

seven years and never really talked before. We never needed to. Meg was always Amy's confidante, the way Jo was mine. Our father was gone. And Mom was always so busy. But Meg and Jo took care of us. Spoiled us, really.

"I'm not like you. I don't know who I am or what I want all the time. There's really only one thing I'm good at, and it's hard to let it go."

Amy nodded. "Your music."

I hugged the bear tighter. Shame swelled inside me. I wasn't talking about my music. "Yes. No. It's not that."

"Is it Colt?"

Once I told . . . But I couldn't tell. My sisters would descend on me with well-meaning questions and suggestions and loving concern, and I'd never have control again.

I nodded instead. "I wanted him to stay," I said, giving her a tiny truth. "At least for a couple days. We've been together two years, and it's good, we're good together, it's just . . ."

"You want to get married," Amy said.

I was jolted, as usual, by her bluntness. "Not married." Meg was the one who couldn't wait to start a family. Anyway, Colt had made it clear — weddings and kids, not his thing. "I'm not expecting a proposal. It's only been two years. Lots of couples are together longer than that without . . ."

"A music contract?"

I closed my eyes.

"Sorry." She stroked my hair, the way Jo used to. "I'm just saying, don't expect too much. He's your first serious boyfriend."

"Daddy was Momma's first love." They practically grew up together, the rich kid from the big white house and the farmers' daughter. As far as I knew, our mother had never even looked at another man.

"Right. And three years ago, she threw him out. So, not the best example," Amy said drily.

Three years ago, Momma had been sick. And then Dad moved out and Jo moved in with Eric. Everyone I loved was moving on with their lives. Without me. Everything I knew was changing, out of my control, and I had been alone in Branson, far from my family, far from home. Colt had been my lifeline then, teasing me gently out of my fears, picking me out of the chorus, taking me out to dinner after the show. Choosing my song. Choosing me, out of all the other, prettier, skinnier, more talented girls fighting for his attention.

"Colt cares about me, I know he does."

"He left you here."

"For my own good. He wants me to get better. We're working on a new album in the fall."

Amy cocked her head. "Whenever somebody tells you something is for your own good, it's because they want something."

"Colt's not like that."

"All guys are like that."

I stared at her in mute distress.

Amy's expression softened. She stroked my hair again. "You're so good, I guess you can't help but see the good in everybody else. All I'm saying is, young love isn't always meant to be. To last. Especially not first love."

"Speaking from your vast experience?" I teased gently.

Amy's face closed so smoothly I almost didn't recognize I was being shut out. "Something like that."

I blinked at her. Maybe I wasn't the only March sister with secrets.

CHAPTER 9
AMY

Young love doesn't last, I'd told Beth. But sisters were forever.

"Aunt Amy! Aunt Amy! Watch me!" Daisy yelled.

Meg and I sat on her front-porch steps, blowing bubbles for the twins as they ran around the yard, colliding occasionally with their large golden retriever mix. The dog was chasing bubbles, too, barking in confusion as they popped and vanished, making DJ convulse in giggles.

I pressed my shoulder to Meg's. "I missed this."

"You should come home more often."

I ignored a familiar twinge of guilt. I'd never told Meg why I stayed away. What was the point? That stupid sexting episode from high school was years ago. And Trey . . . I couldn't tell Meg I'd poached our sister's ex. Plus, Meg loved Trey like a brother. I wouldn't expose him as the guy who broke my heart.

"I've been so busy with Baggage . . ." I said.

If Meg recognized my excuse, she didn't let on. "I saw you talking with Phee yesterday at the reception."

"Ha. You were too busy making out with John to notice me."

She smiled smugly. "I'm a mom. Multitasking is my superpower."

"Don't tell me. You had Drunken Wedding Sex, too."

"Too?"

DJ stopped in front of us, grubby hands on hips. "Bubbles, Aunt Amy."

"Please," Meg coached.

"Bubbles, please."

So cute. "Here." I surrendered the wand with the bottle.

"I want bubbles," Daisy demanded.

So Meg handed over her bottle. The twins zigzagged across the yard, giggles rising in their wake like soap bubbles.

"They're getting so big," I said.

"They turn five this summer." A sideways look. "You should come for their birthday."

I made a noncommittal sound. "They must be starting kindergarten soon."

"In the fall. Daisy is ready. DJ . . ."

We watched as DJ sputtered soap bubbles

all over his shirt.

"I'll do it," Daisy said, grabbing the bottle from him.

He swiped it back, sloshing on his shoes.

"Sharing!" Meg called. She smiled ruefully at me. "So, how did things go with Phee? Is she going to help you finance your new space?"

"Nope. Not without 'conditions.' " I drew the quotes in the air.

"What kind of conditions?"

"She wants me to move back home. Can you imagine the four of us, all living in Bunyan?"

"I don't have to imagine," Meg said mildly. "I can remember. Anyway, Beth won't be here much longer. She's going back on the road with Colt."

"No, she's not. He dumped her from the tour."

"He fired her?"

"Not exactly. He still wants her to write songs for him."

Meg raised her eyebrows. "Well, at least he came to the wedding."

"Maybe he got spooked by the whole family scene."

"Poor Bethie."

"At least she can work from home. I can't."

Meg smiled. "All right, I admit Bunyan isn't exactly Paris, but —"

"Paris? It isn't even New Jersey."

"But couldn't that be an advantage?" Meg pressed. "You'd have an identity as a local, regional designer. The cost of living is cheaper. Your rents would be lower. You already have a good client base in stores. If you developed more of an online presence . . ."

"Why are you saying all this? You're supposed to be on my side!"

"I am. Which is why I think you should consider your options."

Meg had always been a bit of a Momma Hen where I was concerned. But I was not some brainless, fluffy Little Chick. "I am not moving my business to North Carolina. I thought maybe if *you* talked to Aunt Phee . . ."

"Nobody can get around Aunt Phee better than you."

"But you helped write my business plan. And you speak her language."

"What language?"

"Money." Meg laughed. Encouraged, I continued. "I know I don't have enough in assets to qualify for a bank loan. But if you told her Baggage is a good investment —"

"Phee's not a bank. She doesn't care

about assets or return on investment. She cares about family."

"She's surrounded by family. What does she need me for?"

"Why don't you ask her?"

"I guess I could. I have to go over there anyway to say good-bye."

"Exactly. What do you have to lose?" Meg asked.

"Besides my pride?"

"You'll go," Meg said, in her quiet, sure way.

It annoyed me that she was right. "Because I need the money."

My sister smiled. "Because you care about family, too."

The big double bays to the carriage house stood open, exposing a jumble of furniture and stacks of cartons.

"Up here!" Jo yelled cheerfully when I called.

"Watch that table!" Phee ordered, her voice carrying down the narrow wooden staircase.

"Ow."

"Where do you want this, Miss March?" asked a young man's voice. Eric's son Alec.

"Please. Like it or not, we're family now. Call me Aunt Phee."

"Yes, ma'am. Where do you want this?"

"Put it by that wing chair."

I edged my way around a marble-top sideboard and up the steps. How would Phee manage these stairs in a few more years? "Hi, guys. Hey, Alec. Oh, wow. Are you moving in or opening a flea market up here?"

"I see no reason to give up all my things," Phee said stiffly. "I'm downsizing, not dead."

"Nobody wants you to give up your things, Aunt Phee," Jo said. "Robbie, don't touch."

I moved to rescue a lamp from his baby hands and tripped over a table. "Ouch. This room is awfully crowded."

"You should see the kitchen," Jo said. "Or rather, you can't see the kitchen, because it's buried in boxes."

Phee glared. "Aren't you supposed to be on your honeymoon or something?"

"Don't worry, Aunt Phee." Jo grinned. "Eric and I aren't missing out."

"Stop it. I do not want to hear another wedding sex story," I said.

"Hello? Gross," Alec said.

Oops. "Sorry, nephew."

He smiled, a flash of his father in his face. " 'S okay. I don't want to hear about Dad and Jo having sex, either."

"I meant, Eric and I are waiting before we take any kind of trip," Jo said with dignity. "He's so busy getting the kitchen up and running. The students start in a couple weeks. And I need to work on my book. This deadline is going to kill me."

"Fine. Run along. Amy can help me," Phee said.

"If you're sure . . ." Jo glanced longingly toward the stairs. "I really am behind. Do you want to come?" she asked Alec.

Phee snorted. "What's he going to do? Sharpen your pencils?"

"I'll watch the kid," Alec offered.

"Brother bonding," Jo said with a nod. "Excellent."

I listened to them clomp down the old wooden stairs, trying not to feel deserted.

"I suppose you want to leave now, too," Phee said.

I looked at her, standing straight and alone in the middle of all her cherished possessions.

"Aunt Phee," I asked suddenly. "Do you *want* to move into the carriage house?"

She raised her chin. "Of course."

I sighed. "Right." I turned, considering the space. The room ran the length of the building. The ceilings were high. The floors were heart pine. Dormer windows overlooked the pond and the tiny cemetery filled with generations of dead Marches. "You need new curtains. These are blocking the light. And the view."

"I like these curtains. They were very expensive. I've had them for years."

"I can tell. They're dated."

"Classic."

"Old."

"Well, so am I." She glowered. "Just because something is old doesn't mean it should be thrown out."

My heart gave a reluctant tug. "Of course not," I said gently. "But you're making a fresh start here, Aunt Phee. Your style should reflect that. There's a way to be timeless and still be fashionable."

"Humph. I suppose you'd get rid of all the furniture, too."

"Only about half of it. I feel like I'm on an episode of *Hoarders: The Antebellum Edition*."

Her lips twitched. "All right."

"All right, what?" I asked cautiously.

"You can change the curtains. But nothing too sheer. I need privacy."

"You're facing the pond. I don't think the ducks care if you're naked."

When I was little, I loved exploring Oak Hill, stuffed with treasures like Aladdin's cave. All the furniture had claw legs and carving. I remembered sitting under the library desk to dust the talon feet, imagining myself in a dragon's hoard. I hadn't planned on spending the day after my sister's wedding measuring windows and moving furniture for my elderly great-aunt. But no one else was begging for my company. Besides, I had always liked arranging things.

I threw out moldy pillows and curated junk. I dragged a marble-topped jardiniere and a brass can stuffed with dusty peacock feathers down the stairs, replacing them with a delicate table and chair from the stockpile below. Bit by bit, the room took shape. I angled the table in front of a window where Phee could see the view. Angled an oversize mirror on the opposite wall to reflect back the light.

The heavy valances had to go, but I left the drapery panels up.

"You should replace these," I told her as I climbed down the stepladder. "In a lighter fabric, like silk. And this chair could use reupholstering. I'll send you some swatches when I get back to New York."

Phee held Polly close, monitoring my progress. "I see what you're doing. You're trying to get on my good side."

I grinned. "Is it working?"

"You're not going to win me over in an afternoon."

"How long would it take?"

"That's up to you, isn't it? You're the one who wants to redecorate. And of course I still have all of my things in the house that need to be sorted. The attic and the closets."

It began to sink in what she wanted. "Aunt Phee, I can't. Anyway, you don't need a decorator. You need a Dumpster."

"You have a degree in design."

"*Fashion* design. There are people you can hire to do this. Professional organizers. I'm sure Meg could find you one."

"I don't want some stranger pawing through my things."

"Then ask my sisters."

"They have children."

"Beth doesn't."

"Beth is a dear girl. But she doesn't have your sense of style."

The glint in her eyes worried me. "Thanks. But I don't have time to go through your closets."

"Ever heard the expression 'Time is money'?"

I pointed a finger at her. "I see what you're doing here. You think I'll help you because I want your money."

She almost smiled. "Is it working?"

"It could," I acknowledged. I didn't have to be in New York to handle the business side of Baggage — managing online orders and inventory, paying bills and sales tax, posting to social media. But most of my time was still spent on the actual assembly of the bags themselves, cutting and stitching and shipping. "But we're slammed with orders right now. I can't leave my assistant to do all the work alone."

"Hire someone to help her."

"And this would save me money how?"

Phee sniffed. "I suppose I could advance you enough to pay your employees while you're down here."

"Advance? Like, a loan?"

"I will pay you for their time and whatever expenses you incur as a result of our agreement. With the understanding that I am under no obligation to finance your company unless you move your operation to Bunyan."

"Uh-huh. What do I get out of this again?"

"The chance to change my mind," Phee said triumphantly.

Affection filled me. You had to admire the old dragon. She knew how to negotiate. "I can give you a week."

"Two months."

"Three weeks," I said. "And before I start, I need to go back to New York and make sure everything can keep running while I'm down here."

"How long will that take?" For the first time, she looked uncertain.

"A week? Maybe two. I'll be back by . . . Let me see. Memorial Day."

"I could be dead by then."

I hugged her. "Please. You're going to outlive us all."

She patted my back awkwardly.

So, I was coming back home, I thought. Only for three weeks. It would be good to spend some time with my sisters.

"Before you go, you need to get your father's things," Phee said.

"Excuse me?"

"He's already packed," Phee assured me, apparently misreading my dismay. "I told him I was moving in today."

"Where . . . ?"

"The front room. By the stairs."

I opened the unobtrusive door next to the bathroom. Not a closet, as I'd assumed. A second, smaller bedroom over the driveway, facing the house. A single bed, neatly made. An empty table with a lamp. A chest of drawers — bare — a stack of cartons, two suitcases, and an army duffel bag.

Not a home, just a place to stay. Like a monk's cell. It was poignant to see how little my father owned after almost three years of living here.

I peeked inside one of the cartons. Books. "I can't carry all this."

"Take what you can. Ashton can come for the rest."

"But where is it going to go?" *Where is he going to go?*

Phee's mouth tightened like the end of a coral balloon. "That's up to your mother."

CHAPTER 10
ABBY

It's always a mistake to sleep with your ex-husband.

Husband.

Still.

Time was, I was crazy for Ashton March, when all he had to do was look at me a certain way and I couldn't wait for us to be alone. Our daughter's wedding stirred things up. For both of us. I was proud my girls were moving on with their lives. Following their dreams. I kept busy. I was needed. But the truth was, birthing goats and diapering grandbabies were no substitute for sex.

The goats came running from pasture, the ladies nickering for their supper, the kids yelling and bouncing. Clover, my big white Saanen, leaned against my legs, seeking attention. I scratched her scruffy forehead.

I wasn't that girl anymore, grateful Ash had pulled his nose out of a book long enough to smile at me. Last night, the earth hadn't moved. But it had trembled. Habit and nostalgia were powerful things. It felt good to be held, to touch and be touched. Ash and I had a lot of history. Could be I'd always expected too much. Of him and of sex.

Or maybe I hadn't demanded enough. *"The woman makes the marriage,"* my mother used to say. Sometimes I wondered what I'd made of mine.

Dan came from the barn. Together, we separated the kids from their mommas. He was a good worker, quiet and steady and patient with the goats.

I couldn't stop the flush in my cheeks. This morning had been awkward, all the embarrassment of being caught like a teenager with all the responsibilities and regrets of an adult. But he didn't say a word.

When Naomi bolted for the kids' enclosure, I wrestled her back. "Milking time, girl. You'll see your babies in the morning."

"Seems to me she'd be glad for the break."

I looked up in surprise. Dan didn't talk much. Behind his beard, it was hard to know what he was thinking most of the time.

"Hard to argue with maternal instinct." I gave Naomi a rub. "You got kids, Dan?"

"Nope."

186

Which was the closest we'd come to a personal conversation since Ash invited him to Thanksgiving dinner three years ago, another homeless vet needing a berth for the holidays.

"Wanted some once," he volunteered, surprising me. "Wife wanted to wait."

"You're married?" He seemed so young. But then, I'd been a mother at twenty-one.

"Divorced."

"I'm sorry."

He shrugged. *What are you going to do?* "I was gone a lot."

Like Ash. The thought popped up, irresistible. Unwelcome. "Afghanistan?"

"Iraq." *Also like Ash.* "She changed while I was away, she said."

We herded the lady goats toward the milking parlor. "*She* changed," I repeated. It was really none of my business. But he'd been upfront about his PTSD issues when I hired him.

A short nod. "Reckon we both did."

That, too, was familiar.

Opposites attract, my mother said, and for Ash and me it was true. He was thought and I was feeling. He was cool and I was hot. When we were younger, I found his deep reserve mysterious, his mental preoccupation a challenge. I'd taken pride in being the one who could provide him with connection and comfort.

But after his third deployment, he had changed. Not merely distant but . . . gone.

And maybe the fact that I took charge while he was away made it easy for him to go, harder for him to come back again and take his place in the family.

The goats clattered up the ramp. "Deployments are hard on everybody," I said.

"Yeah. Plus, she cheated, so . . ." Another shrug.

Oh. I caught myself sneaking glances at Dan as he latched the goats into their stations and scattered grain in the trough. He wasn't handsome like Ash, but good-looking in a rough sort of way. And kind. "I'm sorry."

"You spend an awful lot of time apologizing." He might have been smiling. Hard to tell with that beard.

"Sorry," I said. Joking.

Yep. Definite smile that time.

I went down the line, squirting, checking, wiping teats as Dan hooked up the cups on the milking machine. Six goats at a time, feed, wipe, milk, sanitize, repeat. We were almost done when I heard a car. Amy, back from Oak Hill.

She jerked open the trunk of the car.

Hauled out a familiar-looking duffel and dumped it on the gravel.

My stomach sank.

Dan followed my gaze out the door. "I got the milking. If you want to . . ."

"Thanks." I wiped my hands on a teat towel and went out. "What's all this?"

Amy reached for a suitcase. "Dad's stuff."

"I see that," I said. "What are you doing with it?"

She lifted her chin. "Aunt Phee said I should ask you."

Anger tightened my throat. At Phee. At Ash.

For thirty years, I'd been the good preacher's wife, the good military spouse. I handled the questions, deployments, and disappointments, the times Ash missed dinner or Christmas, the fact there wasn't any money for summer camps or college. *Don't bother your father. Your father is doing important work. We need to be strong for your father.*

Three years after I kicked him out, he was still missing the important discussions, still leaving the explanations to me.

"You slept with him," said a voice like my mother's. Her exact words when my twenty-year-old unmarried self told her I was pregnant with Meg. *"You deal with it."*

189

"Mom?" Amy asked.

I met her eyes. Blue, like her father's. His princess, he called her.

My days of hands-on parenting were over. But the instinct to protect my children was still there. Whatever was going on between Ash and me — *Drunken Wedding Sex,* indeed — I wanted Amy to think well of her father. And selfishly, I didn't want her to think less of me.

"You'll have to talk to your father."

"Is he here?"

"He's at work." Same as always. Left right after his morning cup of coffee.

Ash ran a nonprofit for returning vets, helping them reintegrate into civilian life, providing counseling for PTSD. I'd mortgaged the farm so he could open it, a storefront ministry in the center of town, after his final deployment.

"He was here last night," Amy said. Wary. Hopeful.

My heart cracked for her, our youngest girl, who tried so hard to hide her feelings and cared so much what other people thought of her.

"He's not moving in, honey," I said gently.

"Does he know that? Because his bags were already packed."

I sucked in my breath.

190

Right on cue, Ash came up the drive, parking behind Amy. He got out of the car, still wearing the pants from his wedding suit and a button-down shirt with the sleeves rolled back. Such a gentleman. I wanted to throw something at him.

"Amy's got your clothes," I said.

He stopped, his gaze flickering from me to Amy.

"I had to leave the books," Amy said. "The cartons didn't fit in the car."

I folded my arms. "Did you pack before the wedding?" *Did you know when you took me to bed last night that you needed another place to stay in the morning?*

A muscle ticked in his cheek. *Say no,* I begged silently. But he wouldn't lie. Not Ash.

"Yes."

I nodded shortly. "You can leave your things in the barn." *Closing the door after the horse had bolted,* I thought with a twist of my heart.

He inclined his head, polite as always. "Thank you." He hesitated. "Perhaps I can sleep in Jo's old room. Only for tonight."

I didn't want him sleeping in my attic, a short flight of stairs away. I didn't want him in my kitchen every morning, drinking my coffee.

"He can bunk with me," Dan said behind me.

How long had he been standing there? "I don't want to put you out."

"You're not." He looked at Ash. "Trailer has two bedrooms."

I wondered if Dan was offering as a friend or a fellow vet, as somebody Ash had helped or as a way to help me out. Not that it mattered.

"Thank you," Ash said with grave courtesy. He turned to me. "If that's all right with Abby."

It was not all right. I didn't want my ex-husband — husband — on my farm. In my space. But where else did he have to go?

CHAPTER 11
BETH

"Are you sure you don't mind watching Robbie today?" Jo said when she dropped him off at the farmhouse in the morning.

"Of course not," I assured her.

"I packed his lunch. But you can give him whatever you're eating. Cut up, of course. He's not picky."

My stomach contracted. I nodded. "Don't worry."

"I only . . . I just need one day to write without any distractions, you know? And Eric has to meet with suppliers all day, and Alec had to go back for finals, and I'm *so* far behind with this book."

"I know."

"I thought things would settle down after the wedding."

"It was a beautiful wedding," I said.

"It was." Jo beamed at me over her baby. "Thank you for singing."

I ducked my head. "It was Colt's idea."

"It was your song."

"What did you think of him?" I asked shyly.

"Colt? I didn't really get a chance to spend much time with him." Jo glanced at me. "He sure likes being onstage."

"He's a wonderful performer."

"Right." She set Robbie down, and he toddled off to play in the hay. "When do you go back on tour?"

"Um, I'm not sure? Colt says . . . He thinks I need a rest."

"Yeah, running after a toddler all day is super restful."

"It will be fun," I said.

And it was.

We played all morning. Robbie was absorbed by everything, completely in the moment, climbing and jumping off hay bales, stomping in puddles by the water trough, breaking into contagious giggles at the baby goats.

I fed him lunch from his little thermal bag. Jo had packed containers of grated cheese, diced melon, and blanched snap peas along with a packet of German teething crackers. I arranged everything carefully on his tray, admiring the pretty colors, the different textures.

Whatever you're eating, Jo had said.

A shadow fell. Maybe I should add more protein. I found some leftover chicken in the fridge and shredded it for him. Robbie dug in, drooling and smiling his wide, nine-toothed smile. Clearly, I was an amazing aunt.

He offered me his cracker, and I gobbled the air by his fist. "Nom nom."

He giggled and held out the cracker again. More smacking noises. More peals of laughter. I laughed back, relaxed. Unguarded.

And then he mashed the cracker against my mouth. *Gack.*

Although . . . It didn't taste terrible, actually. A little bland, like sweet toast. The crackers probably weren't even that bad for you. I mean, they were made for babies. And I was so hungry. I ate another one as I washed Robbie's face and hands. Finished the pack as I wiped down his high chair. I shoved them quickly into my mouth, not thinking, not tasting them, even, hiding the wrapper in the trash.

After lunch, I sat with him on the braided rug in front of the fireplace, singing "Baa Baa Black Sheep," "Old MacDonald," and "Itsy Bitsy Spider" while Robbie bounced and clapped.

"More?" I asked.

"More!"

I searched my mind. I was running out of animals. And songs. I took a deep breath. "I'm being eaten by a boa constrictor . . ."

My stomach gurgled. I ignored it, catching Robbie's snub-toed shoe in my fingers, pretending to swallow him up one delicious baby bite at a time. He squirmed and giggled as I grabbed his knee and ankle. I gobbled his head, and he dissolved in shrieks of delighted laughter.

He was the best audience ever.

"Thank you. You're a lifesaver," Jo said when she came at four o'clock.

"Anytime," I said.

"How's your writing coming along? The new songs?"

I shrugged.

"Writer's block?" she asked sympathetically.

"What? No. Not really."

"Eric always tells me to tell my story."

My throat closed. "I don't know what my story is."

Jo studied me thoughtfully. "Do you still write in that song notebook I gave you?"

"Every day." It wasn't a lie, exactly.

Jo pursed her lips. "My editor says everybody struggles when writing goes from being a dream to being a job. It helps if you

196

remember why you started in the first place."

I smiled. "Like falling in love."

"Exactly. You can't do it to please other people. You have to want it for yourself."

"Like you and Eric."

"Speaking of Eric, do you want to come for dinner tonight?"

The crackers sat uneasily in my stomach. I'd eaten the entire pack. Would Jo notice? "Oh, I can't . . . I don't want to be a bother. You guys are so busy."

"Are you kidding? Eric lives to feed people." Jo grinned. "He thinks you need fattening up."

I managed not to cringe. "It's just . . . You all must have so much to do, with the restaurant opening soon. And Colt's recording a new album in the fall. He wants me to focus on that."

"Mm." Another searching look. "Bethie . . . Is everything all right?"

I'd always been able to talk to Jo about everything. Except this. She was a newly married mother of three with a new house and a deadline of her own to manage. Even if she had the time, she couldn't fix whatever was wrong with me.

And maybe . . . I didn't want to be fixed. I didn't need anybody else telling me what to do right now.

I told myself I was protecting her. But even then I knew I was protecting my secret. Myself.

"I thought I'd work on my music tonight," I said.

And I tried. I really did.

Before I toured with Colt, before I'd ever touched a guitar, I had loved music. The songs from Momma's radio that spoke with the voices of friends, the hymns in Daddy's church that rang with the tongues of angels, the melodies that whispered to me sometimes like my most secret self.

The thing that made me truly me.

The house was quiet. No one was home to hear or judge.

I went upstairs to my little back bedroom, where my guitar sat on the empty twin bed next to mine. Slowly, I opened the case and took out the Hummingbird. There was a chip in the mother-of-pearl inlay from the night Jo threw her shoes across the room, and a scratch on the back from Colt's belt buckle the first time I let him play the guitar. But otherwise it looked the same as the day Mr. Laurence gave it to me, the year I turned twelve.

My heart thumped loud enough to deafen me. I sat on the bed where I'd taught myself to play. Wiped my damp palms on my jeans. I cradled the Hummingbird, curving my body around its familiar shape, feeling the frets and strings like a blind person reading braille. Chord progressions. *Easy.* C major. F major. My fingers were stiff and unresponsive on the strings. G major. A minor. Tight, controlled.

I listened for the music, but there was too much static in my head. How many calories were in a teething cracker, anyway?

I opened my notebook. My cramped writing marched across the pages, black on white, like ants at a picnic. I flipped a sheet. My pencil had dug through the paper, obliterating the lines. There wasn't room for anything else.

My stomach ached.

I picked up my phone. Nothing from Colt.

So I poked around on the Internet. Seventy calories per serving, said the manufacturer's website. Two biscuits. I'd eaten four.

I felt sick.

I went out to the barn.

An hour later, I was drenched with sweat and shaky with exhaustion. Bits of hay clung to my damp skin as I shoveled out the weaning pen, my face on fire. My hands and feet were cold. I was so out of shape. No stamina, that was my problem. One of my problems.

The ground tilted under me. Everything grayed. Blurred.

I stumbled. Something — someone — gripped my shoulders. I sat abruptly, straw prickling through my jeans.

"Here." A man's voice.

A furry bulk pressed against me. I tightened my hold instinctively as it wriggled in my arms. A dog? It butted my face, sharp tiny hooves digging into my thighs.

Not a dog. A goat.

I was sitting on a hay bale outside the barn, a baby goat in my lap.

Dan Harkins crouched in front of me, his gaze on my face. "You okay?"

"I . . ." I drew a shaky breath. The goat — SALSA, said her pink neckband, one of this year's crop of babies — thrust her head under my jaw. I held her closer, clinging to the present, breathing in her warm animal smell. "Yes. Thanks. How did you . . . ?"

"Always works for me."

I smiled. "Goat therapy?"

His eyes creased before his expression sobered. "I got PTSD. The animals can sense it. They let me know when I get in too deep. Mostly they keep me from going under."

200

"I don't have PTSD."

"Panic attacks, then. Whatever you call it."

I shook my head.

"Took me a long time to learn there's no shame in a label." He straightened from his crouch. Glanced down at me. "You ever talk to your dad?"

"No." My father counseled people who truly needed his help, wounded warriors who had suffered trauma in battle, soldiers who had seen and done and experienced horrible things. "My parents worry about me enough already. I can't bother them because I have . . . ." The truth stuck in my throat. "I can handle it," I said.

"Seems to me they'd want to help."

They would. My entire family had cushioned and shielded and supported me all my life. When I pleaded sick to stay home from school. When I left halfway through my first year of college. But I was finally making something of myself. Of my life. It wasn't fair to make them disrupt their own lives to pay attention to me. "I don't want to be a burden."

"He's a good listener."

Outside of his own family, maybe. Between my father and his daughters there was always a thin, palpable barrier, like a plate

201

glass window. I swallowed. I couldn't be mad at our father. My sisters got to be angry. Our mother got to act. *Somebody* in our family had to be the one to keep the peace, to make nice, to understand. To forgive. "Did *you* ever try talking to him?"

Dan nodded. "Your father saved my life. Your dad and your ma both."

Had he served with Dad? But my father was a chaplain — a noncombatant. And Mom . . . "I don't understand."

Dan picked up a rake. Put it down again. I figured he wasn't going to say any more. The smell of hay and goats wrapped around us, dust motes dancing in the light.

"We were part of the initial force to go into Iraq," he said after I'd given up on him speaking at all. "I was eighteen. It was crazy. Like some shoot-'em-up video game. Only it's for real. Craters everywhere. Body parts. Tanks smoldering in the road. We could get blown up any minute, and we just keep pushing forward, under orders, and I've got no control over any of it."

"I'm sorry." I couldn't begin to understand the stress, the horror of what he'd been through. But that feeling of not being in control . . . I could sympathize with that. "Was . . . Was my father with you?"

Dan shook his head. "Not then. But I

talked to him about it. Our convoy is trying to get through, and I see this guy, this herdsman, walking his damn goats along the road. Like, it doesn't matter that there's a war on or who's in charge or who's not in charge. He could get shot, and he doesn't care, because he's got to feed his animals. I told him that story. Your dad. And he brought me here."

"That's why you let him stay with you." Three weeks after the wedding, my father was still living in the trailer behind the barn with Dan.

"That's your ma's decision."

Salsa nibbled on my chin. I scratched between her horn buds. I smiled, a little sadly. "Momma's never been able to say no to Daddy."

"I reckon you underestimate them both." His eyes were grayish green, like lichen. His gaze was soft and steady above the beard. I wondered idly how old he was. "You good now?"

I was. Still sweaty, my heart still jerking in my chest, but I could breathe again. I couldn't talk to Jo, I wasn't ready to talk with my mother, and I never talked to Dad. But somehow, with Dan, I felt heard without having to say anything at all. "Yes. Thanks."

"Anytime." He smiled, making my heart

quicken in a different rhythm. "The goats and I are always here."

CHAPTER 12
AMY

The city, bustling and hustling and full of energy, felt different when I got back from Jo's wedding. Harder. Dirtier. Less friendly. Less like home. The clank and heat of the dry cleaner's downstairs rose to my apartment. The smell of chemicals, the roar of giant fans, seeped into my dreams.

I had hired a new stitcher, a former club band musician named Kyle, who was good with leather.

"He can help you with assembly and packing orders," I told Flo the morning before I left New York. "But I want you to take over the cutting."

I made die cuts, metal templates, for all my designs so they could be replicated in different colors and materials. Every piece was hand-cut and -finished. I prided myself that customization was part of the appeal of a Baggage bag, though I got plenty of clients who simply wanted something "just like

Meghan Markle has." Or whatever influencer I'd gifted, begged, or bribed into displaying my brand that month.

I traced a geometric sunburst vaguely inspired by the Chrysler Building onto ocher vinyl. I no longer had to make every piece myself from start to finish. I could reuse our most popular patterns — the bold, bright graphics Baggage was becoming known for — in a different color palette each season.

But maybe being away would spark some fresh ideas. Give me a chance to play with new designs.

"Don't worry."

"I hate leaving you with all this."

Flo pressed a sweating can of Mountain Dew to her substantial cleavage. "At least you're getting out of the city."

"Bunyan, North Carolina, isn't exactly the Hamptons. Anyway, I'll be working for my great-aunt."

She nodded. "Sucking up for the loan."

"That's the plan."

"You going to see him again?"

My craft knife bobbled. "Who?"

"Please. That guy. The one you haven't mentioned since you got back."

"Probably. It's a small town." And Trey was one of the family.

"So?"

"So, nothing."

"You two hook up at the wedding?"

Drunken Wedding Sex. "No."

"But you did. Before."

"One time. Three years ago." I took a deep breath, steadying my knife against the die edge. "It's over now."

Over almost as soon as we started.

Paris, Then

I turned my head against the hem-stitched pillowcase. At some point during the night, after we made love for the second time (in front of the mirror, hello!), Trey had opened the balcony windows to let in the soft Paris air. The morning light stole through the sheer under-curtains, bathing the room in a gauzy, golden filter.

He lay on his back beside me. I released a breath I hadn't been aware I was holding. He was so beautiful. Those chiseled lips, those exaggerated hands, like Michelangelo's David, all finely formed of smooth, thick marble. One sculpted arm was raised above his head, revealing the soft, black hair underneath. I hugged myself. He was not a statue. Not a fantasy. Theodore James Laurence III was next to me, in the flesh, in my bed. In his bed, which was ginormous, by the way.

My blood thickened in my veins, sweet and slow as honey. I was besotted with his body. I wanted to nuzzle his armpit, lick his collarbone, start at the top and work my way down. The way he had last night. The thought made me blush, heat flowing everywhere.

I'd had sex before. Not as much as my reputation suggested. But I'd resigned myself years ago to the fact that I would never have Trey. So I tried to have something. Normal relationships.

But Trey was different. Special. With Trey, there were all these feelings.

His eyes were still closed. He had thick, tangled lashes, ridiculous on a guy. When he looked at me with those hot, dark eyes — like he saw me, the real me, the grown-up Amy Curtis March, taking me with those eyes, making me hot and confused and happy — I felt special, too.

I shivered, overcome with lust and happiness.

Would he want me to go with him to Italy? There was nothing actually keeping me in Paris. No real job. No apartment. A brief regret surfaced at the thought of what I might be giving up. I stuffed it to the back of my mental closet like last year's sweater.

Momma said love meant thinking more about your relationship than your ego.

I would be happy with Trey anywhere, I decided. So. First Italy — Modena wasn't exactly Rome or Florence, but maybe he would agree to a side trip — and then home to tell the family. What would Meg think? What would our mother say? What would Jo . . .

My mind skittered. Well. Jo was in New York, pursuing the career of her dreams. I probably wouldn't see her until she came home for Christmas. Surely by then we all would have had time to get used to the idea of Trey and me?

She'd probably be my bridesmaid. All my sisters would be bridesmaids. If part of me recognized that planning my wedding after one night of sex (fabulous, amazing, rock-my-world sex) was a little premature, I reminded myself that this was Trey, after all. I'd loved him all my life. Family was important to him.

I could give him family. He could have mine.

The thought made me feel warm and mushy inside. He was practically one of us already. I pictured him asking to speak to Daddy, imagined finally having my father's approval, and melted a little more.

I reached out my finger, trailing my touch along Trey's lovely arm. Tracing his beautiful mouth.

His lips curved in a smile. His gaze, warm and sleepy, met mine. He murmured, "Jo."

I froze. The warm puddle inside me turned to icy slush. "What did you say?"

His eyes opened fully. "What?"

"You called me 'Jo.' "

"I . . . What? No. It was a mistake."

"You bet your ass it was." I scrambled off the bed, almost falling on my butt in my eagerness to get away. *Shit.* I was naked. Exposed. I snatched at the top sheet.

"Amy, I'm sorry." He sat up, the sheet falling away. "I didn't mean it. It didn't mean anything."

I narrowed my eyes. "*What* didn't mean anything?"

"I . . ." He ran his hand through his hair, looking adorably rumpled and confused. "What I said?"

I dropped the sheet and marched across the room to the Louis XV wardrobe, wrenching it open. I ripped the hotel bathrobe from the hanger and wrapped it around me, grateful for its shielding warmth. Like he hadn't already seen everything I had.

"You're stunning."

Tears stung my eyes.

210

"Amy . . . Sweetheart . . ." His voice nearly undid me. "Can we please start over? What can I do?"

I yanked the belt tight. "Show me your phone."

A long pause, measured in heartbeats.

Trey cleared his throat. "Look, the last thing I want to do is hurt you."

Which meant, of course, that he would.

I grabbed his phone from the nightstand. "What's your passcode?"

"This is stupid."

Stupid, stupid. "Show me." My heart beat frantically. Maybe I was wrong. Maybe . . .

He sighed and unlocked his phone. "Can we at least talk about this, please?"

I took the phone and tapped on his messages. Naturally, Jo's name was first on his list. I scrolled through several days' worth of texts, numbness spreading through me.

I miss you.

I'm sorry.

Forgive me?

And — sent yesterday — a picture of the Tuileries Gardens. Taken, apparently, when he'd been with me. Thinking of you, he had typed.

My eyes were suddenly dry and scratchy. Silently, I handed back the phone.

He glanced at the screen. His mouth

211

twisted. "Okay, I know this looks . . . I know how this looks. But it's not that big a deal. We text each other all the time."

"*You* text. You. She's not answering."

"We had a fight."

"You told me you broke up with her."

"We did."

"Then why are you texting her?" *Why did you sleep with me?*

"It's . . . habit, okay? I didn't even think about it."

As if that didn't make it worse.

"Thanks for the explanation," I said politely.

He got out of bed — naked — and walked toward me. I averted my gaze. "Look, I'm really sorry. I care about you, Amy, you know I do, I . . . ."

"This was a mistake."

I had to say it first. If Trey were forced to say it, he would be kind and regretful, and I didn't think I could survive either his kindness or regret.

But if I said the words first . . . Well. I might escape with my pride intact, at least. Trey wouldn't be thrust into the role of villain because I'd chosen to romanticize a one-night stand. If I acknowledged it first — *"This was a mistake"* — maybe one day in the future, the hopefully distant future,

212

months or years from now, we'd be able to face each other over the Thanksgiving table without me wanting to kill us both with a fork.

He was a good person. Even if, at this moment, I wished he were dead. One mistake with me shouldn't cost him his relationship with my entire family.

And maybe, please God, oh, maybe he would disagree with me.

He didn't.

He looked relieved, as if I'd lifted a burden from his shoulders. "Is that how you really feel?" he asked quietly.

I shrugged. "How should I feel?"

He dipped his head to look into my face, his eyes dark and concerned. "Then . . . we're good?"

My throat tightened. He loved my sister. I was, at best, his second choice.

"Don't worry, Trey." I managed a smile. "What happens in Paris, stays in Paris."

I waited until I was in the bathroom to cry, silent, ugly tears in the shower. *Stupid, stupid, Easy Amy.*

All those years stuck playing the princess because my sisters didn't think I could act. I deserved a fucking Oscar.

"Took you long enough," Phee grumbled

213

when I got to Oak Hill.

I paused in the open bay doors, my eyes adjusting to the cavernous dimness. Phee sat on a brocade chair surrounded by piled shelves and furniture, like a dragon guarding her hoard.

I picked my way toward her. "I missed you, too. And it's only been ten days," I added.

"Two weeks. I expected you on Thursday."

It was Saturday. *Suck up,* I reminded myself. Phee was going to be so impressed with my can-do attitude and sunny disposition that I'd be hunting for a workroom in Brooklyn before you could say *fall collection.*

I bent to kiss her cheek, ignoring Polly's halfhearted growl. "You get what you pay for, Aunt Phee. So far, you haven't paid me anything."

"You haven't done anything."

"I've been busy. I can't just take off from work for three weeks. I had to find somebody to help Flo."

"I hired help, too, while you were gone."

I widened my eyes. "A professional organizer?"

Her lips twitched. "I don't need an organizer. I hired Alec."

The teen was stacking cartons in a corner. I grinned at him. "Brave man." My sister had the best stepsons. "You done with school now?"

"Until August."

"Crappiest summer vacation ever."

He shrugged. "I don't mind."

Maybe he didn't. Jo was busy with her deadline, and Eric with the restaurant opening in three weeks. All Alec's friends were in Fayetteville, his older brother away on a soccer scholarship at the University of Maryland.

At least when Momma moved us out to the farm, I'd had my sisters.

"Alec lives here now," Phee said. "It's only appropriate he has an opportunity to learn about his new home. About our family."

I held up a rotary dial phone in the shape of a ketchup bottle. "Our heritage."

"Not all of the furnishings are original to the house," Phee said stiffly. "Obviously."

"How come the house didn't burn down?" Alec asked. "During the Civil War?"

"The Marches were Unionists," Phee said proudly. "Oak Hill sheltered the Union wounded after the Battle of Monroe's Crossroads. Unfortunately, that didn't protect the contents of the house from being lost. Or looted. Or sold off."

"My dad says it's all just stuff."

Phee nodded. "He's right, of course.

Nothing is as important as family. But this stuff, as you call it, is our family's history."

"Yes, ma'am."

"Aunt Phee."

He shot her a flickering look through long, dark lashes. A hint of a smile.

"My mother told me her great-grandmother buried the family silver rather than see it go to support the secessionist cause," Phee said. "It's always been up to the women in this family to preserve things."

"Like buried treasure," Alec said.

"Don't encourage her," I said. "Or she'll make us dig holes under the rosebushes, searching for it."

Another of those sideways smiles.

"I guess this move is pretty hard on you," I said.

"Into the servants' quarters?" Phee asked.

"I was talking to Alec," I said.

He shrugged. "I'm used to it. Mom's in the army. We've never lived anywhere more than a couple years."

"And I've never lived anywhere but here." Phee sounded almost wistful. "Oak Hill has been in our family for almost two hundred years. We didn't build that house. We didn't farm this land. It exists because our family profited from the labor of others. But here we are. From my great-great-grandfather to my father to me. And now to Jo and your father and you." Her severe face softened as she looked at Alec. "I have always loved living here. I hope you will, too."

"Yes, ma'am."

"Aunt Phee."

He grinned suddenly. "Yes, Aunt Phee."

Her answering smile was something to see. I blinked moisture from my eyes.

"Well, don't stand there gawking," Phee said. "We have work to do."

I pivoted slowly, surveying the piles. "It looks like the house threw up in here." Spewing the contents of every closet, attic, and spare room across the carriage house floor.

With Alec's help, I created broad areas. Consignment store. Thrift shop. Dump. We hauled and sorted, getting hotter, sweatier, and dirtier by the hour.

"I could have stayed in New York," I muttered. "I feel like I'm on the subway."

But every now and then a breeze would wander through the open doors, bringing with it the scent of grass and the sound of birds. Or Alec or I would uncover a treasure — a Marine Corps saber from Spain that belonged to an uncle in the First World War, a silver-backed brush from Phee's mother's vanity set, an oil painting from the 1920s or

'30s in the Barbizon style — and Phee would tell a story.

Over the next week, we found a kind of rhythm, dragging, clearing, and cleaning. I took pictures of whiskey barrels and gateleg tables, oil lamps and curio cabinets for eBay and Facebook Marketplace.

"I don't know anything about selling online," Phee said.

"I do," I said.

At night, after I finished reviewing orders and checking inventory for Baggage, I looked up the items online, trying to determine their value. Keep or sell? Sell or donate?

During the day, Alec and I emptied jammed shelves and jumbled drawers, rescued Polly from behind bed frames and stacked canvases, and held up random items for Phee's inspection. Crumbling dried flowers (*Toss*) in a beautiful Revere bowl (*Keep*). A silver epergne from the 1890s. *Sell*. Mildewed magazines, broken cups and saucers. *Toss*. Old vinyl records from the 1960s.

"I'll go through those," Phee said.

"What about this?" Alec asked, holding up a gray mechanical box.

"Keep."

"Toss," I said at the same time.

218

Phee glared. "That canasta shuffler belonged to my mother."

"Aunt Phee, you don't even play canasta."

"What's canasta?" Alec asked.

"It's a card game," I said. "That nobody plays."

Phee sniffed. "Fine." *Toss.*

One of the students from the restaurant, a pink-haired teen a year or two older than Alec, crossed the driveway carrying a plastic pitcher and a stack of red cups, the kind used at church picnics and fraternity parties.

Alec straightened. "Hey, Nan."

"Hey, yourself." She set the pitcher on a tiger oak washstand. "Chef thought you all might be thirsty."

"Thank you, dear," Phee said.

Alec watched the girl saunter back to the house. "Why aren't you working for your dad this summer?" I asked him after the screen door closed behind her.

"Slaving away in the kitchen of the ol' plantation house?" He smiled and shook his head.

I blotted my hot face. "Sorry. I didn't think."

"It's your father's kitchen now," Phee said. "He's creating something very special here with his school and restaurant. You should

219

be proud of him."

"I am. He's a great chef. And a great dad. But I don't want to cook. And when we're in the kitchen — the restaurant kitchen — everything has to be done his way."

I put a coaster under the pitcher. "Oh, like working for Aunt Phee is any better."

"Maybe not." He glanced at Phee. Grinned. "She pays better, though."

"The laborer is worthy of his wages," Phee said.

"Remember that the next time I talk to you about my loan," I said.

Polly yapped, trapped beneath a rolltop desk. "Oh, for Pete's sake." I dropped on hands and knees to retrieve her. "Ouch. Your dust mop bit me," I complained, handing the dog to Phee.

"Poor thing."

"Thank you."

"I meant Polly," Phee said, cuddling the dog. "This heat makes her cranky."

"It makes me cranky, too, but I can control myself."

"You March women are tough to crack," Trey's voice said behind me.

The heat spread, sudden and low.

"Hey, Trey," Alec said easily.

"Alec. Phee. I brought you a little something." He handed her a bakery bag from

Connie's Cupcakes.

"Red velvet," Phee said with approval. "Very nice."

I ran my grimy fingers through my sweat-dampened hair, aware how I must look. How I must smell. Ugh. "Nothing for the rest of us?"

"Hi, Amy." His eyes sparkled. Laughing at me. "You're working hard."

"Some of us have to." I looked him up and down. Instead of his customary dress shirt, he wore basketball shorts and a T-shirt. "The dealership isn't open on Saturdays anymore?"

"I got away. I thought you could use a break. You, too," he said to Alec. "There's a pickup game at the park. Interested?"

Also very nice, I thought. But then, he was a nice person.

"Yeah, I guess. If that's okay," Alec said to Phee.

She waved her fingers. "Go. We've done quite enough for today."

"Coming?" Trey asked me.

"You're confusing me with Jo. I don't play basketball."

"So bring a book."

Also not me, I thought. But neither was being Marie Kondo.

"Come on," he coaxed. "I'll buy you ice

221

cream after."

I should say no. "Is that a bribe?"

"Is it working?"

"*I* want ice cream," Alec said.

"He wants ice cream," Trey said. "You don't want to disappoint a hungry teenager."

I threw up my hands. "Sure. I've never been able to resist" — *you* — "a hungry teenager."

The Bunyan waterfront was a bright patchwork of Americana, as if Norman Rockwell and Grandma Moses had had a love child. Flags flapped. Boats bobbed on the river. Tourists and retirees shared park benches. Joggers and cyclists whizzed around people walking dogs. Knots of parents chatted as their laughing, shrieking children ran around the playground.

The asphalt courts by the Laurence Recreation Center were divided between dads coaching their kids and the pickup game of older teens and adults. The players thudded up and down the court, shirts and skins, Black and White.

Trey was shirtless. And sweaty. And gorgeous. Hard not to notice that.

"He's so hot," a woman beside me said.

I turned my head. It was one of the

playground moms — Meg's friend Sallie Moffat, the buyer for Simply Southern, an upscale women's boutique in town. When I was first starting out, Sallie sold my bags on consignment.

I smiled. "Hey, Sallie."

"Hi, Amy. Ooh, I love your bag. Is that the Duchess?"

"Same style, different pattern." I turned the square tote sideways so she could see. I was proud of the design, *Fleur,* a single stylized flower in bold blue.

"Love it. Why don't I have any of those for the store?"

"I'll make sure you get some. We're a little behind on orders," I confessed.

"So, what are you doing here?"

"I'm helping Aunt Phee move into the carriage house. Trey thought I could use a break."

"Really?" Sallie's gaze darted between me and Trey on the court. "Are you guys . . . together?"

Easy A. The old nickname rose like a finger-pointing ghost. I shook my head. "He's my sister's ex."

"Jo? That was years ago."

"There is no statute of limitations on the Sisters' Code."

"Please. I used to go out with Belle's

boyfriends all the time. If I didn't take sloppy seconds, I never would have dated at all. It's not like there's a surplus of eligible guys in this town."

"We're not dating. We're here with Alec. Eric's son?" Who was running down the court, high-fiving a teammate. So at least somebody was having fun.

"Which just goes to show," Sallie said.

"Show what?"

"Trey must really be over Jo."

Was he? The possibility stole my breath. "He's just being nice," I said. "Trey is like family."

" 'Like a brother,' Meg says."

Not quite. "Speaking of family, is that your baby?"

Sallie glanced over her shoulder at the toddler in a sundress clinging to her father's hand. Her face softened. "Yes, that's our Hayley. I should go before Ned gets her killed on the monkey bars. Enjoy the game!"

Trey's team lost.

Although you could hardly tell from the way they behaved afterward, fist-bumping and grinning. Trey came over, sweaty and cheerful, and reached for his shirt. A light fan of dark hair arrowed from his chest down his stomach, disappearing into his shorts. I remembered the secret pleasure of that soft friction against my skin and blushed.

"Seen enough?"

I jerked my gaze from Trey's torso to his amused face. "Basketball? Yes." I raised my chin. "I'm not a big fan."

"And yet you're ogling."

Busted. "Please. I'm an artist. It's not ogling. It's human study." Although none of the male models I'd drawn in school had looked like Trey, all lean muscle and golden skin.

Alec loped up. "Ice cream?"

"That's the plan," Trey said. "Your aunt Amy needs to cool off."

"Bite me," I said sweetly.

After ice cream, we strolled through downtown, the storefronts refurbished after the recent floods. The windows of Eric's new Taproom gleamed. An art gallery and a gift shop had joined Bunyan's Hardware and Connie's Cupcake Confections on Main Street. A new bookstore had opened where the camera shop used to be.

"Hey, there's Jo's book," Alec said, pointing to *Sisters' Farm* displayed in the front window.

I had a signed copy. I'd even read it. *A warmhearted exploration of family, self-discovery, and change,* the blurb said, and

225

never mind that the character of the youngest sister, May, made me cringe. Well, it was Jo's book. Jo's story.

"And your father's cookbook." *Service* by Eric Bhaer, with a foreword by Jo March.

Stacks of them, with LOCAL AUTHOR stickers. My sister was a celebrity. I stifled the familiar pang of pride and envy.

"I want to show you something," Trey said.

He guided us past the old brick warehouse near the center of town, abandoned now as long as I could remember.

"What's this?" Alec asked.

"Farmers' warehouse," Trey said. "Built in 1904. They used to bring their tobacco here to be auctioned."

"It's big."

"Too big. Granddad's never been able to find a tenant. Costs more than it's worth to keep it standing empty. He'll probably tear it down."

I tipped my head back to study the warm, ancient brick, the multi-paned windows blocked with grime. "That would be a shame."

Trey shrugged. "Tourism will never be able to replace tobacco in this town." He smiled. "And here we are."

I raised an eyebrow. "A shoe store?"

"It's closed," Alec said.

"Owners retired eight months ago," Trey said. "Kids didn't want to take it over, so they let it go."

I peered through the plate glass window at the dusty retail space. Terrible blue carpeting, cheap veneer racks, soulless fluorescent lighting against ugly ceiling tiles. My heart gave a sudden, unexpected thump.

"The second floor is empty," Trey said. "Lots of storage."

"And you're showing me this because . . . ?"

"I thought you might be interested." He shot me a bright, expectant look. "Want to see inside?"

I swallowed against temptation. "It's locked."

"I have the key."

Of course he did. "You own the building."

"Laurence Properties does. Jo said . . . If you were thinking of staying . . ."

"What did she tell you?"

"That Phee was trying to bribe you to come home."

I half laughed. "Bribe or blackmail."

"So . . ." He stuck his hands in his pockets. "You want to go in or not?"

His eyes dared me. *In* or *out*? *Stay* or *go*?

My heart thudded. Leave it to Trey to find

the perfect venue for my dreams. I could love him again without even trying.

And he didn't feel the same way.

CHAPTER 13
BETH

A calico cat perched on the rail of the goat pen. I leaned my rake against the wall and extended one finger for her to sniff. She hissed briefly and then, apparently deciding I wasn't worth even that much effort, ignored me.

"She'll come around," Dan said. "Once she gets used to you."

We were cleaning out the barn while the goats were at pasture. Straw dust tickled my nose.

"I can be patient." I had plenty of time these days. I glanced at him over my shoulder. "We always had barn cats growing up. People dump them by the road. They think because we're a farm, their pets can fend for themselves. But they can't."

"We put out food and water," he said.

I remembered the story he told, about the herdsman walking his goats along the road. Whatever happens, the animals needed to be fed. I smiled. "I'm sure the cat earns her keep."

It was hard to tell behind the beard, but I thought he smiled back. "She's got a family to provide for."

"A . . . Oh!" The calico stood and stretched, revealing herself as a working mom. "She has kittens?"

He nodded, a smile breaking through his camouflage. "Showed up pregnant about a month ago. Want to see?"

The cat followed us into the feed room, where he'd fixed up a box lined with old towels. I peeked into the carton as the calico jumped in. Her babies swarmed over her. Dan reached down, stroking one big finger lightly along the top of a tiny head. My heart tugged in response.

"I used to bring kittens into the house," I said.

"You and your ma. Always trying to save somebody."

"I wish I was more like my mother." Strong. Competent. In control.

"You do all right," he said.

The quiet-voiced compliment was almost believable. "I *am* a farm girl." I waited for him to make some crack about pigtails.

"You more than your sisters," he said.

"Meg is a big help with the books. And Jo

always worked in the barn. But they were already in high school when we moved to the farm."

"You the youngest?"

"No, that would be Amy. But she never liked outside chores."

"I've noticed," he said, a hint of humor in his voice.

"What about you?" I asked shyly. "Where did you grow up?"

"Around. I was a city kid. Sure never saw myself in a place like this. When your ma hired me, I thought I'd died and gone to heaven."

"I'm glad you didn't die."

Gah. What a stupid thing to say. "I'm sorry. I mean, of course you didn't die. I'm glad you're here."

"Me, too. There's plenty of death on a farm. Animals are born. Animals die. You can't get away from it. But there's always life, if you look for it. Life wins on a farm."

I wondered what deaths he struggled to get away from or over. How he managed to be so accepting.

A rasping sound vibrated from the box — the calico, purring, as her pink-toed kittens scrambled over one another.

"The Curtises — my mother's people — aren't a first family like the Marches. Or big landowners like the Laurences. But we've been here a long time. We stick, Momma says."

"But you left."

"Because everybody said that's what I was supposed to do. Follow my heart. Follow my dreams."

"And now you're a star."

The star wasn't me, any more than the shadow was me. I was lost somewhere between them, the bright and the dark. But I couldn't tell him that. I never told anybody. "That wasn't ever my dream," I said instead. "It just happened. My voice teacher thought the audition would be good practice."

Dan was silent.

I watched the kittens, blindly searching for their place. "I'm not like the rest of my family," I said. "I never made any grand plans about what I'd do when I grew up. I never thought of being married like Meg or famous like Jo or starting my own company like Amy. I couldn't imagine myself anything but stupid little Beth, trotting about at home, of no use anywhere but here."

"Sounds pretty great to me," he said. "Being here."

I swallowed the ache in my throat. "Yes. But it's not enough." That's what everybody said. My teachers. My sisters. My mother. Colt.

"I don't see that. You want to be useful? I've watched the way you and your sisters take care of the babies and each other and your ma." He took a breath. Expelled it. Looked at me, genuine puzzlement in his eyes. "How is that not enough for you? It sure as hell would be enough for me."

The moment stretched between us, filled with the purring of the cat and hay specks floating like music in the air.

"Hey, Dan." My mother appeared from the creamery, a bandanna over her hair. "Hannah could use some help with the pallets."

"Yes, ma'am."

"I thought you were visiting James Laurence today," she said to me as he left.

I flushed guiltily. Because I *had* promised. I should go, I should play, I should do it for him, he'd been so kind to me. But every time I reached for my guitar, I froze. "I wanted to give Dan a hand first."

"You want to be careful there, honey," my mother warned. "That's a working cat."

I bent to give the calico a parting pat. "She just needs time to get used to me."

"Beth, these barn cats . . . They're not like Weasley." The cat I'd grown up with.

"They're feral. We give them work and food and a better life than they could have somewhere else. But they're not pets. You don't want to get too close. Do you understand?"

I met her shrewd mom-gaze. "Are we still talking about the cat?"

"Not only the cat. You're spending a lot of time with Dan these days."

"Don't you like him?"

"I do, yes. But how well do you really know him?"

"I know he has PTSD."

"He told you."

"Not much. He's very . . ." *Undemanding. Kind.* "Quiet," I said.

My mother sighed. "He had a rough childhood. Bounced around in foster care, got into fights at school. He enlisted to avoid jail. Did a couple of tours and was finally discharged for slugging his commanding officer."

I shivered. Not in fear. In shame. Compared to Dan's hardships, my problems seemed so small. "You always say we should give people a chance."

"I hired him, didn't I? He's good with the animals. But you're my daughter."

Amy would have made some kind of joke.

Does that mean you love me more than the goats?

"Don't worry, Mom. You can trust him. You can trust me."

She tugged off her bandanna, running her hand through her hair. "I just don't want to see you get hurt."

Hurt? I blinked at her. "He's not violent."

"Not anymore," she agreed. "But he has issues, honey."

"He was a soldier." *Like Dad.* "You can't hold that against him."

My mother gave me another sharp, penetrating look. "I don't hold it against him. I respect him for trying to turn his life around. Dan's a good man. It's not easy adjusting to civilian life, even with support."

All my life, I had relied on my mother's advice, protected by her wisdom, secure in her love. But . . .

"I just want to be his friend. I think he could use one." *And so could I.*

"As long as that's all it is."

That's all it could be.

"I love Colt," I reminded her.

My mother shook her head. "You have such a soft heart."

I smiled. "Dan said I take after you."

"That'll get you in trouble one day," Momma said.

235

No marble lions guarded the Laurence house, a mile down the road from our farmhouse. Only Mr. Laurence himself, with his growly voice and intimidating eyebrows.

The first few months after Trey came to live with his grandfather, my sisters were in and out of their house all the time. Especially Jo. At eleven, I felt too young — and much too timid — to tag along.

"You're a year older than Amy," Jo had pointed out.

But Amy was never shy.

That Halloween, though, Meg and Jo had been invited to a party at Sallie Gardiner's with Trey. Before the party, they were taking Amy and me trick-or-treating in town. Meg, the oldest, was entrusted to drive. I was glad not to go to the Gardiners'. I would have skipped trick-or-treating, too, even in our familiar old neighborhood. But Amy had sulked and Meg had coaxed and Jo promised it would be for only a little while.

Which is how I'd found myself standing in the lion's den that night, facing old Mr. Laurence himself.

Meg had dressed for the party as a demurely sexy vampire. Amy was a glittery rock star. (She had been a glittery princess the year before and a glittery fairy the year before that.)

"And who are you supposed to be?" Mr. Laurence barked at Jo, in period costume.

She grinned at him. "Mary Wollstonecraft."

"Who's that?"

Jo brandished the pamphlet in her hand. "She wrote *A Vindication of the Rights of Woman.*"

"Votes for women!" Trey said.

Mr. Laurence harrumphed and turned those scary eyebrows on me. "And you are . . . ?"

I wore a white tunic Amy had made from a sheet and carried a sword, a play prop borrowed from Jo. I opened my mouth to explain, but no words came out.

"She's Joan of Arc," Jo said.

My face was one hot blush. As if I could even pretend to be that brave.

Mr. Laurence had scowled quite fiercely and then winked, so quickly I almost didn't see it. "You look like Princess Leia to me."

Like a heroine.

Even all these years later, the memory made

me smile. He'd always been so kind to me.

All he'd ever asked in return was to hear me play. I hated to disappoint him.

I climbed the shallow porch steps of the Laurence house and knocked softly. The massive front door opened.

"Beth." Mr. Laurence, still upright and vigorous at seventy-five, smiled at me from the shadows of the hallway. "This is a treat."

I held out the gift I'd brought.

"What's this?" he asked, taking it.

"Colt's CD. He signed it. I didn't want to come over empty-handed," I said apologetically.

His keen gaze met mine. "Thank you, my dear. But I was hoping for a live concert."

"No, I . . ." My voice failed.

"But what am I doing, keeping you standing outside? Come in, come in. Dee, would you bring tea and cookies to the study?" he asked the housekeeper. He looked at me. "If that's all right. I know you're not a little girl anymore, but it's early in the day for bourbon. Even for me."

My whole face relaxed as I smiled. "Tea is perfect."

I sighed in comfort as we settled in his study.

"Cookie?"

Chocolate chip. My favorite. I put one,

untasted, on the side of my plate. The room smelled the same, like bourbon and tobacco. The deep leather chair still wrapped me like a hug. The picture of his late daughter — Trey's aunt, the original owner of my guitar — smiled from his desk, her teased bangs and soft smile fixed forever in high school.

Mr. Laurence caught my glance and smiled. "You remind me of her."

"I'm sorry. I promised I'd play for you today."

"It's good to see you, with or without your guitar. No strings attached." He chuckled at his little joke. "Besides, I can listen to you on this." He squinted at the CD case. "You're on here, right?"

I nodded. "Two songs." The songs I'd written.

"Very nice. I'm proud of you."

"Thanks," I said huskily.

"I should thank you. For giving life to my little girl's dreams."

My eyes were misty. "I always wondered . . ." I stopped.

Mr. Laurence looked at me inquiringly.

"Well . . ." I owed him so much. I didn't want to seem ungrateful or spoil our time together. But something in me — a trace of Jo's fairness, maybe, or Amy's curiosity — drove me to ask, "It's such a beautiful instrument. Why didn't you give it to Trey?"

Mr. Laurence took a cookie and sat back. "Trey had just lost both his parents when he came to live with me. He was hurting, and I barely knew him. That was my fault. But I tried too hard to make it up to him. I didn't know how to help him, so I spoiled him instead. By the time I figured that out . . ." He broke off, brushing crumbs from his fingers. "I had to teach him he can't expect everything to be handed to him on a plate. Trey needed to learn to earn what he wanted."

"But he loves music." I had memories of Trey making playlists, constantly plugged into his iPod or playing music while Jo tried to do homework. "And your daughter was his aunt."

He huffed. "You think the boy inherited some great musical talent?"

"I don't know. I can't judge. Wasn't his mother a singer?"

"A club singer in Miami. Graciela Mendoza." He shot me a look from under bushy brows. "I have one of her CDs, too."

I swallowed. "You didn't approve."

"Gracie was all right. It was my son I didn't approve of. Trey's father. No interest in anything but his own comfort. No discipline. No follow-through." His face twitched. "I didn't want to repeat my mistakes with my grandson. I was glad when Jo got him started running cross-country. You girls were a good influence. But Trey didn't need to take up his time with music lessons and such. I put him to work waxing cars and sweeping the showroom. Taught him to get his hands dirty. I figured he'd learn to appreciate an honest day's work." His mouth spasmed again on one side. "I was lucky he didn't tell me to go to hell."

"Trey wouldn't do that. He loves you," I said.

"He's a good boy. But he doesn't have any fire in his belly. Not like you an' your sisters."

"Not me," I said.

"You don't stand up for yourself. But you . . ." His hand shook. The ice cubes rattled in his glass. "Quick enough to . . . to . . ."

"Mr. Laurence?"

". . . take up ferr ovvurr . . ."

"Are you okay?"

". . . people," he mumbled. His glass dropped from his hand and rolled on the carpet. The ice cubes spilled.

"Mr. Laurence!" I jumped from my chair, reaching to catch him as he slumped. "Miss Dee!"

241

CHAPTER 14
AMY

"Okay. Thanks. I'll be there as soon as I can." Trey slid his phone back into his pocket.

His face frightened me. "What is it?"

"Granddad. He's at the hospital."

"Oh God, I'm so sorry. What happened?"

"Stroke, they think. Beth is with him." His gaze cut to the empty storefront windows and back to me. "I have to go."

"Of course. Do what you need to do." I glanced at Alec, leaning against the side of the building. The teen was engrossed in his phone, oblivious to the grown-up drama around him. "We'll be fine."

"I'll take you home first," Trey said.

Boarding school manners. "I'm coming with you, dumbass. I'll call an Uber for Alec."

His set mouth relaxed in a near smile. "You don't have to do that."

"I want to. Beth could use the support."

Not only Beth. Trey shouldn't have to face this alone. *A stroke.* How bad was it? Would his grandfather be okay?

Alec looked up from his phone. "Jo will meet us at the hospital."

"Jo is coming?" The eagerness in Trey's voice made me wince.

Alec nodded. "Yeah, I texted her. She's going to drive us home."

I felt a surge of affection for my newest nephew. "Brilliant."

Trey hesitated, obviously trying to decide the right thing to do.

When my mother was in the hospital, Trey had done everything he could to help, covering for John at work, bumping me to first class so I could get a flight home from Paris, picking Beth and me up at the airport. He had been so kind. I'd even dared to let myself think that maybe he had reconsidered our postbreakup hookup. That maybe we could start again.

And then on Christmas Eve, he took Jo to Alleygators, leaving me home alone.

Whatever. We were his family. Without us, without his grandfather, he had no one.

"We're wasting time," I said. "Let's go."

I chattered on the drive to the hospital. I always was a nervous talker. I asked Alec about his least and most favorite foods and

243

if he had any weird or useless talents and what he was listening to on his earbuds. Alec, blessed boy, responded politely to his crazy aunt-by-marriage, and every once in a while Trey would glance over.

So maybe he didn't mind the distraction too much.

I shivered as we walked through the emergency entrance doors. After the sunny park, the hospital felt bleak and cold.

I scanned the waiting room. Not so crowded for a Saturday afternoon. Good. An old woman in a wheelchair, her elderly husband by her side. A man with a bloody towel held to his face. A child ignoring her mother's demand to *Get out from under that table right now.* Beth huddled by herself in a row of chairs. Alec and I joined her while Trey went to the reception desk.

"How is he?" I asked.

"I don't know. They wouldn't let me back. They're running tests now."

"Thank God you were there."

Her fingers worried a hole in the knee of her jeans. "I called 911 right away."

Poor Bethie. She had always been Mr. Laurence's favorite. She must have been terrified. I didn't know what to say. I wasn't comforting like Meg or strong like Jo. I patted her hand, stilling the nervous movement, and after a moment she turned her palm up, lacing her long, thin fingers with mine.

The doors swished open, and our mother strode in wearing her usual jeans and work shirt. She went down the row of chairs, dispensing hugs like lunch money, *One for you and one for you . . .* Her scent — animals and hay, so different from the stale, sterile hospital smell — enveloped me. I clung to her, absurdly reassured.

Trey returned from the reception desk. "Abby! What are you doing here?"

His hug was longer than ours. Well. That was his grandfather, lying behind the hospital doors.

"I wanted to see you. Plus, Beth needs a ride home." She drew back to study his face. "How's your grandfather?"

"Stabilized, the nurse said. They won't let me see him yet." His throat moved as he swallowed. "They're doing a CT scan."

"I'm sorry," my mother said.

"He'll be fine. He has to be fine."

She patted his cheek without answering. I wanted desperately to help, to wrap Trey in my arms and let him cry on my shoulder. But his eyes were dry. Also, my mother was watching.

"So, what happens now?" I asked.

"We have to wait. I have to wait," he corrected. "There's no reason for you to stay."

"I want to," I said again.

He quirked an eyebrow. "And you always get what you want."

Not always, I thought with a wrench. I raised my chin, meeting his amused gaze. "Yes."

"Then . . . Thanks." His smile warmed his eyes. "Nice to have company."

My heart contracted and then swelled.

"You've always been there for us," Mom said. *On the outside of the circle, looking for a way in.* "I'll never forget what you did when I was in the hospital. Let us take care of you for once."

"Trey!"

My sister Jo barged into the waiting area, carrying Robbie. I watched as she went straight into Trey's arms and hugged him tight, both of them so tall, his dark, curly head bent over her shiny chestnut hair, matched since they were fifteen.

"How is he? How are you?" she demanded.

I listened as he went through the same non-news, the brain scan, the wait. "The nurse said he'll probably be admitted," he finished.

Jo gave him another sympathetic squeeze

before turning to the rest of us. "I should get you home," she said. To me? To Alec?

"It's no problem if you want to stay awhile," Alec said.

"You are the best," Jo said to him. She bounced Robbie on her hip. "Maybe. Thanks. Just until we hear."

The entrance doors slid open again and Meg came in. "John's watching the kids," she announced. "I brought sandwiches."

I watched my family engulf Trey. I'd missed this, I realized. Team March, united again, the way we had been when Daddy deployed.

Trey's relationship with my family had survived his breakup with Jo. But if they all knew we had slept together, how would they feel? It's not like he would have stayed with me. Not when he really loved Jo. And he needed this, needed them. He'd already lost one family. I couldn't deprive him of mine.

We sat in the scratchy waiting room chairs. Meg dispensed hand sanitizer and sandwiches from the capacious mom bag I'd made for her a couple years ago. Except for Alec, nobody ate much.

"I'm not hungry," Beth said.

"You should eat something," our mother said.

"Oh, I ate with Mr. Laurence. Miss Dee

made cookies." Beth managed a small, strained smile. "Chocolate chip."

When Robbie got bored with the toys Jo brought, I drew silly faces on my fingers and thumbs and put on a puppet show with my hands. Jo smiled at me gratefully.

"Laurence family?" the nurse called.

Trey stood.

We all did. Even Alec, the newest member of the clan, gathering his long legs under him, pulling out his earbuds to listen.

Trey looked around at this demonstration of support, his dark eyes glittering. My mother took his arm. I was so proud of her. Of us. So grateful for our family.

The doctor came out. She looked a little taken aback as the mob of us converged — well, we were a lot — but delivered her report to Trey in a dry, reassuring voice. Apparently the stroke had been caused by a clot, revealed by the CT scan.

"We've given Mr. Laurence a medication to break up the clot and reopen the blocked artery," the doctor said. "We've found that if the drug is administered soon enough, it can reduce the stroke's severity. Even reverse some of its effects. Your grandfather is lucky you got him here as quickly as you did."

"Because of Beth. Thank you," Trey said

to Beth.

She blushed.

"We'll have to watch him extra closely for the next twenty-four hours," the doctor said. "I'll order a repeat CT scan in a day or two to make sure the drugs worked."

"But how *is* he?" our mother asked.

The doctor hesitated. "Conscious. Confused, which is completely normal. And of course he's very tired. We'll continue to assess his condition over the next few days."

"We're admitting Mr. Laurence now," the nurse said. "You can wait for him up in the room if you want."

"All of us?" Jo asked.

"We won't fit," Mom said practically.

"You all can go," Trey said. "You heard her. He's normal. He's going to be fine."

Which wasn't exactly what the doctor said. "What about you?" I asked.

"I'm fine, too."

"We love you," Meg said. "Call if you need anything."

Jo scowled. "I don't like to leave you here alone."

"Go," Trey said. "You have the boys to take care of."

"Hey, I don't need a babysitter," Alec said.

Trey smiled. "Neither do I."

249

"Fine. I'll see you tomorrow," Jo said to Trey.

I watched wistfully as they hugged like two old friends. Which they were.

"I can stay. I stayed overnight with Momma when she was in the hospital," Beth said.

"Because there's only one chair to sleep in." I looked at the nurse for confirmation. "Right?"

"I'm afraid so."

"Which means none of us are staying." I needed to go with Jo to pick up my car at Oak Hill, anyway.

"Your grandfather's on the third floor," the nurse told Trey. "You want to go through those doors to the elevator, and the nurses upstairs will direct you to his room."

We left in a flurry of good-byes, good lucks, and promises to call. I even managed to smile.

But the sight of Trey walking alone down the hall, still wearing his sweaty T-shirt and basketball shorts, broke my heart.

"That boy needs somebody," Jo said on the drive back to Oak Hill.

I glanced in the rearview mirror at Robbie, buckled into his car seat, and Alec, plugged into his phone.

"Not those boys," Jo said. "Trey."

"You know Alec can hear you, right?"

The sixteen-year-old glanced up from his phone. " 'S okay. I'm not listening."

"Did you see him at the hospital with Beth?" Jo continued, undeterred. "Maybe now that she's home, the two of them will finally get together."

"Beth has a boyfriend already."

"Who left her."

"To go on tour."

"Why are you defending him?"

"I'm not. I just don't think Beth is looking for another relationship." And neither was Trey. "Besides, wouldn't that be a little weird for you?"

"What?"

I peeked at Alec, listening to his iPhone in the backseat. Lowered my voice. "If Trey . . . You know."

Jo grinned. "Hooked up with my sister?"

"Now I am really not listening," Alec said.

"Beth doesn't do hookups." But I did. *Easy A.*

"I'm just saying, it wouldn't bother me," Jo said. "Trey's practically our brother already."

"Not my brother," I said. "Anyway, I don't think Beth is his type."

"She could be. Trey needs someone to

adore him."

"Or smack him upside the head with a two-by-four."

Jo shot me a look in the glow of the dashboard. "What is with you two? I thought you liked him."

"I do." *Too much.* "I just . . ."

"Never got over being treated like his bratty baby sister?"

Never got over him. "Something like that."

Mr. Laurence's suite on the third floor of the hospital was decorated like a three-star hotel room with lots of dark wood and an adjoining bath. A large flat-screen TV dominated one corner. An actual lamp cast soft light from a table by the window. Apparently donating a medical wing bought you something nicer than the standard private room.

But no amount of donor money could disguise the hospital bed or the glowing, blinking, beeping machines. Mr. Laurence lay connected by tubes and wires, his face gray above the blue hospital gown. A bruise bloomed in the crook of his arm where they'd jabbed an IV. A clear oxygen tube forked under his nose. Even his eyebrows appeared sparser, tamed. He was sleeping.

So was Trey. He'd pulled the recliner close

to the bed, extending one arm through the raised bar to hold his grandfather's blue-veined hand. Tenderness for them both swamped me.

Trey opened his eyes. For a moment, I stood frozen, lost in the darkness of his gaze, transported back in time to Paris in the early-morning light.

"Amy."

I trembled. "Hey," I breathed. "I thought you might need a few things."

His gaze dropped to the bag in my hand. *"For Mr. Laurence,"* I'd explained at the nurses' station, and they'd waved me through, even though regular visiting hours were over.

Carefully, Trey uncurled his fingers from the old man's hand.

"Don't get up," I whispered. "I'll leave it on the table."

"Stay."

"I don't want to bother you. Your grandfather . . ."

"Is doing much better."

I glanced doubtfully at the bed where Mr. Laurence breathed on, undisturbed. "I should let him sleep."

"He is sleeping. Best thing for him," Trey said.

I remembered how I felt when it was

Momma in the hospital. Despite Trey's assurances, he must be scared.

"Please?" he added.

"Well . . . Just for a minute."

Trey came around the bed. His baggy shirt and basketball shorts made him look like the boy I remembered. Except for the man-stubble. He was broader through the shoulders, too, and there were character lines in his face that hadn't been there at fifteen or seventeen or even twenty-seven. His hair was still dark and rumpled and when he smiled I still swooned inside like a twelve-year-old girl.

"I went to your house. Miss Dee packed you some things. I wasn't sure what you'd need. There are clothes. And, um, toothpaste and stuff." The housekeeper's eagerness to help had not extended to letting me paw through Trey's underwear drawer. He looked at me, his face unreadable. "I hope that's okay."

His arms went around me. My body recognized the feel of him, the hard frame and lean muscles, before my brain registered the hug. I don't know how long we stood, our bodies aligned, our breathing gradually finding a rhythm. When he let me go, my knees were weak and he was half-aroused.

He smiled crookedly. "Thanks."

For the clothes? For the hug?

I cleared my throat. "No problem."

He sat — not in the recliner, but on the banquette under the window, leaving room for me beside him. I eyed the space nervously.

"Can I get you anything?" I asked. "Coffee?"

"No, thanks." He pulled a slight face. "The hospital coffee tastes like shit."

"I remember. I packed you a thermos. It's in the bag."

He grinned. "Marry me."

My heart jolted. I looked into his wicked dark eyes, and even though I knew he was kidding, for a second I couldn't breathe. "Ha-ha."

I poured his coffee and added sugar, fussing over the simple service like a Victorian maiden over her auntie's tea tray.

"Thanks." He cocked an eyebrow as I sat beside him. "None for you?"

"No, I'm good."

The words reverberated through my memory, setting off a sweet ache in my chest.

You good?

I kissed his shoulder. "I am excellent."

"Yes, you are."

The machines whooshed and beeped softly. His grandfather's chest rose and fell.

The sounds of the hospital at night — squeaking shoes and rattling carts and lowered voices — seemed very far away.

"Why didn't you ever call me? After Paris," I asked.

Trey slanted a look at me, a smile teasing his mouth. "You want to do this now?"

I flushed. There were things between us that had never been said. Questions that had never been answered. I was too much a March and he was too well-bred. Both of us were good at avoiding pain. "You're right. Forget it."

"I did. Call you," he said.

"You most certainly did not."

"I texted."

I rolled my eyes. "Everybody texts. It's one step up from sending a dick pic."

He looked away. The lamp illuminated the edges of his profile, hard and perfect as the stamp on a coin. "I guess . . . I didn't want to make things any worse."

"It wasn't that bad," I said, and he laughed, his face relaxing in the way that I loved.

"It was wonderful. You were wonderful," he said. "You were so bright. So busy. So sure of yourself and what you wanted. I didn't want to mess that up. I wasn't part of your plan."

"Clearly, I wasn't part of yours." *Jo was the plan,* he'd said back then.

He looked straight at me, his eyes deep and vulnerable. Almost bleak. "I didn't have a plan," he said. "Why didn't you call me?"

Because you still loved Jo. "Because I was avoiding you. Duh."

"I thought we were better friends than that."

"We were. We are." I struggled to explain. "Which is why I didn't want to be another Brittany."

"Who?"

"Exactly. Or Jennifer or Ashley. Some Tinder date whose last name you can't remember."

"I don't make a habit of anonymous sex," he said. "And it's March."

"Which one?"

"Amy." The quiet reproach in his voice shamed me.

"Sorry, I shouldn't . . . Not now. You don't need this now."

"I care about you," he said. "I've always cared. About you."

He did care. And I loved him. Had always loved him.

"What can I do?" I whispered.

Trey took my hand. "You're doing it. You're here. That means a lot."

My heart dissolved. "We'll always be here for you." *I'll always be here for you.*

He smiled. "The March sisters' motto. 'Whatever happens, we have each other' — Jo says that."

Her ghost rose between us. *"It wouldn't bother me,"* she'd said. He's like our brother, she said.

Who did he have to comfort him and care for him? Besides his grandfather. Besides us.

His thumb rubbed a circle on the back of my hand.

"You should call your grandmother," I said. "The one in Florida."

"I have a better idea." He set down his coffee. Smiled. "Call it a plan."

He tugged lightly on my hand. *Mistake,* my mind screamed as he drew me closer. But I didn't move.

His mouth brushed slowly over mine. His hand cupped my jaw with exquisite care. I knew he was using me for comfort. For distraction. And I didn't mind. Our lips tasted, tested, clung, finding the perfect fit.

I was older now and wiser. As long as I didn't expect anything more, I could give him this. I could have him, this much of him, for at least a little while.

I pulled back and smiled. "So, tell me. What's the rest of your plan?"

CHAPTER 15
ABBY

I was eight years old when my sister Elizabeth died, drowned in the river that ran along the bottom of our property.

Not that I realized it at the time. For two days, all my parents would tell me was that Bitsy had *"gone to the hospital."* I learned later that her body had been put on life support until the doctors finally, mercifully, convinced my mother to pull the plug. All I knew then was that my sister never came home. I lost a playmate I could never replace, a part of me I would never recover.

I learned early on not to bother my already-devastated parents. *"Don't fuss,"* my mother would say when I cried or acted out, and I did my best to be a good girl. To make up, somehow, for the loss of my sister. My parents' grief, after all, was worse than mine.

But I never got over hating the hospital — that place of no return. When I had my babies, when I had surgery on my spine, even visiting poor James Laurence after his stroke, I had to steel myself to overcome my childish fear.

It was a relief to get home.

The security lights flicked on as we drove up.

"I'm going to check on the goats," I said to Beth as we got out of the truck. "Do you want to make us some tea?"

Beth — named for my dead sister — hesitated. "I'm tired. I think I'll go straight to bed."

I studied her thin face in the floodlights. Bethie, my Sensitive Child. I'd never known how to comfort her. "You did good today."

"All I did was call 911," she said.

She never did take credit. Never could recognize her own strength. I wished I could tell her that. "I'm proud of you, honey."

Her smile flickered. "Thanks, Mom."

I watched her climb the steps to the kitchen door and let herself inside before I turned back to the barn, grateful for the goats. Animals were easy to understand. Daughters were harder.

It was good to have Beth and Amy temporarily under my roof again, to consult with Meg about the business side of the farm, to see Jo writing her stories and raising her family in the place where she'd sworn never to return. My girls had choices I had never had. I was glad of that.

But I wondered what would happen to the farm when I was gone. There was only me to keep it going now.

The half-moon caught in the tips of the pines. Tree frogs tuned up for their summer chorus. A dog barked somewhere far away. Maybe I should get a guard dog. Or a donkey. I'd heard donkeys offered more protection against predators than llamas and they didn't bark all night like dogs. But for now, I locked the herd in the barn at night — not because of crime, but because of coyotes.

I undid the latch and walked through the darkened office toward the pens. A few goats poked their heads over the rails as I walked the work aisle. I petted, patted, praised. Paused to give an extra cuddle to Sage, whose first-time mom had rejected her.

The latch clicked, sharp against the quiet of the barn.

"Dan?"

A silhouette filled the office doorway, lanky and elegant. Not Dan.

"It's me." Ash stepped into the barn, the light revealing the angles of his lean, clean-shaven face.

I caught my breath. In the play of light and shadow he looked twenty years old. "You're up late."

He smiled faintly. "I could say the same about you."

I set Sage back in the pen, watching her snuggle with the other babies. "A farmer's day is never done."

"You were out all evening. Everything all right?"

I glanced at him in surprise. Ash had never been particularly attuned to the rhythms and routines of the farm. Or my comings and goings. "No, I had to go to the hospital. James Laurence had a stroke this afternoon. Beth was with him."

He drew a sharp breath. Composed himself. "How is he?"

He sounded very pastoral. "Too early to say. Beth called 911 right away, thank goodness."

"How's Mouse doing?"

I raised my eyebrows. Ash would die for our daughters, but he had generally been more concerned with their grades or the state of their souls than their feelings. "She's upset, of course. James has been like a grandfather to her." In the absence of any other male role models. "I'm worried about her," I confessed.

Ash nodded. "The shock."

"Not just the shock." Something was wrong with our little girl. But she wouldn't talk to me, and I couldn't put my finger on it.

"You should have called me," Ash said.

"I didn't think of it."

"I suppose I deserve that," he said quietly.

I felt a flash of shame. "I'm sorry. I know you and James are friends."

"I meant, I could have helped. Do you need anything?"

"It's a little late for that." Hours too late. Years too late.

Ash regarded me gravely. "Paul says when we bear one another's burdens, we truly fulfill the law of Christ."

I folded my arms. "You know what I *don't* need? I don't need you to preach at me right now."

"No," Ash agreed. Another surprise. He gave me a small, self-deprecating smile. "My own words just seem so inadequate."

"Compared to Paul?"

"Compared to Scripture, yes. Or to you."

I felt myself thawing, softening. It had been years since we had talked. Really talked. "You weren't so tongue-tied when we were dating."

"I was always awkward. But you were so

264

warm. So interested in everything."

I snorted. "I threw myself at you, you mean."

His gaze was steady. "You were easy to talk to. I appreciated that."

"Until you came home from Iraq. You wouldn't talk to me then."

"You made it clear you didn't need my advice. You had everything under control."

I flushed in acknowledgment. "Better than letting everything fall apart. I had to take care of the girls. The farm. We had a routine."

"Which didn't include me."

I waved my hands. "You should have said something."

"Why? The girls were thriving. The farm was thriving. You were doing an excellent job. Better than I would do."

"You could have told me how you felt."

"I didn't want to burden you."

"So you shut me down."

"I protected you."

"From what, for heaven's sake?"

"From me. From the things that I saw. The stories I heard. It's difficult enough for me to express emotions. Even the positive ones. I didn't want all that ugliness to spill on you and the children."

"You don't have any trouble talking to

other people — your soldiers at the mission."

"Because I don't take part in their lives or their problems. I can listen, I can sympathize, and still keep a safe distance. I put up barriers to insulate myself." He smiled wryly. "I might be a better counselor without them."

"You're an excellent counselor," I said.

"A better husband, then."

"I admire what you do for others. But you had nothing left for us. I was your *wife*."

"You *are* my wife."

"Well, it sure didn't feel like it most of the time."

"It did a month ago."

After Jo's wedding.

I felt a flash of heat, embarrassment or desire. "That was a mistake."

"I thought so, too, at first. But I've played it over and over in my mind so many times since then. It felt good." His gaze held mine. "It felt right."

Attraction shimmered between us.

"It felt good."

Moths fluttered around the light, tempting death. If I held out my hand, he would take it. We could go up together to the bed we had shared for thirty years, and I could feel that way again tonight.

Except . . . we weren't twenty anymore. I was too damn old to sneak my ex-husband — husband — into my bed like a teenager smuggling her boyfriend up to her room.

I didn't want Ashton in my house, in my life, disturbing my hard-won balance. Threatening my independence.

"I'm going to bed," I announced. *Alone.* "Good night."

He nodded, his eyes still on my face. "I'll see you in the morning."

I went into the house, shut the door, and turned off the light.

CHAPTER 16
BETH

Amy stood in front of the fridge, muttering. "Three, four, five . . ."

I poured coffee. Black, two packets of Sweet'N Low. "What are you doing?"

"Looking at pictures." The refrigerator doors were cluttered with family photos, magnets, lists, and artwork from the grandchildren. "Six. No, seven . . ."

"Are you *counting* them?" I asked.

"Mm. To see who Mom loves best."

I looked. I couldn't help it. The pictures were stuck up without any order or preference that I could see, candids from Jo's wedding jumbled together with old family snapshots. There was even one of Dad, pushing a stroller with a very young Meg and Jo. He looked so happy, smiling at the person behind the camera. At Mom. My throat knotted at the reminder of the way things used to be, the family I'd never been a part of.

"Nine," Amy said. "Based on the number of photos, the grandkids are winning."

I laughed. "Because they're young and adorable."

Amy pulled a face. "We used to be young and adorable."

"You're still adorable," I said.

In fact, she looked amazing, like the girl in a country music video, in a twirly sundress that was all wrong for farmwork and a fresh face it had probably taken her twenty minutes in front of the mirror to achieve.

"Yeah, but it's more work now." She pulled a carton of yogurt from the fridge. "Want some?"

My stomach cramped. "I'm not hungry."

She tilted her head. "So keep me company."

I wanted to be with her. To be like her. To be normal. "I guess . . . Sure."

She flitted around the kitchen, preparing a pretty bowl of cut-up fruit, setting the table in typical Amy style, with folded napkins and the blue glass bottle from the windowsill stuffed with black-eyed Susans from the yard.

"How's the great cleanup coming?" I asked.

"Know anybody who wants to buy some old furniture?"

"Not really, no."

"Exactly," she said gloomily. "Nobody's looking for a mahogany breakfront china cabinet for their third-floor walk-up apartment."

I nodded. "Too large."

"Too old-fashioned." She slid an empty plate in front of me. "Kind of a shame, really, because the hand carving is gorgeous. I'm going to take more pictures today, see if I can attract some buyers."

She sat opposite me, at the scarred kitchen table where we used to do our homework. It was good to be back where nothing ever changed, not the wallpaper or the salt and pepper shakers shaped like birds or the clock on the wall. I wanted to pull the past around me like a quilt and never go out.

"Just like old times," I said.

Amy speared a piece of cantaloupe with a fork. "Almost. Meg and Jo aren't here."

"Like when we were in high school, then. After they went away to college."

"We didn't hang out together in high school." A twist of a smile. "We should have."

We could have. We were in the same grade. I was sick so often after our father deployed that the school had held me back a year.

270

I smiled. "You were way cooler than me."

"I was a hot mess." Amy wagged her fork at me. "And you were Daddy's little angel."

I winced.

Her eyes narrowed. "What's wrong?"

"Nothing."

I'd had another text from Colt that morning. Hey, Angel. Missing you. And a picture — snapped by one of the roadies? — of Colt singing with Mercedes, both of them smiling, her hair shining under the stage lights, her shoulders shimmering with Sharla's magic powder. She looked fantastic.

Amy put a piece of melon on my plate. Cantaloupe, fleshy and juicy and orange.

The shadow closed its bony fingers around my throat. "I'm not hungry," I said again.

"One bite," she said, like Meg coaxing DJ. "Even one bite shows on camera."

"Like you have to worry," Amy scoffed. "What are you, like, a size 2 now?"

"Numbers don't matter," I said.

But of course they did. They *did*. I picked up my fork, using the side to cut the melon into smaller pieces.

"Anyway, even the fashion industry is becoming more body positive," Amy said. "A lot of major brands are more inclusive now. There's such a thing as being too thin."

"Not according to Aunt Phee."

271

"Appearances aren't everything to Phee." Amy grinned. "It just looks like they are."

I smiled. "You don't need to worry about appearances. You always were the pretty sister."

"Ugh. Why do we do that?"

"Do what?"

"Pigeonhole ourselves. The responsible one, the smart one, the good one, the pretty one."

"I don't know. Maybe for the same reason you count pictures on the fridge?"

"Competition?"

"We wouldn't be the same without one another." Meg was the oldest, Jo was the brave one, Amy was the baby. We defined ourselves by the void that was left when you took the other things away. Or I did.

Amy stirred her yogurt. "I never told you this, but I had problems with body image. Back in high school."

I nodded. "That *mean* Jenny Snow."

Amy put down her spoon. "Well, shit. You knew?"

"People talk." I smiled apologetically. "She still lives here, you know. Jenny."

"She *told* you?"

"Oh no. I, um . . . recognized you."

The image had flashed around the band room, phone to phone. Even before the whispers started, I *knew* her. Watching her strip in our shared bedroom, I'd envied my sister's flat chest, her careless confidence. She was so perky. So perfect, naked and bold.

Amy's blue eyes widened. "The week before homecoming . . . You climbed into bed with me one night. You and your teddy bear. You knew then?"

"You were crying." *Every night for a week,* I remembered.

"Oh, Beth. I love you."

I swallowed the lump in my own throat. "I love you, too."

We'd never been friends, like Meg and Jo. We were too close in age. Too different in temperament. But we were sisters. We shared a world, a past, a secret language made of in-jokes and memories.

Amy squeezed my hand. "Why didn't you ever say anything?"

"Why didn't you?"

"I didn't want you all to know what a screwup I was. But looking back, I wish I'd told you. Told Meg. Told *somebody.*"

She paused, looking at me expectantly.

I stared down at my plate. At the melon, an orange paste by now.

Amy sighed. "Beth . . ."

A knock on the back door. "You ready?"

Dan asked.

Saved. I jumped up. "Let me just put my dishes in the dishwasher."

"Come on in," Amy said. "Want some coffee?"

"I'm good, thanks." But he came in anyway, taking time to scrape his boots on the back stoop.

"What are you up to today?" Amy asked.

"Moving fence." The corners of his eyes creased in an almost-smile. "I got extra gloves if you want to join us."

"Yeah, that will never happen. We're visiting Mr. Laurence today."

"You're taking Aunt Phee?" I asked, grateful for the change in subject.

"No, I'm going with Trey." For some reason, my sister blushed. "I thought he could use some support."

"How is he? Mr. Laurence?" I'd visited him in the hospital right after the stroke. He reminded me of a zoo lion, his mouth dragged in an involuntary snarl, his eyes bright and baleful. He'd been moved to a rehab facility two days ago.

"Frustrated," Amy said. "He can't get his words out, he hates using a walker, and he growls at all his therapists."

"Poor Mr. Laurence." Of course he'd rather lick his wounds in private.

"Trey keeps saying it's temporary."

"What do the doctors say?"

"They don't talk to me. I'm not 'family.' " She put air quotes around the word.

"Anything I can do?"

"You could come with us to see him. You always were his favorite."

"I can handle the fencing," Dan said. "If you want to go."

"No, I told Momma I'd help. Besides, I need the exercise."

Amy gave me a sharp look. But all she said was, "We're not leaving until this afternoon. Around three? We can pick you up."

"Well . . . If you're sure I won't be in the way."

Her blush deepened. "In the way? No. Absolutely not. Why would you say that?"

"I just thought . . . If Mr. Laurence has rehab scheduled . . ." I said.

"Oh, right, okay. So, I'll text you. When it's time to go." She put her mug in the dishwasher. Kissed my cheek. Waggled her fingers at Dan. "Three o'clock. Bye!"

I scraped my plate into the garbage.

"Healthy forage makes healthy goats," our mother liked to say.

It's not true that goats will eat anything, but they liked kudzu. Also poison ivy. Slogging through the brush was hot, slow going.

The sun beat down. After a couple hours moving portable fence, I was damp with sweat. Dan had stripped off his T-shirt, leaving him in jeans, work boots, and gloves. I caught myself sneaking glances at his torso.

He looked strong. Not like a gym addict, but like he lifted 150-pound goats all day. Broad shoulders. Flat stomach. No fat anywhere. He had a battlefield cross tattoo — helmet, rifle, and boots — on one shoulder, and another, dog tags filled with the flag, on his arm.

"Aren't you worried about sunburn?" I asked.

"Nope."

"Or bug bites?"

"I'm not that sweet."

He unspooled another section of fencing. I balanced the roll as he jammed a support pole into the ground with his boot heel. It had rained the day before, and the soil was soft.

A mosquito whined in my ear. I swatted it away. "I don't know what to say."

"About how sweet I am?"

My face was hot. "To Mr. Laurence."

"You don't have to say anything." Dan glanced at me, the creases deepening at the corners of his eyes. "Reckon your sister will do all the talking."

I smiled back hesitantly. Amy *did* chatter, especially when she was nervous. "She's very good with people. And she cares."

Dan paced off another length of fencing. Sweat gleamed on his shoulders. "You're good with people. With animals, too."

"In little ways. Bandaging Barbies. Feeding the goats. Nothing important."

His lips twitched. "You bandaged Barbies?"

"Somebody had to. Jo was rough on toys."

His full smile escaped, and I glowed. I hadn't made someone laugh — made an attractive man laugh, on purpose — in a long time.

We reached a creek bed that cut down to the river. The murmur of the water filtered through the brush. Birds swooped and twittered in the trees. The sky overhead was a deep, dizzying blue.

He crossed the ditch in one stride, carrying the roll of fence.

"He asked me to bring my guitar," I blurted.

"Laurence?"

I nodded.

"So? They got some kind of rule against music where he is?"

"No."

He anchored the fence on the bank. "I don't see the problem."

"So you think I should play for him."

He dug an extra support pole into the rocks. "Don't matter what I think. What do you want to do?"

My chest felt tight. "I want to make him happy."

The fence gapped across the creek bed, leaving an opening big enough for a baby goat to scramble under. I pried a rock the size of my head out of the ground, wedging it in place against the bottom wire. My hands tingled. I straightened, and the world lost color and slid sideways, tilting and whirling away.

"Whoa, there." Dan had me by the shoulders. I grabbed his arms. "I got you." He sat me on the bank, forcing my head to my knees. "Breathe, okay?"

"Sorry." I started to raise my face. "I . . ."

He pushed my head back down. "Take a minute."

I sucked in my breath. Let it go. Gradually, my heart slowed. The creek bank settled into place around me.

"You all right?"

I nodded, shamefaced.

His grip on my neck loosened. "Let me get you up to the house."

"I'm fine." I was clammy. Nauseous. "It's the heat."

"Not only the heat. You need to lay down."

"I don't need one more person in my life telling me what to do." I closed my eyes. "I'm sorry. That was rude. I don't know why I said that."

He fished a water bottle out of his pack and handed it to me. "Because that's how you feel?"

"No. Maybe. I *shouldn't* feel that way." I was supposed to be the nice sister, the easygoing middle child, the peacekeeper of the family. *Ugh,* Amy's voice said in my head. I screwed the cap carefully back on the water bottle. "Thank you for taking care of me. And for listening." My phone played a quick chord in my pocket. I glanced at the text. "That's Amy. I should go."

Dan was watching me, a faint frown on his face. "Sure." He helped me to my feet.

I took a step toward the house. Stopped. "Mr. Laurence gave me my guitar," I heard myself say.

Dan looked at me steadily.

I swallowed. "I used to *like* to play for him."

"Play or don't play, that's up to you. It's your music." Dan's voice was calm. Accepting. "Reckon he'll be glad just to see you."

"I don't think that's enough — just show-ing up."

"Most important thing in life," Dan said.

I held on to that thought as I sat in Mr. Laurence's room at the rehab center. My guitar case stood upright and unopened behind my chair. *The important thing was to show up.*

Trey was being attentive and Amy was at her most charming. Mr. Laurence's eyes moved from face to face, following their conversation with painful attention.

". . . old potpourri, right?" Amy said. "And then Aunt Phee tells me I've tossed out her cherished corsage."

"Puh," Mr. Laurence said. "Punk."

"Pink roses, that's right. At least they were pink once upon a time. How did you guess?" Amy grinned. "Mr. Laurence, did you take Aunt Phee to prom?"

His mouth jerked in what might have been a smile.

A whiteboard faced his bed, with his therapy sessions and the names of his care-givers scrawled in black, blue, and green marker. Speech therapy. Physical therapy. Occupational therapy. It looked like a lot. Was the schedule too much for him? Were *we* too much for him?

280

Trey was talking, something about a cap rate on a strip mall or maybe an apartment building managed by Laurence Properties. Honestly, I didn't understand most of it. Maybe Mr. Laurence had trouble following, too, because he was blinking, his hands plucking the sheets.

"Let me get you more water," Amy said, reaching for the pitcher on his hospital tray.

He guided the cup unassisted. Took a small, cautious sip. Water dribbled from the corner of his mouth. Amy handed him a paper towel as Trey looked away.

"I hired an agency to help with stuff," he said. "When you get home. Get you ready for work, whatever. Just a temporary thing until you're better."

"Duh. Dee," Mr. Laurence said.

"Sends her love. I gave her the week off. She's going to visit her daughter. No point in her rattling around the house taking care of just me."

A — nurse? aide? — in lavender scrubs appeared, smiling at Mr. Laurence. "Well, hello. We having a party in here today?"

"G-girls," Mr. Laurence said.

"But no booze," Trey said. "We left the bourbon at home."

She shook her head at them. "You know the rules. No more than two visitors at a time. We don't want James getting overstimulated." She took Mr. Laurence's blue-veined hand in her dark, smooth one, feeling expertly for his pulse. "Blood pressure's a little up. How you feeling, hon?"

"Could I talk to you a minute?" Trey asked when she was done.

"Should I leave?" I asked Amy after they had stepped out of the room.

"I think we're okay."

"Why did Trey want to talk to her?"

"He's probably bribing her to let us stay." I wasn't sure she was joking.

Trey returned.

"Look who I found in the hall."

"Dad!" Amy said.

The aide reappeared in the doorway. "Family, close friends, and clergy *only.* Oh, Reverend March. I didn't see it was you."

"Hello, Keisha," our father said. He was always so polite. I remembered when my sisters' friends came to our house, how they'd giggle and blush when he walked through the room.

"You know each other?" Amy asked.

"Keisha took care of your mother."

"And the reverend's here all the time," Keisha said.

Of course. Along with stroke survivors and seniors with joint replacements, the rehab

282

center treated wounded warriors with missing limbs and spinal cord and brain injuries.

"I can come back later," our father said.

"No, we'll go." I glanced at Amy. "I don't want to tire Mr. Laurence."

"But you haven't played for him yet," Amy said.

"You came together?" our father asked.

"They came with me," Trey said.

"I have other visits to make today, but I can bring Beth home when I'm done. If you'd like to stay," he added to me.

I looked at the nurse. "Just don't tire him out," she said.

The room was quiet, the hum of fluorescent lights broken only by the rattle of dinner carts, the squeak of rubber-soled shoes, and the murmur from the nurses' station down the hall.

Mr. Laurence watched me without speaking, his eyes like a wounded lion's. The evening sun slanted through the window. I stood to adjust the blinds so the light didn't shine in his face.

"Play or don't play, that's up to you," Dan's voice said quietly in my head. *"Reckon he'll be glad just to see you."*

Maybe I didn't have to be perfect. Maybe I only needed to be present.

283

My heart thrummed. I opened my guitar case. "I'm a little out of practice."

I sat, curled around the guitar, picking softly. The quiet notes vibrated against the silence. I played the old songs I knew he loved, "Sweet Baby James" and Paul Simon's "American Tune." The music sounded stiff. Stilted. My fingers stuttered on the strings.

I looked up, ready to apologize.

Mr. Laurence was weeping behind his closed eyes, a shining track sliding from his temples to the wrinkles of his face. Something inside me melted, rushing like breath, filling my lungs, flowing like water under ice.

I started again, quietly, building the melody, trusting the magic to come. The notes seeped and spilled from my guitar, and I slipped inside the music, letting go, letting the feeling come, carrying me away on cascading riffs and eddies of sound.

I don't know how long I played, caught up in the current, my hands sure and supple, the music pouring from my guitar.

When I looked up again, Mr. Laurence's eyes were still closed, his chest rising and falling in even breaths.

"Well done," my father said from the doorway.

284

I put my guitar away and went into the hall, its walls decorated with crayon rainbows. "I made him cry."

"Crying can happen after a stroke, even without emotional stimulus," my father said. "It's one effect of the stroke on the brain."

"Oh."

"But I believe," he added, "it does his heart good to hear you."

I looked sideways at the compliment. "It did my heart good to play." I shouldered my case. "Are you all done for the day?"

"I'd like to make one more visit. If you don't mind."

"I can wait."

"Actually, I was hoping you'd come with me."

"Me?"

"There's a young man here, a veteran. Apparently, he and his wife are fans of yours. They danced to your song at their wedding — the one you sang for Jo and Eric."

"Miss You More." The one I'd written for Mom and Dad. The one they had danced to.

"I mentioned you were here," my father said. "They'd like it very much — I'd like it very much — if you would sing it for them."

"I don't think I can."

He looked at the guitar case. Raised his

eyebrows slightly.

I flushed. I'd played for Mr. Laurence. "Not for strangers." *Not my songs.*

"It's always been easier for me." My father smiled ruefully. "Helping strangers."

"I'm not like you, Dad."

"I think you are. More than you know. You've always put yourself in the service of others. That's your strength."

Tears welled in my eyes.

He cleared his throat. "I have found . . . Sometimes helping others can help you, too."

All my life I'd hoped for my father's attention. His approval. But if I did this, it couldn't be for him.

"Play or don't play. It's your music."

I asked anyway. "You'll be there?"

"Every step of the way," my father said.

CHAPTER 17
AMY

"Alone at last," I joked.

Trey and I were walking through the rehab center parking lot. Not the most romantic setting. That was okay. We weren't about romance. We were about comfort and caring. Support. Sex.

Not that we'd actually had sex again. Not yet.

He slanted a look down at me, a smile in his soulful dark eyes. God, those eyes. "Sorry about that."

"No 'sorry.' Nothing to be sorry about. You're dealing with a lot right now."

"You, too."

Since that night in his grandfather's hospital room, our relationship — if you could call it that — had been put on hold. Because whatever Trey's eventual "plan" was, his focus was on his grandfather. And mine had to be on Baggage. Sometimes I thought Aunt Phee was softening her insistence that I move my business to Bunyan. But so far she'd evaded all my attempts to get her to invest. To commit.

Kind of like Trey.

Unease fluttered. I wasn't looking for commitment. I was sleeping across the hall from my mother. He was living at his grandfather's with Miss Dee. We had managed a few stolen kisses and one rather memorable make-out session on the porch swing. But we weren't horny teenagers, hooking up in the backseat of his grandfather's car. We couldn't sneak off to the beach like Meg and John when they first started dating. There was a difference — wasn't there? — between sharing a luxury suite in Paris and checking into the Marriott by the airport for a couple hours.

Paris had been a fairy tale. Popping corks and fireworks and fantasy sex wrapped together in an illusion of happily-ever-after.

But if we slept together in Bunyan, it would be real.

For both of us.

My phone vibrated. I ignored it.

Trey, at least, didn't seem in a hurry to make our new status ("It's Complicated") public. But he'd given Miss Dee the week off, he'd said. Which meant — didn't it? — that tonight we could be alone. We could do it and no one would ever know. My insides tingled. My skin buzzed. Thank God I was wearing nice underwear.

I cleared my throat. "I like your car." He'd ditched the Ferrari in favor of his grandfather's massive Lincoln to make room for Beth and her guitar.

He grinned. "Yeah, it's real a chick magnet."

"If you're Aunt Phee, maybe. Country girls go for tractors. And pickup trucks." I sank into the leather seat, keeping my knees together. Breathing in the smell, like the accessories wall at Nordstrom's, leather and money. "Really big trucks. With fog lights and tinted windows."

Amusement warmed his eyes. "Thanks for the tip."

"You're welcome. I figured you might need some dating help."

"Because I have no game."

"True." *Not true.* "At least you're rich."

"That was always my dream. To be loved for my grandfather's money."

We were teasing. Flirting. But there was a snap to his words, bright and hard, like the closure on a bag. "I'm sure some women want you for your body."

"Damn. I was hoping it was my charming personality."

"You can be charming." Prince Charming.

"I hear a *but*."

I shook my head. "No *but*. I just think you're . . ." *Don't spoil this. Keep it casual.* "More," I said finally.

He didn't answer. His hands — lean and long fingered, with squared-off nails — were easy on the steering wheel. But there was a tension in the car now that hadn't been there before, like the echo of an argument we'd never had.

I tried again. "Like when you opened my car door."

"I was being polite. It didn't mean anything."

"Yes, it did."

"I wasn't trying to put you down by asserting my male privilege. Obviously, you can open your own door."

That sounded like something Jo would say. Had said, probably. "It means you're considerate. Kind. You're a kind person." I paused. "Even if you don't have any game."

He smiled. *Success.*

My phone buzzed again. "Sorry, it's probably just . . ." I glanced at my notifications. "Well, wow. That's encouraging."

"What?"

"I took more pictures of Aunt Phee's

furniture today. Those big old cabinets are so 1880s. So I staged them to make them look more contemporary. Added some flowers, some baskets, some bags to the shelves. Pops of color, you know? Contrast."

I opened the app. Stared at my messages.

"Well?" Trey asked. "Do you have a buyer?"

"They sold," I said in confusion.

"That's what you wanted."

"Not the furniture. My bags. All these messages . . ." I scrolled. "They want to buy my bags."

"Good."

I laughed. "I guess. I'll have to connect them to the online store." He turned the car onto the highway, away from the farm. I leaned forward. "Where are we going?"

"I thought we'd grab something to eat." A slanting smile. "Celebrate your sales strategy."

The electricity was back, charging the air, creating an invisible current between us.

Keep it light, I reminded myself. *Casual.*

If we had dinner, I might start imagining this was a date. I'd fool myself into thinking this could turn into a relationship.

And then he'd break my heart again.

I put my phone away. "This isn't Paris, Trey. You don't have to buy me dinner before we have sex."

He slid me a dark, wicked look. "How about McDonald's? That would be quick."

I rolled my eyes.

"Or we can do drive-through," he suggested, straight-faced. "If you're in a hurry."

I let out an unsteady laugh.

"I thought we'd go to The Taproom," he said. "Okay?"

A public restaurant. Eric's restaurant. "Whatever you want. It's your money," I said.

He was being polite, I reminded myself. It didn't mean anything. But I couldn't stop smiling.

The Taproom was packed.

The hostess smiled apologetically. "Sorry, Trey." She didn't look at me. Naturally. If you were female and breathing, you focused on Trey. "Would you like to wait at the bar for a table?"

That round face, the long brown hair . . . "Kitty? Kitty Bryant?" My old classmate, my former best friend, who'd dumped me for Jenny Snow.

"Oh my God, Amy March! I heard you were back."

We hugged, the menus wedged between us. As if the intervening years had never passed. As if my high school humiliation had never happened. "It's good to see you," I said sincerely.

"You, too." She released me, looking me up and down. "You look just the same. I love your hair. And your purse."

"Um . . . Thanks." Color-blocked canvas with my label, BAGGAGE, stitched into the seams of the side.

"Are you joining Meg and John for dinner?"

I glanced over her shoulder at the crowded dining room. "Are they here?"

"It's Saturday night. Everybody's here," Kitty said cheerfully. "Booth in the back. Want me to take you?"

Meg was my favorite sister. John and Trey used to work together at the dealership. But was I ready for my nosy, loving family to get all up into my business? Was Trey?

"We can find our way," he said.

"If you're sure they won't mind," I added.

They did not mind. They were almost finished eating, but they shifted over in the wooden booth and ordered drinks with us — beer for John, white wine for Meg. No one seemed surprised to see us together. Why should they? Meg thought of Trey like a brother.

"Thanks for letting us crash your table," I

said after we were seated. "Who knew Bunyan had a nightlife?"

"It's nice having somewhere in town we can go on date nights," Meg said.

I smiled. "Besides Alleygators."

"There's a place for Alleygators in Bunyan," Trey said. "A place for everybody. That's what good growth is about."

"Lots of new businesses opening up in town," Meg said. "The gift shop, the bookstore . . ."

The town I grew up in had changed. We talked about the changes — the new stoplight at Church and Vine, the restored bed-and-breakfast near the waterfront to accommodate the tourists stopping for a dose of small-town charm on their way to the coast. The farmers' market had expanded its hours and was looking for a permanent enclosed location.

Kitty came back with our drinks, trailed by one of Eric's new culinary students, the pink-haired teen with multiple piercings.

"Hey, Nan," I said. "Nice eyeliner."

She gave me a side-eyed look — *Do I know you?* — and slapped a flatbread on the table. "Shrimp with spring onion. Uh. Compliments of Chef."

Trey smiled at her. "Thanks."

She blushed to match her hair. Another

victim to the Laurence charm.

"Oh, I couldn't eat another bite," Meg protested, taking a slice.

"Sometimes business isn't about profit. It's about community," Trey said, picking up our conversation.

"Unless you're applying for a loan," I said. "Then it's all about profits and assets."

"How are negotiations going with Phee?" Meg asked.

I sipped my drink. "They're not."

"Have you looked into other funding?" John asked.

"The bank already turned me down."

"What you need is a wealthy investor," Trey said.

I laughed. "Are you volunteering?"

He shrugged. "It's worth a discussion with Granddad. He's into local business development."

Was he serious? I shook my head. "I'm not a local business."

Meg smiled. "Not yet."

"Well, let me know if you change your mind." Trey winked. "I know a guy who can get you a break on a lease."

I was not his charity project. Still, it was nice, the four of us together around the table. Relaxed. More like family dinner than a date.

Except every time Trey turned his head or shifted his knee, my thoughts scattered and my pulse went crazy. It was like we were connected, and every touch tugged something inside me. He laid his arm across the back of the booth, and I shivered, feeling that invisible pull along every sensitive nerve. My shoulder prickled from the near-touch of his fingertips.

Meg's gaze tracked from his hand to my face. "So," she said brightly. "What are you guys doing here tonight?"

A crust stuck in my throat. I coughed.

"Amy went with me to visit Granddad," Trey said.

"How's he doing?" John asked.

I threw him a grateful look. He smiled blandly.

"You know the old man. He's indestructible," Trey said. "He'll be home in another week."

"That's a lot of work for you and Dee," Meg observed. "Let me bring over dinner one night."

"Thanks, but we're fine."

"Trey hired a home health aide," I said. "To help with rehab."

"Anyway, the doctor says Granddad's doing great. He'll be running around in no time," Trey said.

Running? I didn't think so. On the other hand, I wasn't a doctor. I hadn't even talked to Mr. Laurence's doctor.

Meg raised her eyebrows very slightly. "Well, that's . . . good. He's your only family, right?"

"Trey has a grandmother in Florida. Have you called her?" I asked him.

"Not yet."

"But you will."

A corner of his mouth lifted. "Pushy, aren't you?"

"It's one of my most attractive qualities," I assured him.

His smile deepened. Something spilled inside me, a bolt of color rolling and unfurling everywhere.

"We should think about getting home," John said.

I pulled myself together. "Yes. Okay. Bye."

"Great to see you," Trey said.

"Oh, but . . ." Meg said.

"We told the sitter nine o'clock," John said.

"Fine. We'll catch up later." Meg glanced again at Trey's arm on the back of the booth. Hit me with the Mother Hen look. "*Call* me."

"Hey, guys."

Trey's gaze jerked over Meg's shoulder to

the door.

Jo.

Of course.

She flopped into the booth beside Trey, squashing him into me. "Ooh, flatbread."

"What are you doing here?" I asked. Stupid question. This was Eric's restaurant.

"I came to celebrate," Jo said around a mouthful of flatbread. "I'm done! Finished!"

"Finished what?" Meg asked.

"*Castles in the Sand.*" Jo looked around at our blank faces. "My book? I just sent my book to my editor!"

There was a chorus of congratulations. Several diners — a cheerful table of gal pals, some bros at the bar, a middle-aged couple with their teenage daughters — turned around to smile.

"Too bad Eric has to work tonight," Meg said.

Jo waved her flatbread at the teenagers, who giggled and waved back. "He wanted to do one more dinner service here before the Oak Hill opening next weekend. I finished the book just in time."

Meg nodded wisely. "Work-life balance is a myth. It's more like a teeter-totter. Sometimes you're up, sometimes you're down. Some days it's tears and tantrums and chaos and car pool, and some days . . ."

She smiled at John.

"It's wonderful," Jo finished.

"Yeah."

I listened, nodding as if I were an equal part of their discussion. As if I had a cute little house in Bunyan and a fat, adorable baby and a husband who loved me best of all.

"Anyway, tonight I'm celebrating!" Jo declared, taking another bite of flatbread. "God, I'm pumped. And exhausted."

"Hungry, too, apparently," Trey teased.

She grinned and ruffled his hair affectionately. "The March women. Eating their feelings since adolescence."

An image of Beth, pushing melon around her plate, slid into my brain. "Except for Beth," I said. "She starves hers."

My sisters both looked at me.

"What are you talking about?" Meg asked.

In our family hierarchy, Meg and Jo were the Big Sisters. They gave advice, they offered insights, they asked about our lives. They knew Beth better than I did. But they didn't live at home anymore. They weren't there at breakfast. "She never eats," I said.

"Everybody diets," Meg said.

"Anyway, she's always been skinny," Jo said.

Meg nodded. "Delicate."

"She's lost weight," I said. "I'm pretty sure she's skipping meals."

"She ate at the wedding." Jo looked at Meg. "Didn't she?"

Did she? I hadn't noticed. Hadn't been watching. My bad. Jo always said I was self-absorbed.

"She helped me serve the cake," Meg said.

"There you go." Jo frowned. "There's nothing wrong with Beth."

Right. Because Beth was perfect.

Maybe if Meg and I were alone, I would have said something else. But I didn't have proof, only a lurking suspicion. I wanted to be reassured, to believe that everything was all right.

Besides, tonight was about Jo.

Eric came out of the kitchen with a rib-cracking hug for Jo and a pitcher of Mother Earth Kölsch for the table. "To my Jo and her new book!"

Trey smiled and raised his glass. "To Jo."

Aw. How sweet. I was not a beer drinker, but I sipped anyway.

"Chef," Kitty said apologetically a few minutes later. "Family at table twelve hoping to speak with you. Somebody's birthday."

"Thanks. In a minute, yeah?"

"Go ahead, honey." Jo grinned. "You don't

want to disappoint your fans."

He grimaced and bent to kiss her. "I will see you after service."

"We should go, too," Meg said after he left to say hello to the other table. "Our sitter's waiting. Sorry we can't stay to celebrate."

Jo waved her apology away. " 'S okay. I can hang with Trey until Eric gets off."

Trey, not *Amy.*

I looked at him, waiting for him to say something. *Willing* him to say something.

Nothing. Crickets. What did I expect? He was a good guy. A good friend. Practically a brother. He wasn't going to bail on Jo.

"Love you. So proud of you," Meg said to Jo.

"Love you, too!" Jo said as they embraced.

Meg and John were going. Leaving me to play third wheel again. It was like that night in Alleygators, like every time the three of us were together.

"I can get a ride home with Meg," I said quietly to Trey.

"What? No. I'll take you."

"It's no problem," Meg said, overhearing.

"It's kind of a problem," Trey said. "Seeing as we came together."

"Wait. What?" Jo said.

"*Together* together?" Meg asked. "You

301

mean, like a date?"

"Not exactly," I said.

"Yes," Trey said at the same time.

I couldn't decide who was more surprised, my sisters or me. Jo's mouth hung slightly open. Meg's gaze was bright and speculative. I'm not sure what my face was doing, but my heart surged in my chest like a high-speed sewing machine.

Trey was choosing me. In front of my sisters. Instead of Jo. He wanted to be with *me.*

Eric returned to the booth. "Jo, someone wants to meet you."

"Eric, Amy and Trey are dating," Jo told him. She didn't look upset, I thought with relief. Only confused.

"One date," I said. "Dinner."

There was no way I was telling my sisters about Paris.

Eric smiled kindly at me. "*Sehr gut.* All in the family, yeah?" He put his arm around Jo. "The girl at the table, the birthday girl, she is a reader. She would like to take a picture with my wife, the famous author."

"Now?" Jo asked.

His eyes crinkled. "You would not want to disappoint your fans."

She laughed and went with him.

Meg turned back to me. "So, when did —"

John nudged her. "Sitter. Nine o'clock."

I loved my brothers-in-law.

They left, John's hand on the small of Meg's back. Across the dining room, Jo was talking with the starstruck teen while Eric looked on proudly. I was happy for them. Honestly. But . . .

"Jealous?" Trey asked.

I wasn't going to swallow my feelings. Not even to save my pride. "A little," I admitted.

"You shouldn't be. Baggage is really taking off." He met my gaze, his eyes warm. "I've always admired your focus."

"Wait. You think I'm jealous of Jo's *celebrity*?"

Trey cocked an eyebrow. "Aren't you?"

"No. Maybe. I guess. We've always been competitive."

"So it's a habit."

I sipped my Kölsch. Set it aside. "Trey, do you remember my nickname growing up?"

He signaled to Kitty. " 'Princess,' " he answered promptly.

"Before that." Maybe not. I was already ten years old when he came to live with his grandfather.

He shook his head.

"My sisters called me, 'Me, too.' " My first words, according to Meg. "Because I said it so often. Whenever Momma let them do something — stay up late or play down the street or go to the movies — I complained until I got it, too. I always wanted what they had."

Kitty appeared at our table and set a cocktail in front of me.

I blinked. "Thanks."

Trey shrugged, like it was no big deal he'd ordered me another drink. He probably ordered drinks for women all the time. "I thought you all shared everything," he said after Kitty left.

Oh, right. We were talking about my sisters. "We did. Which meant someone else always had it first." A new sweater, a new bike, a new lunch box . . . Trey.

"I used to envy you," he said. "Your family. I wanted what you had."

The cocktail was good, sweet and boozy with a hint of bitter. "A goat farm?" I joked.

He smiled, but there was something else in his dark eyes, a trace of sadness, a hint of vulnerability. It always got to me, that Lost Boy look. "You have each other."

"I know. Oh, I know. I'm lucky. But whenever I see my sisters, I feel like I'm twelve years old again. Like we're all stuck

304

in the same roles we had when we were kids."

His mouth curved. "The beautiful princess."

"The spoiled princess. With the smallest speaking part."

"That's not what I see. You are beautiful." He took my hand. "You're also talented."

"Go on."

He grinned. "Hardworking."

"Thank you."

"You know what you want and you go for it."

"I didn't always." He had lovely hands, smooth and strong, like Michelangelo's David. "I wanted to be a great artist. Remember?"

"You are an artist. You were just searching for the right medium."

Something burned the back of my throat, the alcohol or the compliment. I swallowed. "I think that's the nicest thing anyone's ever said to me."

"Then the guys in New York must be blind. Or dickheads."

The cocktail warmed me all the way down. "Let's just say they don't focus on my work ethic." I took another sip of my drink. "My sisters used to say I was all over the place."

"Nope. It took you a while to figure out what you wanted, that's all. But you don't give up."

"Even when I should. Remember my quilting phase?"

"Was that before or after pottery?"

He knew me so well. "After pottery. Before sculpture."

"You tried to make a mold of your hand."

"I *did* make a mold of my hand."

"You got stuck in the plaster."

"And Jo had to cut me out."

I'd never had this with another guy, this common language, this shared history. Like when I got together with my sisters, all of us talking at once, completing one another's sentences, finishing one another's stories.

"Do you still have a scar?" Trey asked.

I rotated my wrist, exposing the thin white line where Jo had stabbed me, freeing me from the plaster.

He stared down at it for a long moment before he turned his hand over, revealing the puncture at the base of his thumb where he'd jabbed himself baiting my fishhook when I was twelve years old.

He smiled crookedly. "We match."

Feeling flooded my chest, a rush of lust and tenderness. I touched the tiny scar with my finger. "Thanks for letting me tag along."

"I didn't always. Remember the time you followed me and Jo in your father's canoe?"

Was he really going there? To the times I'd been unwanted. Left behind. "I was stupid."

"Fearless," he said. "You're not afraid of anything."

"I'm afraid of lots. Afraid of failing. Afraid of disappointing people."

His gaze was steady on mine. "You've never disappointed me."

"Because you don't want anything from me."

"I want you," he said. "But only when you're ready."

He took my breath away. "No expectations, huh?"

"No pressure," he said, his voice scraping low in my stomach, and, oh God, I wanted him, his basic decency, his dark, stormy eyes, his lightning-quick smile.

I wanted him, and it didn't matter this time that it wouldn't last, that it would hurt — so much — when I left and it was over.

No assumptions. No expectations. No pressure.

I moistened my lips. "How about now?"

His gaze narrowed. Heated. "Right." He

reached for his wallet. "Let's get out of here."

My phone was blowing up.

First Meg: Call me.

Then Jo: I can't believe you didn't tell us.

Beth: When are you coming home?

Then Meg again: John says to leave you alone. Are you alone?

"Your sisters?" Trey asked.

"Yep. And my mom. I told her I wouldn't be home for dinner."

He unlocked the front door, holding it open for me. "You want to answer?"

"Not now." I had my sisters' approval. Or at least, they didn't disapprove. Absolution and explanations could wait. "Let me just . . ."

I typed a quick response to my mother — Don't worry — before my phone buzzed again.

Mom: Make good choices.

I huffed with amusement and held the screen toward Trey.

"That sounds like Abby." He stood watching, not touching, as I slid the switch on my phone to MUTE and dropped it in my bag. "You want something to drink? A glass of wine?"

So polite. *No pressure.* Unless he was having second thoughts. Maybe I shouldn't have shown him the text from my mom.

I shook my head, my heart hammering. *Make good choices.*

He smiled, just a little. My girl parts squeezed. "You want to go upstairs?"

"Okay."

Unlike Jo, I'd never been in Trey's bedroom. It didn't look like a teenage boy's room or like a Manhattan man pad. No piles of laundry, no posters or pizza boxes, no tangle of controllers or a black leather gaming chair. There was an actual fireplace and what looked like real artwork on the walls. Lots of books in the built-in shelves. Harry Potter (he and Jo had read the series together) and Stephen King, books about Cuba, travel books and biographies. The color palette was rich and restful, tawny grays and unexpected blues.

The bed — a giant four-poster with spare, elegant lines — looked freshly made.

I tilted my head. "Expecting company?"

Trey tucked his hands in his pockets. It occurred to me he might be nervous. Or maybe I was. "Miss Dee straightened up before she took off."

I wandered closer to the fireplace. The painting over the mantle, an original oil, mirrored the fading view from the window, fields and woods and an old tobacco barn.

There was a photo beneath it. A younger version of Mr. Laurence, with an '80s mustache and a slightly sulky mouth, posed with his arm around a beautiful woman with masses of dark curly hair. "Your parents?"

Trey nodded.

"You have your mother's eyes." Sad and smiling at the same time.

A framed sketch sat on the shelves. I picked it up.

"I remember this." Jo and Trey playing at the beach on some long-ago day trip, Jo slogging into the water, Trey's lean body cutting a wave. I had sketched them, finishing the drawing in watercolors when we got home.

"You gave it to me."

"I didn't know you kept it."

He raised an eyebrow. "Why wouldn't I?"

"My sister's picture. In your bedroom. All these years."

"It's your drawing." Another half smile. "Your gift to me."

That smile . . . It unlocked all kinds of things in me. All kinds of feelings. "Damn, you're good."

"So are you."

"As an artist."

"Not only as an artist," he said.

Warmth flooded through me. He cared about me. He always had. He thought I was talented. He said I was fearless. Maybe it was time to prove it. If not to him, to me.

I slid the straps of my sundress off my shoulders, pushing it down my thighs to the floor.

His eyes met mine. Hot. Intent. "Nice underwear."

"Are you sure you're heterosexual?"

His lips quirked. "Signs point to yes."

I raised my chin. "Most guys don't notice what a woman is wearing."

"If the woman is you, they do."

I blushed, more flustered by his compliment than by his obvious erection.

He stepped closer. "I remember Bastille Day, three years ago."

"The fireworks."

"The gardens in the afternoon." He reached out, brushing the backs of his fingers along my hot cheek. "You were wearing a blue dress, with the sunshine on your hair. And for days afterward, when I closed my eyes, all I could see was the reflection of your hair, like the sun burning in the sky."

His words painted a picture in my head, seared into my brain. I closed my eyes. I could feel the heat of his body, the warmth of his breath as he leaned closer. He brushed his lips over my eyebrow, his beard scraping my cheek. He smelled so good, like laundry soap, like bergamot and Theodore Laurence. My Trey. He pressed a kiss to the corner of my mouth. I was drowning or maybe I'd forgotten how to breathe.

I swallowed and leaned back a little. "Your turn."

He looked at me, one brow raised, and then his teeth flashed against his stubble. His smile sizzled down to my toes. He pulled at his buttons. Yanked off his shirt. He was skinny in the sketch, a thin, beautiful boy. Now he was hard and lean, a dusting of dark hair over his golden skin.

Who needed fireworks? Not me.

He cupped my face. His mouth was soft and searching. Hot. My hands slid up his ribs, around his waist, and then we were kissing again, kissing and kissing, like I was meant to kiss him and only him for the rest of my life. I stumbled on my dress, and he grabbed me, steadying me, before he tripped, one foot caught in his jeans. We fell to the bed.

I laughed. "Very smooth."

"I told you I have no game." He raised his head, his eyes dark and liquid. "Not when it comes to you."

"How about condoms?"

"Condoms, I have."

Finally, his pants were off. His body was on top of mine, in mine, pressing me into the mattress, and oh, I'd missed this. Missed him, all his hard angles and warm, smooth skin and tensile weight. Missed the way we fit together.

Nobody else was the same.

Apparently I didn't need dinner to lose my heart again. All it took was a look.

CHAPTER 18
ABBY

Even without looking at her name, I would have known the text was from Amy. Out to dinner! Don't wait up, followed by a string of emojis — a smiley face, a kissy face, a heart.

Big on signs of affection, short on details, that was my Amy.

When the girls were growing up, Meg was the rule-follower and Beth the peacekeeper. Jo never got into the kind of trouble a mother could protect her from. But Amy . . . She was so eager to be popular, so determined to grow up as quickly as possible. Amy had been a challenge.

I gave a stir to the chili simmering on the stove. I should let it go. Let her go.

My nest had been so empty. It wasn't only the girls I missed, but Meg's clothes on the floor and Jo's scraps of paper, Beth's music and Amy's messes, the arguments over who sat in the front seat or spent more time in the bathroom. I missed who I was when they lived at home, when they still needed me.

My chicks might be back in the nest, but their comings and goings were no longer my business. Still, habit — or concern — made me wipe my hands and reach for the phone.

Time? I typed.

Three dots wavered on the screen. Amy, replying. Late. Love you!

Like that was reassuring.

Honestly, I'd been looking forward to dinner with my girls again, Amy, my baby, and Beth, the last to leave home.

At least they were together. I hoped they were having fun.

Make good choices, I typed, and she texted back emojis for laughing hard and fingers crossed.

My girls weren't teenagers anymore. It was no longer my job to worry about their safety or wonder whether their behavior was appropriate for the Reverend March's daughters. But old habits were hard to break.

The scales were slowly tipping in our relationship. Now they worried about me. How's your back, Momma? How's the farm? How are you doing with Daddy gone?

My phone rang. Beth, this time, apologizing for being late. "I wanted to stay with Mr. Laurence."

I gave the chili another stir. "Where's Amy?"

"With Trey."

My mom antennae quivered. *Late. Don't wait up.* But this was Trey, I reminded myself. He used to chauffeur the girls all the time. And he'd always had a soft spot for Amy.

I lowered the heat under the pot. "Need me to come get you?"

Like she was a ten-year-old calling from school with a stomachache.

"I'm good. Dad's bringing me home."

Oh. "That's nice of him."

Ash had never shared car pool duties when the girls were young. I didn't expect he would develop a deeper relationship with our daughter simply because he drove her home this one time. But who knew? Being stuck in the car had always made the kids chatty. Anyway, it was good Ash and Beth were spending time together. Girls needed their fathers.

We ended the call. I felt a sudden longing for my own dad, a comforting memory of whiskers and tobacco. My father was a farmer who spoke mostly in grunts or not at all, who believed girls should be married and wives should be good cooks. But he taught me to fish when I was five, sitting beside me for hours in the johnboat, baiting my hook with chicken livers, untangling my line, grabbing my rod when I almost fell in. He taught me to drive a truck, barreling across the fields and back roads in his battered pickup, smoking Camels and listening to George Strait on the radio. And the day he walked me down the aisle to marry Ash, he stopped at the back of the church and offered me the car keys, and never mind that Ash was the catch of the county and I was already pregnant with Meg.

"You're a strong woman, Abigail May," he'd said, patting my hand on his arm. *"You don't want to marry this boy, you'll be just fine on your own."*

And I was. Fine on my own, I mean, now that my parents had passed and Ash had moved out and the girls were grown and gone.

I sighed and got out the Tupperware.

I was writing labels on masking tape — CHILI and the date — when I heard a car pull up. I flipped on the outside light and opened the back door.

Ash unfolded himself from the car. He looked the same and not the same as the boy who used to wait for me thirty-five years

317

ago, same lean face and thoughtful eyes, same bony wrists and shoulders. His thick chestnut hair was graying now. He needed a haircut.

No wonder the church ladies brought him casseroles when I was in the hospital.

Beth retrieved her guitar case from the trunk.

"Chili's still hot," I said.

Beth smiled and shook her head. "I'm not very hungry."

"You need to eat something."

"I had a candy bar at the rehab center. Sorry," Beth said. "I'll get some later."

I looked at Ash. "What about you?"

He smiled, just a little. "Are you asking if I've spoiled my appetite?"

I snorted. "I packed some in a Tupperware for you and Dan. If you're hungry."

"That was kind of you."

His smile had faded. Foolishly, I wanted it back. "Or I suppose you could come in."

We looked at each other for a minute. The tiny lines around his eyes deepened. I felt a throb of the old attraction. "Thank you."

So, there we were, the two of us getting ready for supper, as if I'd never kicked him out.

He opened a drawer. "You moved the forks."

"I'm surprised you noticed."

He moved around me, setting the table. "I did live here for fifteen years."

"But you didn't use to be so handy in the kitchen."

"You mean, I couldn't find the coffeepot without your help," he said drily.

I smothered a laugh. "To be fair, I never asked you to do much."

"I never offered. I like to think I've learned something since we separated."

I nodded. "How to take care of yourself."

He met my gaze. "That I should have taken better care of you."

Oh. I cleared my throat. "How do you like living with Dan?"

"He's a good man. Quiet. Keeps to himself."

"You must appreciate that."

He shrugged. "I'm getting used to it."

I didn't know how to respond. When our girls were young, I was always telling them to hush. *"Don't worry your father." "Don't bother your father." "Your father is working,"* I'd say whenever Ash holed himself up in his office for hours at a time.

Did he actually miss their noise?

I brought the food to the table. "He and Beth are spending a lot of time together."

"And that worries you," Ash said quietly.

"Because of his combat experience."

"I admire his service. But he has issues."

"He's dealing with them."

"By talking to you."

"You know I can't discuss that." *Subject closed.*

Just as well. Despite the intimacy, the familiarity, the, oh, the *comfort* of eating dinner together, Ash hadn't really changed. He had issues, too.

"This chili is very good," he said.

"Thanks."

We ate.

Ash lowered his fork. "Soldiers aren't supposed to need help. Especially not emotional help."

"I've noticed."

Red stained his cheekbones. "I wasn't talking about myself."

"You never do."

"There's a . . . stigma to seeking counseling. I used to stock my tent so that my men would have an excuse to stop by and talk."

I smiled, remembering. "We were always sending you movies and candy and books and stuff."

"Your care packages helped a lot of homesick soldiers."

A fall of notes drifted down the stairs. Beth, playing guitar. It was nice to have music in the house again. I was glad she had played for Mr. Laurence.

"You helped them," I said. "I just baked cookies."

Ash shook his head slightly. "I can offer support and resources. I can facilitate group discussions. But I'm not a medical professional. There's a limit to what I can do."

I gave him a steady look. "Are we still talking about Dan?"

The flush spread across his high-bridged nose. But he surprised me by answering. "Dan has made a lot of progress. He isn't relying on me. He's doing the work."

"He's a good worker," I acknowledged.

"But Beth is your daughter."

"Our daughter," I reminded him.

"I wasn't much of a father."

I couldn't argue with him there. Anyway, it wasn't my job to make excuses for him anymore. "It's never too late."

His eyes, light as ash, met mine with odd intensity. "Isn't it?"

My heart pounded. "The girls know you love them."

He smiled wryly. "Indeed."

I got up to clear the table.

"Because of you," Ash said. "I always counted on you to connect us."

I concentrated on stacking the dishes. "I

didn't mind. Maybe that was the problem. I was always in the middle."

He carried his plate to the sink. "You were a wonderful mother." He stopped behind me. I could feel his heat all along my spine, not touching, just . . . there. "*Are* a wonderful mother," he murmured.

I drew a shaky breath. "I could have set a better example. For the girls."

"I don't see how." His breath was warm in my ear.

"I should have spoken up when things bothered me."

"It's not your way to complain."

"No, I just shut down," I said.

"It's hard to admit when something's wrong. To face your fears. Sometimes it's easier to shut down."

"Ignore your problems, and they'll go away?" I shook my head. "That didn't work for us. I want our daughters to fight for what they want."

He turned me in his arms. His gaze searched mine. "What do you want, Abby? What are you scared of?"

I'm scared I want you. "I'm afraid to need you."

"I love you."

"You left me."

"You asked me to go."

"You'd already made your decision. To go to Iraq after my parents died. To go to a conference in D.C. when I was in the hospital. You never asked what I felt, what I thought, what I needed."

"I was wrong."

"It doesn't matter."

"It does. I was so caught up in what I believed I was called to do, I forgot my first duty was to you and the girls. I'm sorry."

"It's too late for that now."

"Never too late, you said. Abby." He took my hands in his. Strong hands. Steady hands. Familiar hands. "I love you," he repeated.

"I'm sorry, too," I said, and my voice was shaking. "Sometimes love isn't enough."

CHAPTER 19
BETH

The following Thursday, I was back in the rehab center outside Staff Sergeant Carlos Cruz's room. His wife, Jessica, followed me into the hall.

She handed me her phone. "From our wedding day."

I looked down at the photo. She looked radiant, dancing with the groom in his dress blues. To "Miss You More," they'd told me. I glanced at her now, in her stretched T-shirt with her hair pulled tight. The ponytail dragged at the tender skin at her temples, giving her a faintly surprised look. Like life wasn't supposed to turn out this way.

Her husband was in a wheelchair. They'd never dance like that again. But something in the way they'd sat, listening to me play, their hands clasped on his truncated thigh, their bodies canted together . . .

"You look beautiful," I said sincerely. To her? To the woman in the picture? "You're very brave."

She shrugged, swiping at her tears with the edge of her palm. "For better and for worse, you know?" She tucked the phone away like something precious, her smile a fleeting shadow of the happy bride's. "Thanks for the song."

Her words rode with me in the car. *"For better and for worse . . . Thanks for the song."*

I'd written that song for my parents. "Miss You More." Back when I'd imagined their love would last forever, perfect and un-changing.

Not so perfect now. They'd changed. Mom seemed so sure of herself these days. So independent. Dad seemed so . . . lost. Or maybe they were the same people they'd always been and I saw them differently. Was the change in them — or in my new, adult perspective — for the better? Or for worse?

The words surged, fitting themselves to a tune. I hummed in snatches as I drove, phrases coming and going in my head like a radio station fading in and out of range. I could feel the music swell inside me, bigger than hunger, filling my stomach and chest and the palms of my hands. A chord, a chorus, melody and lyrics winding together. My fingers itched for a pencil. For my note-book. For my guitar in the backseat.

When I walked into Oak Hill, Jo was behind the bar, wiping glasses. "Yay! You're here."

"Do you have a pencil?" I asked abruptly.

"I . . . Sure."

I scribbled on a coaster. Two lines that felt true. Authentic. Not my story, but still . . . my voice. Maybe I could write a song — tell someone else's story — without my own guts spilling all over the page. "Thanks." I stuffed the coaster in my pocket. "Okay. What can I do?"

"Tell me we're going to be ready to open tomorrow night."

I smiled. "You'll be ready. Everything looks amazing."

The dining room gleamed. Amy was at the hostess station, surrounded by buckets of flowers and dozens of vases. Alec was at the other end of the bar, polishing flatware and flirting with a pink-haired teen in a black bib apron. Meg was setting tables with mismatched plates.

"Are those Aunt Phee's dishes?" I asked.

"Great-grandmother's china," Meg said.

"Or great-great-grandmother's. Or somebody's great-great-aunt. There were boxes and boxes, all these different patterns, just sitting in the attic," Amy said. "Aunt Phee didn't want to sell them, and she said she was tired of waiting for us to get married to get rid of them."

"Meg and Jo are married," I said.

"Oh no," Meg said. "John and I do not need a formal dinner service for twenty-four."

"Speaking of wedding china," Jo said. "What's with you and Trey?"

Amy focused on her flowers, her tongue sticking out. "Well, that was a supersmooth transition. Aren't you supposed to be a writer or something?"

"Have you seen him again?" Meg asked.

"Hard to avoid him," Amy said. "He lives next door."

A mile down the road.

"Uh-uh." Jo waggled a glass at her. "No dodging the question."

Poor Amy. I took a step closer to the hostess stand in solidarity. Our big sisters' concern could be overwhelming. "They went to visit Trey's grandfather," I said.

Meg raised her eyebrows. "We know that. We saw them at The Taproom after. And then . . . ?"

"And then . . . I guess we're working that part out," Amy said.

"What time did you get home on Saturday?"

Amy stabbed a stem into a vase. "We need

to talk boundaries. You do realize I don't have curfew anymore."

Meg looked at me.

I threw Amy an apologetic glance. "I don't know. I didn't hear her come in. She's really, really quiet."

"Sneaking up the stairs," Jo said.

"Not sneaking," Amy protested. "Walking."

"Quietly," Meg pointed out.

"You and Trey." Jo shook her head. "I did not see that coming."

Because we'd been blinded by his devotion to Jo.

"They like the same things," I said. "And Trey's always looked after Amy."

"He looks after all of us," Jo said. "We've been friends since we were kids."

"More than friends. Family," Meg said.

"But not in a creepy, incestuous way," Amy said.

Jo grinned. "You don't feel like you're kissing your brother?"

"*No*. Jo!"

"Just asking."

My sisters were like hawks, circling. I held still as a rabbit, as if any movement would divert their attention to me. At least they weren't asking about Colt.

"Please ignore the aunties," Alec said to

the pink-haired girl.

"Are you kidding? This is better than watching *The Bachelor*."

"You're not mad? That we're dating?" Amy asked Jo.

"Of course not. I want you to be happy. You and Trey both. I always felt guilty I couldn't . . ." Jo broke off, vigorously polishing a bar glass.

"So, are you two serious?" Meg asked Amy.

Amy shrugged. "There are feelings. Obviously. We care about each other. But we both agreed we're not going into this with any expectations."

"That's probably wise. What?" Jo asked when Meg shot her a look. "Trey's always been a man whore. I wouldn't want Amy to get hurt."

"Or Trey, either." I shifted my gaze to Amy. "I mean, you're going back to New York soon."

"I was. I mean, I am. Next week."

"I hear a *but*," Meg said.

"But . . ." Another shrug. "I keep thinking about what you said the other day. About how it would be cheaper if I moved my business to Bunyan."

Meg frowned as she folded a napkin into a precise rectangle. "Does this decision have anything to do with Trey?"

"There is no decision. I haven't decided anything yet. But he did show me a building. An empty storefront near the tobacco warehouse."

"The old Shoe Box store?" Meg asked. "That's a good location."

Amy crinkled her nose. Adorably, the way she did everything. "You sound like Aunt Phee. But it *is* a beautiful space. I always planned on opening my own shop. Just not here. Or so soon."

"I can run the numbers for you if you want," Meg said.

"Thanks." Amy sighed. "I mean, if I can't get financing any other way . . ."

"You'll figure something out," Meg predicted.

I liked listening to them like this, sharing their plans and dreams, a counterpoint to the music in my head. Part of their discussion and yet apart.

The floor beneath the hostess station was littered with tiny leaves and droplets of water. I found a broom and began to sweep up.

"You shouldn't relocate for a relationship," Jo said.

"Eric did," Amy reminded her.

Jo grinned. "I was one factor. There was

330

also a baby. Plus, we were both ready to leave New York. And he saw an opportunity in Bunyan."

"I thought you moved for me," Alec said.

Jo patted his arm. "Of course we did. Our entire lives revolve around you and your needs. You and your brothers are the center of our universe."

There was more truth in that, I thought, than either of them would ever admit. My prickly sister had lost her heart to her boys.

Alec grinned. "Good to know."

"Come on, Center of the Universe," the girl beside him said. "Chef wants us to stock the bar fridge."

"It would be wonderful if we all lived closer," Meg said wistfully as the teens headed to the kitchen.

Amy nibbled on her thumb. "Yeah. But —"

"There's always a *but* with you," Jo said.

Amy tossed her head. "Look who's talking."

"What's the problem?" Meg asked.

"There is no problem. Yet," Amy said. "But Trey — he's one of us. What if this relationship thing doesn't work out?"

"What if it does?" Meg asked.

"Either way, it changes things," I said. Habits were comforting. At least your life was predictable. Even if you were miserable.

"Life is change," Meg said. "Like Mom and Dad or me and John or Jo and Eric. That doesn't make the next phase better or worse. Just different."

Jo rolled her eyes. "Very profound."

Meg smiled, unoffended. "But true."

"You and Trey . . . It does shift the dynamic," Jo said.

"Exactly," Amy said. "I don't want things getting weird. Or awkward. Bad enough if we have to see each other at the holidays. What if we were living in the same town?"

"Things might be weird for a while," Jo said. *Speaking from experience?* "But we can deal with awkward. The question is, What do you want? For your business and from Trey."

"That's two questions," Meg, the accountant, said.

Jo elbowed her.

Amy sniffed. "I'm not afraid of risk. But what about Trey? Except for his grandfather, we're all he has."

Meg and Jo exchanged glances. "I guess only he can answer that," Meg said.

I swept, lulled by the mindless task, falling into the familiar rhythm of working with my sisters. *"Whatever happens, we have each other,"* we used to say. For better or for worse.

The words tumbled in my head, forming a string of melody. I caught myself humming, keeping time with the broom. *In good times and in bad . . . Whatever happens —* something something — *what we once had . . .*

Alec and the girl, Nan, returned with fruit for the bar. Jo went back to her glassware. Meg continued to line up forks with mathematical precision.

"So, you want to hang out sometime?" Alec asked.

"Alec, stop harassing my staff," Eric said.

I blinked, raising my head.

Jo's husband had appeared from the kitchen, his professional chef's coat unbuttoned at the neck.

Alec grinned at his dad. "You hit on Jo when she worked for you."

Jo laughed. "He's got you there, Chef."

"Actually, Jo hit on him," Meg said.

"It's true," Eric said solemnly. "I cannot resist her." He kissed his wife before turning to me. "Beth, you have missed lunch. I will cook for you."

My stomach growled. The words and music scattered.

"Oh, that would be . . . Don't you have to

get ready for the opening?"

"All will be well. The kitchen is ready. The students . . ." He smiled at Nan. "You are almost ready, yeah?"

"You bet. I mean, yes, Chef."

"Besides, tomorrow is a soft open," Eric said.

"Soft open?"

"Friends and family," Jo explained.

"So, basically another wedding," Amy said.

Eric smiled at me. "I make your grandmother's chicken and rice. With a few changes. Come and taste."

A whisper rose inside me, like smoke gliding across the ground.

"I will tomorrow," I said. "It sounds great. But I already ate. At the rehab center."

"What were you doing at rehab?" Meg asked.

"Visiting Mr. Laurence," Jo guessed.

"Not only Mr. Laurence." I started loading Amy's finished vases onto a tray, keeping my head down. "Dad asked me to play for some of the patients he sees."

My sisters glanced at one another.

"How often are you going?" Meg asked.

"Almost every day this week," Amy said. I shot her a hunted look. She shrugged. "Hey, you told on me. Payback's a bitch."

Meg made a *hmm* sound, not judging, just . . . Okay, totally judging.

"How's the songwriting coming along?" Jo asked.

I carried the tray to the tables, distributing the vases one by one. "It's coming."

"Have you sent anything to Colt yet?" Meg asked.

"Not yet."

She frowned. "Do you still get paid while you're off the tour?"

I'd never asked. I felt stupid. I would have to search for my show contract. Check my bank balance. "I have money coming in from my songs. Residuals."

"And you're writing the new ones, right?" Jo said. "When do you start recording?"

I panicked. They meant well. Of course they did. But why couldn't they let it go? *September,* I should have said. Or maybe, *That's up to Colt.*

But what spilled out of my mouth was, "Leave me alone. I don't know, all right? I'm working on something. It's not ready."

"Why are you so mad?" Jo asked.

"I'm not mad." I was shaking. I set the tray down.

"Honey, we didn't mean to upset you," Meg said.

Jo nodded. "We nag because we care."

335

"It's okay to set boundaries," Amy said.

"Even with us," Jo added.

"Especially with us," Amy said.

They hovered around. I looked at their loving, concerned faces, and the anger — if that's what it was — drained away. "I didn't mean . . . I shouldn't be so bitchy."

Meg patted my arm. "That's not being bitchy. That's . . ."

"Expressing yourself," Jo said. "You need to work on that."

"I know. I'm sorry."

Amy shook her head. "She means you should lose your shit more often. It's good for you."

Jo smiled ruefully. "Good for us. We overstepped."

"It's because you're so nice," Meg said.

"Too nice," Amy said.

"Considerate," Meg corrected. "You care what other people think. How they feel."

"You make me sound like a pushover."

"Not a pushover. A little Fanny Price, maybe," Jo said.

"Who?"

"Jane Austen. *Mansfield Park*?" She shook her head. "Never mind. The thing is, Fanny gets a bad rap because she's young and shy and always worried about doing the right thing. Her family treats her like dirt. But

336

she's really the best of them all. The moral center of the novel."

Their kindness brought tears to my eyes. I almost told them then. But the words stuck in my throat. How could I let them down, when they were being so understanding? How could I show them my worst, when they believed the best of me? I swallowed thickly. "I love you," I said instead. "All of you."

Meg hugged me. "Love you more."

"Love you best," Jo said.

"Jeez, does everything in this family have to be a competition?" Amy's nose wrinkled. "Not that I don't love you, too."

I was still a little shaky when I pulled up to the house a few hours later. I sucked at confrontation. Expressing myself, Jo called it. I pulled a face. I'd never been any good at opening my mouth.

Except when I sang.

I sat a moment in the car, trying to summon the strength to go inside. The lights were on in the kitchen. Momma, fixing dinner.

The shadow coiled inside me. I could go for a run, I thought. Or . . .

I dragged my guitar from the backseat.

The feed room was quiet, with a musty,

mineral smell from a dozen bins of organic alfalfa pellets, organic dairy pellets, supplements, kelp, and salt. Plastic totes full of baby bottles, towels, and little goat sweaters filled the wooden shelves. The sling for the baby scale hung on the back of the door. I opened the guitar case and sat on a stack of feed bags piled on the floor, cradling the Hummingbird.

Three chords and a chorus to tell my truth. Or somebody's truth, real and raw and honest. Could I do it? Was I brave enough?

I thought of the patients at rehab: Brenda Richards, struggling with balance after a mortar blast. Of Ray Jones, adjusting to his prosthetic arm. Of Jessica and Carlos Cruz, taking cautious steps forward in their new life together. Not victims, but survivors, every one.

Life is change, Meg had said.

For better or for worse.

The calico cat stuck her head above the flap of the carton. I took a deep breath and began to play.

I don't know what pulled me out of the song. A sound. A rise in the temperature of the air. I felt the weight on my bent head and when I looked up, Dan was propped in the feed room door, motionless as a barn beam. Like he'd stood there awhile.

My hands stilled on the strings. My heart raced. "I'm sorry. I didn't think anyone could hear me."

"Got an audience right there." He nodded toward the carton in the corner.

The kittens. I smiled. "They're not very critical."

"You got the goats."

"Harder to please."

"You got me."

Something about the way he said it, low, scraped my nerves and set them humming like guitar strings.

I was dying to know what he thought. "I hope I didn't bother you."

"Haven't heard that one before."

"The song? It's not finished."

He scratched his beard. "Reckon it's your music. Your call."

He didn't like it. I bent over my guitar, hiding my disappointment. Not a fan of country music, he'd told Colt.

"It sounded pretty perfect to me," he added.

My head jerked up. "You didn't think it was too . . . sad?"

"Nope. Honest. You write what you know. What you feel. People get married, move on. Sometimes they don't move on to-gether."

"Like my parents."

Dan gave me a surprised look. "Abby and Ash? There must be some reason your dad's still bunking with me. But I hear him talking in his sleep. He loves your mom."

I frowned, confused. "Oh."

"I was talking about me."

My heart swooped. "You're married." Momma tried to tell me. I didn't really know him at all.

He nodded, holding my gaze. "Was. Before I went to Iraq."

"I'm sorry. That it didn't work out, I mean."

"I'd just joined up. She thought she was marrying a hero. I couldn't be that for her, so . . ." He shrugged.

"It's hard when people expect so much of you," I said softly.

"Guess she found it someplace else."

This time the anger felt good. Warranted. "She cheated."

"Can't say I blame her." The calico cat emerged from its nest and twined around his ankles. "I was pretty rough for a while after I got out."

"Not now," I said.

"Not so much now." He reached down to

340

scratch the cat under its chin. "Still get angry sometimes."

The cat's purring filled the feed room. A copper-and-ash kitten ventured out of the box, and was promptly pounced on by its siblings.

"I had a fight with my sisters today," I heard myself say.

Dan continued to pet the cat without comment.

"Not really a fight," I amended. "They were actually very supportive."

"Your sisters are good people."

"They're wonderful. Which makes it worse. They're only trying to help. I shouldn't snap at them."

He glanced up. "Kind of hard on yourself, aren't you?"

The shadow rose like the Ghost of Christmas Yet to Come, dark and accusing. "I don't think so."

Dan straightened. All of his movements were smooth and slow. No wonder he was so good with animals. "Your dad got me going to those meetings of his for a while. You know?"

I made an affirmative noise. My father had lots of meetings in the basement of the church where he'd once served as pastor. Veterans' support. Grief recovery. Alcoholics Anonymous.

"Yeah. So some of the God talk, that's not really for me. But a lot of it made sense. Everybody's got their own shit to deal with. The first step is, you need to accept that you've got shit. You've got to want to fix your shit. And then you have to accept that you can't fix your shit without help."

The darkness inside me seethed. My personal shadow. Could I let it go? Did I want to?

"You think I need help?"

He was silent. Leaving the answer, the decision, up to me.

I liked him so much. I wanted to get to know him. But I was afraid to let him know me. The real me, with my darkness and my flaws.

Jo's question to Amy came back to me. *"The question is, What do you want?"*

"Eric and Jo are opening the Oak Hill restaurant tomorrow," I said.

His gaze was level. Steady. "I heard that."

"Yes, well, it's dinner. For friends and family?"

"Abby said. I told her I don't go out much."

My little courage failed. "I understand. I just thought . . . I was just wondering if you might like to come anyway. As a friend. With me," I added in case that wasn't clear. As if that would make a difference.

"With you."

I thought . . . Was he smiling, behind the beard? I nodded, my heart surging in my chest.

"I reckon I could do that," he said, and thank you, yes, that was definitely a smile. "That'd be real nice."

343

CHAPTER 20
AMY

The dining room at Oak Hill was full of guests, the tables loaded with drinks and flowers. My arrangements looked amazing, if I did say so myself. Outside, the terrace twinkled with lanterns and fairy lights, pale against the rays of the evening sun. The family was all seated together at two long tables. Mom, next to Robbie in the high chair, with Dad across. Meg and John with the twins between them. Alec, on the other side of Beth.

Tonight was Jo's show, Jo and Eric's. I had to admit, I was feeling kind of proud of her. Of them. Of our family.

"It's a shame your grandfather couldn't be here tonight," Aunt Phee said.

Trey pulled out her chair, and my insides gave a slow, warm squeeze. He was one of us. Always. But there was a special glow to the night because he was here with me.

"I tried to talk him into it," he said. "He

claims he's not good company yet."

Phee sniffed, settling Polly on her lap. "Doesn't want to be seen using a walker. James always did have too much pride."

Nan bustled by with a tray full of plated salads, her pink hair a cheerful contrast to her all-black server's outfit.

"Need help?" Alec asked.

"As if." She pocketed a spoon off the floor. Handed a clean one to Robbie. Flashed them both a smile. "But I'll be cut loose by eleven. If you want to hang out."

And maybe she wouldn't leave him hanging, I thought. Maybe he wouldn't break her heart. Maybe some young loves were meant to be. To last. I glanced at Trey, waiting for him to take the empty place between Beth and me. But before he sat down, Dan wedged in.

I arranged my face in a smile. "Hey, Farm Boy. You here with Mom?"

"With me," Beth said, blushing.

"Oh. Okay." I scooted my chair over, making room, hoping it wasn't obvious Dan was messing with the seating arrangements. "Trey, grab a chair."

"I can't stay."

"You . . . Why not?"

"I'm spending the evening with Granddad."

I searched his face. "Is everything okay?"

"Yeah. But his aide gets off at four, and Miss Dee has to go to her daughter's. Something with one of the kids, she said. So it's just me and the old man tonight."

Some of the shine rubbed off the evening. "Were you going to tell me?"

"I didn't want to bother you. I figured I'd slip out."

So, no. He hadn't planned on telling me anything. We didn't have that kind of relationship. My throat felt scratchy, like I'd swallowed a toothpick.

He bent and kissed me, a light, casual brush on the cheek. The kind of kiss you gave your sister. "See you later."

And he was gone.

My hands curled in my lap as I stared down at my salad. *No expectations.*

"He's leaving," Phee said.

I picked up my fork. "I noticed."

"You're letting him go?"

"I can't stop him." I stabbed a piece of baby kale. "And Mr. Laurence shouldn't be alone. He needs company."

"I'm disappointed in you," Phee said. "I thought you had more backbone. If you want something, you should go for it."

I shot her laser eyes. What was I supposed to do? Tackle him?

346

Jo bounced by, dragging Eric with her. He wore chef whites, a black bandanna around his head like a pirate. "Hey, gang. How is everything?"

A chorus of compliments rose from the table. "It's so good!" "Love the baby beets!" "Delicious!"

"I am proud of you," Phee said.

No, *I'm disappointed in you* for Jo. No sirree.

"You are pleased?" Eric asked Phee.

"My parents used to give the most wonderful parties. You have brought them back."

A look passed between them. *"Sehr gut,"* he said quietly.

"Because of you." Jo stooped to kiss her check. "Thanks, Aunt Phee."

"It's all wonderful," I said. "I'm sorry Trey had to leave early."

Jo nodded. "He told me."

Of course he did. Because it was her party. Eric's big night. And because they — Jo and Trey — were BFFs.

"I thought . . . Do you mind if I pack two dinners to go?" I asked. "For Trey and Mr. Laurence."

"Nan will help you," Eric said. He signaled her over.

"Three dinners," Phee said. We all looked

at her. "James needs company. I'll bring Polly."

"Because nothing says *Get well soon* like an ankle-biting little dog," Jo said.

Eric smothered a grin with his large hand.

"Maybe you should stay here, Aunt Phee. I'll probably be gone awhile."

"We'll need four dinners, then," Phee said, undeterred.

Uh, no. Nope. "That's sweet of you, Aunt Phee, but —"

She raised her chin, a gleam in her eyes. "We'll take my car."

I rang the doorbell, my heart thumping. I was nervous, I realized. About seeing Trey, a guy I'd known most of my life. Which was stupid. I was here on an errand of mercy, damn it.

He opened the door. "Amy." His voice was surprised. "Hi. What's this?"

I shifted the carton in my arms. "I brought dinner."

He smiled. "Dinner, flowers, and . . ." His gaze slid over my shoulder. "Aunt Phee."

The dog yipped.

I smiled wryly. "And Polly."

"We came to see James," Phee announced. "Don't leave us standing here on the porch. Invite us in."

"Yes, ma'am." He took the box from me, his eyes alight with laughter. "Where do you want this?"

"The kitchen? Unless you've already had dinner. In which case, I can put everything in the fridge."

"No, this is great. I was just about to nuke us something in the microwave."

I'd always admired the Laurence house, the dark wood, the antique rugs, the smell of furniture polish and old money. Not my style — too traditional — but very elegant. We crossed the foyer to the library. Mr. Laurence sat in his customary leather chair on one side of the fireplace. He was wearing what I thought of as his rehab clothes, a gray T-shirt and sweatpants. His hair stuck up in tufts on one side. Even with the slackening of his face, I could see the resemblance to Trey — the long, straight nose, the high, wide forehead.

"Hey, Mr. Laurence," I said softly. "I figured since you couldn't come to the party, we'd bring the party to you." He stared at me, his jaw working. "You know, like a picnic? We could set up trays in here."

"No," he said.

Well, that was clear.

"James and I are too old for picnics," Phee announced. "He and I can visit while you

349

set the dining room table."

"Sure. If that's what you want. Is that all right with you?" I asked Trey's grandfather.

He made a grunt that could have been assent.

Trey carried the box to the kitchen.

"You sure it's okay?" I asked. "Us being here?" *Me, being here.*

"Very okay. It's good for Granddad to have company." He grinned. "Unless the dog bites him."

"Or Aunt Phee does."

His chuckle released something inside me, iridescent as a flight of soap bubbles. I arranged the food on plates, fresh Southern ingredients with a German twist, a nod to Eric's mother. *Rouladen* made with heritage pork. Schnitzel with chowchow. Rabbit stew with pillowy potato dumplings.

"Amy, seriously . . . This is great."

The bubbles expanded, swelling my chest. "Eric made everything."

"But you brought it." He kissed me, a brief, hard kiss. Not particularly lover-like, but my pulse scrambled anyway. "Thanks."

"The food will get cold," I said.

"Right." Another lightning grin. "Don't want Phee to come looking for us."

I picked up the flowers. He grabbed the

plates. Together, we went into the dining room.

"This was very nice." Phee dabbed her lips with a napkin. "But it's getting late. We should go."

Reluctantly, I stood. It wasn't that late. But Mr. Laurence must be tired. He'd done great all through dinner — *great* being a relative term for a patient recently sprung from rehab. He seemed to enjoy his stew. He smiled and nodded to the stream of gossip and reminiscence from Phee. Now he sat with Polly curled in his lap, his hand resting on her silly topknot. My heart tugged.

Celebrate the small victories, the Internet had advised.

Trey touched his arm. "Come on, Granddad. Let's get you upstairs."

His tenderness brought tears to my eyes. He was such a good grandson.

"We can see ourselves out," Phee said.

"I'll stay," I said. "I don't want to leave Trey with all the cleanup."

"Don't worry about it," Trey said. "This has been great. Thank you both so much."

"Don't be silly," Phee said. "You can take her home?"

"I'll be fine, Aunt Phee."

She sniffed. "You're a grown woman. I suppose you'll make your own arrangements." She picked up her dog. "Good night, James."

He smiled — a real, recognizable smile — before pushing to his feet, using the arms of his chair. I held my breath, afraid he would fall as he reached across the table. He tugged a flower from the vase I'd placed and handed it to her. "Pink," he said.

She blushed to match the flower. Two old friends, sharing a memory of what might have been. The poignance jabbed my heart.

Gripping his walker, he turned to me. "Thank you," he said clearly.

"You're so welcome." I squeezed his arm. "I had a lovely time."

His eyes brimmed. "Yes."

Impulsively, I kissed him, his unshaven cheek rough against my lips. "Good night."

He nodded and stumped away.

Trey was watching, his black gaze unreadable. "I'll be down soon."

"Take your time. I've got dishes to wash."

I listened to their voices — to Trey's voice, warm and low — as he coaxed and coached his grandfather up the stairs.

"He likes you," Phee said.

"Beth is his favorite."

"You need to stop comparing yourself to your sisters."

"I will if you will."

She huffed in acknowledgment. "That was a good thing you did tonight for James."

"It was fun."

"You should say thank you when someone pays you a compliment."

"Why, thank you, Aunt Phee," I said, drawling my words like a Southern belle.

Another puff like laughter.

"I'll miss you," I said.

She arched an eyebrow. "I thought you couldn't wait to leave."

"I can't work remotely forever. My business is in New York. My life." My chance to prove that I could make it in the city Jo had called home.

"Your family is here."

"I'll miss them, too."

And Trey. The toothpick was back in my throat. I swallowed.

Phee regarded me, a dragonish gleam in her eyes. "Have you changed your mind about staying?"

No. Maybe. "Have you changed your mind about the loan?"

"Yes, I believe I have."

I blinked. "Excuse me?"

"The money is yours. My investment in

353

you. You've earned it. No strings attached."

"I . . . I don't know what to say."

"I find that hard to believe."

"I . . . *Thank* you, Aunt Phee." I flung my arms around her, making Polly wriggle and bark.

"You're welcome. We'll set up a meeting at the bank tomorrow." She patted my back stiffly before stepping away. "Let's go, Polly. This girl has dishes to do. And lots to think about."

I put the food away and stacked the dishwasher, moving automatically, trying to sort my thoughts, bright and jumbled as the workroom scrap bin. I was washing the wineglasses when Trey came downstairs.

"How's your grandfather?"

"Tired. Happy." He smiled. "Lot of excitement for one night."

He came up behind me, putting his arms around me to tug me against his chest. I leaned back, enjoying the warmth and angles of him. *Excitement.* Yes. It tumbled inside me, a kaleidoscope of colored shards. "I talked to Phee before she left."

"She's really something."

I turned. "Yes. Trey . . ."

He took advantage of the change in our position to kiss me, a long, lush, indulgent kiss. I felt myself going under, my busy thoughts submerged in sensation.

"Thanks," he said when we came up for air.

"Thank *you*. Was I saying something before you turned my brain to mush?"

He grinned. "Phee."

"Yeah."

"Thanks for bringing her."

"She didn't give me much choice." I traced the line of his nose, distracted by its perfection. "Why do you think they never got together?"

He let me go, rolling up his sleeves, reaching for a dish towel. "They dated in high school. Maybe the timing was never right for them."

Trey and Jo dated in high school.

"Or they weren't right for each other," I said.

"Or he went away and met somebody else."

Also like Jo.

You need to stop comparing yourself to your sisters, Phee scolded in my head.

I plunged my hands back into the dishwater. "What was your grandmother like?" I asked.

Trey started drying the wineglasses, another tiny, shared intimacy. Like playing house. "I don't remember her. When I was born, my father and grandfather were barely speaking to one another. I remember he went to her funeral. My father."

I was greedy for these glimpses of the bits he usually kept hidden: his corded forearms beneath his rolled-up sleeves, the childhood he'd tucked away at fifteen. For the private Trey, who sometimes felt like mine.

"You didn't go with him?"

"I was at boarding school."

Until his parents died, and he came to live with the grandfather he'd never known. No wonder our family had seemed like a haven.

A terrible tenderness welled in me for the boy he'd been then, the boy I remembered, moody and charming. For the man he had become, lonely and loyal and kind. The jitters I'd felt on the porch were back, like I was on the threshold of something more than here and now. Something solid, sustainable, and lasting.

Apparently I had expectations after all.

"I talked to Aunt Phee. About my business loan."

His quick, dark eyes focused on my face. "How did that go?"

"It was . . . Actually, it went great." I told him, the sentences spilling out. With the financing from the loan, I could fill my current orders, expand my operation, hire more help. Spend more time developing new products and custom designs. I could move to Bunyan or stay in New York.

He listened, a slight flex between his brows. "What are you going to do?" he asked when I was done.

I was relieved. And disappointed. I wasn't looking for declarations or promises. I'd been home barely three weeks. We'd been together — an acknowledged couple, having sex — for seven days.

And you've been in love with him your entire life, a voice whispered in my head. So, yeah, okay, it would be nice if he expressed a desire for me to stay.

"I don't know." I took refuge in Phee's words. "It's a lot to think about."

He stuck his hands in his pockets. "You could make a real difference in this town. If you moved your business here."

I exhaled. So he wasn't opposed to the idea of me staying. "Or I could fail miserably."

A glimmer of a smile. "Have a little faith."

"In Bunyan?"

"In yourself."

How could I think logically when he said things like that? "It was almost easier when I didn't have a choice," I confessed.

"You're lost in New York," he said. "Here you could be somebody."

"One of the March sisters."

"One of the smart, successful March sisters."

"New York is the fashion capital of the world. If I can make it there, I can make it anywhere."

"That's what Jo used to say."

"I am not Jo," I said through my teeth.

"No," he said quietly. "No, you're not." I don't know what my face did, but his changed swiftly. "Christ. I didn't mean it like that."

"Like what?"

"Like whatever you're thinking that made you look that way."

"I'm sorry if you don't like the way I look."

He took his hands out of his pockets. "Amy . . . I'm sorry."

I pulled myself together. He wasn't trying to hurt me. "I'm sorry, too." Three *sorry*s. We were breaking our own record. "It's all just been . . . kind of a shock."

"How can I make it better?"

"You can't." *If I have to explain it to you, if you don't feel the same way, you can't.* "I need to figure this out myself."

"Come to the library." And oh, didn't that sound lord-of-the-manorish, I thought, torn

358

between amusement and the desire to hit him with a leftover bottle of Eric's wine. "I'll pour you a drink and we'll talk."

"I don't want to talk."

"Okay." He took me in his arms and held me while I stood there stiffly, fighting tears. Wrapped in his good, clean Trey smell, citrus oil and starch. Feeling the strong, steady beat of his heart against mine. Slowly, the tension bled from my muscles. With a little sigh, I laid my head against his shoulder. "It's okay," he murmured. "We don't have to talk."

"Good."

"Yet," he added.

At all, I thought.

Stay? Or *go?*

I tightened my hold around his waist. Tilted my head up. "Take me upstairs."

CHAPTER 21
BETH

The dining room was thick with laughter and talk, the rattle of flatware and the smell of good food.

"You're not eating," Momma said. "Are you all right?"

I swallowed, instantly on the defensive. Forced myself to smile. "I ate my salad." Three pieces of baby kale. No beets, because of the sugar. "Anyway, I'm saving room for dessert."

Across the table, Meg raised her eyebrows. Jo broke off her conversation with Alec to glance from my plate to my face.

Boundaries, Amy had said. But Amy wasn't here to blunt the force of our sisters' attention.

I dropped my gaze to fiddle with the phone in my lap. No texts. Nothing.

"Have you heard from Colt?" Meg asked.

"Not lately."

Dan was silent beside me.

Colt had barely messaged me at all since I'd been home. No, *I miss you.* No, *How are you feeling?* No, *You're the only woman I want to spend the rest of my life with.*

Not that I was expecting the last one.

"Did you send him your song yet?" Jo asked.

"Jo, stop. You asked her that yesterday," Meg said.

A burst of voices, the clatter of dishes, broke out from an adjoining table. Dan was rigid beside me.

"You asked her." Jo grinned, her face full of laughter and apology. "So it's my turn."

I took a breath. At least we weren't talking about my dinner anymore. "Actually, I did. This morning."

"And . . . ?" Jo asked expectantly.

And . . . I was afraid. What if he didn't like it? What if he did? What would I do?

I moved my fork an inch to the left. "He has a show tonight. I'm sure he hasn't listened to it yet."

Dan pushed his chair back abruptly. " 'Scuse me."

I watched him go, a piece of me trailing after him.

"He's going to love it," Jo predicted.

He? Colt.

"You're so talented," Meg said.

Dan crossed the dining room, shoulders braced against the din, and went out the doors to the terrace.

I stood. "I'll be right back."

"Beth . . ."

"I want to hear about Colt."

I met three pairs of concerned, curious eyes. My sisters. Our mother. "Not now," I said.

Apparently I had boundaries after all.

I found Dan sitting on the low stone wall overlooking the garden, his profile outlined by the fading light.

"Are you all right?" I asked softly. Hearing the echo of my mother's words. Not an attempt to control, I realized, but a desire to make things better.

"Yeah." He stood, stiff as a soldier on parade. "Sorry. I'm not much good in a crowd."

I took a cautious step closer, like he was something feral I could startle into flight. "My family can be a bit much."

"They love you."

"They do." Another step. "I'm not comfortable with crowds, either."

He relaxed a fraction of his military posture. "Must be hard to get up onstage every night."

I smiled. "It is."

362

"So why do it?"

"I . . ." No one ever asked me that before. *"Follow your dreams,"* Momma urged. *"Use your talents,"* Daddy preached. *"Take your shot,"* Jo had said.

I shrugged. "This is what I'm supposed to want."

He was quiet, letting the words stand in the stillness. *Supposed to.*

"Why did you come tonight?" I asked.

"It was worth it. To be with you."

I felt a flare of pleasure and distress. "You can be with me anytime. Every day at the farm."

"I'm thankful for the farm. A lot of my buddies died, in Iraq and after. Your ma gave me a place to live and a reason to keep on living. But the deal is . . ." He looked away, out over the wall to where the pond gleamed and the shadows gathered. "I haven't let myself be all the way alive. I've been . . ." He broke off, searching for words.

"Stuck." I knew the feeling. Caught in the shadowlands between living — recovery — and death. Clinging to your familiar walls, even when they were no longer a refuge, but a prison.

He nodded once. "You asking me to dinner made me think how things could be. How I wanted them to be." He drew a hard breath. "Like I had a chance at making them different."

I wanted to touch him. I curled my fingers against temptation. "We don't have to go back in."

"I do. This is my chance. My choice." His mouth bent in a near-smile. "Might take me another minute, though. You go on. It's your sister's party."

"Jo can wait. I can wait." I gave him his words back again, like a gift. "It's worth it, to be with you."

Another harsh breath. He met my gaze, his eyes raw and honest. Like he saw me, the real me, not the thin, flat, distorted image I dragged around. Not the somebody else he wanted me to be. And then we were touching, my fingers on his face, his hands in my hair. He kissed me, or I kissed him, kisses soft as breath and necessary as air. Yearning filled me. My body tingled to life, like a leg prickling with returning circulation.

I broke the kiss, dropping my forehead to Dan's chest to avoid looking him in the eyes.

"I'll take you in," he said huskily.

I nodded, overwhelmed with happiness and guilt.

We went back to the dining room. Another course was already on the table. I smiled at my father. Talked to my sisters and Alec. Wondered. *What if things were different? If I made them different?*

"Corn bread?" the pink-haired server asked, waving tongs over a basket.

The darkness rose, wraithlike.

"Thank you," I said.

I stared down at my bread plate, my heart pounding as if I were about to go onstage. Or jump out of an airplane.

No one was watching. I picked up the golden square. Sniffed it. It smelled so good, like Momma's cooking and Granny's kitchen, like buttermilk, molasses, and home.

How many calories? A hundred? A hundred and fifty? *Think of the butter,* the shadow whispered, tugging me back to safety. *The carbs. The regret.*

I put the corn bread down. Picked it up again.

One bite. *My choice.*

Defiantly, I tore off a corner and put it in my mouth. My brain exploded, fat and sugar detonating the pleasure centers like hard drugs. I chewed, testing the grit of cornmeal between my teeth.

Jo frowned at me. "Are you all right?" she asked, and this time I didn't hear judgment. Only love.

I swallowed. Blinked. "Fine."

I should have known better. I did know better.

But for the next few days, I let myself hold on to hope, clutching the possibility like a teddy bear against the personal monster in my closet.

There are no weekends when you live on a farm. Oh, Saturday is the farmers' market, and Sunday was always for church. But every day the animals need to be milked and watered and fed. I'd always liked the rhythm, the routine, the predictability of it all.

Habit was a powerful thing. Obviously, I reckoned, I couldn't change everything all at once. So, Monday morning, I got up as usual at five thirty, checked my phone — no messages from Colt — and went for my regular run.

I didn't enjoy running when I started. Not like Jo, who had been on the cross-country team in high school. Keeping track of my miles was a kind of affirmation — a gold star on my secret report card. But gradually, I'd learned to like it. As long as I was putting one foot in front of the other, I didn't have to think too hard about anything else, like how much my shins hurt or why

I'd kissed Dan or what I would do if Colt hated my song.

When I got home, the sun was up. The goats were out, the babies bouncing like popcorn in the green field. I let myself quietly in the back door.

My mother, in barn clothes, was sitting at the kitchen table, writing out a grocery list. "You want to be careful, running in this heat."

I slipped by her. "That's why I went early."

"Well, drink some water. Have you had breakfast?"

She meant well. I knew that. I opened the fridge and froze, paralyzed by the well-stocked shelves. There was so much *food*. How could I possibly choose?

"How about some coffee?" Mom asked.

Black, two Sweet'N Lows. *Easy.* I smiled at her in gratitude. "Thanks, Momma."

Amy came downstairs.

"You're awfully dressed up," our mother observed.

"Going to the bank today." Amy reached by me. "Got the loan from Aunt Phee."

She grabbed a yogurt. I took one, too, relieved of another decision.

"That's wonderful," I said.

"And then what?" our mother asked.

Zero grams of fat, said the small print on

the yogurt carton. Seventeen grams total carbs, eleven grams of protein. One hundred twenty calories. Less, if I didn't eat the fruit on the bottom. I got a spoon.

Amy was talking, something about driving back to New York this week. Her new hire had quit, and Flo needed her there.

"You know your own business best," our mother said.

Amy grinned. "That's very good, Ma. Have you been practicing?"

Our mother smiled. "A mother's job is to teach her children not to need her anymore. Sometimes I have a little trouble accepting how well I've succeeded with you all."

"Aw." Amy hugged her. "Love you, Momma."

Our mother patted her.

"We'll always need you," I said.

"I love you girls, too." Mom cleared her throat. "Well. The cheese won't make itself."

The screen door swung shut behind her. Amy propped against the counter as I peeled open the yogurt, aware of her watching, weighing every bite that went into my mouth.

We weren't the kind of sisters who talked. I mean, to each other. Not about anything meaningful. Not before this summer.

I had a chance to make things different, I

reminded myself. The way I wanted them to be.

"How does Trey feel about you going back to New York?" I asked.

For a long moment, I thought she wouldn't answer. But maybe she was trying to change, too, because after a pause, she said, "Trey and I don't talk about his feelings."

I could relate.

"That doesn't mean he doesn't have them," I said. "Sometimes the more you feel, the harder it is to say anything."

"The song of our people. I should put that on a T-shirt," Amy said. "I've never told Trey how I really feel, either. I'm afraid he'll freak out. Or worse, feel sorry for me."

"But, Amy, you're so beautiful. So confident. I'm sure Trey cares about you. He's probably just afraid of being hurt." *Again.* "Everyone he's ever loved has left him." His parents. His family in Florida. Jo.

"He hasn't exactly asked me to stay." She straightened her slim shoulders. "Anyway, it's my life. My business. I have to figure this out for myself."

I nodded, because, really, what could I say?

"Enough about Trey. What's up with you and Farm Boy?"

I flushed and stirred my yogurt. "Nothing. He went with me to the opening."

"Meg said you were kissing at the restaurant."

"That wasn't . . . I wasn't . . . I have a boyfriend. Colt."

Amy pursed her lips, looking, for a moment, remarkably like Aunt Phee. "Well, Colt can definitely help you more, career-wise."

I winced. "You make it sound like I'm using him."

"Please. You won the guy a Grammy. I'm just saying, maybe you're using each other. He fits into your life. The life you want."

"Or I fit into his."

Amy looked at me with her keen blue artist eyes that saw so much and gave away so little. "What does that mean?"

I floundered, taken aback by her directness. "I hate being on the road."

"But you love Colt."

"He's so wonderful. I can never deserve him."

Amy frowned. "That's bullshit. He loves you. He chose you."

"Sometimes I wonder if he loves me or if he just wants my songs." If he still wanted my songs. Checking my phone had become a kind of compulsion.

Amy looked at me kindly. "And what do you want?"

I don't know, I almost said. But my sister deserved a better answer than that.

And maybe I did, too.

"I want to write songs." *Real* songs, that told the truth. That told my story. I swallowed hard. Or at least . . . "I want to feel . . ." *Safe.* "Loved, I guess. I want what Mom and Dad had. Or what I thought they had. I want a home, a place I belong, like Meg and John, and a guy who looks at me the way Eric looks at Jo."

"You want to be seen."

I nodded. But did I really? "To be accepted," I said. With all my flaws and secrets.

Amy sighed. "Me, too."

I smiled. "Your old nickname."

"Yeah." She smiled back crookedly. "Seems we're both still comparing ourselves to our sisters."

Defined by who we were not.

Shadows of Meg and Jo.

371

CHAPTER 22
AMY

I heard the car before I saw him, the red Ferrari muscling up the drive of the carriage house. When I went downstairs, Trey was leaning against the driver's-side door, wearing Wayfarers and leather Rainbows, another perfectly pressed button-down shirt untucked over khaki shorts. My heart sighed and flopped at his feet like Polly displaying herself for a belly rub.

"Let me guess," I said. *"Ferris Bueller's Day Off?"*

His grin flashed. "Want to play hooky?"

Yes, please. "I can't," I said with regret. "I've got so much work to do."

The new images on social media had boosted sales. My phone screen had broken out in a rash of notifications, likes, comments, and tags. I needed new posts, fresh content to keep my followers coming back.

Maybe Trey would pose for me. In black and white, that wild dark hair, his lean, hard chest framed by the panels of his white shirt (unbuttoned, of course), those black eyes laughing at the camera as he held a purse with the Baggage logo . . .

Best marketing ever. There wasn't a woman in the world who could resist him.

He nodded at the box in my arms. "Fetching for Phee?"

I blinked, recalled from my photoshoot fantasy. "I'm getting her old photos scanned." We'd spent the day sorting through pictures. It was strange seeing my father preserved in Phee's eyes, a toddler with fat knees and cheeks, a tall boy with a shy smile. "Also, I have to pack. I'm driving to New York tomorrow."

Trey shot me a glance, his eyes hidden by sunglasses. "You've already decided to leave, then."

"Everyone he's ever loved has left him," Beth whispered.

But I'd put my heart out there before. I wasn't doing that again. Not without some kind of sign from Trey.

"I'm keeping an open mind. But my stitcher quit. Flo can't fill the orders by herself. If I don't go back soon, I won't have any business to go back to."

"Too bad. I was going to give you a tour of that shoe store. I brought the key," he added in a low, deliciously dirty voice. Like he was promising to show me his secret sex dungeon.

I tilted my head. "That's always been my dream. That one day you'd pick me up in a red convertible and drive off with me to . . . the Shoe Box."

Okay, my childhood fantasies had not included a tour of an empty storefront in downtown Bunyan. But the rest of it? Trey, listening to me, wanting to be with me, giving shape to my dreams? It was all I'd ever wanted.

His eyes lit with laughter. "So that's a yes."

An answering smile uncurled in my heart. "Maybe. Are you going to feed me?"

"That's part of the plan."

There was a plan. That included me. My chest filled with butterflies.

"Go," Phee said from behind me. "You're no good to me mooning around here."

Since offering me the loan, she hadn't tried to talk me into staying in Bunyan. Maybe she thought Trey would.

Maybe I wanted him to.

"Mooning?" Trey murmured as he opened my door.

"Shut up," I said, and got into the car.

He took me in the back way, unlocking the

door and leaving me there while he walked through the empty showroom to turn off the security system. The evening sky had clouded over on the drive into town — a summer thunderstorm rolling in. Inside the building, the air was stale, warm, and dark.

I felt along the shadowy wall. "I can't find the switch."

"I've got you."

I was waiting for the overhead fluorescents to flick on when Trey returned in a pool of light, carrying a lantern. "Mood lighting?" I joked.

He grinned. "I wanted you to see the place in the best possible light."

"Ha-ha. What are you hiding? Water damage? Mice?"

He shook his head. "In real estate, you learn to look for hidden potential. Watch your step."

He steered me across the showroom, one hand on the small of my back. My skin tingled at that light, possessive touch. He raised the lamp. A quilt was spread over the ugly blue carpet in the space created between the brick wall and a cheap veneer shelving unit. The light fell softly on a vase stuffed with flowers. There were pillows. Candles. All the trappings of romance.

I looked from the picnic basket to the

champagne chilling in a bucket of ice, and the butterflies in my chest took flight in a flurry of color and joy.

"I . . . Wow."

"Glad you like it." He popped the bottle. Poured.

Bubbles swirled in giddy counterpoint to the butterflies. I took a cautious sip. "What are we celebrating?"

"I was hoping . . . Your decision to stay in Bunyan."

Holy freaking cow. Was this . . . More than a sign. Was this . . . *it*? I trembled. "Trey, I . . . I don't know what to say."

"You don't have to say anything yet." He smiled and topped off my glass. "The lease is yours. Whatever you want. Whatever you need. We'll work it out."

The lease.

I set down my wine. "Let's not get ahead of ourselves." Great advice. Too bad I hadn't followed it. "I'm not playing store, Trey. Baggage is my business. My life. My livelihood. I can't afford for it to fail."

"You won't fail. You're too good."

"Thanks." I unpacked the basket — chicken salad sandwiches studded with grapes and pecans, two bags of chips, strawberries dipped in chocolate. "This looks amazing."

"I stopped at Connie's."

"Good choice." I laid everything out on real cloth napkins he'd obviously brought from home. "I just . . . I don't know if I can make it work here."

"You can make it work anywhere. Bunyan is a great business location."

"If your last name is Laurence," I muttered around a mouthful of food.

"What are you saying?"

I swallowed. "You're Theodore James Laurence III. That gives you a certain advantage in this town."

"You're part of this community, too. More. I didn't grow up here like you did. All anybody ever saw when they looked at me was rich Mr. Laurence's spoiled grandson from Miami. The boarding school brat. Lucky bastard. Never had to work a day in my life. Everything handed to me. Everybody watching, waiting for me to screw up like my daddy."

I set down my sandwich. "It's not that different growing up as the preacher's daughter."

"But everybody respects your father. Everybody admires the Marches. Your mother. Your sisters, too. I admired you. Hell, I wanted to be one of you."

So much that you wanted to marry Jo? So

much that you'd settle for . . . me? I pushed the thought away. "You're not that boy anymore, Trey. You don't have to prove yourself to anybody."

"Except my grandfather."

"Your grandfather loves you."

"He thinks I'm a slacker. Like my dad."

I hesitated, aware of trespassing on quicksand. "You're not your dad. But you're not exactly . . ."

He cocked an eyebrow. "Fulfilling my potential? I've heard that before, thank you, Teacher."

"I don't want to fight with you."

"No, please." He took a brownie, gestured with it grandly. "Go on."

"Maybe you could step up a little. At work." Cinderella telling Prince Charming to get off his horse and clean the stables.

"There's more to life than business."

"I know that."

"Do you?"

Ouch. Outside it was raining, pattering on the roof, splashing in the street. "All I'm saying is, your grandfather's not getting any younger. And now that he's had a stroke . . ."

"Granddad's fine." Trey's voice was flat and hard.

O-kay. I needed to let this go. His parents

378

had both *died*. He didn't need me to remind him that his beloved grandfather had recently, er, suffered a major health event.

I wanted to be seen, I'd told Beth. I wanted to be heard. Time for a little honesty, maybe.

"He's making wonderful progress," I said gently. "But maybe if you were more focused on work, he could concentrate on getting well."

"I think I know what my grandfather needs better than you do," Trey said stiffly.

"He needs you."

"And your family needs you."

"Not the same way. You're a good person, Trey. You're generous and kind. But you're wasting your advantages. Being good is not enough. My father was good, and it never got my mother anything but alone. You have to show up."

"You're the one who keeps running off. Paris. New York. I'm here. I do everything he asks of me."

"But you could do more."

"Look, I owe him. I get it."

"Not because you owe him. Because you owe this to yourself." I folded and refolded the napkin in my lap. "Don't just do what you have to do. Do what you want."

"It's not my business. It's his. It gets along

fine without me. You said you're afraid of failing?" He shook his head. "There's nowhere for me to go but down."

"So it's easier not to try?"

"You don't understand. I can't be my grandfather."

"You don't have to be. You care about people. You care about this town. You have such a good heart. You're just . . ." *Afraid to have it broken. Don't say that.* "You just have to be yourself," I amended. "The man you might and ought to be."

Silence fell, filled with the hissing of the rain.

He looked at me with those black, black eyes, a twist to his mouth. "Guess I was wrong."

"About what?"

"It's not my grandfather I have to prove myself to. It's you."

CHAPTER 23
BETH

Here's the thing about starving yourself.

In the beginning, there's this sort of honeymoon period, when denying yourself feels really good, when it makes you feel special. In control. It's only later you realize that you're not. Your behavior starts to control you. And the things that once attracted you and made you feel good — the hunger, the purging, the compulsive exercise — aren't working anymore. You hide what's happening, not for the power your secret gives you, but from shame. On some level, you know what you're doing is bad for you. Might kill you, even. You're no longer in love with the shadowland. But by then, you're afraid to leave.

Like an abusive boyfriend, anorexia owns you.

But if I could make a plan not to eat, I reckoned, I could make a plan for eating, too. I'd done it before. But not at home.

Being home, I told myself, would make the difference.

When Amy came downstairs and got a yogurt, I got a yogurt, too. Protein was important. And calcium.

We ate breakfast together at the kitchen table, and when she set a bowl of strawberries between us, I ate three, feeling virtuous and healthy. I would miss her when she was gone. Or would it be a relief when she wasn't here, appraising me with her eyes? I wanted both the reassurance of her presence and the absence of her judgment.

She was tapping on her phone, commenting, liking, and responding to social media posts.

I still hadn't heard from Colt about my song. Or anything else.

Eventually, she looked up and smiled. "Did you go running this morning?"

Every morning. I nodded warily. I had developed a lot of bad habits since I'd left home, but running was a good one. I always felt lighter, stronger, when I ran.

She touched my arm. She was always doing that, patting, stroking, comfortable in her body in a way that I was not. "Well, don't overdo it, okay?"

I didn't want to be reminded that I'd tried this before. The eating. The not eating. All of it. I didn't want her to say, *Something's wrong,* because it would be true. To ask, *What's the matter?* because then I would have to lie.

So I turned her concern back on her. Deflecting. Evading. I was good at that. "You were home early last night. Did you have a nice dinner with Trey?"

"He packed a picnic. Sandwiches and champagne."

I smiled. "Sounds romantic." And fattening, but Amy didn't let things like that bother her.

"It was." She toyed with her spoon. "And then we had a stupid fight and he brought me home."

"Oh, Amy," I said, genuinely dismayed. "What happened?"

"I was hoping for some kind of sign from him, I guess. Like a lovesick teenager. But we're obviously focusing on different things right now."

"You'll make up," I predicted. "Next time you're home."

"Probably." She sipped her coffee. "The thing is, I was thinking of sticking around. Now that I have a choice. I'm proud of Baggage, proud of building my own name, my own brand, my own business. But I miss our sisters and Momma and the kids. Even

Dad and Aunt Phee. I miss the river and the blue sky. I even miss this town sometimes. I can make it in New York. But it's not home."

"Then why go back?"

"I need to be sure I'm making the decision for the right reasons. I *know* there's more to life than work," she said. Like she was continuing an argument, responding to something I hadn't said. "But work's important, too."

I nodded encouragingly. "You've always wanted to be successful. And you will be. Wherever you are."

She shrugged. "How do you define success?"

I stared at her.

"Well." She drained her coffee cup and left it in the sink. "I have to hit the road. Miss you."

She held out her arms and we hugged.

"I'll miss you, too." A piece of truth that I could give her.

She pulled back and looked in my face. "Take care of yourself."

"I will," I promised.

I tried.

But her question stuck with me for days after she left. *"How do you define success?"*

I had written a Grammy-winning song.

384

My boyfriend was a country star. But I'd never shared my family's dreams for me. They were too big. Too overwhelming. I'd found myself instead in small, furtive acts of autonomy and rebellion, measuring myself in tiny increments, a bite, a pinch, a number on the scale, a reflection in the mirror.

Who was I without those things? How did I define success?

It was harder to eat normally without Amy's example. I kept up a semblance at dinnertime, under my mother's watchful eye. But the weight of her attention pressed on me.

"You're too thin," she said one night at supper as I cut my chicken into smaller and smaller pieces.

I felt burdened by her concern, by the pressure to be good, to be strong, to be happy.

"I'm fine," I said, and she had to accept that, like it or not. Wasn't that what she'd told us girls for years?

But it was even worse when Momma wasn't around. The next morning — a Monday — after my run, I prowled the kitchen, restless in my own skin. Dissatisfied. Empty.

Colt still hadn't called. I'd texted him on

Saturday before his show. Knoxville, according to the tour schedule. He hadn't messaged me back.

I ate my yogurt, but I wanted something else. Something more.

I opened the cabinets, searching. I opened the fridge. But whatever I wanted wasn't there. Not food. Not even the satisfaction of not eating.

"How do you define success?"

My phone jangled with the opening chords of "Miss You More." "Colt?"

"Angel! Baby! Where the hell have you been?"

I clutched the phone, desperate for connection. "Right where you left me." *Six weeks ago.*

"You had me worried, sweetheart. I almost sent Jimmy down there to check on you."

His concern assuaged me. "You don't have to do that. I'm fine."

"Yeah, good. Although, hey, I'm sending the car anyway. We've got almost a week before we got to be in Atlantic City. Thought we'd make a stop in Nashville and lay down the track for your new song."

"What?"

"Your song. 'For Better or Worse.' Great little ballad. Can't wait to hear it in the studio."

My heart lifted. "You like it?"

"Love it. We're all lined up to do the vocals on Sunday."

And sank. *Oh. No.* "Colt, I can't be ready to record in three days."

"Listen, you don't have to do a thing. No press, no appearances. I cleared it all with Dewey. We'll lay down the instrumental tracks before you even get here. You just show up and sing."

My resistance faded in the face of his certainty. "But . . . Three days."

"Got to keep it flowing, babe. Fans don't wait anymore for you to put out twelve or fifteen songs at once. It's all about throwing out content."

Amy would jump at the chance. But this was my life. My business. My song. Not something to be thrown out in a hurry to appease Colt's fans.

I gripped the phone tighter. I was sweating, from the run and nerves. "I'd like to think about it."

"We already booked the studio. If you can't get up here, Mercedes can sing it."

A compromise? Or a threat? Distress spiked my heart rate. "It's not Mercedes's song."

Colt expelled an impatient breath. "Obviously you'd get credit. Just like always."

I wavered. He was offering me an identity. Something solid to hold on to. *Beth March, songwriter.*

"Look, angel, I *want* to do the song with you." His voice turned coaxing. "It'll be great. You'll be great. Let me send Jimmy. We'll record the vocals and get you home before you know it."

My defenses crumbled like a castle of dry sand, and Colt rushed in like the tide.

Of course he got his way. He always did.

Even after I ended the call, I could feel the pull of him, feel myself dissolving in a swirl of expectations and anxiety. *Do this. Or that. Be thin. Be normal. Be more like your sisters.* I was desperate to shore myself up somehow, to fill the void with food. To eat something. Or puke.

Puking would be good. The yogurt I'd eaten curdled in my stomach.

I swallowed self-loathing. I needed to move. Breathe. Escape.

I burst out the back door, still in my running clothes, the impulse natural as flight.

"Dan!"

Relief washed over me. He was standing in the sunlight. I drank in the sight of him, his body hard and knotted as a rail, his thick, soft hair and full, soft beard. We hadn't been alone — truly alone, the two of us — since he kissed me more than a week ago.

My heart steadied, ridiculously calmed.

His eyes met mine. "What's wrong?"

Like he saw me in all of my confusion and distress. Like I didn't have to hide. That, too, should have been a relief.

But . . . Hiding was a habit. It's what I was good at.

"Nothing." I managed a smile. "I talked to Colt. He, uh, he loves the song."

"Congratulations."

"Thank you."

"You don't sound too happy."

"I am." I smiled harder to prove it. "He . . . He wants me to record it. This week."

Dan hitched his thumbs in his belt loops. "So you're leaving," he said, no judgment in his tone.

I flinched anyway. "Only for a few days. He's sending a car."

He waited, his expression neutral behind his beard.

"It's a duet," I said. "If I don't go, he'll sing it with somebody else."

"I don't know much about the music business," he said slowly. "But it's your song."

"No one would ever hear my songs without Colt. I *owe* him this. It's not like I *want* to go. I don't have a choice."

"There's always a choice," he said.

The silence pulsed between us.

"You don't understand," I whispered.

"So tell me."

I opened my mouth. Shut it, the weight of my secret balling like shame in my stomach. I couldn't tell him what I wanted. What I feared. I'd never told anyone.

Dan nodded, once. "You change your mind, you let me know."

I watched him go with his long, lanky stride. A wounded warrior who had somehow found the courage to accept his failures — his shit, he called it — and go on living.

He wasn't going to fight for me or fix me or rescue me. I had to do it myself.

And I wasn't strong enough.

CHAPTER 24
ABBY

My daddy never ate cheese from a goat. Never went to a restaurant where they would serve such a thing. My parents were homesteaders, subsistence farmers who left me the house and the land and a tolerance for dirt and hard work. But it wasn't until they died and Ash went to Iraq, leaving me to raise four girls on a captain's pay, that I figured on goats as a way to make money.

I taught myself from books, experimenting in gallon glass jars in the kitchen, converting the old mule barn into a dairy, selling what I made at the farmers' market. Our neighbor Hannah Mullett, who taught science at the middle school, gave me a hand in the cheese room. But back then I did most everything myself.

Not like now. I had Dan now, to help with the farm, and Meg, to help with the books. Two part-time employees for wrapping and labeling, and a handful of volunteers from the 4-H club and the ag program at the community college. But I still liked working alone in the quiet creamery, only the hum of the lights and the quiet agitation of the vat pasteurizer to keep me company.

The air was moist and rich with whey. I turned out the drained curd from the perforated molds, placing the small rounds on racks. When the racks were full, I salted and dusted them.

"What's that?"

My heart gave an unwelcome flip. He stood at the creamery door, tall and lean, with a sensitive mouth and cool eyes. A good-looking man, my husband. When I was laid up in the hospital, every single woman for miles around — and some married ones, too — had been to our back door with a casserole.

"Ash."

"Yes?"

I smiled. "No, I meant . . . I'm using ash. Oak charcoal powder."

He came closer to see. "What does it do?"

Like Jo, he'd always been a good student. Valedictorian of our high school class. Doctor of divinity from Duke. *"Better with a book than a shovel,"* my daddy said. It hadn't been a compliment.

"Neutralizes the surface acid so the mold

can grow." I'd had only two years of community college before I got pregnant with Meg, but I'd read plenty since taking over the farm. I slid the rack of seasoned cheeses on to the rolling shelves. "Develops the rind."

"Interesting."

I picked up the salt shaker. "You've never been interested in the farm before, Ash. What do you want?"

"I'm going to the rehab center. I thought I'd see if Beth wants to come along."

"She's up at the house." Working on her music, I hoped. A light had gone out in my little girl, and I didn't know how to bring it back. Music, I thought, would help.

"It must be lonely for her with Amy gone," Ash observed.

I shot him a glance. He'd never been particularly interested in our daughters, either. Seemed that was changing. "Maybe. She won't talk to me."

He stepped forward, taking the other side of the rack as I transferred it to the shelves.

"Thanks," I said, surprised.

He straightened, sticking his hands in his pockets. "Must be lonely for you, too."

"They're not children anymore. It's been over three years since the girls left home. Time for all of us to move on."

He met my gaze. "Are you asking me to move out?"

I busied myself with the salt. "You can't live in that trailer forever."

"Fair enough," he said. "You've been generous, letting me stay this long."

Generous? Or stupid. I'd never had much sense where Ash was concerned. "You got someplace to go?"

"I'll find something." A pause. "I've been recommended for a clinical pastoral care position in D.C."

This was the Ash I knew. All our lives, he'd made decisions about his career without consulting me, leaving me to deal with the consequences.

I'd told him once if he left not to come back. But it still hurt when he listened.

"When do you go?" I asked, proud of my steady voice.

"They haven't made a formal offer yet," Ash said.

I feathered a fine layer of ash across the rack. "You're welcome to stay until then."

"I might not be right for the position. Or it may not be right for me." He lifted my finished rack. Slid it into its slot with precision. "Did you ever imagine being somewhere else?"

"You mean, did I think I'd be a fifty-four-year-old divorced goat farmer?" I asked wryly.

"We're not divorced." His eyes were light and clear as ice. "And I was speaking geographically."

I shrugged. "Where would I go?"

He tilted his head. "Where would you want to go?"

That was new. Him, asking.

The farm was my heritage. I'd never pictured myself living anywhere but here. But what came out of my mouth was, "The Loire Valley."

His brows raised. "France?"

I flushed, embarrassed by my dream. By my pronunciation. "Not to live. Just for a visit. The cheese cultures I use are manufactured there." I'd seen pictures, like something from a storybook, tiny farms and gilded palaces and strange, stiff, styled gardens. "I'd like to see where they come from, that's all."

"Abby . . ." He took my hands.

My phone rang in my pocket.

I pulled free. "I should get that."

I didn't recognize the number. Probably somebody selling extended car warranties or time-shares in Florida. I answered it anyway, before I made a bigger fool of myself. "Hello?"

"Abigail March?"

Definitely a robocall. "Yes?"

"This is Megan Fitzpatrick. From Cape Fear Regional? I'm sorry to tell you that your daughter Beth was brought into our emergency department this morning."

Collapsed, they told us at the hospital. A passing driver found her on the side of the road and called 911.

There was more, but I couldn't seem to process. Facts and phrases swam at me, elusive as fish in murky water. *Dehydrated. Tachycardic. Seizure.* The last one leaped out at me. Possible heat exhaustion, they said.

They wouldn't let me into the trauma room.

"I want to speak to her doctor," Ash said.

A woman in scrubs came out. I looked at her badge for her name. Forgot it a moment later.

No, I said in reply to her questions, no history of seizures. Epilepsy, no. Diabetes, no. Medications? Was she on drugs?

I shook my head.

"Not that we're aware of," Ash said, wrapping his fingers around mine. I gripped his hand, grateful for its warmth. "What's wrong with her?"

"That's what we're trying to find out," the woman said. "Her electrolytes are out of whack. Glucose in the toi— That is, her levels are very low."

"I want to see her," I said.

She gave me what I'm sure she intended as a reassuring smile. "We'll get you back there as soon as we can."

Time crawled. Meg and Jo came, along with John and Eric. Had Ash called them? The girls sat in the chairs on either side of me, almost as if they were protecting me.

"We should call Amy," Jo said.

"I'll do it," Meg said.

Ash was speaking in a low voice to Eric and John. He spent a lot of time in hospitals, of course, comforting the wounded and their families. But he wasn't there when Amy got her ear tubes. Or when Jo broke her arm. Or when Meg had her babies.

Meg looked up from her call with Amy. "Anorexic."

"What?" Jo said.

Meg's eyes were wide and troubled. "Amy thinks Beth might have anorexia."

No, I thought. And then, *Of course.*

"Should somebody tell the doctor?" Jo asked.

"I'll talk to her," Ash said. He went to the desk.

The girls glanced between us, puzzled and frightened by this reversal in our usual roles. I tried to rouse myself to reassure them, but my brain was frozen. My hands were cold.

Oh God, Beth . . .

Ash came back. "They're moving her up to a unit. They want to keep her overnight for observation."

"Is she . . . ?"

"Stable," Ash said.

"Conscious?" Meg asked.

"Is she going to be all right?" demanded Jo.

"She will be." Ash looked at me as he answered. Using his pulpit voice, sure and low. *The voice of God,* Jo once called it. I wanted — so much! — to believe in him. "We can go up and see her."

She looked so small, swaddled in a pale blue hospital gown, stark against plain white sheets. Bethie, my baby, my sensitive middle child. Her eyes were closed, her hair spread matted and stringy on the pillow. A bank of beeping, blinking, pulsing machines did the work of her depleted body, pumping her full of fluids and oxygen.

I couldn't breathe. She was so thin. She looked so young, like herself at nine or ten, like my sister, Bitsy.

Who died in the damn hospital.

Anorexic. She was starving herself. Why hadn't I known?

"You'll get better. You have to," Jo said fiercely, holding Beth's hand. "I'll make you better."

Beth didn't open her eyes.

"She needs sleep," said the nurse monitoring the machines. "We're going to have to kick some of you out."

"I'll stay with Mom," Meg said. My responsible eldest.

"You go home to your children," I told her.

"I'm not leaving you here alone."

"I can stay," Jo said.

"Momma?" Meg asked.

As if they were children again, arguing over who got to sit in the front seat or eat the last piece of pie. I wanted to send them to their rooms. But I knew that they needed to be here. "I . . ."

"Go home," Ash said. "I'll stay with your mother."

The girls looked at me.

"It's all right," I assured them.

"You'll call us," Meg said.

I nodded.

"If there's any change," Ash said.

They looked at him, surprised. Resentful.

As if he'd taken something from them. Maybe he had.

"I'm not going anywhere," Jo said.

"Dear heart." Eric touched her shoulder. "Let your parents be with Beth tonight. She will need you in the morning, yeah?"

Jo stood and flung herself into his arms.

We shared kisses and hugs before they left, Jo crying silently, Meg with her head on John's shoulder.

I sat in Jo's vacated recliner and took Beth's hand. I'd always been glad she'd inherited her hands from her father, beautiful hands, musician's hands, lean and long and elegant. I should have noticed how skinny they were. Now they were cold and unresponsive.

Hours went by, measured by her breath and the beep of the machines. I was only dimly aware of Ash, upright in the room's only other chair, a quiet, familiar presence.

The hospital staff came and went. To take her vitals, to check the equipment, to bring a dinner tray.

"Why?" I said to Ash. "She's not eating." *Starving herself,* I thought with a catch in my throat. "She's not even awake."

"I ordered it for you," Ash said.

"I'm not hungry."

He raised his eyebrows, very slightly. I

400

flushed and ate, though I couldn't have told you what it was. Hospital food.

She woke once. "Momma."

"I'm here, baby."

Her eyes met mine and flooded with tears. "I'm sorry. I'm so sorry."

"Ssh."

"I'm scared."

"It's all right. You're going to be all right," I said. An impossible promise.

"I'll make you better," Jo had said.

She slept again.

Her recovering body needed rest, the nurse said when she came at the shift change. Tomorrow there would be more tests — a bone scan, another blood panel, a psych evaluation. But for now, her heart rate had stabilized. The doctors would see us in the morning.

Beyond the windows, the sun went down. The lights dimmed. Ash sat in the hard plastic chair across from me, our daughter between us, like when she was a little girl and crawled into our bed after a nightmare.

"I failed her. Failed all of you," he said quietly. He raised his head. His eyes were wet. I couldn't remember the last time I'd seen him cry. When Jo was born?

My throat ached. "We can't fix what's past. We just have to . . ." *What?* I swallowed. "Move on as best we can."

"You've always done that," he said.

Had I? I wondered. I hadn't done my best for Beth. She hadn't come to me. But I was grateful he said it anyway.

My back was stiff. My arm cramped from being held in one position so long, but I wouldn't let go of Beth's hand. I dozed, my head on the side of the mattress.

"Abby. Abigail." My husband's voice. "Lean your chair back."

I roused, thinking I heard one of the babies cry. "The girls . . ."

"The girls are fine. You need to rest."

"Beth. What if she needs me?"

"I'll wake you."

The chair shifted under me. I clutched the arms. "Aren't you leaving?"

"No." Something warm covered me. A blanket. "I'm right here."

I believed him. Somehow, impossibly, I slept.

CHAPTER 25
AMY

The last available flight from LaGuardia to Fayetteville got in at midnight. *After* all the car rental counters closed.

I hauled my overnight bag from under my seat. I could ask one of my sisters to make the forty-five-minute drive to the airport, I thought as I walked through the deserted terminal. Or . . .

"Trey!"

He was waiting beyond the checkpoint. I flew into his arms, feeling them close around me. "Oh, Trey, I knew you'd come."

"Of course."

Of course. I closed my eyes, safe in his embrace. Even when we were fighting, Trey showed up. He didn't need to prove himself to me. I raised my head. "But how did you know my flight?"

He gave me a squeeze before he let me go. "Meg told me."

"How is she? How is Beth?"

He slipped my bag off my shoulder. "Is this all you brought?"

"I didn't really have time to pack." I fell into step beside him, fatigue warring with adrenaline and the Venti Caramel Macchiato I'd downed in Charlotte. "Beth?"

"At the hospital. I'll take you there in the morning."

I shivered.

He slanted a look down at me. "You okay?"

I nodded. "It's just . . . We've got to stop meeting like this."

A wisp of a smile touched his mouth. "My grandfather."

"And Mom." Three years ago, after Paris, Trey had come to the airport to pick me up so I could be there for my mother's back surgery. "Only this time I feel so guilty. I keep thinking if I'd been here . . . If I'd said something . . . Maybe Beth wouldn't have gone running. Or she would have gotten help."

"Hey." He put his arm around me. Gave me a little shake. "You can't blame yourself. Whatever's going on with Beth, it started more than a week ago."

I turned my face into his shoulder, absurdly comforted.

"Come on. Let's get you home," he said.

Home.

The farmhouse was dark. My parents were at the hospital, Trey said.

"Both of them? But Dad was such a dud when Mom was in the hospital."

Trey shrugged. "People can change."

"Not that much."

"Maybe it's different when it's your kid." He looked up at the darkened house. "Meg said you could spend the night at their place."

"No." I'd already texted her. "I'm not waking up her family in the middle of the night."

And if I couldn't be with Beth tonight, I wanted to stay here. At least I'd feel closer to her at home.

The floodlights flicked on. Dan came around a corner of the barn, looking like he'd just rolled out of his bunk. Checking on intruders?

"Dan." I almost hugged him, which would have embarrassed us both. "Hi. It's me."

"How's your sister?"

"I haven't seen her yet. We're going to the hospital in the morning."

"Tell her I said . . ."

What? I wondered. What could you possibly say? *Feel better. Don't kill yourself. Eat a sandwich, for God's sake.*

"The kittens miss her," he finished.

That. That's what you said. "You could tell her yourself."

He rubbed his jaw with the back of his hand. "She can have visitors?"

"I think so," I said cautiously. Unless . . . Maybe she was in the psych ward. Where did they put anorexics? If she were anorexic. "Have you talked to Mom?"

A short nod. "I'm taking care of things until she's back."

"Great. That's great," I said awkwardly. "Thanks. Really."

"Let me know if you can use a hand," Trey said.

"You any good with goats?"

"It's been a few years," Trey said evenly. "But yeah."

Because he used to do chores with Jo, I remembered.

"Appreciate it." Dan shifted his gaze to me. "Good to have you back."

"Thanks. Good to be back." I made a face. "Well. Not good, exactly. It's . . ."

"Important," Dan said.

I nodded. *Oh, Beth . . .*

Trey carried my bag into the dark, quiet

406

house. I turned on a light. The shadows scattered, but the emptiness was still there. A Beth-size hole opened in my chest.

"I can stay," Trey said into the silence.

I sagged with gratitude. "What about your grandfather?"

"He'll be fine. Dee is there if he needs anything."

"Where will you sleep?" I asked, and flushed. Stupid question. Naturally, he expected to sleep with me.

"Wherever you want." He touched my neck. "You shouldn't be alone tonight."

A little sizzle sparked from that light touch, radiating from his fingertips, spreading warmth through my body. So, okay. Maybe sex was the natural response to crisis — something about affirming life or the survival of the species.

But there was no way I was sleeping with Trey in my parents' bed. Or in the attic that used to be Jo's. Or in the twin beds I once shared with Beth.

We laid down together in Meg's old room, him stripped to his boxers, me in an old T-shirt. The mattress dipped in the middle, making us roll together. He smelled good, I thought, pillowing my head on his hard arm. His hand rubbed idle circles on my back, and in that moment, I didn't have to think. I didn't need to act. I was home. So . . . Sex. Okay. It could be a relief to feel something besides worry and grief. At least sex would be a distraction.

He stroked my hair, pushing a strand from my face to tuck behind my ear. "Go to sleep."

I almost rolled my eyes. *As if.*

"You want to shower?"

I opened bleary eyes to see Trey's face smiling at me at very close range across the pillow. The morning sun made patterns on the wall beyond his head. "You . . . I . . . Um."

He grinned. "I'll go first. Don't want you to drown in there."

He kissed my nose and got out of bed. I watched him go, his messy, dark hair, his lean, smooth back, the indent where his boxers dipped low, and my insides ran with colors like a paint box in the rain, tender shades of yellow, rose, and crimson.

It felt like we'd passed some kind of test or barrier last night, moving into fresh and unfamiliar territory. He was not only the family friend who picked me up at the airport. He was more than the childhood crush I sometimes had sex with.

Theodore James Laurence III. My Trey.

"Hey," I called softly. "Thanks for being here." Did he hear the echo of his words from his grandfather's hospital room?

He turned in the doorway, his smile lighting his dark eyes. "Always."

Always, here in Bunyan? I wondered. *Always* here for our family? Or . . . I hugged my pillow tight. Here for me. *Always.*

I heard the water turn on in the bathroom and went downstairs to make coffee.

While it brewed, I checked my phone, scrolling through likes and comments on social media, reading texts from my sisters and mother. Beth was still on an IV. She'd eaten a piece of toast for breakfast. Hard to tell from Mom's text if this was good news or not.

There were no messages, no replies, from Beth.

A long black limo slid down the drive and parked by the barn.

Colt. She must have called him. Texted him.

A wave of fury swept over me and just as quickly receded. It wasn't Colt's fault Beth was . . . Well. Sick. I'd read a bunch of stuff online. There was no one cause for an eating disorder. And no easy cure. Most of the websites suggested anorexia was the result of a combination of factors. Perfectionism.

Anxiety. Genetics. Low self-esteem. Stress.

Touring with your country superstar boyfriend? Getting thrown *off* the tour by the country superstar boyfriend? Ticked a lot of boxes.

Still, he was here. I was prepared to forgive him. Not everything. But a lot.

But it wasn't Colt who got out of the luxury car. I recognized the driver guy, Jimmy, from the wedding.

I thought about dashing upstairs for some shorts. Shrugged instead and opened the back door. "Hey."

He nodded, his gaze politely on my face. "Hi. Is your sister ready?"

I crossed my arms over the T-shirt. "Ready for what?"

"Colt's recording. He sent me to pick her up."

"Are you fucking kidding me?"

"Is there a problem?"

I narrowed my eyes. "He doesn't know?" *Beth hadn't told him.*

"Know what?"

"Beth is in the hospital."

"Shit. I'm sorry." Jimmy's face crinkled in what appeared to be genuine concern. "Is she okay?"

I shrugged. "Holding her own." *Stable,* our mother's text said.

410

"What was it, an accident?"

The weight of my sister's secret pressed on me. Colt wasn't only Beth's boyfriend. He was her boss. Jimmy's boss. If she hadn't told him . . . "I can't really say."

"But what do I tell Colt?"

I set my hands on my hips. "You tell that piece of shit he can ask her himself."

I stopped in the doorway of Beth's room on my way to the shower. My heart wobbled at the sight of her guitar, silent in a corner. Her teddy bear, waiting on her bed.

The walls still displayed her childhood posters, Hannah Montana and Harry Potter. Her books and stuffed animals were neatly lined on the shelf, frozen on the cusp of adulthood. Like Beth herself. A wave of longing for my sister swept over me.

I grabbed her bear and hugged it tight, knocking the journal on her bedside table. It fell open on the floor. *Oops.* I reached to pick it up.

I wasn't snooping.

Not really.

But I missed her so much, and the notebook was a part of her, the place where her music came from. Her childish, looped handwriting, scrawled and scratched out, danced across the lines. I recognized the words of her song, "Smooth as You." Smiling, I turned the page.

It looked different, the writing darker, as if she'd pressed into the paper. Tight, hard letters. Numbers, dug into the page. Steps. Crunches. Calories. Inches. Pounds.

My stomach quailed. This was . . . Beth? Or her illness, compulsively transcribed into a notebook. I flipped through page after page of cramped, black writing. Like graffiti on a wall, like scars cut into her skin. All this time, she was bleeding. She was killing herself, and we never knew.

I wished I'd never seen it.

CHAPTER 26
BETH

I wanted to get better. I did. I didn't want to be the person my family all worried about.

But I flinched from their concern. I could feel myself shrinking inside my hospital gown, pulling away, closing in, closing off. Like when I was fifteen and my mother took me to the gynecologist for the first time. In my head, I knew I should be there. But I felt exposed. Anxious. Violated.

I had a problem. Obviously. That didn't mean I wanted to talk about it.

I took refuge in being polite, cooperative, answering everything in my softest voice, not giving them anything they could use against me. Like the Mouse my sisters called me, small and secretive, I cowered, my heart beating rapidly inside my ribs.

As if, by being good enough, quiet enough, I could somehow escape their notice.

There was another doctor coming this

afternoon, Momma said, to talk to me.

A psychiatrist, I thought apprehensively. "Are you and Daddy going to be here?"

"If you want us," my father said.

I shook my head. *No.*

Mom sighed. "Well. I'm going to go home and change."

"I can stay," my father said.

I swallowed. "I'm okay. One of the nurses is going to help me shower, I think."

He nodded, accepting defeat.

"I'll be back in a few hours," my mother said.

"And then can I go home?"

"We'll see."

"Momma, I'm fine," I said, but the lie didn't work anymore, for either of us. "I want to go home," I amended.

"We have to wait for your test results," my father said.

My mother changed the subject. "Your sisters want to see you."

I didn't want my sisters. Their questions. Their well-meaning interference. I didn't want to see myself through their eyes.

"Tell somebody," our mother used to say. *"If someone ever bullies you or hurts you or asks you to keep a bad secret."* It was good advice to four growing girls. But what did you say when you hurt yourself? What if the

414

secret was mine?

I turned my head away. "I'm too tired."

"Even to see Jo?" my mother asked.

Jo — fierce, loving Jo — would try to fix me. It was easier to hold myself separate, inviolate, apart.

"Maybe later."

"Or Amy," Mom said. "She flew in last night."

"She didn't need to do that. I'm not dying."

My parents exchanged glances. I flushed. My seizure had scared them. It had scared me, too. For once, I couldn't view my body as something under my control.

Maybe it wouldn't be so bad to see Amy. And maybe then they would all leave me alone.

"I thought you could use some company." Amy stood in the doorway of my hospital room, my teddy bear in the crook of one arm.

I mustered a smile. "You didn't need to come all the way from New York."

"Not me." She tucked the plush toy into bed beside me. "Mr. Bear."

A rush of affection closed my throat. "Oh, Amy."

She kissed my forehead and took a seat by

the bed. "You washed your hair," she observed.

"The nurse helped." I picked at the sheet. "They don't want me to be by myself. In case of falls."

"As long as you don't slit your wrists in the shower."

A shocked giggle escaped me. "Amy, that's terrible!"

"I know."

"Anyway, I couldn't . . . I would never . . ."

"Throw up?" she asked. "Kill yourself?"

I gaped. Her words solidified in the air, taking on new weight and meaning. *I know.*

The instinct to hide, to deny, to lie, rose like panic inside me. "How?" I whispered.

She shrugged. "I see a lot of models. And . . . there's this."

She laid my notebook on the bed between us.

I couldn't breathe. Shame squeezed my lungs. My throat. She must have seen. Everything I'd been hiding, my secret, written over and over in black and white.

I know.

"I brought you something else, too."

She dug in one of the bags she carried and set another notebook on the bed, the spiral kind that children take to school. I touched the rainbow cover, tracing the glittery hearts and stars with one finger.

I opened it to the blank, lined pages. Looked up in question.

"I thought you might . . . I don't know," Amy said. "Want to make a fresh start?"

Tears blurred my eyes.

"Are you mad at me?" she asked.

I shook my head. I still couldn't speak. But my chest unclenched a little, like a fist easing open.

"Sorry about the design," she said. "It was all they had in the gift store."

I swallowed thick tears. "It's perfect."

"And so sparkly." Our eyes met. "I love you, you know."

"I love you, too."

When I reached across the bed, she took my hand. I gripped hers, hard.

"The good news is, your electrocardiogram is normal. There seems to be no permanent damage to your heart muscle." Dr. Patel (*"Call me Eileen"*) glanced at the clipboard on her lap. "Electrolytes . . . Well. I'm sure your primary care physician will want to monitor your kidney function, and they may refer you to a nephrologist — a kidney specialist — as well. The bone scan shows some density loss, especially in your wrists. But that can be reversed, if you adjust your diet. Physically, there's no reason you can't be discharged."

My mind skipped over the news about my bones to seize on her last sentence. "So I can go home."

She folded her hands, making the multiple gold rings on her fingers sparkle. "Beth, do you know why you're here in the hospital?"

My gaze dropped to the covers. Of course I knew. But the words stuck in my throat.

"Your BMI is dangerously low," she said gently. "In your health history, you indicated your last period was five months ago."

I didn't have to say anything. My secret was . . . okay, not safe. Not even much of a secret anymore. But the not-telling was as much a part of me as the not-eating. Which meant telling must be important, too.

"A fresh start . . ." Amy had said.

I couldn't force the secret past my throat. But the notebooks were still on my bed. I handed the used one to Dr. Patel.

Her hand hovered. "May I?"

Wordlessly, I nodded.

She opened it. I looked away, fidgeting with the covers.

"Ah," she said after a minute had passed. She closed the book. Waiting.

"Do you want to talk about it?" she asked at last, kindly.

No, no, no, an inner voice howled. I'd already revealed too much.

"Thank you for sharing your notebook," Dr. Patel said after another pause. "That was very brave. Mindful eating is important to recovery. I often suggest that people with eating disorders keep a food journal. Not just a record of what you eat, but how you're thinking and feeling about food."

And there it was. Here *I* was. A person with an eating disorder.

I repeated the words, testing them. Practicing. "I have an eating disorder."

And heard Dan's voice in my head. *"The first step is, you need to accept that you've got shit."*

"You smiled just then," Dr. Patel said.

"Oh." I flushed, embarrassed. "I was remembering something a friend of mine said. About how you have to accept that you have a problem before you can fix it."

"And do you want to fix it?" asked Dr. Patel.

"And then you have to accept that you can't fix your shit without help."

Something stirred inside me. Not exactly hope bursting into bloom, but a cautious unfurling — a thin green tendril of possibility.

"You know," I said slowly. "I think I do."

I didn't go home after all. Not that night. I ate my dietician-approved dinner under Mom's watchful eye, chewing and swallowing my "medicine" while my parents shared a cafeteria tray. Family meals and support were a critical part of my treatment plan, Dr. Patel said when she came back to help me talk with my parents. To tell.

Part of me — the shadow part — resented the loss of control. And yet it was a relief to yield responsibility to my parents, to be a child again. Food had dominated my life and thoughts for almost a year. There was a strange freedom in having all choice removed except the basic decision — to eat or not to eat. Anyway, the meal tray was better than a feeding tube.

At the same time, I felt uncomfortably full. Stretched. Stuffed. I needed time alone to digest. Not just the food, but the consequences of telling.

Who was I without my secret? I'd known, once. I wanted to be that girl again. To get back to the way I used to be. Happy. Healthy. Whole.

"You should go home," I told my parents after dinner. "Get some sleep."

My mother's jaw hardened in a way I knew well. "Your father can leave. I'm staying."

I didn't have the energy to fight her. But I had an unexpected ally. "Whatever you want," my father said. "We have to trust her. She knows what she needs," he told my mother.

Momma folded her lips, but I heard what she would not say. Trusting me was what got us here.

"I'll be fine," I said. Less a lie, this time, than a promise.

Eventually, she let herself be persuaded. I watched them go, sorry to be the cause of another disagreement. Yet there was something absurdly comforting about watching them leave together, my father's hand at the small of my mother's back.

My phone vibrated on the hospital tray table. Jo, again, or Colt. I let it go to voice mail, touching my distended stomach tentatively under the covers. I felt bloated. Gross.

I took a deep breath. It would take time, the dietician had warned, for my body and my brain to adjust to being fed. My thoughts jerked and rattled like a carnival ride. Obviously, I would never get to sleep.

I woke gradually, roused by a change in the

air, a smell, a sound, an awareness. Someone was in the room with me. Not an aide, I saw when I opened my eyes.

Dan was sitting in the hard plastic chair by the window, his ball cap pulled low over his forehead.

My heart lightened. "Hey."

"Hi."

Through the blinds behind him, the setting sun streaked the sky. Visiting hours must almost be over. "How long have you been here?" I asked shyly.

He rubbed his beard with his knuckles. "Awhile, I reckon. I didn't want to wake you."

He'd watched me sleep. Which could have been creepy. But instead, it felt . . . sweet. "You make a very good guardian angel," I assured him.

It was his turn to flush. He ducked his head, fishing around in the bag at his feet. "Brought you something."

I smiled. "I don't need anything." My room was full of flowers and balloons, magazines and books. A ridiculous outpouring for a two-day hospital stay. My sisters, denied the chance to visit, had overcompensated. Colt had sent fifty long-stemmed red roses with a card, *To my angel.* I wondered if he were recording without me. If Mercedes were singing my song. "I have too much to carry down to the car already," I said.

"I'll take this back with me," Dan said. "Probably breaking enough rules as it is."

He found whatever he was reaching for and set it on my bed.

A kitten. One of the calico kittens from the barn. It teetered toward me, its pink toes gripping the blanket, its tail as upright as an exclamation point.

I reached out an unsteady hand. The kitten flinched and then curled around my fingers. I scooped it up, its fur against my cheek, breathing in its lovely, musty baby smell, milk and pee and hay.

Tears flooded my eyes. "But how did you . . . Why did you . . ."

When I looked up, Dan was smiling. "They missed you," he said simply. "I couldn't bring them all."

My smile wobbled into existence.

"I'll be fine," I'd promised Momma. I don't know if she believed me.

But this time, I thought it might even be true.

CHAPTER 27
AMY

"Sisters' Night Out," Meg said contentedly as we settled into our booth at The Taproom. "We should have done this before."

"We have," Jo said.

"Not all of us. Beth and I were always too young," I said.

"Or too far away," Beth said.

"Well, it's nice." Meg smiled across the table at Beth. "Good idea."

"I can't really take credit," Beth said. "Dr. Patel suggested it as part of my homework this week."

She spent a long time with the menu, I noticed. Not in a kid-in-a-candy-store kind of way. More like a vegan at a steakhouse.

My heart hurt for her. "You okay?"

"I've got this." She smiled. "I practiced with Dr. P."

"I didn't think," Jo said remorsefully. "Is this hard for you? Going out to eat?"

"A little. But food has always been about

424

me saying no. I have to teach myself to say yes."

She was so brave.

"Good job," Meg said after Kitty had taken our orders. "To Beth."

We raised our glasses.

Her face glowed. "Progress, not perfection, Dr. Patel says."

"I'm proud of you," Jo said. "I feel guilty I didn't see what you were going through."

"Don't feel bad. For a long time, I didn't admit it to myself," Beth said. "How were you supposed to know?"

"Why didn't you say something?" Jo asked.

"Because as long as it was a secret, it was under her control," Meg said.

"Says the control freak."

Meg smiled.

"But we could have helped," Jo said.

"Or judged," I said. "We're good at that."

"You still could have told us," Jo insisted. "We love you. We're your sisters. Sisters shouldn't have secrets from one another."

Beth stared down at her place setting.

"I'm guilty, too," I blurted.

"You tried to tell us," Meg said kindly. "That night we were here with Trey."

"No, I meant . . . I have a secret, too."

Beth raised her head.

"This isn't about you," Jo said.

"I think," Beth said in her gentle way, "Amy's trying to distract you."

"Oh." Jo grinned. "Sorry."

"So, what's your secret?" Meg asked.

I took a deep breath. "I slept with Trey."

"Good for you," said Kitty Bryant, returning with a basket of hush puppies. "Anybody need a refill?"

Jo snickered. Even Beth was smiling.

"You're both adults," Meg said after Kitty had left. "And you've been together for, what? A couple weeks now."

I cleared my throat. "No. I mean, yes. I mean, before that."

"You slept with Trey before?" Beth asked.

I nodded.

"When?" Meg asked.

"In Paris." *Three years ago.* I watched my sisters do the math.

"Wow," Jo said.

"I think we need more wine," Meg said.

"I'm sorry," I said to Jo.

She waved my apology away. "Please. You were a baby."

"Twenty-two. And you're my sister. And he was your boyfriend."

Jo nibbled a hush puppy. "This was in Paris, right? After I broke up with him. So he was already my *ex*-boyfriend."

426

I blinked. "You're taking this awfully well."

"I am, aren't I?" Jo grinned. "Which tells you everything you need to know about our relationship. Trey is like a brother to me. Plus, I'm crazy about Eric."

"Is that why you stayed away so long?" Meg asked. "Because you felt . . ." She paused tactfully.

I squirmed. "Guilty. Yes. Well, that's partly the reason."

"I figured you just wanted to get the hell out of Bunyan," Jo said.

"Not really. I mean, high school sucked, but it's over. I've moved on."

"It's not over if you're letting what happened then stop you from doing what you want now," Beth said.

Jo popped another hush puppy. "Somebody's been talking to her therapist."

"What happened in high school?" Meg wanted to know.

I hesitated. But . . . *Sisters shouldn't have secrets from one another.* "I went to a sleepover at Jenny Snow's, okay? She took some pictures. And the next thing I know, her brother is showing my tits around school."

"That little shit weasel," Jo said. "I'll put him in a book and kill him. Jenny, too."

I smiled at her gratefully. "It doesn't matter anymore." And it didn't, I realized with some surprise.

"Then why did you leave?" Beth asked.

"I guess . . . I wanted to be a success. To prove I could make it on my own."

"And now that you have, you can come home," Jo said. We all looked at her. She shrugged. "That's how it worked for me."

"I'm not you."

"Well, duh."

"So, what now?" Meg asked. "Are you going to stay in Bunyan?"

I'd never loved my sisters, or valued them, more than at this moment, when we were all together. When we had almost lost Beth. My heart brimmed. I wanted this, I realized. Wanted them around me, part of my life. "I might. I mean, I have this great location all lined up."

Beth smiled. "And this great guy."

A blush burned my cheeks. "That's up to him."

"I call bullshit," Jo said.

"You're a March," Meg reminded me. "You want something, you go get it."

"We believe in you," Jo said.

"We want you to be happy," Beth said.

Not simply successful. *Happy.*

I tried to picture what that would look like. My sisters around the table, just like this, and a little shop in the town where I grew up, down the street from my father's old church and my brother-in-law's new restaurant. All of it the same and not the same, at once fresh and familiar — Sunday dinners at the farm and birthday parties with my niece and nephews and my mother coming in from the barn. And me, here, part of it all.

And Trey.

My heart swelled. My eyes were wet with tears. I laughed. "Fine. What the hell." I was going to do it, I thought in wonder. I was going to go for it. I raised my wineglass. "To Bunyan!"

"To Baggage," Meg said.

Jo smiled. "To sisters."

Beth met my eyes. "To a fresh start," she said softly.

I didn't want to wait another minute.

Two hours later, after dropping off Beth at the farmhouse, I stood on the front porch of the Laurence house, my heart knocking against my ribs.

Trey opened the door, his unbuttoned shirt over a pair of jeans, as if he'd thrown it on to answer the door. His chest . . . That was some chest. All that beautiful golden skin, that dusting of dark hair . . .

"Hi. Everything all right?"

429

I jerked my gaze to his face. Right. It was almost ten o'clock. The way our families' luck was running, he must be expecting another trip to the emergency room.

I nodded vigorously. "Everything's fine. Good. Great, in fact."

His mouth pulled up at one corner. "I guess you had a good time with your sisters."

"I'm not drunk," I blurted. Not even tipsy. But I was buoyant with my decision, eager to share my love, my life, my family with him. "Is your grandfather . . . ?"

"In bed. Come in." He drew me across the threshold, and then we were kissing, hard, sweet, wonderful kisses, my hands inside his shirt, his fingers in my hair.

"Trey." I drew back, giddy with lust and excitement. "I have to tell you . . ."

He tugged me toward the library. "In here."

"Miss Dee . . . ?"

"Watching *The Great British Baking Show* in her room."

So we were alone. More or less. The rush of heat swept me to my toes. I wrapped my arms around his neck. "I have something to tell you," I said between kisses.

His mouth, his hot, beautiful mouth, trailed down my throat. "You're not wearing underwear?"

I giggled. "No. I'm staying."

"Great. Let's go upstairs."

I tugged on his thick, silky hair. "Listen to me. I'm staying in Bunyan. I want the lease on the shop."

He raised his head, an arrested expression in his dark, dark eyes. "Seriously?"

I nodded, brimming with anticipation, bubbling over with plans.

"Amy, that's great," he said, which was apparently all the urging I needed to run off at the mouth.

". . . still have to talk to Flo," I said, and then something about needing to get out of my lease in New York and something else about how long renovations would take and how I couldn't afford to fall behind on orders during the transition. Chattering. Gushing. *Gah.*

And Trey, the blessed boy, listened and nodded, making encouraging noises and doing nothing to stem the flow.

At last, I pulled myself together, leaning back in his arms. "And what about you?"

He tucked a strand of hair back from my face. "What about me?"

"What are your plans?"

"I don't have any."

"You said you did. When your grandfather

was in the hospital."

"That's right, I did." He smiled into my eyes. "And here we are. You can be my plan."

My heart swelled. It was everything I'd ever wanted. It had to be enough. But my brain was stuck on auto loop. I kept hearing his words in Paris, after Jo broke up with him.

"Jo was the plan . . . There is no plan."

"I'm a person," I said. "Not a plan."

"Well, obviously."

"I'm not a substitute for whatever else is missing from your life."

He drew back. "Something's bugging you. What am I missing?"

My heart panicked. *Shut up, shut up, shut up.*

"Trey, I'm not staying in Bunyan to be your trophy" — wife, *don't say* wife — "girlfriend. But I have to know. Do you love me?"

"Of course I love you," he said promptly, and then spoiled it. "I love your whole family."

"But do you love me more than you loved Jo?"

He half laughed. "It's not a contest."

"That's not an answer."

He met my eyes. His face sobered. "I love you differently."

432

"That's pathetic."

His brows flicked together. "I'm sorry you think so. It's the best I can do."

I swallowed. "I don't believe you."

"Amy. My feelings for Jo . . . They're in the past."

"Then why don't you let them go?"

"You're the one who keeps bringing them up!"

I stared at him, my eyes leaking and my face like stone.

"My relationship with Jo is part of me. Part of who I was. Before I was a disappointment to everybody."

He was breaking my heart. "Then you're selling us both short," I said. "Trey, I love you. Not the boy you used to be, but the man you could be now. I'm ready to make a life with you."

Well, shit. My hand flew over my mouth. I hadn't meant to say that.

He raised his eyebrows. "It's a little soon for that, isn't it?"

"We've known each other fifteen years."

"And you've been home a week."

"Almost two months."

"And then you left," he shot back. "How long before you leave again?"

I stared at him, realization dawning. "This isn't even about me, is it? It's about every-

433

body else who's ever left you."

He glared. "That's stupid."

"Yes, it is." I was suddenly, gloriously, furious. "You know what? Forget the lease."

"But the location's perfect for you."

I tossed my head. "How do I know? Maybe something better will come along. I wouldn't want to take a chance and lose out."

"Amy, be reasonable. You can't give up something you want because you're afraid of a little risk."

"Nope. No way. It's too big a commitment."

He held my gaze. The air charged between us. He sighed, running a hand through his hair. "Okay, I see what you're trying to do here. But, Amy . . ."

"Screw you, Trey. I deserve better than to be your plan B. I deserve everything. And if you won't give it to me, I'll be fine without you."

His jaw set. "So I was right. You are leaving."

"Wrong. Again. You don't want to be my lover? Fine. But I'm not letting you wriggle out of being my landlord."

CHAPTER 28
ABBY

Mothers don't sleep, the saying goes. We just worry with our eyes closed.

For years, I lay alert for the cry, the cough, the footsteps coming up the stairs after curfew. The flush of the toilet. The phone call in the middle of the night.

Old habits are hard to break.

"Mom?" A whisper.

I stirred. Amy stood in the doorway of my room, her hair haloed in the light from the hall.

"What is it, baby?" What was she doing home? I'd reckoned she'd spend the night with Trey.

"Are you awake?"

I bit down on a smile. *I am now.* I raised on one elbow. "Come in. What's up?"

She perched on the edge of my bed, the way she used to when she'd come into my room to beg a ride into town or to tattle on her sisters. "I've decided to move my business to Bunyan."

"Beth told me." Not the best answer, I thought as soon as the words were out of my mouth. It was Amy's news. Maybe she'd wanted to share it herself. "That's wonderful."

"Are you . . . disappointed in me?"

"Of course not. Why would you even think that?"

"You always told us to follow our dreams."

"Because I want you to be happy. I can't be sorry if that means you're moving home." But something was wrong.

"I have to go back to New York first. Not to stay," Amy added. "But I can't expect Flo and my delivery guy to fill all the orders themselves. I figure I can hire a contractor here to rough the space out, and then I'll be back in a couple weeks. In time for the twins' birthday."

"A contractor?"

"I'm signing a lease for the old shoe store."

"So you've talked to Trey."

She nodded, her eyes stormy.

"And . . . ?"

"And he offered me a break on the rent." Her face crumpled. "He doesn't love me, Mom."

"I'm sure he does."

"Not enough." Her blue eyes welled. "Not

as much as I love him." She burst into tears, flinging herself onto the pillows.

My poor baby. I stared down at her bright blond head, my heart aching for her. I'd always been better with my hands than with words, better at bandaging scrapes than bruised feelings. I stroked her hair. "Then he's not as smart as I thought he was."

"It's not his fault," Amy said. Defending him, the way I used to defend her father.

Maybe not, any more than it was Ash's fault. In every relationship, somebody loved and somebody was loved, my mother used to say. Love was rarely equal.

But that didn't make it hurt any less.

Amy cried in big, wet, ugly sobs, like a child. I missed those days when I could fix her problems with a kiss and a cookie. Or at least make her forget them. I patted her shoulder.

Beth hovered in the hall, drawn by the noise. "Is she okay?"

"I'm fine," Amy wailed. She sat up abruptly, tears streaking her cheeks. With her red eyes and swollen face, she looked about five years old. "My heart's broken, but I'll get over it."

Beth handed her the tissue box from the bathroom.

"Thanks." She blew her nose.

"Trey will miss you," Beth said. "Maybe when you get back . . ."

Amy's face hardened, suddenly adult. "He's had three years," she said. "Three years since Jo broke up with him and fell in love and had a baby and got married to somebody else. If he was going to miss me — if he really wanted me — he's had plenty of time to do something about it. I'm not waiting around for him anymore."

A lump formed in my throat. "That's my girl. I'm proud of you."

"Mommy, can I sleep with you tonight?" Amy asked.

Mommy. The word ripped my heart. That hadn't been my name in a long time.

"Me, too," Beth said.

I scooted over in bed. Threw back the covers. "Get your pillows."

Love is letting go, they say. But sometimes it was sweet to hold them tight. To be Mommy, at least a little while longer.

Three days later, I took Amy to the airport.

When I got home, Ash was sitting on the front porch steps. He stood politely as I got out of the car, almost as if he were waiting for me.

"I suppose you're leaving next," I said.

He raised his eyebrows. "I just got back."

He was wearing what I thought of as his hospital visitation clothes — pressed khakis and a button-down shirt with his stole neatly rolled and stowed in the breast pocket. "I meant, for D.C. Have you been offered that job yet?"

"Yes. I'd be providing support to the staff as well as veterans and their families. The salary is generous. And the benefits, obviously, are very good."

That was that, then. I was happy for him. Of course I was. I didn't want him living the rest of his life in a trailer, struggling to raise funds for his storefront ministry. It was time he moved on. Time we both moved on. "Congratulations. I'm sure you'll do a wonderful job."

"I didn't give them an answer. I told them I had to talk to you."

That was a first. "It's not my decision."

"You're my wife."

"Ash . . ." My mother's crepe myrtle were all in bloom, clusters of pink flowers framing the front porch. "You know I can't leave the farm."

"Because of the girls."

"Not only the girls. But Amy is coming home. And Beth needs me. The grandkids are here. My life is here."

He studied me with those cool, light eyes.

Nodded once. "Then so is mine."

I was shaken. "We're not together any-more. You should do what's right for you."

"I am your husband," he said. "You told me once that love is not enough. But love isn't only a feeling, Abby. It's action. It's time — past time — for me to act like a husband. Your husband. Love does not insist on its own way, but bears all things, believes all things." He smiled ruefully. "Hopes all things."

I crossed my arms, as if I could keep my heart inside. "You're quoting again."

"First Corinthians." His gaze met mine. "From our wedding day."

My breath caught. "I remember." I remembered the rest, too: *Endures all things* was part of it. And *Love never ends*. "But Ash . . . what will you *do*?"

He put his hands in his pockets. "I thought I'd go up to D.C. and talk to the folks there about other options. There's a lot of need in these rural counties for clinical pastoral care, especially with all the bases around. I imagine there would be travel involved. Fay-etteville. Goldsboro. Jacksonville. But I would hope to be quartered close to home."

"This isn't your home anymore."

"Wherever you are has always been home to me."

440

My heart cracked. I looked down at the grass, starred with fallen flowers. "I don't know what to say."

"Say you'll come with me."

I was skeptical. "To D.C."

"Only for a few days."

"Ash, I haven't taken a day off in twenty years. I can't drop everything because you want me to tag along to a meeting."

"We can work around your schedule. And the trip would be for you, too."

"What are you talking about?"

"There's a place there. Hillwood. It's a big house with a bigger garden and a really large collection of eighteenth-century French art and furniture. It's not the Loire Valley," he said stiffly. "But I thought you might . . . like it. It's only three days."

I gaped. He had *listened.* He was trying.

I couldn't remember the last time Ash had given me a gift I hadn't picked out for myself. Something I hadn't asked for or shopped for. Something I didn't need. Didn't even know I wanted.

But oh, how I wanted this. Wanted to hope again.

Which made me a fool, I reckoned. "A trip isn't going to fix us, Ash."

"I know."

I snorted. "You could at least try arguing

441

with me."

He smiled a little. "Do you want me to?"

"Maybe," I admitted. "Maybe if we'd argued more, we'd still be together. Maybe if I'd told you what I wanted . . ."

"You tried. I didn't listen."

Denial hadn't worked. Maybe it was time for honesty. "You were too focused on what you felt called to do. And I was too busy picking up the pieces."

He regarded me for a long moment. "What *do* you want, Abby?"

"I want you to go to counseling."

"With you." It wasn't a question.

I stiffened. *I* wasn't the one who needed help dealing with my emotions. Or maybe I didn't want to accept responsibility for my part in what had gone wrong. I nodded.

"All right," he said slowly.

My chest lightened, a rush of buoyancy like . . . Well. Like hope. "And I want to go with you to D.C.," I said.

CHAPTER 29
BETH

Jo took me to the beach. Because, she said, the ocean makes everything better.

I hadn't been to the beach in years. I really didn't want my sister — or anybody — to see me in a bathing suit. But Jo hadn't given up on the idea of fixing me. She needed my help with Robbie, she said, and Alec was bored, and Eric was busy with the restaurant.

Besides, I was practicing saying yes.

So we went, a day trip on a Tuesday, when it wouldn't interfere with my three-times-a-week outpatient therapy. Jo, her boys, and me.

Alec lowered his window as we crossed the bridge, letting in a warm blast of salt air and car exhaust. A white crane hunted the weeds below. My heart lifted, soaring like a gull over the blazing water.

Jo turned right onto the island, past shops painted passion fruit pink and Bahama blue, past the boardwalk with its rickety rides and racks of tie-dyed shirts. The scent of coconut sunscreen and fried doughnuts wafted through the car windows. The sidewalks were crowded with boys in board shorts and ball caps and girls with flat stomachs in tiny string bikinis.

I shrank inside my sweatshirt, dreading their bright, judgmental eyes. It was July, the height of the season, when most rentals would be full and the beaches would be crowded.

But Jo kept driving, past the condos, down a long flat road where luxury vacation homes stood out from the rows of sun-bleached bungalows like flamingos in a line of gulls. She parked at a quiet access near the island's point, where beach grass waved and orange sea oats bloomed. We carried the cooler, the blankets, the baby tent, and a basket of sand toys along a splintery walkway over the dunes, trudging across the soft, shifting sand to an unspoiled stretch of beach.

"How about here?" Alec said.

Here was quiet. No one else was here except a few fishermen casting lines into the surf. A woman read in a chair, her feet in the water. A family on vacation crowded into the scant shade of an umbrella.

Something inside me relaxed. "Here is good."

Alec set up the baby tent. I slathered Robbie in sunscreen while Jo set out our lunch. As supervised meals go, it was very nice. Alec ate three peanut butter and jelly sandwiches. I managed half, seasoned with sand and lotion, and thirty-four grapes and a bite of banana.

It was still an effort to eat.

After lunch, I took a walk, resisting the urge to repeat my morning's three-mile run. Reminding myself to breathe, to be, to feel the sand between my toes. When I got back, I stripped off my sweatpants to sit with Jo and Robbie at the water's edge, the baby in a diaper and a sunhat, Jo in a one-piece suit. Her hair was falling down and the suit was bunching up and she looked totally happy, comfortable in her shape. Her body. I felt a twinge of envy. Alec glided his skimboard along a long flat stretch of beach, picking it up, dripping, and throwing it down again.

Everything was bright and flat and clear, the shadows shortened by the noonday sun. Alec's body cut the air like a sail, the shallows curling in his wake. The waves rolled out and whispered in. Robbie kicked his pink toes in the water, sending droplets sparkling. My legs, sticking out beside Jo's, looked very pale. My knees were big and knobby. Were my thighs fatter than two weeks ago?

"You're getting better," Jo said suddenly. "I know you are."

I grasped a handful of wet sand, letting it trickle through my fingers. "I want to. Get better, I mean. I'm trying."

She turned her head and looked at me. "What's it like?"

I stared out at the curving blue horizon, avoiding her eyes. "I have this noise in my head all the time. Like another person living in my brain. Every day I lost a little of myself. I'm still not sure I'll ever get it back. It's like the tide, Jo, when it turns — it goes slowly, but it can't be stopped."

A sound escaped her. She pressed a hand to her mouth, her eyes brimming. I put my arm around her.

She leaned her head against my shoulder. "Let's build a sand castle."

"What?"

"The way we used to. Remember?"

A smile started, deep inside. "I remember."

We scooped and shoveled, finding a rhythm, digging a pool just beyond the reach of the water. We piled the sand high, dredging gloppy handfuls to create spires and towers. Robbie patted the sand with starfish hands and gouged it with his shovel. Occasionally the towers came down, slumping with their own weight or smashed by Robbie's feet. It didn't matter. We shored them up and built again. Alec saw what we were doing and came to help, abandoning his board and teenage dignity to deepen the moat, diverting the water.

A wave ran up the beach, churning the pool, leaving behind a line of treasures in the sand. Specks of shells. Ribbons of seaweed. A broken feather.

"Tide's coming in," he said.

Another surge, threatening the foundations. Our castle would never survive. But the cycle would go on between the sand and the restless sea, storm and tides constantly taking away and replenishing the beach.

The ocean makes everything better.

I picked up the feather and stuck it on top of the tallest spire.

When we trooped to the car at the end of the day, sticky and sandy and sunburnt, I looked back over my shoulder. Down by the line of water, the brave white feather still fluttered in the breeze.

A black limo was parked in the shadow of the barn. A man was sitting on the porch

447

swing, like the star of a country music video. My heart bumped.

Jo peered through the windshield. "Is that . . . ?"

"Colt." I got out of the car. "Hi. What are you doing here?"

He sauntered down the front porch steps. "Waiting for you. For the last two hours." He leaned forward. His warm mouth pressed mine. "Good thing you're worth it."

"You should have texted."

"I wanted to surprise you." He drew back, smiling. "You look great."

I touched my face, immediately conscious of my sunburned nose, my salt-crusted hair.

Jimmy appeared from the limo with an armload of red and gold flowers like a pageant queen's bouquet. He nodded to Jo as she got out of her car. "Hey."

"Hi."

Colt ignored them both, taking the flowers to give to me. "These are for you."

I took them, overwhelmed. Bewildered. "Thank you."

His blue eyes twinkled. "Don't thank me yet. I got you something else, too."

Not a kitten.

"I thought you were on tour," I said.

"Got a break. Had to see my best girl." He started to take me in his arms, but the bouquet was between us. "Jimmy," Colt said without turning his head.

"On it." Jimmy relieved me of the flowers, setting them on the polished black hood of the limo.

Colt took my hands in both of his. I stiffened, aware of our audience.

"What are you doing?" Jo asked.

But she was talking to Jimmy, who had raised his phone. Alec opened his car door and was hanging over the window, watching us.

"How . . . How is Mercedes?" I asked.

Colt shrugged. "She's good. Says hey."

"That was nice of her. How did the recording go?"

"I've been listening to the tracks. Three damn days in the studio, and it still wasn't as good as your demo." His grip tightened on mine. "The song isn't the same without you, angel. Nobody's got what we've got. We're magic together, baby. I came to get you back."

Panic choked me. "I can't go back, Colt. I'm not ready."

"I know I didn't give you what you need. But I need you. I shouldn't have put this off so long."

"Put off what?" Jo asked.

"You never would have got sick if I'd done

this six months ago. But I'm ready to do it now. For better or for worse, just like in the song. We'll get ourselves married, lay down the new album, and be back on tour in the spring. You'll see. You'll be fine. Everything's gonna be great."

"Colt, I can't go anywhere. I'm in a program."

His gaze swept over me. "Getting a little beach therapy?"

I flushed. "A counseling program. For people with eating disorders."

"You mean, like rehab."

"Sort of."

"Okay. So, you see a shrink for a couple months. Whatever you want. Whatever you need. You want to go to Hawaii for the honeymoon, that's fine with me."

Jo folded her arms. "She hasn't said yes, asshole."

He glanced over my shoulder. "You're the sister, right? The one who got married. I sang at your wedding. Six million hits on YouTube."

I wanted to sink with humiliation. My knees were shaking. "Colt . . ."

"It's all good, angel."

"You're not listening to her," Jo said.

He frowned at her. "Excuse me, you're interrupting a private moment."

"Dude," Alec said. "You're live-streaming this whole thing."

"Not streaming," Jimmy said from behind his phone. "Recording."

Ignoring them, Colt lowered himself to one knee. Right there on the gravel drive. His golden hair gleamed. He reached in his pocket. "Angel, make me the happiest man in the world." And oh, golly, that was a ring box in his hand. He opened it, and an enormous diamond flashed in the sun.

"Holy crap," Jo said.

"Gonna have to edit that out," Alec said.

"Marry me," Colt said.

My heart crowded into my throat.

Say yes, urged a voice like Dr. P.'s. Wasn't that what I was supposed to learn? To say *yes* to eating and to living. *Yes* to music and to love.

I looked down into Colt's blue eyes. He was handsome. Smiling. Sincere. Confident of my answer.

Maybe even . . . *Yes* to myself. *Yes* to *my* dreams.

Gently, I tugged my hands free and took a step back. "No."

CHAPTER 30
AMY

"You did a good job," our mother said, looking around the remodeled storefront.

Jo rolled her eyes. "Way to overwhelm her with the compliments, Ma." Our mother laughed.

Beth smiled and put an arm around my waist. I hugged her back, feeling her light, sharp bones, the slight padding of muscle on her shoulders. Had she put on weight while I was gone?

"The renovation looks amazing," Meg said.

"I hired Eric's contractor," I said. The guy who did the dining room at Oak Hill, a vet who also worked for Laurence Properties and was recommended by my father. I was back in Bunyan, where everybody knew everybody else's business. It worked for me.

"Well, then, he did a good job," our mother said.

I smiled. "Thanks, Mom."

The old Shoe Box had been transformed, stripped to its original bones. The ugly blue carpet was gone, exposing newly sanded hardwood floors. The natural light from the plate glass windows revealed the tin ceilings and exposed brick walls, lightly whitewashed and daubed now with color.

My worktable occupied pride of place in the center of the store, separating the industrial racks, bolts, and bins in back from the retail space in front, so I could see the entrance and the customers (*please, God, let there be customers*) could watch the bags being assembled as they browsed.

The only thing missing from my dream store was the sign over the door in the shape of a handbag, with my logo, Baggage.

The sign, and Trey.

Yearning stabbed me. I missed him so much — the laughter lurking in his eyes, his enthusiasm, his generosity, his kindness. His belief in me.

"I'll be fine without you," I'd said.

But I hadn't expected him to drop so completely out of my life. So much was changing. Stupidly, I'd expected him to somehow still be there.

"I haven't heard from Trey lately," I'd remarked to my sisters when I got in two days ago. Like, not a word. No call, no text, no e-mail. Not even to ask how work was progressing on the store.

Meg and Jo had exchanged glances, completely unfooled by my casual tone.

"He's been away," Meg said kindly.

I gaped. "Where?"

"Florida?" Her tone made it a question.

Jo nodded. "To see his grandmother, he said. I thought you knew. He said it was your idea."

My heart thunked. Because . . . Obviously, I was glad he had listened to me. I was happy he was reconnecting with his family. It was a big deal, a big step, news worth sharing. Just . . . not with me. He hadn't told me.

His silence throbbed like a splinter, painful and impossible to ignore.

"He said he'd be back for the twins' birthday," Meg offered.

So there was that.

And there was Baggage.

For the past three weeks I'd been in New York, working sixteen- and eighteen-hour days to fill orders and build enough inventory to meet demand during my move. I contacted vendors and suppliers, went out to lunch with the Manhattan boutique buyer who gave me my first chance, and took Flo out for a long, martini-filled thank-you dinner at Gusto.

And I walked. In Central Park. Down Fifth Avenue. Along Canal Street with its makeshift stalls selling knickknacks and knockoffs to tourists.

New York would not miss me.

But there was a part of me that would miss New York. That would always be grateful to the city for the chance to prove myself.

"And now that you have, you can come home," Jo had said.

I didn't need to run away to find myself anymore. I knew who I was. For better or for worse, I was always and forever one of the March girls. Not the pretty one or the smart one, the talented one or the spoiled one, although a little of all those things was in me. I was myself, Amy Curtis March, and I was home where I belonged.

Jo ripped open a carton. "Where do you want these?"

Right. We were supposed to be unpacking. "The mahogany china cabinet in front." A gift from Phee, along with a set of cherry bookshelves, an oak farm table, and two large antique cupboards.

Jo began to stack sample bags randomly on a shelf.

"I'll do that," Meg said, rescuing my display.

"Where's the rest of your stuff?" Jo asked.

"This is it." My precious sewing machine had traveled with me in the car.

"Your furniture? Your clothes?"

"I didn't have much furniture to start with. I gave away most of my things." Or threw them away. "I'm living at the farm now." To save money, until I could find a place in town.

"Everybody's moving back home," Beth said contentedly.

"Including Dad," Jo said.

"Mom can use the help," Meg said.

Jo grinned. "I can see Amy now, mucking stalls in her Louboutins."

I stuck out my tongue.

"Actually, I could use all of your help for a few days," our mother said. "Later this month."

Meg frowned. "Are you all right?"

"I'm fine." Mom busied herself breaking down a carton. "I might be going away for a few days, that's all. Dan can handle most of the work, but it would be nice if you girls could pitch in."

"Where are you going?" Jo asked.

"To D.C."

I stopped sorting tools. "You're taking a vacation?"

"By yourself?" Meg asked.

Our mother's face turned pink. "I'm going with your father. We're visiting some gardens, and he's taking me to a French restaurant."

Meg and Jo exchanged glances.

"I thought you were angry at him," Jo said.

"I've been angry nearly every day of my life. But I didn't admit it for a long time. Anger doesn't help anybody unless you use it to make a change."

"You did," I said. "You kicked him out."

Our mother smiled wryly. "That was a change, all right."

"Dad's changed, too," Beth said.

"He's trying. Going to counseling," our mother said. "We both are."

Beth's thin face transformed in a smile. "Maybe they'll give us the family rate."

Jo snorted.

"At least Dad's upping his game," I said.

"Only if Mom really wants to go to D.C.," Jo said.

Our mother laughed. "Actually, I want to go to France. But a French restaurant in D.C. is a very nice start."

"It shows he's listening," Meg said.

Beth nodded. "It's the thought that counts."

"Unless diamonds are involved," I said.

"Colt gave Beth a diamond," Jo said. "She

turned him down."

"Good. He's an asshole."

"Go, Beth."

"He isn't . . . It wasn't . . ." Beth blushed. "I didn't need some grand gesture. The flowers, the ring, the proposal . . . It was all about him. It wasn't about me."

My throat knotted. Trey was good at gestures — champagne, fireworks, first-class tickets, rides from the airport. Plus, he'd offered me a break on the rent. Maybe Mom was right. He was trying. Maybe that was enough.

I love you differently.

And maybe not.

"I knew Eric loved me when he gave me a cookbook and wrote *Tell your story* inside," Jo said.

"John took me to the beach where we had our first date," Meg said.

"Dan gave Beth a kitten," I said.

"That's adorable," Jo said.

"Until it starts sharpening its claws on the furniture," our mother said.

I nudged her. "Come on. You know you love Patches."

"But how do you feel about Dan?" Meg asked Beth.

A shadow fell across our sister's face. "I need to get better."

458

Which was no answer. Or the only answer. Beth needed to focus on herself now. Self-care first. Survival first.

"Not every road leads to romance," our mother said.

"Beth's on her own journey," Jo said. "She doesn't need a sidekick."

"Except us." I gave her a hug.

Beth squeezed me back, her eyes shiny. Her arms were skinny and frail. "I still have a long way to go."

For a minute I was afraid.

"You're not alone," Meg said. "Whatever happens, we have each other."

The bells over the door jangled. I turned as a woman entered the shop with a little girl around Daisy's age. Recognition pricked me. Did I know her?

I smiled politely. "I'm sorry, we're closed. I hope you'll come back next week."

"Hi, Jenny," Meg said.

The woman's glance darted to my sister. "Hey, Meg."

Jenny. I narrowed my eyes. Jenny Snow, Queen of the Mean Girls, was in my shop.

"What do you want?" I asked, earning a sharp look from Momma.

"I saw your sign. In the window?"

HELP WANTED.

"Yes?" I asked. Not encouraging. Hey,

459

karma was a bitch.

Her fingers twisted the strap of her bag. "So, are you hiring?"

"Do you have any sewing experience?"

"No." She raised her chin. "But I've worked retail."

My gaze traveled over her ordinary bag, her cheap shoes. I waited for the rush of mean satisfaction before I told her to get the hell out of Baggage. And felt . . . nothing.

The little girl at her side played with the bright tags hanging from the display.

I sighed. It had taken me a while to get here, but I knew something about behaving badly because you were jealous and insecure and desperate for attention. I wasn't that girl anymore.

Maybe Jenny wasn't, either.

"Let me get you an application," I said.

After she left, Jo said, "I thought you didn't like her."

I shrugged. "Back in high school. I'm older now."

"Wiser," Momma said with a glint of approval.

"Maybe."

"Kinder," Beth said.

I shot her a grateful smile.

"Jenny's had a tough time since her divorce," Meg said.

"She's a hard worker. It's not easy, raising a child on your own," our mother said.

Jenny was divorced? With a child. But she was only my age. I watched her and her daughter walk down the street.

A white van pulled up to the curb outside.

"You expecting workers back today?" Jo asked.

"No . . . It's probably a delivery." I'd ordered new storage bins.

My sisters joined me at the window. Like we were kids waiting for the ice cream truck. Or teenagers, watching for Trey to ride over on his bike.

"Maybe it's flowers," Meg said. "To celebrate your opening."

But no, I could read the writing on the side now. COOPER SIGNS.

"It's your store sign!" Beth said.

"It can't be." Two weeks, George Cooper had told me when I approved the proof.

He got out and walked around to the back of the van. My heart fluttered in anticipation. But what else could it be?

A big, black pickup parked behind him. His crew. The driver's door swung open. Work boots, jeans, wild dark hair . . .

It was Trey.

My heart went from flutter to full-on

pound. He lingered a moment on the sidewalk, talking with George, and then they both disappeared behind the van's rear door.

"I'll be right back."

"I'll come with you," Jo said.

Beth bit her lip. "Oh, I don't think . . ."

"She's got this," our mother said.

"I was only —"

"Not now, Jo," Meg said.

"Oh," Jo said. "Gotcha. Okay."

But I was already out the door.

Summer rose from the sidewalk in shimmers of heat. Sunlight flashed from windshields and painted the street in bright contrasts. I stepped into the shadow of the van, blinking to adjust my eyes.

Trey and George Cooper stood between the open van doors, carrying a large hanging sign shaped like a handbag between them. BAGGAGE, the sign announced in jaunty letters. And below that, OWN IT.

"Oh." Tears sprang to my eyes. I pressed my hands to my mouth. "It's perfect."

George grinned. "Glad you like it."

They took two steps up the curb and leaned the sign against the building so I could take a better look.

"I love it," I gushed. "I thought it wouldn't be ready for at least another week. Thank you!" I hugged him.

"Well, now." George patted me in an avuncular sort of way. "Mr. Laurence told me how important the job was to you."

My gaze flew to Trey on the sidewalk. His eyes were dark on mine. "Thank you!" And then, of course, I had to hug him, too. It would be too awkward if I didn't.

So I did. He wrapped me up, pulling me against him. Yearning washed through me. I closed my eyes, absorbing his heat, all his lean and lovely angles, breathing in his familiar smell, bergamot and cotton. My fingers clutched his shirt. His arms tightened around me. It almost hurt, being held this close and yet being separate. Not knowing how he felt or if he could give me what I asked him for.

But he was here. I didn't want to let him go.

George cleared his throat. "When you all are done there, I could use a hand with this sign."

Right. I took a step back. Pulled myself together. I nodded toward the pickup. "I see you took my advice about the truck."

"Country girls go for tractors," I'd told him. *"And pickup trucks."*

Laughter leaped in his eyes. "Are you a country girl now?"

463

I tossed my head. "I moved down here, didn't I?"

His smile warmed me to my toes. "So you did."

"Want to come in when you're done?" I asked. "I'll give you the tour."

He hesitated. "Actually, I have a meeting."

"Oh." A little warmth leaked away. I'd imagined the sign was, well, a *sign.* But Trey was always generous.

"Maybe later," he said.

"Okay."

"I'm getting a bid from a contractor on the old tobacco warehouse. We're looking to turn it into an enclosed space for the farmers' market."

"Trey, that's wonderful!"

He shrugged. "I'm not the builder. I'm just the money guy."

"And the idea man," I guessed.

He glanced away. "I was thinking about what you said. How I needed a plan. I don't have any real talent or passion like you and your sisters. But I have connections. Or Granddad does. This development is something that could be good for the town. The least I can do is see it through."

I jammed my hands on my hips. "Don't you dare talk about yourself that way. You have *vision,* Trey. You believe in people. You help them realize their dreams. The way you did for me. I think it's amazing. You're amazing."

He looked back into my eyes. "I'm just trying to make myself into the man you said I could be. The one who can be worthy of you."

Oh, Trey. You are. You are everything. Tears stung my eyes. I opened my mouth, but no words came out.

Anyway, George was watching. And my sisters. And our mom.

Trey smiled crookedly. "I should give George a hand. I'll see you at the birthday party."

CHAPTER 31
BETH
***

Patches stalked a trailing balloon ribbon across the porch. I tied it up out of the way before the kitten pounced and choked on it.

We were decorating for the twins' birthday party at the farm. Red, yellow, and blue balloons floated from the mailbox and picnic tables. "No theme," Meg had stated somewhat apologetically. "I just want everybody to have fun."

But Amy, being Amy, had transformed leftover paint and moving boxes into a cardboard carnival. Pop-up playhouses identified the plastic pool turned fishing hole and the face painting station. Colorful signs pointed the way to the petting zoo at the baby goat enclosure, the scavenger hunt in the hay, and the boat rides down at the dock.

"Everything looks amazing," I said.

Amy straightened, stretching her back. "Thanks for helping."

"I'd rather be here than in the kitchen."

She shot me a quick look. "Too much food?"

I smiled. "Too many people." Mom, Meg, Eric, and Jo were all in the house, prepping to feed the entire family and a dozen or so five-year-olds.

"This family." Amy rolled her eyes. "All we do is eat." She clapped her hand over her mouth. "Shit. Forget I said that."

I laughed. "It's okay. Actually, that's one of the things I missed. Just being able to sit down with you all for a meal."

"You were always at the table."

"Unless I found something to do in the kitchen. But I was so anxious all the time, about eating or not eating, that I couldn't enjoy my own family. And then I'd go to my room alone and fantasize about recipes on the Internet."

"Like food porn."

That's exactly what it had been. A secret, compulsive addiction. "Yes."

"And now you have the chance to have a healthy, satisfying relationship."

I eyed her cautiously. "Are we still talking about food?"

"Unless you want to talk about Colt. How is the bad boy of country these days?"

"I don't know." I concentrated on twining

crepe paper along the porch railing. "I haven't heard from him."

"Asshole."

"I did turn him down," I reminded her mildly.

"He could at least check in to see how you're doing."

"He's hurt. I hurt him. I hurt his pride. I think Colt really loved me. He told me all the time how beautiful I was. How talented."

"Well, you are."

I picked up Patches, brushing my cheek against her kitten-soft fur. "It was like he was in love with his idea of me. His angel. His muse. I just couldn't be who he wanted me to be anymore."

Amy nodded. "I get that. It's exhausting, being on all the time."

"The funny thing is, I thought starving myself made me . . . I don't know. Better. Stronger. Special."

"Bethie, you *are* special."

"Actually, it turns out I'm pretty typical. Just another stupid girl with an eating disorder."

"You are not your eating disorder. Anorexia is a part of you. And, okay, right now it's kind of a big part. But it doesn't define you."

She sounded so sure. She sounded . . .

Like Dr. Patel. "When did you get to be so smart?"

Amy tossed her head. "I've always been smart. It's just taken everybody a while to notice."

Dear Amy. She didn't let anybody put her in a box. I smiled at her, my eyes damp. "You do like to play dumb sometimes."

She grinned. "If it gets me what I want."

I carried a bucket to the spigot and began filling little balloons with water from the hose. My phone vibrated in my hip pocket. I dried my hands on my jeans.

Amy glanced over from laying out supplies to decorate loot bags. "If that's Colt, tell him to go to hell."

I didn't recognize the number. "Hello?"

"Hey, girl. It's Dewey. Dewey Stratton?"

"Hi. I know who you are." We'd met at the Grammys. Dewey Stratton, A&R, signed Colt to the label.

"Heard your demo."

My mouth was suddenly dry. "Colt played it for you?"

"What?" Amy said. "Who is it?"

I flapped my hand to hush her.

"Listen, I don't know what's going on with the two of you," Dewey was saying, "but I'm calling to let you know the label's got five certified gold-record artists —

women — who'd love to debut this song at the Grand Ole Opry anytime you say the word."

"I don't know what to say."

"Say yes."

"But . . ."

"I know what you're thinking. You let me handle Colt. You two got a contract?"

"I don't think . . . I never signed anything." Not for my songs. "But . . ."

"That's all I need to know. Who's your manager? Because the label sure would love to tie this down."

"Tie down . . . ?"

"A songwriting deal. Long term."

"I'm . . . I'm kind of on a break right now."

"Who is it?" Amy whispered. "What do they want?"

"Colt said. You're taking some time for yourself."

I could barely hear him over the pounding in my ears. I nodded as if he could see.

"I can respect that," he said when I didn't answer. "This is a tough business. We can work with you on that."

"Did Colt tell you I'm not going on the road?"

"Honey, we have a stable full of talent itching to tour who couldn't write a hit song if Dolly Parton and Taylor Swift were holding the pen and whispering in their ear. What we don't have is the next Gretchen Peters. The new Diane Warren. I'm betting that could be you."

"But I don't . . . But why?" I asked.

Dewey chuckled. "The label likes Grammys. Your new song, 'For Better or Worse'? That's real special. You got a real gift. Something to say. Let me talk to your people, and we'll get this contract thing worked out."

I don't know what I said after that.

"Well?" Amy asked when I ended the call. Her eyes were hopeful. Worried.

"That was Dewey Stratton. The label wants to offer me a songwriting contract."

"Oh my God. Oh my God, Bethie!"

"He wants to call my people," I said dazedly. "I don't have people."

"I will be your people."

For some reason, this struck me as funny. I laughed. "You don't know anything about the music industry."

"So what? Trey will know where to start. Oh my God." Her face lit. She grabbed my arms. "We have to tell everybody!"

She dragged me to the kitchen, shouting the news. Everybody pressed around, Mom and Dad, Meg and Jo and Eric. I was swarmed, surrounded by family, filled with love. Swamped by hugs, congratulations, and questions I couldn't answer. Jo cried.

"What's going on?" John asked, appearing at the door, Daisy and DJ in tow.

The twins' birthday party was in twenty minutes. Sometime during the explanations, I slipped upstairs to change my clothes. My reflection stared back at me, stunned and happy and with, yes, a hint of pride.

The spiral notebook was by my bed. Empty, the way I had been for so long.

A sweet heaviness settled in my stomach. A fullness, a softness, an ache. I listened to my family's voices, coming up the stairs. *You have something to say.*

I flipped open the glittery cover. Stroked the blank pages.

For the first time in a long time, I thought I could see how to fill them up again.

CHAPTER 32
AMY

Birthday pennants fluttered in the breeze. The sky was hot and blue. The farmyard teemed with chaos, color, and life like that painting by Miró, *The Harlequin's Carnival*. Five-year-olds were everywhere.

I was painting, too. Face painting — butterflies, rainbows, and kittens on the girls; tigers, pirates, and dinosaurs on the boys.

"Very gender normative," Jo said when she stopped by my "booth" with Robbie on her hip.

"Hey, I'm a commercial artist," I said. "I give the people what they ask for."

I painted a lightning bolt on Robbie's forehead, like Harry Potter, and Jo and Robbie wandered off smiling.

The water balloon toss had started, bright bombs splashing on the ground. I noticed tall Alec taking a lot of hits, one of them landed by pink-haired Nan, who was here as his . . . date? Beth was comforting one of

473

the party guests, Jenny Snow's daughter, whose balloon burst in her hands before she had a chance to throw it.

Mom came around with towels and Meg with Popsicles. Our father and John were supervising the fishing hole. Eric strode around with DJ on his shoulders. Dan was in the baby goats' enclosure with Daisy and Sallie Moffat's little girl.

Trey came up from the dock, where he was in charge of boat rides. The two kids with him dashed off to join the balloon toss, Robbie toddling in their wake. Trey lingered, talking with Jo.

Carefully, I repaired a bumblebee on Kaylee Upton's cheek before sending her back into the water battle.

"I was talking to Trey," Jo said.

I wiped nontoxic glitter from my brush. "I saw."

"You don't mind, do you?"

"Of course not. You're friends." Best friends.

"And we're sisters."

I met her eyes. Brave, loyal Jo. "Sisters' Code?" I asked ruefully.

Her smile flickered. "He loves you, you know."

"I know." Even with so much left unsaid. And I loved him. Of course. I turned her

474

question back on her. "You don't mind?"

"No. Now I don't feel so guilty about dumping him. It just goes to prove there's a right person for everyone." Jo's gaze sought Eric and returned to me. "I'm so glad you're the right one for Trey."

My throat thickened. "I always looked up to you. Without you following your dream, I don't know if I would have had the courage to chase mine."

"Ha. As if anybody could stop you."

Was that true? If Trey had loved me three years ago the way I wanted to be loved, would I have created Baggage?

Meg came up holding Daisy's hand, Beth following with DJ. "The twins have something to say to you."

Daisy scuffed the ground with her toe. DJ sucked solemnly on a Popsicle.

"Kids?" Meg prompted.

"Thank you, Auntie Jo," they chorused. "Thank you, Aunt Amy."

"Aw. You're welcome," I said.

"Love you, little monsters."

"So nice to see my girls together," our mother said.

She looked relaxed and happy, her hair escaping its bandanna, our father at her elbow.

Jo grinned. "Nice to see you together, too."

"Weird, but nice," I said.

"I'm very proud of all of you," Mom said.

"We both are," our father said.

There was a shriek as Chris Murphy fell into the water trough and was rescued by John.

"Kill me now," Meg said, and went off, smiling, to get more towels.

My face painting duties done, I wandered toward the house. Miss Hannah was sitting with Aunt Phee and Mr. Laurence in the shade of a crepe myrtle. I bent to kiss her cheek.

"When does your new shop open?" Hannah asked.

"Two weeks. I have to get the workroom set up first. Flo is coming down to help me catch up on orders."

"Will she move down here?"

"Probably not," I said.

"When hell freezes over," Flo had said when I asked her if she were willing to consider a move. *"I love you, but I'm not leaving Mami and Papi and my sisters' kids for any job."*

I knew exactly how she felt.

"I'm recommending her for a position with Louis Vuitton New York," I added.

"So you'll be hiring locally," Phee said.

I nodded. "Jenny Snow on the retail side,

476

to start. And I'll need at least one more person to help with assembly."

Mr. Laurence twinkled at me from under his eyebrows. "Nice to see new businesses moving into downtown."

I smiled back. "You would know. Trey was telling me about your plans to convert the old tobacco warehouse."

"What plans?" Phee asked.

I was aware of Trey, approaching from the porch. "For the farmers' market."

Mr. Laurence glanced from me to his grandson. "Farmers' market?"

"I've been getting bids on the work," Trey said. "I wanted to have the plans before I talked to you about it."

Mr. Laurence grunted.

"Right now, the sellers and the buyers are limited by the weather," Trey said. "If we had something that could serve the community year-round —"

"It's a great idea," Mr. Laurence said. "Start small. Expand hours on the weekends and then add more days. And vendors."

Phee nodded. "Antiques."

"Artist studios," I said.

Trey glanced at Eric. "I thought, food trucks. Maybe a brewery."

"I like your vision, son," Mr. Laurence said gruffly.

Trey flushed with pleasure, shoving his hands in his pockets. "It was Amy's idea."

"It was not," I said.

"Better reward her, then," Mr. Laurence said at the same time.

Trey cocked an eyebrow. "Want a boat ride, little Amy?"

I raised my chin, aware of our family watching our every move. "I can row."

"You rowing me, while everybody watches? No way."

"Give me an oar, then. We'll row together."

We ambled down to the dock, where the flat-bottomed johnboat was tied up.

"Nice day," Trey said when we were floating with the current.

It was a lovely day. The river murmured over trees and stones. The sun sparkled on the water.

I bit back a smile. "You brought me down here to talk about the weather?"

"No." He cleared his throat. "Actually, I thought I'd be doing this over dinner. Or in the moonlight. Hire a flash mob or an airplane banner or something. But . . ."

My heart trembled. "We have a lot of history with this boat," I said. When I was twelve, Trey and Jo had taken the boat out together. I had tried to follow, with disastrous results. "You saved my life."

"You changed mine. Amy . . ."

I stopped him, taking my fate and my oar in my own hands. "What did you mean, differently?"

"What?"

"You said you loved me differently than Jo."

"Well, yeah. Because I do."

Right. I closed my eyes, willing the pain away.

"Because I loved her the way a boy loves a girl. But you . . . I love you the way a man loves a woman. Amy, look at me. Please." I did. He watched me anxiously, everything I ever wanted to see in his dark eyes. His heart. Our future. "I love you. Will you marry me?"

The moment hung suspended, floating between the blue sky and the bright river. The sound of children's screams and laughter drifted down the bank. Life wasn't perfect. But there were moments like this one that felt perfect, shimmering with happiness, shining and transient as reflections on the water.

My heart overflowed.

"Yes," I said.

EPILOGUE
ABBY

Too many cooks spoil the soup, my mother used to say.

But not today, I thought. Not on Thanksgiving, with my family all gathered together at Oak Hill.

The restaurant was closed for the season, but Eric had been in the kitchen since early morning. I'd baked pies — pumpkin, apple, and chocolate pecan. Meg brought mac and cheese. "Not from a box," she said smugly. "I used Jo's recipe from last year." Even Phee contributed her hummingbird cake.

"And what did you make, missy?" she asked Jo.

"Green bean casserole," Jo said.

"With the crispy onions?" Alec asked hopefully.

She grinned. "Absolutely."

Bryan glanced over from the football game he was watching with John. "I love crispy onions." His attention darted back to the

TV. "Come on. Just throw the ball!"

"It's all about clock management," John said in his coach voice.

This past Sunday, Jo and Eric had made the three-hour drive to Winston-Salem — Alec practicing his highway skills behind the wheel — to watch Bryan's last soccer game of the season and bring him home for the holiday. Maryland was knocked out in the second round of the tournament, but beyond grousing to John (*"I hate losing to a North Carolina school"*), Bryan seemed to be recovering from his team's disappointment.

Amy and Trey arrived in a flurry of hugs and hellos, bearing wine and a harvest centerpiece. Part of me missed the pinecone turkeys she'd made in second grade that always sat on the Thanksgiving table at the farmhouse. But the flowers were lovely. I admired her arrangement and accepted a glass of wine from Trey.

He poured wine for Phee and Meg. "Dan?"

Dan was sitting apart with Patches on his knee. Daisy perched beside them, chattering nonstop. He smiled briefly. "I'm good, thanks."

My motherless boys.

"I'll take a beer," Alec said.

Jo smacked him lightly. "In your dreams."

481

"It's too early to drink alcohol," said Wanda Crocker, who had nowhere else to go for the holidays. "I'll have some sweet tea."

"I'll get it," Nan said.

"No, no," Eric scolded, emerging from the kitchen. "You are a guest tonight."

Nan lived with her folks in the trailer park on the outskirts of town. Talk was her parents drank their holiday dinner. I didn't know them well enough to say. But their daughter was a fine young woman.

"I'll help," Alec said.

Love filled my chest. Our family was growing, expanding the walls of my heart. "We can all pitch in. We're all family here."

Amy squeezed Trey's arm, making the enormous rock in her engagement ring flash. "Officially, soon."

"Oak Hill is a home again," Phee said, feeding a cracker to her dog. "The way it was meant to be."

I looked at Ash, lying on the rug in front of the fireplace, with DJ and Robbie. Maybe he was finally the man he was meant to be, too.

His new job took him away a lot. Which was fine. I'd always been independent. But now when he came home, he was really *there*, in ways he hadn't been before. I

482

couldn't ask for more.

Robbie knocked down the tower of blocks, and DJ patiently built them up again. The twins had started kindergarten this fall, in separate classes. It seemed to me the boy was coming into his own, out from the shadow of his sister.

"Have you guys set a wedding date yet?" Jo asked.

"We thought . . . in the spring." Trey glanced at his grandfather, sitting by the fire. "We don't want to wait too long."

"Do you have a venue?" Meg asked.

Amy shook her head. "Not yet."

"Wherever Amy wants," Trey said.

Phee sniffed. "You're very agreeable."

Trey winked at her. "Because she's always right," he said before he went off to talk to his grandfather, their heads close together, their profiles lit by the fire. Discussing the wedding? Or the opening of the new farmers' market?

"You could have the wedding here," Jo said. "At Oak Hill."

Amy's eyes shone. "You wouldn't mind the fuss?"

"Well . . ."

"There is no fuss," Eric said. "It is no trouble at all. We will make a special menu, yeah?"

483

"Hey." Alec came back from the kitchen, waving a glass of sweet tea in one hand and his phone in the other. "Beth's song is on Spotify!"

"No surprise," Jo said. "It's a Christmas song, right? It's playing everywhere."

"Not 'Leave a Candle in Your Window.' The new one!"

" 'For Better or Worse'?" Meg asked.

Amy was scrolling on her phone. "It's on iTunes, too." She tapped. The singer's voice, pure and powerful, filled the room.

"Oh my God," Nan said. "Is that Carrie Underwood?"

Beth nodded. "She's so nice. Dewey thought . . . She wants to record 'Shadowland,' too." Dewey Stratton, some executive with her record label. "I might go up to Nashville. To do background vocals."

"I'm so proud of you!" Jo exclaimed.

"I couldn't have done it without you. All of you."

I looked around at them, my girls, my family, trying to preserve them in my mind like a snapshot pressed in the pages of a book, like a memory captured in one of Jo's stories or Beth's songs, seeing the patterns repeated in the next generation — in Alec's thoughtful eyes and Daisy's bright chatter, in the curve of DJ's cheek and Robbie's smile.

"That's wonderful, sweetheart." I hugged her tight. "I hope you're always this happy. All of you."

Beth leaned her head against my shoulder.

"We've had some rough spots," Jo said quietly.

"And some smooth sailing," Meg said.

Amy stuck out her chin. "I'm not afraid of storms. I'm learning how to sail my ship."

I opened my arms to embrace them all.

Outside, the leaves turned red and gold and blew away. Troubles would come. They always did. But we would get through them — as we always had — together.

And in the meantime, there were moments like this.

Moments to hold on to. To look back on and remember.

AUTHOR'S NOTE

I was ten years old when my grandmother gave my sister and me a copy of *Little Women.* She probably figured it was an appropriate story for girls. Which it is.

Meg, Jo, Beth, and Amy aren't sidekicks or sweethearts, but the heroes of their story. I remember wishing I could live in Orchard House, so I could act in plays and write a newspaper and all the rest of it. I wanted to be book-loving Jo March, munching apples and scribbling in her attic room. With Jo as my model, some of those wishes even came true.

But as I grew up, things I'd sort of skipped over on first — or second or tenth — reading struck me for the first time or in a different way. At its heart, *Little Women* is about the sisters' journey — their different paths to adulthood. Jo is always at the center, the star and interpreter of the narrative. But I started to wonder, was there more to the story than Jo (or even Louisa May Alcott) told us?

Even though the story is timeless in some ways, it's also a product of its time. Obviously women now have options — and issues — that Alcott's characters didn't face. I wanted to tell the sisters' story in a way that reflected my changing, grown-up perspective. I wanted to make it accessible to modern readers who aren't familiar with the original. So I aged the sisters up to their twenties, which I think of as the contemporary "coming-of-age," and reimagined their story as women's fiction in what I hope is a fun, fresh, relatable way.

Of course, there's a huge challenge in reimagining a classic because so many readers know and love the original, and they're going to bring their own feelings and memories of reading *Little Women* (or watching the movie) to your book. I'm not sure you can ever live up to that kind of expectation. You can only be true to yourself, to your own experience, your own emotions.

So that's what I did. Some of *Meg & Jo* and *Beth & Amy* reflects research I did on Louisa May Alcott, and some is a deep dive into my own life. I set the story in North Carolina, where I raised my family, and took all my love for *Little Women* and what it meant to me at different points in my life and brought that to my story.

This past year was tough for all of us. Writing about the March sisters gave me a sense of family and connection at a time when we're all missing family and longing for connection. *Beth & Amy* is a comfort read, yes, but it's also about three different women, two generations, who struggle and come out the other side stronger than before. It's hopeful and heartwarming and, yes, romantic. The March women — all of them — speak to me, because I carry each of them inside me. I have been Meg, balancing the demands of being a daughter, wife, and mother, and Jo, fighting for creative expression and a relationship between equals. I have been Beth, struggling with her secret in emotional isolation, and Amy, ambitious and eager for recognition and approval. And I am Abby, always defined as Marmee/Momma and yet a woman with her own drives and dreams.

They have been my companions, offering a kind of road map on the path to becoming my best self. They inspired my journey in so many ways, as a writer and a woman. Growing up, I wanted to live in their world. Now, in *Meg & Jo* and *Beth & Amy,* I get to share their story, my story, my homage to

Little Women.

I hope you'll find some of your story here, too.

ACKNOWLEDGMENTS

First of all, I need to thank Louisa May Alcott, whose story *Little Women* informed and inspired *Beth & Amy* (and *Meg & Jo*).

Thanks always to my amazing editor, Cindy Hwang, and to Claire Zion for getting behind this story. I'm so grateful to Angela Kim and the whole Berkley team, including Danielle Keir, Brittanie Black, and Jessica Plummer for their good work in getting this book out into the world, and to Colleen Reinhart and Laura K. Corless for making it so pretty.

Thank you to my wonderful agent, Robin Rue, and to Beth Miller of Writers House, for their thoughtful insights and for holding my hand.

To my mom, whose resilience amazes me.

To my sister, Pam, with love from "Me, too," and my fabulous sisters-in-law, Mary Keefer and Ginny Grisez.

To my writing sister, Brenda Harlen, and

my deadline pals — Jamie Beck, Tracy Brogan, Sonali Dev, Sally Kilpatrick, Falguni Kothari, Priscilla Oliveras, Barbara O'Neal, and Liz Talley — who cajoled and cheered me on into finishing this book.

I'm grateful to my neighbors, Kathy Hamilton and Lisa Jackson, and thankful for the places and people in North Carolina, the little towns, family farms, and small businesses that inspired bits of this story. Special thanks to designer Holly Aiken (check out her amazing bags at hollyaiken.com), Celebrity Dairy (celebritydairy.com), and Prodigal Farm (prodigalfarm.com).

Thanks to Diane Spell for sharing her experience as a Cuban American in North Carolina; and to my niece, Julie Rose McMahon, for her stories of being an American in Paris.

Thank you, Jean and Spencer, Andrew and Celia, and Mark and Katie, for expanding the walls of my heart. And to the next generation, Katerina Abigail, Jackson David, and Julia Alexandra. "However long you may live, I never can wish you a greater happiness than this."

To Michael, for giving me the courage to write the hard parts.

And finally to you, dear readers, for your

time and the chance to share my stories. Thank you so much.

■ ■ ■ ■

READERS GUIDE

BETH & AMY
VIRGINIA KANTRA

■ ■ ■ ■

QUESTIONS FOR DISCUSSION

1. What scenes or lines from the original *Little Women* do you recognize in *Beth & Amy*? What struck you as most different?

2. Amy feels guilty for having sex with her sister Jo's ex — "a clear violation of the Sisters' Code." Do you believe in a similar code? What makes Amy's choices in Paris and three years later in Bunyan okay or not okay?

3. When Beth arrives for the wedding, her family reacts to her changed appearance. "Look at you," Abby says. "You're skin and bones." And Phee replies, "You can never be too rich or too thin." How do their comments reflect the messages women hear about their bodies? How do other characters in the story feel or talk about weight or appearance?

4. Why do you think the author chose to include Abby/Momma's point of view in this story? What did it add to your understanding of the characters?

5. At what point in the story did you realize Beth had an eating disorder? Why doesn't she confide in her family about her anorexia? Why do you think it took her family so long to recognize her problem? Have you known anyone who has struggled with an eating disorder? Have you discussed it with them? What do you think is helpful to say or not say? (Want to learn more about eating disorders? You can find resources and support at nationaleating disorders.org.)

6. Several romantic relationships in the book involve missed opportunities and connections — Abby and Ash, Jo and Trey, Amy and Trey, Beth and Colt, Aunt Phee and James Laurence. How were these resolved? Were you satisfied with the resolutions? Why or why not?

7. Do you agree that Beth and Amy are "defined by who we were not. Shadows of Meg and Jo"? How does birth order affect the sisters' relationships? In what ways do

they embrace or reject their family roles? How does their closeness, comparison, and competition affect their choices?

8. Amy refers to Trey as "Prince Charming" and herself as "Cinderella." How accurate is this description? How does their relationship stay the same or change?

9. When the March sisters go out to dinner, Beth says, "Food has always been about me saying no. I have to teach myself to say yes." What are the turning points in the story where the characters say *yes* or *no*?

10. In Louisa May Alcott's time, many young women died in childhood or childbirth. The original Beth dies of scarlet fever. Why do you think the author chose to give Beth an eating disorder instead? Were you satisfied or dissatisfied with the decision not to kill off her character?

11. At the end of the book, Abby thinks Ash is "finally the man he was meant to be." Do you agree or disagree? In what ways do the other characters become their best selves?

ABOUT THE AUTHOR

New York Times bestselling writer **Virginia Kantra** is the author of thirty novels. Her stories have earned numerous awards, including two Romance Writers of America RITA® Awards and two National Readers' Choice Awards.

Meg & Jo, her debut women's fiction novel, received starred reviews from *Publishers Weekly* and *Booklist* and was praised by *People.*

Virginia is married to her college sweetheart, a coffee shop owner who keeps her supplied with caffeine and material. They make their home in North Carolina, where they raised three (mostly adult) children. She is a firm believer in the strength of family, the importance of storytelling, and the power of love.

Her favorite thing to make for dinner? Reservations.